Death at Daffodil Inn

Also by R. L. Killmore

A Cinnamon Falls Mystery

Death at Daffodil Inn

R. L. KILLMORE

SIMON &
SCHUSTER

London · New York · Amsterdam/Antwerp · Sydney/Melbourne · Toronto · New Delhi

First published in Great Britain by Simon & Schuster UK Ltd, 2026

1 3 5 7 9 10 8 6 4 2

Simon & Schuster UK Ltd, 1st Floor
222 Gray's Inn Road, London WC1X 8HB

Simon & Schuster Australia, Sydney
Simon & Schuster India, New Delhi

www.simonandschuster.co.uk
www.simonandschuster.com.au
www.simonandschuster.co.in

The authorised representative in the EEA is Simon & Schuster Netherlands BV,
Herculesplein 96, 3584 AA Utrecht, Netherlands. info@simonandschuster.nl

Simon & Schuster strongly believes in freedom of expression and stands against
censorship in all its forms. For more information, visit BooksBelong.com

A CIP catalogue record for this book is available from the British Library

Paperback ISBN: 978-1-3985-5032-2
eBook ISBN: 978-1-3985-5033-9
Audio ISBN: 978-1-3985-5034-6

Typeset in Sabon by Palimpsest Book Production Ltd, Falkirk, Stirlingshire
Printed and Bound in the UK using 100% Renewable Electricity
at CPI Group (UK) Ltd

MIX
Paper | Supporting
responsible forestry
FSC® C013604

For Riley, our Angel.
The world is brighter because you're in it.

Cinnamon Falls
& Asheville

Daffodil Inn

Cinnamon Falls
Main Town

Reeds & Roots

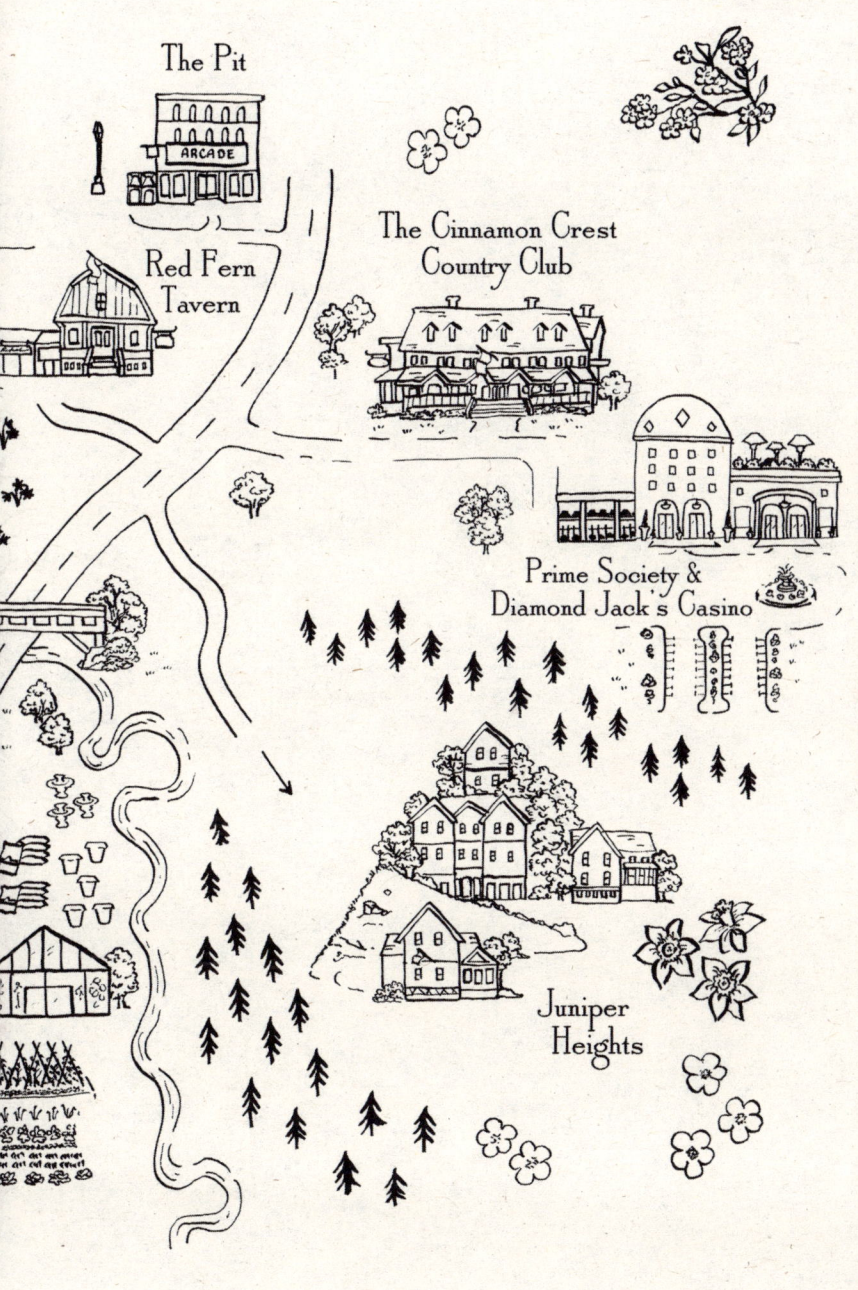

The Pit

ARCADE

Red Fern
Tavern

The Cinnamon Crest
Country Club

Prime Society &
Diamond Jack's Casino

Juniper
Heights

Chapter 1

Saturday

Morgan

Let the record reflect that Morgan Vanessa Taylor was not one for hosting large extravaganzas, especially the kind where the entire town is invited to your front yard. But when your parents own 'the quaintest bed and breakfast with relaxing riverfront views that features a never-ending field of breathtakingly beautiful daffodils', you have no choice but to memorize the website copy, grit your teeth, and fall in line.

The Daffodil Jubilee, Cinnamon Falls' Annual Spring Festival, was the worst idea her parents had ever come up with. Her mother claims that Morgan loved it as a child, was excited for it even, but back then Morgan would have agreed that the Earth was flat if her mother had told her so, especially if it meant having her attention for more than five minutes at a time.

To an outsider, the Daffodil Jubilee looked like any other small-town festival in Anywhere, USA, but to the residents of Cinnamon Falls, the Jubilee meant that spring had arrived like a promise kept, warm and golden. It was an excuse to shake off winter's shivers, and get out of the house, sip lemonade, and post scenic photos for your same ten followers.

Little ones got lost in the hedge maze or hunted for plastic eggs behind manufactured tufts of grass, while everyone else enjoyed the live music, local vendors, and the star of the show: a garden of yellow and white daffodils that stretched as far as the eye could see.

It began as a simple invitation almost thirty years ago when the Taylor family planted daffodils in the overgrown garden behind their newly restored farmhouse-turned-bed and breakfast. Their business venture marked a fresh start for the family, and the Taylors spread the word far and wide for residents, travelers, neighbors, and friends, to celebrate the start of spring. They came and had been coming ever since.

Her father, Wesley Taylor, had worked in hospitality all his life. When he was a young man, he'd served cold drinks on hot summer days to flirty aging women over at Cinnamon Crest Country Club in Asheville. Through the years he'd moved up to breakfast attendant, then server. The customers raved about his service so much that he was promoted to front desk attendant, then manager, where he'd spent the majority of his career until he'd had the cockamamy idea to open up a bed and breakfast of his own.

As the story goes, when Morgan's parents heard that a riverfront property on the outskirts of Cinnamon Falls was on the market, they'd jumped at the chance to buy it. With their combined life savings, they willingly bought an unkempt piece of land housing a run-down shack that had long since been abandoned.

It took years of sweat equity, dozens of tearful nights and shouting matches, but the Daffodil Inn Cinnamon Falls knew now was her parents' idol; a symbol of their life's hard work encompassed in eighty acres of rich, rolling greenery that had been transformed to hold a charming estate, neighboring a field of daffodils that stretched along the quiet riverside.

Morgan's birth, however nominally exciting, paled in comparison to the unbridled joy in her father's eyes when the Inn finally opened for business just a few months after she was born. Morgan didn't remember the opening, since she was fast asleep in her mother's arms, but she'd seen (and dusted) the commemorative picture almost every day of her life. It hung proudly in the great room over the brick-laid fireplace, encased in an ornate golden frame. There was nothing more important than the Inn, not even their own daughter, from Morgan's point of view.

Over the years there had been plenty of soccer games, debate team matches, and dance competitions her parents missed (or conveniently forgot) because they were busy with the Inn. There was always work to be done; beds to be made, linens to be washed, dishes to be served, mantels to be dusted, weeds to be pulled and grass to be trimmed. There was never enough time for both. Precious childhood memories be damned.

As much as Morgan resented the Daffodil Inn for cutting her parents' attention in half, she also knew that helping her parents was her duty. So when they'd asked her to cancel her long-awaited spring break plans with her best friend, Nia, she begrudgingly spent the week at the Inn preparing for the Jubilee instead.

Every year The Daffodil Jubilee transformed Morgan's backyard into a patchwork of green, yellow and white tents that fluttered in the breeze like petals dancing in the sun.

This year would be no different. The Taylors couldn't have prayed for better weather. The golden sun kept winter's chill at bay and Morgan was glad she opted for her quarter-length sleeved shirt.

She watched as children squealed with sticky fingers and wide eyes; cheeks painted with daffodils, butter-flies or fairy wings. The signature scent of cinnamon buns from Rosie's old recipe mingled in the air with the sweet bite of kettlecorn, funnel cake, and the tang of spicy-sweet barbecue smoke. In the distance, Rodney McIntire and the Macs, Cinnamon Falls' most popular folk band, played a rendition of a classic oldies tune while parents snapped along in their lawn chairs, reminiscing.

Morgan ducked inside an empty tent next to Benny Johnson's meat smoker. The BBQ Joint owner had been smoking a mouthwatering brisket all day. Wiping her forehead with the back of her hand, Morgan took a deep breath, inhaling equal parts smoke and stress. It was as good a hiding place as any; it got her away from the crowd and her nagging mother, for a brief godsent second. She adjusted the laminated badge in the shape of a daffodil laced around her neck and scanned the festival grounds from her vantage point. Everything *seemed* to be going smoothly.

Just a few more hours, her brain told her.

'Is it a good sign that no one is shouting your name or asking where the extension cord is?' Nia Bennett appeared beside her, sunglasses perched on top of her head, holding two frosted bottles of lemonade. She stopped short. 'Sorry, were you supposed to be hiding?'

Nia always had terrible timing; realizing the obvious a little too late. They'd been best friends since the first grade, when Morgan enrolled at Morningstar Elementary, and had been stuck together ever since. They'd survived the complicated and traumatic death of their mutual best friend, Sienna, and her mother, Rosie, and were embarking on a new adventure together: Nia's wedding to Cinnamon Falls' top cop, Jesse Shaw.

Today, Nia wore her recently dyed honey brown

curls in a high ponytail, gold hoops glinting in the sun as she tilted her head with a knowing smile, finally catching on. Her maxi dress, covered in yellow daisies, fluttered in the breeze, and her vendor apron, pressed with The Cinnamon Scoop logo, still bore a faint smudge of dried cinnamon-swirl ice cream from the cones she'd been serving all morning. She was beautiful in a confident and easy way. Nia never had to try too hard for attention, or acceptance for that matter. Morgan admired that she knew exactly who she was and didn't waste any energy on being validated.

'Not anymore,' Morgan grumbled, snatching one of the bottles from Nia and twisting off the cap hungrily. 'No one asking for me is either a good sign or a sign of the apocalypse.' She held up the bottle to her best friend, a silent thank you. 'Been running around like a chicken with my head cut off since sunrise. I needed this.'

'You pulled it off again,' Nia said, glancing around the green with a proud smile. 'This might be the best jubilee yet.'

Morgan opened her mouth to deflect Nia's compliment when she noticed movement outside of the tent; her hiding place threatening exposure. Near the game booths, William Reed stood behind his daughter, Angel, helping her form at the basketball contest. His hand guided hers gently, his other muscled arm braced against the game's frame. When Angel's ball hiked too high and thunked off the rim, Will handed the attendant another dollar and let her try again. Angel's determined expression made Morgan's heart melt.

Nia followed her gaze. 'You should go talk to him.'

Morgan scoffed, her eyes darting away. 'You're out of your mind. Angel is in my kindergarten class.'

'She *was* in your kindergarten class,' Nia clarified. 'She's in second grade now and that makes her father fair game,' Nia added with a smirk. 'Come on, you had to see the way he looked at you during the school's spring fundraiser last week.'

'He was looking at the snack table,' Morgan muttered.

'Trust me, it wasn't the brownies that had him in a trance.'

Suddenly flushed, Morgan took a long sip of lemonade. Her eyes drifted back to Angel as she giggled, reaching up to accept a blue unicorn from the game's attendant. She was too short, so Will handed the toy to his daughter with an exaggerated flair, bowing in a deep curtsy. Angel hoisted her winnings in the air, unleashing a victorious battle cry.

An older woman journeyed over, a shock of burgundy hair swept into soft waves pinned to one side and a smile of pride set deep in her eyes. Eleanor Langford. She'd been staying at the Daffodil Inn since Monday, and was always impeccably dressed, like life was her runway. Today she sported a flowing floral kimono with dramatic ruffles that dragged the ground when she walked. Morgan could spot a

Frankie Templeton custom with her eyes closed. She was a walking billboard for The Velvet Fox Boutique.

Eleanor's bejeweled hand clutched a delicate teacup to her chest like it was a prized possession and Morgan wanted to believe it was her daily requested chamomile tea, but knowing Eleanor, it could have been straight vodka. Angel showed her prize off to Eleanor, who gasped in delight and joined the girl in a hip shaking victory dance.

'I have to finish breaking down with Dad.' Nia tapped her phone, bringing Morgan back to the moment. Nia listed on her fingers. 'Then I'm heading home to shower, and take a nap, in that order. You know how I love to sleep through alarms, so I might be a little late for Petals N' Promises.'

'Fashionably, I hope,' Morgan called after her as she walked away.

'Obviously!' Nia responded. 'Save me a cinnamon bun and' – she cupped her hands over her mouth – 'save a dance for that tall drink of trouble.' She pointed not so subtly to Will behind her cupped hand. Morgan resisted the urge to flip her friend the bird in case a child was watching. The last thing she needed was for it to get back to her mother.

The rest of the afternoon passed without incident, and despite it being solely responsible for the sharp and intense pain between Morgan's ass cheeks, the Daffodil Jubilee was on its final act, the Petals N' Promises Dance.

The dance began just as the sun dipped low behind the trees, casting an ethereal glow over the fields of nodding daffodils. The real magic happened at night, under a sky of sequined stars, transforming the backyard into something out of one of those expensive home magazines.

The tents, tables and chairs were cleared from the space and a makeshift dancefloor was laid over the soft grass; the music, a mix of local musicians and old soul records, spilled across the lawn, blending in with the effortless laughter of couples in love, and the soft clink of cocktail glasses.

You can do this, Morgan told herself. *It's just another Jubilee. It'll be over in–* She looked at the face of her smart watch. The timer ticking away in the top corner told her it'd only been twenty-two minutes since the dance began and she was already over it. She took a deep cleansing breath, like the nightly meditations she fell asleep to told her to, in order to calm the galloping horses in her heart.

Normally, Morgan would have rejoiced this time of night. In just a few short hours, the hellish day she'd been dreading since the new year would be behind her. She could go back to her normal life and sleep in her own bed without her mother managing her every move, just like, she was sure, Vanessa preferred. Morgan was used to her mother's frostiness by now. Ever since Morgan moved across town to a place of her own, it wasn't like Vanessa ever called to catch up if it didn't involve the business. Morgan could have run away and joined the circus as a bearded woman and her mother would have still commented an airy, 'that's nice' over the phone.

Vanessa Taylor wasn't all bad. She showed her devotion through work. In her mind, work meant action. Action yielded results and she had no time for trivial matters of the heart like affection.

Morgan climbed into the gazebo that should have been bulldozed years ago. It was as old as the land it sat on – weathered paint, stripped from the salt of the river, unruly nails jutting out this way and that – but her mother was adamant about keeping the 'vintage charm' of the bed and breakfast, whatever that meant. Morgan's arches were screaming in her five-inch wedge heels and her stomach was praying for a break from the girdle she wrestled on earlier in the evening. It was keeping her breasts hiked up to her nostrils in her strapless gown, so some sacrifices were worth it.

She eased onto the wooden bench, turned and hooked her arm over the edge, careful not to get a splinter, to get a good view of the river dawdling past her, smooth and undeterred, until it reached the ocean miles and miles away.

A chorus of crickets and frogs sang their nightly

ballad, serenading her, while mosquitoes worked to dodge her quick reflexes. It was unusually warm for April, heat pressing in around her, but the nearby river offered her a welcome breeze like a stolen kiss from a lover.

On the horizon, she couldn't make out where the river ended and the sky connected. Tiny white spheres dotted the night sky creating a kaleidoscope of constellations that Morgan used to know by heart when she was in school. Now, it looked like a complicated map that she couldn't read. The stars reflected on the water like schools of glow-in-the-dark fish, swimming away from Cinnamon Falls. Morgan wished she was going with them.

She took a sip of the drink perspiring in her hand, a strawberry margarita, heavy on the muddled strawberry and heavy on the tequila. She sucked hard, ready to inhale the drink in one sitting. A chunk of strawberry tangled itself in the suction and shot to the back of her throat like a heat-seeking missile.

Morgan doubled over, hacking out a cough that made her eyes water. Finally, she spat out the death-determined strawberry and it landed with a splat near a pair of hard-bottomed shoes standing at the gazebo's entrance.

Through teary eyes, Morgan catalogued the man in front of her from the bottom up. Black snakeskin dress shoes stuck out underneath a pair of cuffed dark wash denim jeans that stretched across his thighs in a way that made her mouth water – and not from nearly suffocating.

It was just her luck to choke when the finest man in Cinnamon Falls was standing in front of her, clutching the most perfect bouquet of cream and yellow daffodils, her favorites. William Reed was the kind of handsome that Morgan hadn't ever experienced before. In a small town, most men had been spoken for since they were in diapers. Will was a transplant, thank goodness, by way of Macon she'd heard, and suspiciously rumored to be single.

He sported a black round-neck T-shirt that was tucked behind a snakeskin belt that matched his shoes. Morgan, a woman in favor of intense color coordination, appreciated his effort. A plum-colored blazer hung off his athletic shoulders, almost shimmering under the moonlight, and even underneath the heavy fabric she admired the muscles sculpted by years of intense, sweaty yard work.

His expression shifted from concern to humor as his full, incredibly kissable lips folded into a smile revealing two rows of astonishingly white teeth. His long locs were twisted into a ponytail, making his buttercream complexion the star of the show. His button nose crinkled with an incoming laugh and his kind, smiling brown eyes made Morgan's skin flame with embarrassment.

With Will she played it safe, keeping things light, friendly and surface level. She'd certainly never had the guts to ask about his relationship status. He didn't even look like the relationship type. A man that handsome surely kept a revolving door of women chomping at the bit for their turn at him. She was not going to be one of those women, desperate for a second glance or a flash of his smile, even though in reality she could run for president of his fan club.

Besides, friendship was something Morgan excelled at; that was her lane. Messy, fairytale love stories were for someone else, someone softer and less complicated. Morgan had made peace with being the funny best friend in everyone else's love story. It was easier that way, keeping her crush buried deep in the quietest corner of her heart, where she stored all the things she didn't dare want *too* much.

'Those for me?' Morgan croaked. She batted away a few tears that had escaped and righted herself, sucking down gulps of precious air.

Will looked down at the forgotten flowers, straightening a few of the crumpled petals.

'Yeah,' he responded shyly, a hint of rose coloring his cheeks. 'I was going to . . . sorry, are you okay?'

'Fine,' Morgan replied, sitting her drink down next to her. 'Didn't know strawberries were so blood-thirsty.'

He smirked. 'Note to self, ixnay the strawberries.' He stuffed his free hand in his jeans, rocking back on his heels. Morgan gestured for the flowers.

'Sorry,' he said for the second time. He took a step

toward her and his shoe caught on something under-foot. He pitched forward, losing his balance.

Their foreheads collided in a startling jolt, sending a shockwave of pain reverberating through Morgan's brain, stunning her. Stars popped behind her eyes and she let out a pained *oomf* as Will's solid frame slammed into hers.

Stumbling backward, Morgan desperately grasped for the railing to gain her balance. The wooden bench bit through the fabric of her lavender gown; splinters piercing the soft skin of her thighs. The flowers went flying from Will's hands, toppling over the guardrail and floating downriver.

Will landed on top of her, his solid arms locking her body underneath his. In different circumstances, Morgan would have probably welcomed and enjoyed an encounter of such with Will, but just like every other time in her life, things just *had* to go wrong.

'I am so sorry,' Will said breathily, scrambling to his feet. He held out his hand and pulled Morgan upright so quickly she had to brace herself against his rock-solid chest, her vision swimming.

It wasn't lost on her that their faces were a breath apart; their mouths perfectly aligned. If Morgan were a princess in a storybook, her Prince Charming would lean forward, primed for a kiss, the music intensifying as fireworks exploded in the distance, washing their bodies in pops of sparkling lights. But Morgan was no Cinderella.

She brushed herself off and looked up at him, mortified. 'At least we're tied up in awkward moments.'

Will looked down at her, a mischievous sparkle in his eye. It'd been one school year since Morgan taught his daughter. But she recognized that look from a mile away. It was the same expression Angel gave her when she was about to disrupt her entire kindergarten class.

'Let's see if we can go two for two.' Will hooked one finger under Morgan's chin, directing her lips to his.

Time stopped.

All other anxious thoughts dropped out of her head: this dumb party, her aching feet and bleeding thighs seemed like trivial matters to this moment.

The frogs' song hit a crescendo and Morgan wondered, just for a split second, if her life was truly about to become something out of a romance novel. Will moved in, shuttering his eyes closed, and Morgan's legs turned to Jell-O. He was inches away . . . centimeters . . . just a whisper of breath trapped between their waiting mouths . . .

A scream shattered the night, animalistic and guttural, that sent a blast of lightning down Morgan's spine. They shot apart, their romantic moment fluttering away in the passing wind.

Morgan met Will's panicked eyes and without saying a word, she sprinted out the gazebo, clearing the steps in one leap, and charged toward the Daffodil Inn.

'Morgan!' Will called after her. 'Wait!'

Snatches of conversation filtered past her as she muscled her way through the crowd of spectators who looked on with curious and horrified expressions. She reached the center of the crowd where the hedge maze had been erected weeks prior, thanks to Will and his father, owner of Reed & Roots, Cinnamon Falls' best landscaping company. Morgan had pretended not to watch Will out of the second-story window as he'd worked shirtless and sweaty underneath the April sun, anchoring the bushes into the ground one by one to build the complicated tapestry of greenery.

'What is it?' she asked the crowd gathering at the lip of the maze.

Caleb Brewster and a group of seniors at Cinnamon Falls High stood around, their faces ghostly pale. Beside her, Will arrived out of breath, searching the crowd for his daughter.

'Angel!' He screamed against the murmurs of the crowd getting louder with each passing second.

Then, Morgan received the worst news of the night. Caleb's pointer finger shook in the direction of the maze. 'Miss Morgan, there's someone in there . . . dead.'

Chapter 2

Eight Hours Earlier

Will

Like every other crisp Saturday morning, William Romeo Reed found himself elbow-deep in the damp soil outside of his father's greenhouse. Sunlight stretched across a pale sky, glinting off dew-slick grass, while a cheerful chorus of robins sang a sweet song. Behind him, the screen door creaked with every shift of the breeze, carrying the faint sweetness of honeysuckle tangled along the fence line. Will pushed his sleeves higher, earth smudging his forearms, and worked with a quiet satisfaction alongside the Grow Squad; half a dozen teenaged boys from Cinnamon Falls High who needed an outlet, something to get into other than trouble.

With varying degrees of effort, they removed weeds from the soil, more interested in elbowing each other than the dirt. The program, run under the family business, Reed & Roots Landscaping, wasn't just about planting tomatoes and pulling weeds. It was survival. And for some boys, it was the first time they'd seen something grow because of them, not in spite of them.

Will had just finished staking a row of tomato cages when he'd overheard his father's familiar drawl floating across from the adjacent plot.

'That right there,' Calvin said, pointing at a cluster of tall, elegant stalks crowned in bell-shaped blooms in soft pinks and purples, 'is foxglove. Beautiful, right? Attracts bees, hummingbirds, and all kinds of pollinators. But hear me good, do not touch it. It's poisonous if handled the wrong way.'

Will dusted his hands off on the thighs of his cargo pants and watched as some of the boys took a collective step backward, impressed but wary. Calvin moved on to talk about irrigation flow and Will caught eyes with Caleb Brewster, who stayed back from the group.

He was tall for sixteen; lean and wiry, growing like a weed. He sported a permanent scowl carved into his face like a mask he'd grown too comfortable wearing. His uncle, former Cinnamon Falls Police Chief Vernon Prescott, had worn the same one. After Vernon was exposed, fired, and sentenced for his role in the cover-up of the murders of Sienna and Rosslyn Rose, Caleb had spiraled. He went from being the golden child of Cinnamon Falls to the town pariah. Kids at school whispered behind his back, and in front of his face, too. Some said that Caleb would end up just like his uncle, that it ran in the family.

The rumors seemed to hold some weight since he'd made new friends from Atlanta who showed up in town with souped-up cars and heavy chains. Will had been around long enough to know that guys like that weren't hanging around for the scenery. Caleb was into something deep, and Will was doing his damndest to pull him out of it.

It didn't help that Caleb's mother, Rhonda, had all but cornered Will in Bones' Barbershop last winter, tears clinging to her lashes, begging him to find something, anything, to keep her son safe and out of trouble. That was how Caleb ended up in the Grow Squad.

He'd barely said a word the first few sessions. But Will saw how intensely he listened, how he lingered next to the plants a little longer than the others. Will knew there was still something reachable in him; something real.

'What's up, Caleb?' Will called to him.

Caleb shrugged, kicking at a clump of soil with the toe of his boot.

'Nothin', he replied. Will didn't like to converse early in the morning either, so he didn't take it personally.

Will leaned against his shovel. 'You got any plans later today?'

'Man, it's seven in the morning,' Caleb complained. 'All I can think about right now is getting back into bed.'

Will chuckled. 'You should swing by the Daffodil

19

Jubilee. Remember that plot y'all helped plant last fall? The flowers have bloomed like crazy.'

Caleb's face stayed unreadable, but Will caught the brief flicker of pride behind his eyes. The other boys gathered around, curious now.

'You serious?' Jeremiah English asked, rising on his tiptoes in excitement. 'We can go?' Jeremiah was the youngest of the group, his eyes still bright with possibility.

'Yeah,' Will said, grinning. 'Bring your family, too. Come out and see what your hands built.'

While the other boys celebrated, Caleb leaned against the fence, arms crossed. 'What's the catch?'

'No catch,' Will replied. 'But y'all need to find something decent to wear. Don't show up lookin' like you just rolled out of bed. You got a suit?'

Caleb shrugged and mumbled, 'I got a bunch of my uncle's stuff.'

'A suit for flowers?' Carl Weathers snorted. 'I ain't tryin' to wear no bowtie or nothin'.'

'It's not just flowers. There's live music, food trucks, photo booths, the whole town comes out. At the end of the night is the Petals N' Promises dance, you need the suit for that.'

The boys exchanged playful glances. Will knew what that meant. Girls.

'What you wearin', Mr. Reed?' Caleb asked.

Will didn't hesitate. 'Purple.'

Their laughter rippled through the quiet fields. A

spooked bird jetted from a tree overhead. Will rolled his eyes.

Caleb smirked. 'Purple? What, you trying to match somebody?'

Will didn't answer at first. His gaze drifted across the field where the sunlight filtered through the daffodils, a breeze bending the golden blooms in soft waves. In his mind, he saw Morgan Taylor, laughing, head tilted, probably in some purple silky loose-fitting dress that would make his heart stumble over itself. He hoped today would be the day he could finally ask her out.

'Maybe,' Will said at last, more to himself than the group, a quiet smile tugging at his lips. 'Y'all just worry about showing up, aight?'

They each reached in for a pound and scattered to help Calvin with the last of the compost bags. Will hung back for a moment longer, watching them. Caleb, in particular. He'd been trying so hard to keep the kid close; to keep him from sliding off the edge of something he couldn't undo.

If giving these boys something to take pride in could shift one of their futures it was worth every aching joint in Will's body. He headed for the shed to pack up the tools, already thinking about what shoes he'd wear to match his blazer.

That evening, in his room at the Daffodil Inn, Will was so nervous that his stomach was threatening to reintroduce his breakfast. When was the last time he'd been this nervous? Not since Angel was born.

He shook out his nerves, giving his reflection a silent pep talk in the floor-length mirror while his daughter looked on, bored. She sat cross-legged on the extra double bed in their shared room and gave him a skeptical once-over before continuing to scribble away on the tablet that had become her third arm since her mother bought it for her last Christmas. Will hadn't been pleased about it, especially considering that he and Tanya had agreed to keep Angel screen-free.

There was nothing wrong with drawing tradition-ally with pen and paper, artists have done it for centuries, but he couldn't say no to Angel's eyes pleading to keep it. He was terrified of her resenting him in her adolescent years, especially for doing it all on his own.

Some battles weren't worth the victory. He was satisfied knowing that his baby got to see her mother at Christmas for once, healthy and smiling. Truthfully, he hadn't thought about another woman since he and Tanya decided to part ways just after his daugh-ter's third birthday. Besides, Angel had kept him busy enough.

But Morgan Taylor was different.

When he'd seen her during Angel's first day of school, greeting all the new students, it was like time slowed. Her magnetic personality, knee-weakening smile, and whip-sharp sense of humor had him feeling *things* he thought he'd forgotten about. That year, he'd kept his distance, admiring her from afar (heavy on admiring). But now that Angel had moved on to the second grade with a different teacher, he was going to make an effort to get to know the *Miss Morgan* Angel spoke so highly of.

There had been plenty of times over the past year that they could have conversed about something other than Angel. But every time he got within range of her, it was like his brain took that opportunity to shut off.

Tonight, he vowed, would be the night. He'd picked his outfit carefully the day before, hoping to coordinate with purple-obsessed Morgan. He had to do this right; impress her, capture her attention, something that would break him out of the box of friendship they'd been toying with since meeting. It was something about her; the way she held his name in her mouth, or how her eyes always seemed to roam him, that made him think there was *something* between them; something worth exploring.

'What do you think?' He turned to Angel, bracing himself for her scathing assessment. One thing about Angel was that she never told a lie, not even a little white one to preserve her father's feelings. The deep purple blazer he'd had dry-cleaned and pressed specifically for the Petals N' Promises dance arrived from Marsha Pickens over at CinnaSudz in perfect condition. He looked good enough for his standards; his daughter's were something else entirely.

Angel pulled her pair of hot pink unicorn headphones off her ears and looked up at him properly. An ache shot through his chest. She looked more and more like her mother with every passing day.

The soft pink party dress complemented her deep ebony skin, making her brown eyes stand out. The 3D applique butterflies gave her dress a dreamy and whimsical look. When Angel had sent him a picture for the exact dress she wanted for the Petals N' Promises, he obliged with a tight smile. It'd cost him a fortune, but Angel was a good kid – the best thing that ever happened to him – and he vowed to always give her what she asked for, within reason, of course. He remembered giving Frankie Templeton over at The Velvet Fox his card details with his eyes closed.

The pink butterfly barrettes clipped to the side of her hair buns had Angel resembling a storybook garden princess. He was getting better at styling her hair. He was used to straight lines and buzzing clippers, but he took his time to learn some new styles, mostly buns. He was grateful for his daughter's patience.

Will wasn't afraid to admit that he struggled with parenting alone; whether to give too much or not enough. He knew he overcompensated for her mother not being very present in her life, but those were the cards he was dealt. Excuses were tools for incompetent men. Will was not one of them.

Angel gave him an uninterested thumbs up. 'Looks good, old man.'

He rolled his eyes. Last week she'd overheard Will's conversation with her grandfather, when Will jokingly called him an old man for complaining about knee pain. She'd been a nuisance ever since.

'Again with the old man stuff,' Will grumbled, turning back to his reflection. 'If I'm old, your grandpa is ancient.'

'Two things can be true,' she replied, flourishing her pointer finger in the air.

Her sarcastic timing was impeccable. But Angel had been advanced for as long as Will could remember. At nineteen months, she was having conversations with him, and once she'd started school, there was no stopping her from talking to anything with a pulse. It was a running joke within his family that Angel had never met a stranger in her life, and he had no doubt that she would leave the Jubilee with a new friend. She'd become fast friends with a senior (only in age) staying at the bed and breakfast with them this week, Miss Eleanor, and he knew she was itching to go downstairs to find her.

'Are you ready yet?' Angel inquired with a sigh that signaled her patience was dwindling.

The Daffodil Jubilee had fallen on the week of Angel's spring break, and having Eleanor to hang out with gave Angel something to do other than playing with her tablet, while they stayed at the Inn. Their bond made Will feel like less of a douchebag for not putting his daughter in science camp or swimming lessons like the other parents at Morningstar Elementary.

Will had to make a living, and Wesley and Vanessa Taylor were shelling out a pretty penny to keep the Inn's grounds looking pristine until the Jubilee. The Taylors graciously offered Will a place to stay while he worked the grounds, and to look after Angel while he was working at the barbershop. Every day, he diligently made the thirty-minute drive into town to cut hair during the day, and drove back out to the Inn to pull weeds and cut grass with his father under the evening sun.

The days were long; exhausting, actually, but when he returned to the Inn in the evenings, and Angel would tell him of the adventures she'd had with Eleanor that day, it was all worth the sacrifice.

The hard part was over now. The daffodils were in full bloom; the maze had been installed. The acres of grass had been mowed into stripes, the weeds pulled and treated. The landscaping was spectacular, if he did say so himself. His night was shaping up to be perfect.

'Go ahead.' Will relented now, pointing his chin toward the door. 'Find your buddy. I'll see you down there in a minute.'

Angel jumped up, tossing her tablet on the bed.

She slipped her shoes on at the door, a pair of white patent leather ballerina flats. Before she got too far, she turned to him.

'You look nice, Dad.' She beamed and shut the door behind her.

Will puffed his chest out a little bit more. He did look good, and he hoped it was enough to catch Morgan's attention. The second she had a minute alone, he was going to swoop in with a handful of freshly clipped daffodils and they would spend the rest of the night slow dancing in each other's arms. That was how it played out in his head, anyway.

The door closed behind him with a soft click. There was no turning back now.

He journeyed downstairs, passing the bustling kitchen toward the back door. Eddie Rutherford, the caterer of the Jubilee, shouted directives to someone unseen. Inside was a flurry of activity as wait staff passed each other in a blur, loading and unloading trays of hors d'oeuvres for the partygoers.

A young lady in a standard black uniform squeezed past him in the narrow hallway, a wide silver platter covering her face, blond braids peeking out from underneath. Will ducked just in time to miss smashing into it. He made it to the back door without incident and stepped out into the spring night.

The air was cool and fragrant, the scent of blooming daffodils wafting over the lawn. Sunlight was fading, giving way to the soft indigo of the early evening.

Strings of golden lights twinkled above the grounds like fireflies caught mid-dance.

The Inn had been transformed; tables draped with white linen lined the stone path, vases bursting with yellow and white daffodils at their center. Music floated from hidden speakers tucked in the shrubbery, the soft pluck of an acoustic guitar accompanied the murmur of laughter and the clink of cocktail glasses and silverware as the guests worked on their appetizers.

'Mr. Reed!' Will stopped when he spotted Caleb and Jeremiah together at a table, ties crooked and jackets hanging off their wiry frames. Both boys were shoveling food into their mouths like they hadn't eaten in days, grinning at each other between bites.

Will reached over, giving each one a dap. 'Lookin' good, fellas.' Will plucked at Caleb's oversized shirt. 'A little wrinkled, but good.'

'Lookin' like your uncle shrunk and left them clothes for you,' Jeremiah joked around a mouth full of something chewed to bits.

'Where you get those shoes from? Clowns R Us?' Caleb shot back, their howls of laughter curling into the night. Will felt a swell of pride that they'd shown up at all, sitting with their heads high.

He clapped both of them on the shoulder. 'You boys clean up better than I thought,' he said, though his eyes started to wander across the lawn.

Jeremiah smirked, elbowing Caleb while they watched Will.

'Love struck,' Caleb singsonged, earning another round of laughter.

Will shook his head, trying not to grin as he backed away from the table.

'Save room for dinner,' he muttered.

With their laughter trailing behind him, he slipped into the crowd, scanning for one face: Morgan's.

Will followed the path, passing couples in their spring best: linen suits and floral dresses. Judging from the crowd, the Daffodil Jubilee was a town favorite, coming in second place only to the Fall Festival. Cinnamon Falls, and all its traditions seemed silly at first when he and Angel arrived almost three years ago, but the little town was growing on him, fast.

He caught sight of Morgan sitting alone in the gazebo, watching the river dawdle past. As he moved toward her, his heart revved.

Her dress, lavender, soft as a spring morning, clung to her curves like it'd been sewn onto her body. It nearly undid him at the seams. It wasn't flashy like all the other women's choices, with gaudy rhinestones or glitter. The strapless neckline framed her collarbones like art in a museum. Tiny sculpted flowers were placed strategically along the bodice and down her ample hips; a garden blooming from the inside out. Even her shoes, strappy wedge sandals, made him want to do something ridiculous, like offer to carry her through the grass just so they wouldn't get dirty, or undo them with his teeth.

Her hair, pulled up into a complicated braid style, brought out her cheekbones, making her doe-like eyes the star of the show. He wanted to say everything he'd been thinking, but she looked so radiant, it stopped him cold in his tracks and TV static filled his brain.

As if it couldn't get any worse, he would stumble over his own feet, colliding face first with the woman he daydreamed about, sending the flowers he spent the entire winter and spring cultivating from root to bloom toppling over the gazebo's edge. And just when things reached a level of unforgivable mortification, then came the scream. The magical moment he planned down to the last possible detail, fizzled into the night right before his eyes.

All Will could think about as he trailed behind Morgan, was Angel. He spotted her, slipping through party-goers' legs, fighting her way through throngs of people gathering at the maze. Relief flooded him like a cool shower. It wasn't his baby that was hurt. He could breathe again. But what could have possibly happened? He hooked one arm around her waist, pulling her backward out of the chaos.

Angel's eyes, wild with fear, landed on his. 'Dad! I heard them say it's Miss Eleanor!'

No. Will's heart plummeted to his feet. Angel wrestled to get out of his grip, contorting herself, bucking against his strong frame. He pulled her in tighter, locking her to his side.

'Let me go!' She hiccupped, tears streaming out of her eyes, her tiny fists beating against his arms. 'It's her! I know it is! I couldn't find her anywhere!'

Will placed her down and dropped to one knee, making sure to keep a solid grip on his daughter's arm so she didn't get too far from him.

'Tell me what happened,' he said, trying to keep his voice level among the absolute chaos exploding around him. Throngs of people stampeded by, running wild this way and that. He didn't want Angel to get more upset than she already was. He kept glancing around through the crowd but couldn't spot Morgan. Where had she gone that quickly?

'It's Miss Eleanor! In there!' Angel cried as she pointed over his shoulder toward the hedge maze.

Will was torn. As much as he wanted to see what was happening, he had to take Angel someplace safe and out of the ruckus. She was his only priority right now.

He grabbed her hand, and Angel dug her heels in the soft grass. 'I'm not leaving without Miss Eleanor!'

Will pulled her in closer, coming face to face with his daughter. She swiped at her wet nose with the back of her hand. Her eyes were fierce with determination.

'Stay right here,' he advised. 'Do not move, do you understand me?'

'But . . .' Angel protested, crossing her arms over her chest.

'I'm going to find Miss Eleanor, okay? I'll be right back.'

She nodded just as Morgan's mother, Ms. Vanessa, was rushing past. She skidded to a stop when she noticed Will and Angel.

'Will! Thank goodness!' She clutched her hands over her ample chest. 'What's happening? I can't find Morgan anywhere!'

'I'm going to find her.' He gestured to his daughter, his eyes pleading in a way that he knew another parent would understand.

'I'll look out for her,' Morgan's mother promised as she reached down to grab Angel's hand. 'Let's get inside.'

'Two minutes,' he promised Angel, with a kiss on her forehead.

Then, he jetted into the maze.

Chapter 3

Morgan

Morgan used to think that the worst thing about Cinnamon Falls was its size. When she was younger, she remembered being terrified of the too-tall trees, and the nights blacker than shadows, illuminated only in snatches by the lightning bugs playing in the open fields next to the Inn. The sky seemed never-ending, stretching beyond the expansive grounds of their home, as far as she could see. Back then, everything felt out of her reach.

Now, she realized, the worst thing about Cinnamon Falls was the mortality rate. Why was someone always dying? And why, of all nights, did it have to be tonight?

Eleanor Langford stared up at Morgan with lifeless eyes. Her burnt-orange silk dress clung to her frail frame, lace-trimmed sleeves grazed her wrists and a vintage bejeweled brooch in the shape of a fox was fastened to it, just above her heart. Her simple gold kitten heels sat askew, inches away from her pale, veiny feet.

33

A headache pulsed behind Morgan's eyes, a dull throb that echoed the thrumming of her heart. Death really did have the worst timing.

'Come on, now,' Morgan groaned, crouching down until she was close to Miss Eleanor's body, silently pleading with her to stay on this side of the veil, expecting the woman to sit upright in an explosion of laughter as if this was some elaborate prank. But there was no movement, no breath. Just eerie stillness.

Eleanor and her late husband, Thomas Langford had once owned the Daffodil Inn, long before her parents decided to buy it. And yet, Eleanor never truly let it go. Like clockwork, she returned every year, checking in exactly one week before the Jubilee, much to her mother's chagrin.

The moment Eleanor's name hit the reservation list, Vanessa would spring into action, barking a never-ending list of orders. Every corner had to be swept, every baseboard scrubbed, every speck of dirt or dust banished to the ether.

Because if it wasn't, Eleanor could sniff it out, and comment on it. Loudly. She had a critical eye and an indiscriminate sharp tongue that often accompanied an arched brow and folded arms. From the time she checked in until she left, she offered a laundry list of unwanted opinions ranging from the paint colors to the arrangement of the furniture.

Over the years, Morgan had become an expert at navigating her moods. She was her father's child after all, hospitality was in her bones. Morgan always made sure to place Eleanor in the Garden Suite, the room with the best views of the wild daffodils that blanketed the field beside the Inn, Thomas's favorite. In his last days, Thomas would often request a slow drive past the Inn to marvel at them; and after he passed, Eleanor clung to those memories by having an annual staycation at the place he'd loved the most.

Every morning Morgan would watch Miss Eleanor drink her chamomile tea on the back porch and then mosey between the rows of flowers, crouching down to smell them or to stroke a velvet bloom between her fingers. Sometimes, Morgan would hear her talking to them, or maybe to her husband, she wasn't sure because she never interrupted. All she knew was that the flowers seemed to light something in Eleanor from the inside. And now, it'd been extinguished, with only a shell of a woman left behind.

'Pssst,' she whispered.

Eleanor didn't move.

'Miss Eleanor?' Morgan whispered again.

The body didn't stir.

Morgan leaned over, placing one finger underneath the woman's nose. No warm breath expelled.

'Don't do this,' she whispered to the skies. 'Not tonight.'

Morgan was just about to put her finger to Miss Eleanor's neck to feel for a pulse when the garden maze exploded ahead of her. A chunk of bush toppled over, making way for Will as he shouldered through the greenery, leaving a man-sized hole in his wake.

'Made a shortcut,' he muttered, brushing off the leaves caught in his suit jacket. He plucked a twig from behind his ear and brought his attention to Miss Eleanor, looking between her and Morgan.

'Dead?' he asked. His Adam's apple bobbed in his throat as he crept closer.

Morgan nodded, the weight of the truth pushing her backwards on her bottom. The grass was cool under her palms; the hard earth beneath her was a steady reminder that she wasn't dreaming. This was real.

'What the hell happened?' Will asked breathlessly.

'Caleb said he and his friends were trying to find the center of the maze and when they found it, Eleanor was just lying here, dead.'

'You think she's been out here all night?'

'Someone would have seen her before now. What am I going to do?' she mumbled aloud to no one in particular, her mind zooming with existential thoughts. If she didn't figure this out in the next few minutes, Morgan was going to be next on the deceased list once her mother got a hold of her. The garden maze had been Morgan's idea. She expected it to be a hit, not to backfire in her face. This would only give her fuel to tell Morgan 'I told you so!'

'I'll call Jesse,' Will suggested. 'He'll know what to do.'

Jesse was merely a detective and Morgan was past

that. She needed a physicist. Someone who could figure out the science behind time travel so she could go back to fifteen minutes ago when all was right with the world. She brought her legs to her chest, resting her forehead against her knees, bracing herself for the inevitable long night ahead.

'Hey, man. I know it's late, sorry to wake you. Oh, you weren't sleeping? Good. Listen, I'm at the Daffodil Inn with Morgan,' Morgan heard Will say. She looked up to see him clutching his cell phone to his ear, his voice low and thick with tension. 'We've got a bit of a situation.' He scrubbed the back of his neck and then pushed one hand into his pocket.

'Yeah, and I think she's dead . . .' Will looked to Morgan and silently conferred, 'Yeah, no pulse. Roger that. Thanks, man. See you in a minute.'

He turned back to Morgan. 'Jesse is on the way. He said to touch nothing and to clear the area as much as we can.'

Clear the area?

'What about the party?' Morgan couldn't stop the tears that pushed themselves out of her eyes. Months of planning had gone down the drain in a matter of seconds. Everything was ruined.

Will looked at her with an expression so gentle she wanted to morph into a pool of liquid. 'I think . . . it's over, Morg.'

Logically, Morgan knew that she would have to end the Jubilee early. But it felt like she was ripping her heart out of her own chest. How would she break the news to her parents? All their hard work whittled down to terrified residents and a dead body.

Will reached down to help her up, offering a hand attached to a veiny forearm. She took it and before she could get her footing, she was upright again, bracing herself against the concrete slabs that doubled as pectoral muscles under his shirt. Under normal circumstances, she would have loved to stay there, a breath apart from a man as fine as frog hair. But her night was turning out to be anything but normal.

'You okay?' he asked, his eyes searching hers, one hand bracing the small of her back, steadying her.

She was certainly *not* okay. Morgan shook her head. 'I don't think I can do this.'

'I'll be right there,' he promised. He pushed tangled branches out of the way and guided her through the man-sized hole in the bushes. 'Watch your head,' he advised.

Together, they stepped through five more jagged openings, with Will dutifully making sure that her or her dress didn't get snagged, until they reached the outer edge of the maze.

'Start at the beginning.' Chief Noelle Raines crossed her arms over her chest. Her gaze flitted around the Daffodil Inn's rustic kitchen, taking it all in. Morgan wondered what Raines was thinking while her eyes trailed the reclaimed oak beams that spanned the length of the ceiling, courtesy of Old Man Milton's barn house renovation several years prior. Morgan always loved how the warm blend of natural materials gave the tight kitchen a larger feel; that was her mother's magical touch.

Food filled every inch of the marble countertops; cramped with dozens of tiered trays of Eddie Rutherford's carefully crafted hors d'oeuvres: delectable brie and fig crostinis, wedge garden salad skewers for the conscious eaters, bacon-wrapped jalapeno poppers for a little spice, single serve charcuterie presented in adorable little mason jars that Eddie called 'jarcuterie', garlic parmesan shrimp bites, and sundried tomato basil roll ups wilted on tiered trays while they waited.

Morgan and Eddie had spent the past two weeks agonizing over the menu. Now, Eddie leaned against the door jamb, a sickly green tint crawling over his skin. This was his first big event as the new owner of Rosie's Diner after Rosie was tragically killed. It wouldn't have been a Cinnamon Falls celebration without her award-winning cinnamon buns. Eddie had made sure to include them for dessert, cutting them into bite-sized spirals.

It was near 10 p.m. and Chief Raines managed to still be suited up in uniform. Morgan wondered if she ever took it off after being sworn in. It was the only time she'd ever seen the woman smile.

'Where's Jesse?' Morgan inquired. Raines wasn't the friendliest cop on the block and she needed to see a familiar face; someone who could soothe her fears; someone who could stop the thoughts from spiraling in her head.

'At the maze,' Raines responded curtly. 'The beginning, please,' she insisted, never looking Morgan's way. Her pen was poised over her notepad with a mechanical patience.

Vanessa took a deep, shuddering breath while seated on the dining bench at the farmhouse style island, her hands wrung together so tightly her knuckles had gone white. Both Morgan and her father, Wesley, flanked her on both sides, keeping her steady.

Vanessa was not a person built for surprises. Any unpredictable inconvenience could send her into a tailspin. A death on their property was DEFCON Level 1 for her family. The fallout from this would be worse.

The news coverage . . . the rumors . . . the losses . . .

Her family . . . They could lose everything.

Don't think like that, she told herself. *Think positive thoughts*. But inside all she felt was a black pit of doom growing in her stomach. Her skin flamed, dots clouded her vision, and it felt like the walls were marching, inching closer and closer toward her.

'We were near the stage,' Vanessa began, her voice soft but steady.

Wesley jumped in, nodding. 'We were talking to

the new mayor, Sterling Tate. He pulled us aside to congratulate us, talkin' about some big plans for the town. Then people started screaming and . . .' He looked toward Vanessa, his throat working, but no words emerging. 'He never got to finish.'

Chief Raines lifted her gaze briefly. 'And you saw nothing?'

'Nothing,' Vanessa reiterated. 'Sterling was mid-sentence when we heard the scream.' Her voice cracked. 'We . . . had no idea someone had been hurt, let alone that it was Eleanor.'

Raines scribbled some more. 'We'll follow up with Mayor Tate. Tell me about the victim.'

'She was a regular guest here,' Wesley stated. He shook his head, like the answer had to gel together in his mind. 'She came every year for the Jubilee.'

Raines' eyebrows rose. 'Is that right? About how long had she been here before tonight?'

'Five nights, since Monday. She and her husband used to own the house before we bought it and changed it into a bed and breakfast. She likes to come back from time to time and reminisce.'

Vanessa grunted and Raines picked up on it immediately. 'Not a fan?' Raines asked, her pen scribbling quicker along the page. Morgan craned her neck to see what she was writing, but was too far away to make it out.

Her mother pushed air through her teeth. 'She was very . . . particular,' Vanessa replied, finding the right words to say. 'But we welcomed her like we would any other guest.'

'Hmm,' was all Raines said in response.

Vanessa looked at Wesley with pleading eyes, then Chief Raines. 'What now? We've got a backyard full of people. What do we do?'

Raines stuck her pen in the pocket of her shirt and folded her notepad closed in slow, measured movements. 'You're going to have to shut it all down, Mrs. Taylor. I'll give you some time to get these people out of here. We'll help with guiding the traffic and all that. In the morning, we'll come back, talk to the rest of the staff, and go from there.'

No. Morgan had to stop this waking nightmare. *Wake up*, she willed herself. This was their biggest night of the year. The profits made from tonight would normally carry them through winter's dry season until the next spring arrived. They couldn't just *shut it all down*. It would kill their business. There had to be another way.

Morgan released her fists, staring down at the palms of her hands where her nails dug crescent shapes into her skin. She rose so quickly the room spun.

'I'm going to find Jesse,' she declared and exited the room before anyone could stop her.

Chapter 4

Will

After Will made sure Angel was upstairs tucked away under the covers, he spotted Jesse Shaw pulling up the gravel driveway in his police cruiser. A moment later, Grace Whitfield arrived in her midnight black Caprice, her expression grim. Guests stood around, mouths agape at the scene unfolding, their phones sweeping back and forth while they recorded. Now that the coroner had arrived, every lingering doubt had vanished. Someone had died at the Jubilee.

A sinking feeling settled in his gut and Will knew things had taken a turn for the worse. Cinnamon Falls had *just* returned to normal after Rosie's death. By morning, every detail would be retold in group texts and over checkout counters. Tonight would be fodder for gossip for the next six months.

It all felt surreal. One minute he was with Morgan, her soft frame pressed against his, and the next, he was staring down at the lifeless body of a woman his kid adored more than anyone. The joy of the evening dissolved into a sobering chill that hadn't lifted.

An icy wind pushed through the fields, reminding Will that winter wasn't long gone.

The Taylors didn't deserve this. Vanessa and Wesley were good people. They'd opened their doors to him and Angel without hesitation, gifting them a week of comfort and care they hadn't experienced since he moved away from Macon.

They'd treated him like family.

Lionel cooked anything Angel requested, something she unabashedly took advantage of, and Ms. Vanessa doted on them both, ensuring their needs were met before he had a chance to request anything. Miss Eleanor had been Angel's constant companion all week, teaching her how to speak up, stand tall, and think for herself. The girl had grown sassier overnight, but Will hadn't minded. It was the most fun he'd seen her have in a while.

Eleanor didn't deserve to pass on the night she cherished the most. A crowd of women in pastel gowns crossed the lawn, lifting their dresses to avoid the damp grass, heels wobbling with each step. The party had long since ended, but the consequences were just beginning.

Will clenched his jaw. The worst feeling in the world wasn't grief, it was helplessness. And he wasn't about to stand around in sticky, formal clothing, whispering behind his hand and speculating like everyone else.

He didn't know how, but he was going to find out what happened. For Angel. For the Taylors. For Miss Eleanor, too. No matter how long it took.

Will jogged toward the maze, passing newly appointed Mayor Sterling Tate, clad in a light gray tailored blazer and casual but comfortable slim cut navy chinos. A yellow daffodil printed pocket square hung loosely out of the blazer's pocket. His crisp white dress shirt boasted no tie, his top button undone in a relaxed fashion.

Will knew what it was like to be an outsider in a tight-knit place like Cinnamon Falls. The even-toned politician did a lot of shaking hands and soothing fears as he guided guests down the gravel driveway to their vehicles. It was the first time the new mayor had been seen outside of Town Hall. He had practically lived there since Mayor Lyons was ousted. Tonight was meant to have been his big debut; a chance for the whole town to get to see their new commander in chief.

There were rumors that he'd been appointed by the state government to 'fix' the town. Harold Bones, Will's boss, owner of Bones' Barbershop, and the town's number one rumor resource, said Mayor Tate used to be some kind of government accountability expert in Atlanta, the person people called to clean up a place after a tragedy, especially one as sinister as a murder. As Will passed him, he wondered how Mayor Tate would handle another death in Cinnamon Falls.

Mayor Tate directed an elderly couple to their car

with a pleasant nod. He looked polished and calm under pressure. Had anyone filled him in?

'Mayor Tate,' Will called out, extending a hand.

The mayor turned, flashing a smooth, practiced smile, collecting his hand with a firm shake. 'Evening!' he boomed. 'You need help getting to your car, son?'

Will shook his head. 'I'm a guest here. My father's Calvin Reed, we own Reed & Roots.'

Recognition flickered across the mayor's face. 'Ah, yes! I met your father earlier this evening. I complimented him myself on the landscaping; the daffodil beds are perfect. Beautiful work.'

Will nodded. 'Appreciate that. We worked hard. I helped design the hedge maze, too . . . though I guess that part's not going over so well anymore.'

Tate shook his head, pushing his hands in his pants pockets. 'Earlier in the day it was a hit. The kids loved it. Shame about the situation. I'm hearing the police have it all under control; just a matter of clearing folks out now.'

Will was right. Tate had no idea how tragic the night had become. The fixer had a lot of fixing to do. 'Eleanor Langford should still be here, celebrating. She loved this place.'

The mayor froze. The flicker of alarm in his eyes was swift, unmistakable, like a man spotting a fuse already lit. He took a quick step back.

'Well, I should check in with law enforcement, offer support. If you'll excuse me, Mr. Reed.' Tate didn't wait for a reply. He pivoted on his heel, and flipped out his cell phone, barking orders. He hurried down the gravel path toward the front entrance where a black truck swooped in and Mayor Tate climbed inside. Will watched him go, but that strange look clung to the edge of his thoughts.

Will glanced upward at his bedroom from the mouth of the maze. Everything had gone wrong so quickly.

His room was dark on the inside, curtains drawn, which meant there was a strong possibility Angel was pretending to be asleep. His daughter was curious and it was only a matter of time before she moseyed over to the window or crept her way down the back stairs to get a front row seat to the commotion. Every second they hadn't moved Ms. Eleanor's body was a second too long. Sooner or later Angel was going to find out that she'd been right. Her favorite person was no longer. The thought of breaking his daughter's heart brought tears to his eyes. How was he going to explain this to her?

He ducked back into the maze, following the pattern he'd memorized after installing it until he reached the center.

'Don't move, please,' Grace called out to him as he approached, holding one gloved hand out. She was crouched down next to Ms. Eleanor's body, studying her closely.

Grace and her older brother, Gage Whitfield, ran

the Whitfield Family Mortuary. From the little Will
knew about her, she was all business, all the time.
Her long hair was pulled back in a tight ponytail, a
headlamp rested on her forehead. She wore a long
black coat over her jeans and T-shirt, with deep
pockets, that Will was sure were lined with the tools
of her trade. Will stayed on the outer edge of the
scene, respecting the invisible perimeter she'd drawn,
giving her all the space she needed.

Jesse stood over her shoulder, hands fisted on his
hips. They met eyes and nodded, giving each other a
silent but somber greeting. When Morgan had told
Will that Ms. Eleanor was dead, the only person he
thought to call was Jesse. It helped being good friends
with a detective. He and Jesse had grown close after
Will started cutting his hair weekly. A reluctant client
had turned into a solid friend, and nights like tonight,
Will was especially grateful for him.

Jesse studied the woman lying in the grass. 'Looks
like Eleanor Langford.'

Grace's camera flashed, lighting up the area,
temporarily blinding the group.

The hair stood up on the back of Will's neck. He
felt Morgan before she appeared beside him. He fought
for eye contact with her, but she didn't turn her head
in his direction. She'd been crying. She slapped at her
wet eyes just as she started to step over the hedge.
Without thinking, Will placed one hand in front of
her, stopping her from going any closer.

At the same time Grace warned, 'Not so fast, girly.'

After scribbling on his notepad, Jesse brought his pen to his mouth. He cocked his head to the side, getting another good look at her.

'Was she a guest here?' Grace asked. Another flash popped and Will was scared that the sudden blaze of light would erase his memory.

'Yeah,' Morgan responded. She ran a hand through the braids that had come loose from her knotted hairstyle. Will noticed that some were highlighted with an electric purple. 'Checked in on Monday. We always give her the Garden Suite.'

Morgan pointed up toward the room that hung off the edge of the house. French doors that led to a private balcony were slung open, curtains flapping in the breeze. An interior light was still on deep within the room, glowing from the inside.

'Always?' Jesse questioned.

'She comes every year and stays for the Jubilee,' Morgan explained.

'Is it possible that she fell?' Jesse asked, glancing from Miss Eleanor to the balcony and back. All four of them craned their neck upward. It was a long way down, and she would have surely broken a limb with a fall that far.

'No way,' Morgan said first. 'Someone would have seen an old lady leaping off the ledge.'

'What *exactly* happened?' Jesse asked, using a nasally voice that Will had never heard before.

Is this his cop voice? he wondered.

It felt like yesterday when Jesse had been neck-deep in a murder case that rocked Cinnamon Falls to its core. By the time the dust settled, the town's beloved and longtime mayor, Asad Lyons, and police chief, Vernon Prescott, were both exposed for corruption in the murder of Sienna Rose and her mother, Rosslyn, affectionately known as Rosie, the previous owner of Rosie's Diner.

It wasn't just a small scandal, it was an earthquake; the kind that split trust down the middle and left folks picking through the rubble of what they thought they knew about their small wholesome town. It caused a shake up in the community so severe, people were just now starting to breathe easier and gossip about petty neighborhood drama instead of cover-ups and courtroom verdicts.

'That's what you're supposed to figure out!' Morgan fired back. 'One minute I'm choking on a strawberry and the next I'm sprinting through the crowd because someone screamed like they were being murdered.'

'Who?' Grace and Jesse asked at the same time. Will searched the skies for an owl.

'Dunno,' she answered through tight lips. 'Caleb Brewster was the one who pointed me into the maze.' Morgan crossed her arms over her chest, her eyes darting between Grace and Jesse. 'Where's Nia?'

Jesse straightened at the mention of his fiancée's

name. Another flash popped as Grace went back to work. Will coughed to break the silence that was getting louder by the second.

'Home, asleep,' Jesse quipped. 'The Jubilee wiped her out. Now back to this—'

'I don't see any evidence of foul play, Officer Shaw,' Grace cut in, all business. 'I'd have to get her back on my table to know more, but I don't see any defensive wounds or unnatural bruising of any kind. Old age, perhaps?'

'So, what, she just *chose* tonight to kick the bucket?' Morgan asked.

Will coughed a laugh into his fist again. It was *not* funny at all, but Morgan had a way to make almost any situation a comedy hour.

'Unfortunate, but it's not like you can choose when you go,' Grace commented.

Jesse spoke into the radio mounted on his shoulder. 'Get Gage up here with the gurney. We're taking the body back to the morgue.'

Seconds later, Terrance Chambers and Gage Whitfield arrived. Terrance was Jesse's partner at the Cinnamon Falls Police Department. The slim man peeked in, crouching low through the maze holes Will left.

'We won't be able to get it through here,' Chambers reported. 'We'll have to cut the hedge down before we can move her.'

'Will knows the way,' Morgan volunteered.

'Got everything you need?' Jesse asked Grace who was stripping off her gloves with a wet smack.

She nodded. Will and Morgan stepped aside as Terrance and Gage stepped through the maze. They flanked Eleanor's body on each side.

'Ready?' Jesse asked. The men nodded in unison. Jesse hooked his hands under her arms, while Terrance supported her midsection and Gage held her legs. In one movement the men rolled her to the side.

'Wait!' Grace cried, her camera flashing back to back. 'Forget everything I said,' she announced. Crouching down, she flipped a new glove out of her back pocket and reached for something just beneath Eleanor's body. A gasp escaped her lips.

She pulled her hand back. The white latex glove was slick with blood shining in the sliver of moonlight. In her grasp was a tiny ceramic teacup, its dainty swirl pattern obscured by dark crimson. Morgan's face twisted in confusion, then recognition. She slapped a hand over her mouth. The cup dangled off Grace's pinky finger as she held it in the air, assessing it.

'I'm going to take this back to the lab, but this isn't what killed her.' She crouched again and Will saw it at the same moment Grace did – a glint of metal. The blood-soaked fabric gave way to reveal a hilt of a thin-handled knife, buried deep in her back.

Grace stood slowly, her face pale. She turned to the group, her voice grim.

'Detective Shaw, you have a murder on your hands.'

Chapter 5

Morgan

Morgan's heels echoed through the empty house; a sharp contrast to the chaos happening outside. Out there, all hell had broken loose. Distant sirens whooped, closing in, while red and blue lights covered the premises. Uniformed officers swarmed the driveway, directing traffic that began to bottleneck at the entrance.

In the kitchen, her parents were still in their Jubilee clothes. Her mother stood at the sink, her fingers gripping an unopened bottle of wine as though she'd been contemplating downing the whole thing. She spun around just as Morgan entered, the train of her black one-shouldered, rhinestone studded dress whipping around her coke bottle frame in a dramatic *whoosh*. Her father sat at the head of the long island, eyes glazed, tie loosened, his palms lying flat against the table like he needed it to keep him upright.

Neither of them spoke. Morgan wasn't sure that they were actually seeing her in front of them; too busy calculating how much damage was done to their reputation of a safe, peaceful harbor – now a crime scene.

Chief Raines was gone. Eddie Rutherford, too. Daphne, their family border collie, scurried across the checkered print tile to reach her, her paws tip-tapping across the floor. She was too big now for Morgan to scoop her up in her arms so she sank to the floor instead, holding Daphne close. Judging from the way Daphne was shaking, she was terrified. Morgan planted soft kisses to the top of her head, reassuring her that everything would be okay, even if she didn't believe it herself. She scratched behind Daphne's ears, raking her fingers through her soft, black and white fur. Her tail swished back and forth before resting on the tile.

'Had to let her out of the basement, she wouldn't stop crying,' her mother mumbled, gesturing toward Daphne. Vanessa looked over at Morgan, her eyes glassy with tears.

'Can you believe in this whole house I can't find the damn wine opener?' She slammed the closest drawer shut, silverware rattling around inside. 'What did they say about Eleanor?'

'Grace won't know anything for certain until she gets her to the morgue,' Morgan replied, wondering if she should tell them everything. The truth pressed against her chest, heavy like stone. Silence, she decided, was worse than bad news. 'She . . . found something,' she added.

Her father finally looked up, his steely gaze locking onto her.

'A teacup under Eleanor's body.'

Vanessa blinked like her daughter was speaking in code. 'She's always walking around with one. Found them everywhere she went.'

'And a knife,' Morgan reported, holding Daphne closer. 'Eleanor was . . . murdered.'

Vanessa's body stilled. The wine bottle in her hand tipped to the side, and she barely caught it in time, sitting it down on the counter with a thud.

'No,' she whispered. The word slipped out of her mouth like it had startled her. Her hands flew to her mouth, then to her chest. 'No, no, no.' She shook her head, backing away as if the news was something physical, running toward her.

Her face drained of color. 'Here, in this house?' Her voice was rising now, panic clawing its way to the surface. She spun around to the window, peeling back the curtain.

'Vanessa . . .' her father started.

His wife continued, frantic. 'We need to get everyone off the property now.' The window over the sink gave her the perfect vantage point to see the entire backyard. If it were daytime, she could see straight to the river. 'Before Elaine Matthias shows up and we're in tomorrow's paper with the headline: Death at the Daffodil Inn.'

She turned to Wesley, eyes wide. 'Tell me this isn't happening. Tell me this night isn't ruined!'

Morgan hung her head. 'A woman is dead, Mom. We need to—'

'Yes, I know that,' her mother hissed. 'And trust me, no one is more devastated than your father and me. But that doesn't mean we just stand here while these people trample all over my flowers! They're ruining them!' she fussed. Daphne pushed her nose under Morgan's legs as her mother continued ranting.

'That Raines woman scared the photographer *and* the caterer so bad with her questions that we had to send them home.' She waved toward the untouched piles of food staring back at them. 'Do you know how much we paid for those brie crostinis? And the shrimp? Wesley, the shrimp!'

'You're worried about shrimp right now?' Morgan asked, incredulous.

'It's not about the shrimp—' Wesley jumped in.

'I'm worried about the Inn, Morgan!' Her mother emphasized, tears crowding her eyes. 'Your father and I worked our entire lives to build this place into something respectable; something enduring that could last way beyond us, beyond you! Do you know how fragile a reputation is in a place like this?'

Wesley stood slowly. 'Now, Vanessa,' he warned, his

voice deep with an authoritative baritone. Daphne's ears perked.

'No, she needs to hear this, Wesley.' Morgan's mother faced her, her eyes narrowed. 'Our entire lives are in this place, and now there's been a murder on our front lawn!'

Technically, it was the backyard, but Morgan didn't think this was the time for semantics. She looked between her parents, panic and disappointment lining their faces, like it was her fault. Why was everything always her fault?

'Do you think I *wanted* this to happen?' Morgan's voice cracked under the pressure that was building inside of her.

'No, honey, of course not,' Wesley started.

Vanessa opened her mouth to respond, but pressed her lips into a thin line instead. She turned back to the window, watching the lights flash across the lawn. Silence blanketed the kitchen. Morgan would have preferred to hear the voice sounding off in her mother's head than receive her cold shoulder. She braced herself for the eventual blame, even if her mother never said it. Besides, it was Morgan who pushed for the garden maze.

Vanessa rubbed her temples in slow circles and continued, 'Everyone needs to leave. I want this place cleared.'

Morgan crossed her arms. 'We can't just kick all the guests out! What do you want me to tell Zara and the Pruitts? Thanks for coming out, sorry about the corpse. Don't forget to leave us a five-star review!'

'Morgan,' Wesley warned. He shrugged back into his blazer and held his hand out to his daughter. 'We'll worry about the guests another time. For now, let's clear the lot and get these people to their cars.'

Morgan relented, taking his hand in hers as he pulled her to her feet. It was best that they left to diffuse the tension. Another word from her mother in her 'I'm so disappointed in you' tone was going to make Morgan burst a blood vessel, and they had enough tragedy for one night.

Vanessa took two handfuls of shrimp in her mouth as she busied herself with rifling through the drawers again. Morgan figured she was on the hunt for that missing corkscrew.

Her mother didn't look up as she said, 'And tell them not to walk through my flowerbeds.'

Daphne padded alongside Morgan while she and her father made their way to the door. Wesley pushed it open and Morgan stepped out first. The air met her with a sharp spring chill, crisp against her cheeks, but beneath it lingered something heavier; an undercurrent that clung to the chaos like the night was holding its breath.

People were slowly filing toward the street, murmuring like bees in a disturbed hive. Some were crying, others were whispering, craning their necks over the maze with a mixture of curiosity and fear that only comes when something terrible happens to someone else.

Morgan took a deep breath and put on the face she reserved for mandatory school assemblies and fundraisers.

'We're so sorry, everyone,' she called out to the crowd. 'Please head home safely. We will have more information soon. For now, we have to let the police do their work.'

'Do you know what happened?' someone from the crowd shouted.

Her father stiffened beside her. 'No,' he lied. 'We don't.'

Hours later, Morgan stepped out of the side door and planted both feet in her backyard. Her wiggling toes rejoiced, free from the shackles of pinching high heels. She dug her heels in deeper, the soft, cool grass welcoming her presence. Darkness enveloped her while moonlight glowed hauntingly against the slow-moving river.

The laughter and music from earlier were gone now, replaced by nature's nightly noise. Toads croaked without ceasing while the cicadas and crickets added to their orchestra. When she shifted her weight to pull out her cell phone, the motion sensor light popped on, bathing her in a warm but lonely glow. The aftermath of the frenzied night revealed itself.

The Daffodil Inn, her childhood home, looked like a natural disaster had blasted through it. The once pristine maze Will and his father worked so hard on was wrapped in yellow police tape. Chairs sat abandoned, overturned, in various states of collapse, surrounding the makeshift dancefloor. Stained pastel tablecloths that cloaked the high-top bar tables billowed in the passing breeze. Cups, silverware, and shattered plates glittered in the grass trampled beneath boot prints that crisscrossed this way and that.

If it weren't two in the morning, she would have screamed. She pushed down the lump in her throat. Morgan hugged herself, but the tears slipped through anyway. Crying always made her feel weak, like she'd let someone see the cracks inside her. She'd grown up chunky in a small town where anything bigger than a stick was frowned upon. She should be the queen of pressure.

She unlocked her phone, revealing a barrage of missed notifications; tags, messages, videos and mentions. One video was trending, primed to go viral; a slow pan of the police tape with dramatic music over the caption 'Killer garden party.'

Someone commented: 'So much for Southern hospitality.'

Another comment: 'Never coming to this place again. Night ruined.'

Her breath hitched. She couldn't bring herself to read the Inn's reviews. Bad press meant bad reviews; bad reviews meant no bookings, and no bookings meant . . .

Just as her vision tunneled, a familiar voice cut through the noise.

'Morgan?'

She turned quickly, blinking hard to clear the tears, and stowed her phone away. Will stood a few feet away, Daphne panting at his side, tongue hanging out of her open mouth. A thin T-shirt was tucked into a utility jacket that clung to Will's broad frame. He clutched Daphne's hot pink leash in one hand, a half-empty bottle of beer in the other. He must have taken her for a night walk, Daphne's favorite. Everyone needed a moment of solitude to recuperate from the drama, she thought.

'Hey,' she said, trying to clear her throat without making it obvious. Daphne galloped over to her excitedly. Morgan leaned down to pet her head and then the dog laid down beside her feet. 'I thought you and Angel would have gone home after everything.'

'Didn't feel right leaving without checking on you,' he replied, stuffing his free hand into his jacket pocket. 'Plus, it's late. I wouldn't dare wake Angel up now.' Will gestured to Daphne. 'Saw this one sniffing around, figured she needed a friend.'

'She has a thing for walks at night,' Morgan said.

He stepped up beside her, quiet for a moment, the

toads' croaking filling the silence. Morgan appreciated it. She didn't need empty words of comfort right now. She needed someone to share it with.

She wished Nia were here. Her best friend always knew what to do. Nia solved Rosie's murder on sheer determination alone. She had a little help from Jesse, but Nia wouldn't stop, even when it cost her the family business. It took a whole year, but they'd rebuilt, and The Cinnamon Scoop was stronger than ever now. Morgan wanted to believe that the same thing was possible for her parents, but she couldn't focus on some future salvation out of sight. She didn't have time for that. All she had right now was the disaster in front of her.

'The Inn is doomed,' Morgan finally said aloud.

Will waited. Morgan continued.

'All my mom cares about are the daffodils. My father is mortified and I'm just . . .' She wrapped her arms around herself. *Trying not to cry*, Morgan thought.

'You're holding it together better than most,' Will responded. 'I saw you out there earlier.' He gestured toward the front porch. 'I think you're doing the best you can given the . . . circumstances.'

Morgan shook her head, hugging herself tighter. 'Everything feels like my fault,' she mumbled.

Will nodded slowly. Morgan pretended not to notice how the moonlight reflected off his deep skin tone, and how from her vantage point, his lips made the perfect shape of a heart.

'Nothing that happened tonight is your fault, Morgan. This isn't on you.'

'I feel so . . . guilty,' she responded.

He took a long sip of his beer and let out a breath. 'Yeah, I get that,' he replied after a while. The tone of his voice made her turn to study him. He wasn't smiling anymore. 'When I was a teenager, I was always the one who messed up. Skipped classes, got in fights, all sorts of crazy stuff. Almost fucked up my dad's business because of it.'

'Crazy stuff,' she mumbled, her mind racing with thoughts. Who was Will before he came to Cinnamon Falls? Would she ever find out?

'I drove my dad mad. He'd constantly compare me to my brother.'

Morgan raised an eyebrow. There were two of him? 'Let me guess, your brother's a neurosurgeon with a nurse for a wife. They've got a perfect kid and golden retriever named Biscuit.'

At her feet, Daphne grumbled.

'Close,' Will laughed. 'He's a cardiologist and his wife's a CPA. I've got twin nephews, Jayden and Jordan, all straight As in school, nothing less; and they've got two fish, Bert and Ernie.'

Morgan snorted. 'Of course they do.'

The corner of Will's mouth lifted in a small smile and he took another swig of beer. 'My dad's land-scaping business was always supposed to go to me. But after I . . . strayed off the ideal son path, he stopped mentioning it.' Morgan noted the tension in his jaw while he continued, 'I went to barber school, started cutting hair. Figured if I wasn't getting in on the family business I could make my own way, you know?'

Morgan knew about the complications of a family business more than anyone.

'When I was growing up, all I wanted was to be normal for once. I convinced my parents to let me go to public school instead of being homeschooled by a woman who still called Georgia's capital Marthasville.' Will snorted a laugh in response. 'Then, there were two Morgans in my first-grade class, so I started wearing purple to set myself apart. I didn't want to be the *other* Morgan or the girl whose parents owned the Inn. I just wanted to be . . .' Morgan bit her lip. 'Seen for who I am, not for what everyone wants me to be. Just me.'

Tears pricked her eyes and she willed them away. She'd done enough crying for one night. 'I used to think my mom was bulletproof. Even in slow seasons, we somehow found our way through.' Morgan blinked rapidly, fighting the emotion swelling in her throat. 'I don't know if we can fight our way through this one,' she whispered. 'The reviews, the media, the police – how do you come back from something like . . . murder?'

Will set his bottle down on the ground and turned to her, full on.

'We'll figure it out. You and me. Your family did me a solid and a Reed always pays his debts. We'll put our heads together, find out who did this, and clear your family's name. You're not in this alone.'

She looked up at him, and for a fleeting moment, the fear, the pressure, the crushing weight of responsibility paused.

'Why are you being so nice to me?' she asked, her voice barely above a whisper.

'Because I see you,' Will replied. 'Even though you want to, deep down, you won't quit. That means something to me.'

The words hit her like a warm gust of wind. She smiled for the first time in what felt like days. Then, he held out his hand.

'I, um, never got to give you those flowers, or this dance.'

Morgan scoffed, her heart beating in surround sound in her chest. 'There's no music.'

Will held one finger over his lips as nature's nightly orchestra cocooned them. 'There's plenty.'

He waited patiently while Morgan looked between him and his outstretched hand. He was acting like this night wasn't a mess, like they had time for a dance when everything was ruined—

'Tell your brain to shut up,' Will cut in, a smirk dancing on his lips. 'Everything else can wait.'

Morgan placed her hand in his. Then, as if pulled by an invisible thread, he drew her in. His arms wrapped around her waist and she rested her head on his chest. She held on to the one steady thing in a world that felt like it was tilting under her feet.

He swayed and she followed. Under the blinking stars and the scent of crushed daffodils, they danced, heart to heart, serenaded by nature's ragtag band.

Chapter 6

Sunday

Will

Will jolted awake, his insides stirring. He never ignored a gut feeling. Something was wrong. He lay still in bed, straining his ears for the sound that woke him out of his sleep. All he heard was silence in return, and silence was always suspicious around a tiny human.

Will cracked his eyes open, one at a time, taking in the sunrise just beginning to filter through the sheer blue curtains at the window. He pushed himself up and stretched out the tension in his back until it gave a satisfying release. He couldn't wait to get back home to his king-sized mattress and the dividing wall between his and Angel's bedroom. As much as he was enjoying the time spent in close quarters with his baby girl, he was looking forward to some parental privacy.

Looking across the room, Will quickly discovered that Angel was not snoring in the bed opposite him.

The covers were thrown back like she'd left in a hurry. Two quick steps across the room and he found that her sheets were icy cold.

With sleep still deep in his bones, he walked to their adjoining restroom.

'Peach?' he called to her behind the closed door. She didn't answer, though it could have been because she had a love-hate relationship with the nickname her maternal grandmother had given her when she was a baby. When Tanya brought Angel home from the hospital, she was wrapped up tight in a pink blanket. Tanya's mother, a Georgia-bred woman through and through, started calling her 'my sweet little peach', affectionately named after the peach state itself. The name stuck around. Tanya and her mother, however, did not.

He slid the pocket door back.

Empty.

It had taken Will hours to fall asleep last night. The scream had been replaying in his head on a loop, with Angel's gut-wrenching cries following and Grace's chilling statement waiting in the wings. He had to find his daughter. If he still felt haunted, there was no telling what she was feeling.

Dashing out of the room, Will was careful not to slip on the thin runner that stretched from one end of the hall to the other. He took the steps two by two, the antique hardwood rattling under his weight, until he reached the ground floor.

He found Angel seated in the great room, in her matching pink pajamas with one sock missing. Daphne was working said sock between her teeth, curled up beside Angel while she scratched away on her iPad. A teacup with barely an inch of tea sat abandoned on the table next to her. It had the same design as the one Grace found last night.

Angel and Miss Eleanor had a morning routine; they'd watch the sunrise and enjoy their tea together. Afterward, they would walk the daffodil fields. He wondered how long Angel had been waiting for Miss Eleanor to arrive. The pang in his heart snatched his breath away. He pinched the bridge of his nose to stop the tears. He could cry later.

Sometimes, he wished he had a partner, someone to lean on, someone who could take the lead on navigating a conversation about death. He stayed up late reading parenting books when Tanya was pregnant and none of them had the chapter: *How to Tell Your Seven-Year-Old That Her Best Friend Isn't Coming Back*.

Now wasn't the time for wallowing about his lack of help. He had to be strong for Angel. If she asked about Miss Eleanor, he would tell her what he knew within reason. But if she didn't, well, he didn't have a plan for what that meant.

Angel didn't look up as Will got closer. Daphne's ears pointed to the sky as he cleared his throat, announcing his presence. She whipped around and placed her paws on the back of the sofa, her generous tail swiping across the screen of Angel's tablet, blocking her view.

'Move, Daffy,' Angel complained, scrambling to grab Daphne's tail, which only wagged faster and faster out of her reach.

Will leaned down to give Daphne a few morning scratches and she repaid his kindness with happy swipes of her tongue on his forearm. Angel still hadn't turned around. He noticed her unicorn headphones tight over her ears, so he tapped her on the shoulder.

'Mornin', sunshine,' Will started, funneling all the bass he could muster in his voice.

Angel removed the headphones and saved the sketch she was working on before looking up at her father.

'I was thinking pancakes,' she said matter-of-factly, like they hadn't spent the night wrapped in police tape.

He could tell that she wasn't okay, not by a long shot, but it was clear that she didn't want to talk about it yet. Despite her age, Angel had no problem expressing her opinion, whether good, bad, unwarranted or requested. Will constantly wondered if growing up without a mother left a hole in her life. And now, he wondered if losing Miss Eleanor would set her back in a different way. It was one thing to lose a loved one, it was another thing entirely to lose someone who was chosen family; a friend.

'Let's pack up and then we can hit the Toasted Pecan?' Will offered.

She looked up at him, sleep caked in the corners of her eyes. 'Do they still have those cinnamon pancakes with the honey syrup?' She looked so much like her mother sometimes it made him ill. Tanya could have saved them all so much heartbreak if she hadn't . . .

'And the maple butter,' he added in, keeping his voice even despite the fact he wanted to break down. He wished he could take Angel's pain away; rewind the clocks back to last night when she was a garden fairy princess in her expensive butterfly gown. How he was feeling now, he'd buy twenty more dresses if it made his daughter smile even a bit. 'You can get as much whipped cream as you like.'

Angel's lips lifted in a sad smile. Even a half smile was still a victory in Will's book.

Will grabbed the teacup and walked to the kitchen while Angel dashed upstairs, Daphne on her heels. Ms. Vanessa was seated at the kitchen table, nursing a steaming cup of coffee, her expression vacant. The ceramic mug trembled slightly in her hand, a betrayal to the stillness she fought to maintain.

He crossed the room, placing the delicate teacup in the dishwasher and closing it gently. It snapped shut, the sound unusually loud in the heavy silence of the early morning. Will leaned against the counter.

'We're gonna head out,' he said softly. 'Angel's got a taste for pancakes.'

Vanessa looked up and blinked. Will noticed that yesterday's makeup was still present on her lined face. He wondered if she'd slept at all, or stayed up, rooted to the kitchen floor all night.

'Of course,' she said after a beat. 'I'm just sitting here waiting for the police to arrive. Chief Raines said they'd be here bright and early. Thank you for staying; for everything. I know she adored Eleanor.'

'She did,' Will replied, his voice thick. 'So did I.' He paused, rubbing the back of his neck. 'You've been good to us, Ms. Vanessa. I don't take that lightly. Thank you for opening your doors to us, despite everything going on.'

She nodded, offering a tepid smile. 'You're welcome, Will. You and Angel are welcome anytime.'

Before he could reply, footsteps thundered overhead and continued down the steps. Daphne arrived first then Mr. Pruitt appeared in the doorway with his wife close behind, their stuffed suitcases' wheels rolling against the hardwood floor.

'We're checking out,' Mr. Pruitt, a wiry man in his mid-sixties, announced. He quickly pulled his brown newsboy cap down around his large ears, and jutted his chin forward in a way that made him look perpetually annoyed with the situation. The deep crease between his brows that had likely been formed sometime during the Nixon administration never relaxed. Mr. Pruitt's khakis were crisply ironed and hemmed over his rubber-soled trainers.

Beside him, Mrs. Pruitt adjusted the strap of her oversized paisley handbag, her lips pressed into a disapproving line. She wore a pink wool cardigan over a white blouse buttoned all the way to her neck. A thin gold chain sported a crucifix nestled beneath her collar. Her salt and pepper hair was held back by a thin headband, not a strand out of place. She scanned the kitchen from behind a pair of bifocals, like she expected dust – or sin – to leap out of the corners. Will glanced at the rooster-shaped clock on the wall. It'd just reached 6 a.m.

Vanessa shot to her feet. 'Oh, please don't rush off. Lionel will be here any minute to start breakfast, and I'd be more than happy to comp your stay for the night—'

'Vanessa, that won't be necessary.' Mrs. Pruitt clutched her husband's arm like he'd float away. 'No offense, but we don't want to spend another minute here. I thought this would be a good experience for us but I have to say it's been nothing short of a nightmare.' She sniffed, jutting her chin toward the sky. 'A murder? What sort of place is this? And for us to be *questioned* by the police!'

'She cried all night,' Mr. Pruitt added.

Mrs. Pruitt's hand flew to her forehead. 'The emotional distress I'm under,' she stuttered, 'I . . . I just can't spend another second here.'

'We need to get on the road,' Mr. Pruitt said curtly, avoiding eye contact.

Will watched the exchange in silence: Mr. Pruitt's shoulders squared and indignant, Vanessa's rounded in defeat. The Daffodil Inn had gone from quaint to cursed overnight. He couldn't blame them, but the sight of Vanessa's face crumpling made his chest ache.

'I understand,' Vanessa said, her voice catching despite her best effort. 'Safe travels.'

They disappeared down the hallway. Will heard the front door open and close, leaving behind a lingering chill.

Vanessa exhaled sharply and looked down at the coffee on the table, now cold. 'That's the third cancellation this morning,' she murmured. 'I'm scared to even check my email. More hate grams, I'm sure.'

Will shifted his weight, then stepped closer and gently touched her arm. 'This isn't your fault. The police are going to take care of everything. You'll get through this.'

She looked up at him, eyes glassy. 'You think so?'

He held her gaze. 'You're stronger than you think.'

A few seconds passed before she nodded. 'Tell Angel she can keep the teacup if she wants.' Vanessa retrieved it out of the dishwasher and gave it a rinse.

'She'll love that,' Will said, his voice soft.

As he turned to go, he paused in the doorway, glancing back at the woman who had treated him and Angel like family. Vanessa slumped back onto the bench, returning her gaze to the cup in front of her like it could tell her a fortune. He trudged up the stairs, the weight of grief and unanswered questions followed closely behind.

The Toasted Pecan was already busy despite the early morning hour, filled with regulars murmuring over coffee and last night's news. On the mounted TV near the service counter, a ticker traveled across the bottom of the screen. Will was too far away to read it but judging from the way heads turned when he walked in, he was sure it was about the Daffodil Inn.

It was no secret that Reed & Roots had done the groundskeeping prior to the Daffodil Jubilee. Word traveled faster than the speed of light in Cinnamon Falls and everyone was talking about the body in the maze.

Angel selected a booth near the window, even though Will would have preferred a table at the back of the restaurant. Will took the seat facing outwards out of habit, always ensuring that he never had his back to the door. His father taught him that. Maybe Will's father could break the ice and get through to Angel, who had barely uttered any words since earlier that morning. Just when he was about to pull out his phone to make the call, he spotted Clarissa Hargrove, owner of the down-home style diner, on her way to their table.

She was the human embodiment of comfort: plump,

polite, radiating warmth. Her hair was cut in a tidy gray bob that suited her round face perfectly. She moved through the diner like she had all the time in the world, greeting regulars by name and making conversation with each customer about small details in their personal lives. As she approached, her soft features lit up at the sight of Angel.

'You want the usual?' Will conferred with his daughter who had begun to scribble on the corner of the kid's paper placemat with the provided red crayon.

She nodded. 'Extra whipped cream, please?'

There was no way he was going to say no.

'You got it, Peach.'

Will watched as Clarissa's broad smile melted into a solemn look as she reached them. He wondered how long he'd have to deal with this.

'I heard about what happened at the Jubilee. You two okay?' Her eyes darted between Will and Angel, who was now too busy mastering the kid's menu word search to be bothered with conversation. Will wished he, too, had a distraction before him instead of having to engage in a conversation disguised as a way to dig for gossip.

'Fine,' Will replied with a polite smile. Small talk was like currency in the South and he had a negative balance. Even though he'd lived in Cinnamon Falls for a little over three years now, he was still considered an outsider; they'd blame his lack of manners on that.

'Good to see you again, Miss Angel,' Clarissa moved on. 'How are you today?'

'Hi, Ms. Hargrove,' Angel responded sullenly. 'My dad is going to order my breakfast for me this time because Miss Eleanor isn't with me today,' she reported like half the town hadn't heard by now.

'I see,' Clarissa responded, her cheeks flushing red, giving Angel a sad smile. 'We're all a little upset about that. From what I remember, you two got chamomile tea first. I'll bring that out for you, honey. You ready to order any food?'

Will started, 'Can the little one here have a cinnamon swirl pancake, extra whipped cream?' Angel nodded her approval. 'I'll have the breakfast sampler with sausage.'

Angel pretended to stick her finger down her throat and gag. 'I was hoping you'd get the bacon.'

'I bet you were,' Will joked. It was part of the reason he got the sausage, so that he could actually enjoy his meal without having to share it. He gave Clarissa a knowing look that meant to add a side of bacon for them to share anyway.

Angel wiggled out of the booth, announcing that she was going to use the restroom. He moved to go with her, but Angel stopped him in his tracks.

'I'm not a baby,' she sneered. 'I can go by myself.'

'Yes, ma'am,' Will responded.

Clarissa snickered while they watched Angel navigate her way across the diner.

'She's such a riot,' she commented. 'A true diva. She had the whole restaurant in stitches last time she was here. I didn't expect to see her with the likes of Eleanor Langford though.'

Will raised an eyebrow. 'I take it you're not a fan?'

'Your daughter might be the only person in Cinnamon Falls who was.' Clarissa's voice took on a careful, practiced neutrality, the kind used when one was trying to avoid a scandal but still tell what they knew. 'I'm not one to speak ill of the dead but Eleanor wasn't exactly well liked around here.' She picked something invisible off her apron. 'She'd burnt all her bridges a long time ago.'

Will's ears perked. 'Oh yeah?' He knew Morgan's mother wasn't a fan of Eleanor, but he didn't think the whole town had a vendetta against the woman. She'd always been pleasant to him, but there was a possibility he didn't know Eleanor the way the long-time residents of Cinnamon Falls did.

Clarissa offered a pointed look. 'Let's just say Eleanor had a way of making you feel small if you didn't meet her standards. She was all pearls and posture, but the tongue behind those smiles? Sharp as a box cutter. Thomas kept her on a tight leash, but after he died, it was all downhill from there. Now, I can understand grief. I lost my Wilbur just shy of ten years now, but that don't mean you go around treatin' kind, hard-working people any kind of way.'

Will said nothing in response. He figured Clarissa

had much more to say. 'I had it out with her the time she came in here during a Sunday brunch rush and demanded I turn the music down, saying it was giving her a headache. Do you know she called the cops on me? Bud Wade woulda gave me a noise violation if I hadn't known him all my life. I've had a jazz brunch on Sundays longer than she'd been living here.' She crossed her arms over her chest. 'That was Eleanor for you, a bunch of unwanted opinions she wasn't afraid to express. Ask Vanessa, I know she and Eleanor exchanged words a bunch of times. Eleanor had all the money in the world, but not a lick of humility. I hate to say it, but no one here is sad that she's gone.'

Will scoffed, finding that hard to believe. The Eleanor he knew was kind and generous. 'She's lived here most of her life, there's gotta be somebody who'll miss her.'

'Well, maybe the people at the library.' Clarissa considered this with a dismissive lift of her shoulders. Will felt like he'd turned a spigot and now Clarissa wouldn't stop talking. He glanced over his shoulder for Angel, but she was still inside the restroom.

'The library?' he echoed.

'She donated to the Friends of the Library fund every year like clockwork, even invested in the reno- vation a couple years ago. It got her name on a plaque and everything. It's still there, I'm sure. That's all she would talk about, how she got her name on a building. Hell, anybody with the funds can do that.'

Clarissa clammed up as Angel tapped Will on the shoulder and squeezed in the booth beside him.

'I'll get your order started, and I'll be back with your tea,' Clarissa said brightly, before walking off.

Will made a mental note that Eleanor had a laundry list of enemies. But did they dislike her enough to kill? He needed a second opinion but first, he needed to talk to someone who was there in the last moments of Eleanor's life.

He fired off a text to Caleb Brewster: **Call me.**

Will's gaze drifted toward the window, the wheels in his head already turning.

When the pancakes came, Angel finally smiled. Will wished he could bottle the moment forever. The extra whipped cream was molded into the shape of a happy face. He clamped his mouth shut as Angel drowned her pancake in maple syrup. The sugar rush she would feel after eating would be worth the crash later. Angel poked around on her plate and took a small bite. Then she took another, before placing her fork down. It melted in the mound of whipped cream until it disappeared entirely.

'Is Miss Eleanor really dead?'

Will froze mid-sip of his coffee. There it was: the moment that had come too soon. Will prided himself on never lying to his daughter. That meant she was privy to a lot more than a second grader should know, but he always wanted to be honest with her, even if it hurt him in the process. There was nothing that mattered more to him than Angel. She deserved the truth.

'Yeah, Peach,' he said finally. 'She is.'

Angel frowned, turning away from him like she was working out a complicated equation in her head. 'But wasn't she a nice lady?'

Will thought of the Eleanor Langford he knew; boisterous, elegant and friendly. She didn't treat Angel like a child, but like a companion. An equal. Despite what Clarissa said, it wasn't just Angel who was devastated about Miss Eleanor. He was too.

'She was a very nice lady,' Will responded gently.

'Then why would someone kill her?' she asked.

Hot coffee slipped down the wrong pipe. Will's throat burned when he croaked out, 'Who said she was killed?'

'I saw Miss Grace before you made me go to bed. She came to our classroom one time for Career Week and she told us that she works at the place where all the dead people are. She said she takes pictures of them and stuff. Jason Richardson asked her if she goes to crime scenes. I didn't know what that meant but I watch *Andrew Guy, P.I.* with Grandpa and I heard him say it once, too.'

'I don't know, Angel,' Will said, stunned. 'But Uncle Jesse and the police are going to figure it out. Eat your pancakes.'

'But, Dad,' Angel whined. 'How will they know who—'

'Listen, Peach. Sometimes bad things happen to good people,' Will explained, hoping to soothe her concerns. 'It's not our job to understand why. We're going to leave that to your Uncle Jesse. For now, we are going to take care of the people around us, okay? Eat.'

Begrudgingly, she picked up her fork.

'Fine,' she sighed.

Will gave her a moment, watching her twirl pancakes in the syrup without taking a bite.

'You two spent a lot of time together this past week,' he said gently. 'Tell me again where you guys went.' Will remembered Eleanor asking his permission before gallivanting off with his child, but apparently he'd missed lots of the small details.

'We went *everywhere*.' Angel perked up. 'First the library. Miss Aisha let me check out the books by myself. I have to wait for the green check and the machine goes: *boop*! That's when I know it's checked out. Then we went to the place with all the foxes to pick up Miss Eleanor's dress for the Jubilee.'

'Wait a second, The Velvet Fox is where I bought your dress. You mean to tell me I could have ordered one for cheaper—'

Angel snickered. 'Mr. Frankie made one special just for me.' Angel beamed. Will shook his head. Once again, he'd been duped by his daughter into paying for an expensive piece of clothing. She was going to be hell on his pockets as a teenager. 'He even let me wear lip gloss with glitter in it!' Angel's smile deflated immediately. 'I wasn't supposed to tell you that.'

Will interjected, 'Hold on—'

Angel talked over him. 'We went to talk to Mr. Hartley at the big white building.' Angel tapped her pointer finger to her mouth, thinking. 'Oh, Miss Eleanor took me to get her hair done, too. After that, we went to visit a man named Thomas and a little girl who lived in the ground. We had to be very quiet and Miss Eleanor was really sad.'

'Sad how?'

Angel shrugged. 'She said she used to have a daughter too, but not anymore. She didn't smile much and we had to sit still for a real long time.'

Will's chest tightened. The people who lived in the ground had to be Eleanor's late husband and their child. She must have taken Angel to the cemetery. He hadn't realized how much Angel knew about Eleanor.

'She really liked hanging out with you,' Will said, brushing a crumb of pancake from her cheek.

Angel's eyes lowered. 'It was like having a fun grandma. I liked her, a lot.'

Will gave her hand a gentle squeeze. 'I know, Peach. Me too.'

If Will's car ever graced Main Street with Angel in the passenger seat, they had to stop at The Cinnamon Scoop. Angel hadn't touched the pancakes she begged for after their conversation about Eleanor, but Will always knew how to cheer her up: a vanilla shirley temple. Two scoops of their signature vanilla ice cream, smothered by a large helping of cherry syrup, topped with a fizzy soda that always made Angel hold her nose. Will needed a quiet moment to make the phone call he'd been dreading all morning, and Nia always had a way of cheering Angel up.

The overhead bell dinged when Angel pushed her way inside the chilly parlor. The place was empty except for Nia behind the counter, humming to herself as she organized the toppings in the glass case.

'Are you kidding me?' Nia squealed. 'Is that my favorite girl in the world?'

'Miss Nia!' Angel beamed. She jetted to the service counter, pulling herself up on one of the stationary stools.

'Where have you been, my girl?' Nia asked, hand hovering over the cherry syrup. 'The usual for the queen?' she asked in a posh voice.

Angel's pointer finger made another appearance. 'Extra cherries, please,' she directed.

Nia winked at Will. 'Coming right up, your highness.'

While Nia and Angel made conversation, Midnight, Nia's Bombay cat, leapt on the stool next to Angel.

'Midnight!' Angel squealed. 'I haven't seen you in forever!'

While Angel harassed the cat with questions regarding her whereabouts, Will stepped to the side to make a call to Tanya. He had three missed calls and two voicemails waiting for him. He didn't have to be a fortune teller to know his child's mother must have seen the news this morning like everyone else.

She answered on the first ring.

'Are you out of your mind, Will? Where is my baby? Put her on the phone! Why didn't you answer last night?'

Will pinched his fingers to his nose to quell the instant headache. 'Do you want to speak to her or do you want to fuss at me?'

'You, first,' she answered. 'Because you know better than to have my daughter at a crime scene! Why didn't you call me back? I was worried all night!'

'It was two in the morning—'

'Do you even hear yourself right now? They're saying there was a *murder*! For all I know it could have been you!' Will was sure she'd wished for that more than once in her lifetime. 'What the hell were you doing with Angel at the scene of a murder?'

'She didn't see anything,' Will lied. 'I got her to bed before the police showed up and locked everything down.'

'She's seven, she shouldn't even know what the police look like!' Tanya screamed.

Will's fingers tightened around his cell phone. 'Do *you* really want to have this conversation with me?' He gritted his teeth, lowering his cadence so Angel couldn't hear.

Tanya didn't respond, but he could hear her ragged breath on the other side of the line.

'Do you need me to remind you of the day I got full custody? When you fell asleep at the wheel with her in the backseat? Or did that instance slip your mind?'

'That's not fair, Will. I'm—'

'What's not fair is me doing all this alone. What's not fair is me having to explain to *our* daughter that her favorite person isn't alive anymore. I was doing what I thought was best, okay? Shit got hectic last night and you questioning my every move isn't making this any easier. It's my job to protect her, and that means I get to decide what she does and where she goes until you're stable again.'

Tanya was crying now. He could hear her sniffling whimpers through the phone. No one on the planet could bring out a reaction in him like she could. He knew his anger was a secondary emotion. Underneath it all, he was so incredibly disappointed in who Tanya Jackson turned out to be. They had so many dreams and she'd crushed them all the day she put Angel in danger.

'I'm not the same person, Will,' she said through a muffled cry.

'I hope not,' he replied dryly. He'd heard it all before.

They were quiet for a beat and he wondered if he'd said too much. He was angry, sure, but he never wanted to hurt Tanya. She was the mother of his child, and he only wanted what was best for her so she could be there for Angel. Whatever they had between them was long gone, but he still loved her, deep down. She was family.

'I need to see her,' Tanya declared.

'It's the first week of school after her spring break. I can't break her routine and pull her out right now. I'll bring her to your mother's house in Macon this weekend, okay?'

'Okay,' she replied. 'Can I speak with her?'

'Peach!' Will called over his shoulder and held the phone out to his daughter. Angel leapt off the stool, Midnight squished against her chest. 'Come say hello to your mother.'

Chapter 7

Morgan

Morgan woke up to the smooth sounds of old school R&B. Even with her door closed she could hear a woman crooning desperately about her sweet love. That only meant one thing: her mother was raging, on a Sunday no less.

Vanessa Taylor was a creature of habit. On Sundays she was up early, dressed to the nines. She never missed a church service if she could stand it. Today must have been one of the days that sat her down, understandably so. If her mother graced within five feet of All Saints Tabernacle the congregation would've swarmed her in the parking lot with prying, incessant questions. Morgan couldn't fault her mother for not wanting to face a bunch of nosy, judgmental parishioners. Besides, there were more important things to focus on than people's opinions, like saving their business.

Morgan was still grappling with the fact that last

night was actually real. Eleanor Langford was *murdered* and the Daffodil Inn's reputation was hanging on by a thread.

Morgan wished she could undo last night. The dead body part of the evening, not the slow dancing under the stars with Will. She could still feel his strong arms locking her in his embrace. She could have stayed there forever. But could she have experienced one without the other? That was the ironic part of her life. For every magical thing she experienced, there was disaster waiting just ahead to smack her back down to reality.

'Thank you, cruel world,' she mumbled aloud.

She was supposed to go back to her apartment today. If everything had gone according to plan, she would have been there first thing, smoking out of the door. Her parents would have had a successful weekend, with reservations flooding their online system over the coming weeks. They'd be celebrating over freshly ground coffee, cinnamon rolls, and maybe some leftovers from the annual affair. She would have fulfilled her yearly daughterly duties and could return to her quiet, two bedroom apartment without a care in the world.

The mood in the house was heavy, she could feel it in her gut. Today would probably be worse than last night. As the music got louder, her mother's signal for her to get out of bed, Morgan figured she'd waited long enough delaying the inevitable.

She threw off the covers, turning around to immediately reset the bed, making sure to tuck the sheets tight in the corners like her mother taught her. She fluffed the pillows, chopping the center to make them stand upright. She smoothed the comforter so there would be no wrinkles, until the room looked exactly like it did on the website.

The Wildflower Room was her favorite. Before her parents began renovating the Inn, it had been her childhood bedroom. The soft yellow and lavender tones combined with a side view of the daffodil fields made it feel like her own secret world. It had a bay window with a cozy reading nook that made the best place for naps on long summer days. Her parents decided to keep the bay window and replace the paint with a busy but elegant floral wallpaper, but underneath it all, it was still Morgan's favorite place.

She rifled through her luggage for a pair of leggings and a T-shirt. She was in and out of the bathroom, refreshed and ready to work, in less than ten minutes. She didn't need the volume to go up another notch.

Careful not to wake the Pruitts next door, Morgan closed the bedroom door softly behind her. The Sunbeam Room at the far end of the hall lived up to its name. The walls were painted a butter yellow with hand-painted daffodils dancing across the ceiling's border. Morgan picked the whitewashed furniture out herself, including the spacious dresser and rocking chair. Several years ago, her mother decided to add in antique floral chargers from the second-hand store behind the brass bed frame because Eleanor claimed the walls were 'too empty'. Mrs. Pruitt called the room 'charming and romantic' when she first checked in, which made Morgan feel much better about her mother's gaudy design choices.

Mr. and Mrs. Pruitt were flower enthusiasts celebrating their second honeymoon of their second marriage, and Mrs. Pruitt was not ashamed to tell it. The quirky couple reconnected after their fortieth high school reunion, and realized they'd been sweethearts after all. Mr. Gilbert Pruitt, a suspender-wearing retired antique dealer, was a quiet and curious man, always pressing a flower into his pocket to save for their shared scrapbook, The Pruitt Path, while Mrs. Marlene Pruitt, a buttoned blouse type of woman, was more talkative, not by much though. They did nothing without each other.

On the way downstairs, Morgan passed Will and Angel's room on the left, the Bluebird Room. On the bedroom door her father had hand painted two blue birds that fluttered over the brass knob in a flourish. It was the only room with double beds and entirely blue decor: pale blue toile wallpaper with whitewashed furniture. The ensuite bath had a rainfall showerhead and it had the second-best views of the sunrise in the mornings.

The door was slightly ajar and Morgan toed it

open the rest of the way, finding it empty. She would have loved a chance to say goodbye, even though she'll see Angel around at school. She wanted a chance to thank Will for all his help, or maybe it was an excuse to see him again after last night.

In the short time they'd spent together yesterday, she learned more about the man than she ever knew before. Before, he was Angel's *fine* father who all the teachers would salivate over when he picked up his daughter from school. He had a calm, collected swag about him that made him both mysteriously dangerous and irresistible. Morgan had read enough romance novels to know that single dads were the hottest, but life had told her, over and over again, that she was nobody's main character.

She passed Eleanor Langford's room just off the staircase; the Garden Suite, everyone's favorite. It boasted a four-poster, king-sized bed wrapped in vintage daffodil print linens with soft sage walls and botanical artwork. It was the only room to have a clawfoot tub. It was also the only upstairs room to offer a private balcony that overlooked the blooming daffodil fields in their entirety. It was perfect for a long soaking bath, journaling, or manifesting a new life, not that Morgan would know, of course.

She slowed and against her better judgment, peeked inside, expecting to find a group of officers cataloguing Eleanor's belongings for evidence. Instead, she found it empty, like Eleanor had just left for her morning walk. Morgan pushed it open further, revealing the opulence of the room. She'd never get over the stunning garden view no matter how many times she'd seen it.

Through the French doors she spotted rows of daffodils stretching in the morning sun, deceptively serene for the trampling they experienced just the night before. Chunks of the garden had been crushed under the shoes of frightened guests or careless police, she didn't know. Even though some of the daffodils had been flattened, Morgan still found the breath-taking beauty in the scene before her.

Eleanor's bed was neatly made. A few floral dresses hung in the antique chestnut armoire towering against the far wall. It was part of the original house; the one piece that was too heavy to move during renovation. The chestnut grain had aged beautifully over time, darkening, and glowing a warm gold from where the light from the French doors hit it just right. The armoire's doors, carved with a daffodil motif, were thrown open, like she was just here, deciding what she wanted to wear for the day.

Morgan pulled the door back fully; the hinges creaked with a sigh, revealing hand-carved shelves that supported all of Eleanor's beauty products: an array of makeup, brushes, mascaras and powders, perfume, deodorant and hair spray. A black beaded bag sat open, its contents spilling out; a receipt from the general store, her card holder featuring a stack of credit cards, and an old-school flip phone. Morgan hadn't seen one of those in ages.

A small bench folded from the side paneling to create a makeshift vanity. Behind the bench was a toddler-sized cubby hole concealed by a latch. When Morgan was little, it was how she stayed hidden for hours when Lionel, the Inn's cook, searched all over the house for her. She was still the hide-and-go-seek reigning champ.

Inside the room, still on the dresser, was an opened welcome basket that Vanessa made for every guest who stayed at the Inn. With meticulous detail, her mother would put together a unique gift for each guest based on their preferences from their reservation. Miss Eleanor's included chocolate-covered pretzels from Guy's Grocery; a variety of artisanal chamomile teas, courtesy of Hailey Hamilton over at Cinnamon Grove; a few easily forgotten toiletries that Morgan normally picked up in bulk from Sylvester James, the general store: a spare toothbrush, shampoo and conditioner; and a jar of strawberry jam, courtesy of the ripe soil from Old Man Milton's farm. It was the best fruit in the South, let Morgan tell it.

On the nightstand there stood a picture of Miss Eleanor, and who Morgan assumed was her late husband, when they were much younger. The grainy black and white photo showed them enthralled in a kiss so intimate that Morgan felt like she was intruding. Eleanor's lips were pursed, her eyes shuttered closed with an expression of the utter relief women feel when they've found the one. Her husband, Morgan assumed, looked like he was mid-laugh, their bodies tangled together in an intense moment of passion.

'Damn,' Morgan mumbled. She didn't know if she'd ever get to experience anything like that. The stolen moment she spent dancing in Will's arms was romantic enough, if you were a fan of mosquito-bitten ankles and the serene snores of an asthmatic collie.

Morgan dipped into the bathroom, finding it the same as the rest of Miss Eleanor's room, lived in, like she'd simply left for a brief moment and would be coming back any second now.

Suddenly, hearing the distinct whistle of her mother as she padded up the stairs, Morgan dashed out of the room just in time to meet Vanessa at the top step, who was cradling a basket of clean towels fresh from the laundry room. Her long hair was thrown into a sloppy bun, still sporting the rhinestone picks from the night before. Had she been going all night?

Vanessa looked up at Morgan and she answered her own question. Rings of black eyeliner still rimmed her eyes and the glitter eyeshadow, although smudged, had remained. Bags rested under her brown, almond-shaped eyes and it felt like Morgan was staring in a mirror.

'You strip your bed yet?' her mother asked, lips pursed, all business.

Morgan couldn't even get a 'good morning' before her mother started barking orders?

'Good morning to you too,' Morgan muttered, stepping around her to descend the stairs.

'Wait!' she called to her daughter, stopping Morgan in her tracks. 'Lionel is in the kitchen, don't go down there bothering him about cooking you breakfast. I need him to figure out what to do with all that left-over food.'

'I was just—'

'Tiana needs to wash the linens when she gets in so make sure that bed is stripped. I don't need to hear a bunch of excuses from that girl about why these sheets weren't laundered.'

'I'm not sure that's going to matter—'

'Your father went to talk to Mr. Reed to see about fixing the daffodils and removing that damned maze,' she added.

'Ma, I don't think you can do that—'

'And Daphne has been dying for a walk and I don't have time to mess around with that dog. You know how she likes to go all over. I've got too much to do today.'

'Do you plan to wake the whole house?' Morgan gestured around her at the blasting music.

'Will, Angel, and the Pruitts checked out before the sun came up this morning. Zara went out a while ago. It's just the three of us.'

Vanessa stomped past her and down the hall toward the linen closet. It was clear that she wasn't in the mood to have a conversation about anything other than work.

Of course not, Morgan thought. She shook her head in disbelief. Was her mother trying to ignore the fact that Eleanor was murdered? Resuming operations as normal seemed counterproductive, especially since nothing about this was normal. Their lives had been forever changed. Morgan desperately wanted to ask if her mother was okay. But she'd learned through years of trying that her mother wasn't one to share what her heart was feeling. She buried it all under tasks, a checklist of to-dos that came before distractions like emotions.

Vanessa dropped the basket to the floor and began folding the towels in perfect rectangles. She looked over to see Morgan still standing by the stairs, studying her.

'Did you hear me?' She sighed, gearing up to repeat her marching orders. Morgan felt like she was sixteen again and under her mother's thumb. As long as her mother was alive, things had to go her way, and nothing else mattered.

'I heard you, Ma. Loud and clear,' Morgan replied. She walked downstairs in search of Lionel and hoped he could make her one of his famous omelettes without her mother noticing.

97

The Farmer's Omelette was the best thing on the Inn's breakfast menu. Lionel always made perfectly fluffy eggs, and the salty crunch of the bacon, topped with the explosion of smoky flavor from the sausage made Morgan dance a jig on the bench. Daphne followed her fork with the precision of an Army trained sniper, waiting for a piece of anything to fall from it.

Lionel was one of her father's best friends. They'd been coworkers at The Cinnamon Crest Country Club since they were young, and kept each other close while they moved up the ranks. When Wesley told him that he was opening up his own bed and breakfast, he brought his most trusted friend along for the ride. Lionel had been part of the Taylors' story for so long, Morgan thought of him as her uncle; someone she could go to who would actually listen to understand, not to respond or scold.

A warm breeze danced around the kitchen from the open window above the sink, an indication that summer was well on its way. Lionel was suspiciously quiet for a sunny Sunday morning. Normally, he would have commented on the weather, or the golden daffodils, or even Daphne's expert timing in snatching runaway food. The caramel-skinned man worked silently, his lips pressed together in concentration, his meticulously arched eyebrows furrowed.

Morgan watched the obnoxious diamond studs in both of his ears shake while he rough chopped a pan of steamed shrimp on the cutting board at the island.

Every few minutes he would toss a shrimp off the side for Daphne to snap up faster than the speed of light.

'You can say it.' Morgan broke the silence first, placing her fork down.

'What, that you all have spoiled this dog to no end?' Lionel shook his head and tossed another piece of shrimp over the side. Daphne's mouth snapped once and then she licked her waiting lips. Was she even swallowing?

'I'm sorry, you're the one giving her shrimp for breakfast,' Morgan pointed out.

'She's just standing here lookin' sad. I came in this morning and she didn't have any water in her bowl, no food. She was starving. Y'all left my girl for dead.'

Morgan rolled her eyes. 'We had a rough night, okay?'

Lionel gestured to the refrigerated trays of food that her mother had left for him to make a miracle with. 'I can tell.'

'What's everyone saying?' Morgan asked sheepishly, fiddling around with the few pieces of her omelette she had left. It was still early, just after 8 a.m. but gossip never slept in long. 'I haven't had the guts to look since last night. I'm sure Elaine Matthias has it as front-page news today.'

Lionel shook his head. 'It's not good, that's for sure. Tiana called me last night after she left the Jubilee,' he started, lowering his voice in case her mother was around.

Tiana was the part-time housekeeper. Two days out of the week, and a few hours on Sunday afternoons, she deep-cleaned the Inn. She was younger than Morgan by just a few years and had dreams of being a Hollywood actress. Morgan didn't know much about her thespian capabilities, but she did know she had a flair for the dramatic, and exaggeration was her best skill. Morgan was sure that whatever she told Lionel, it was incorrect.

Lionel continued. 'Said they found poor Miss Eleanor dead in the daffodil fields and people were scrambling to get outta here.'

'She got one part right,' Morgan replied. 'The garden is ruined.'

'Vanessa had to be hot about that.'

They shared a knowing look. Morgan didn't think her mother would ever get over it.

Morgan asked, 'You think she's seen the stuff online yet?'

Lionel twisted his lips. 'Oh, she's seen it. She's in her drill sergeant mode this morning. I'm not about to get in her way and I suggest you do the same.'

Just then, the doorbell rang. Daphne unleashed a few warning barks as she and Morgan walked to the front door.

She pulled the door open, ready to explain to whomever it was that the Daffodil Inn was closed. Morgan geared herself up when she recognized Nia clutching two iced coffees and a bag from Rosie's

Diner. She knew it contained Rosie's cinnamon rolls, Morgan's favorite.

Nia held up the coffee like a peace offering. 'I got one with the cinnamon crunchies on top and the other with sweetened cold foam because I didn't know which version of you I was going to get this morning.'

Morgan let out a small, broken laugh as Nia stepped inside. Daphne sniffed her vigorously.

'You didn't have to come,' Morgan managed, her voice cracking despite her best effort to play it cool.

'Of course I did, you're my best friend,' Nia said plainly. She sat the food on the table in the foyer and pushed her sunglasses on top of her head. Her brown eyes studied Morgan. 'Where else would I be?'

'It's Sunday, you usually have to work at the shop—'

'I made Niles take the rest of my shift. Plus, I've been seeing all the chatter online. I know what that feels like. I had to come see you.'

Morgan pressed her lips together, trying to breathe past the tightness in her chest. She didn't realize how much she'd been holding back until she was face to face with the one person she had needed all night.

'Everything has just . . . gone to shit and I don't know what to do,' Morgan started, her words coming out faster than her breath could handle. Her chest heaved and her nose stung with tears.

Nia opened her arms and Morgan hesitated for just a half second, stutter-stepping into the hug. Once she was there everything cracked open. The grief, fear, embarrassment, and relief flowed through her while she embraced her friend.

'I've been trying to hold it together. I didn't want to cry in front of Momma, or all the people,' she hiccupped. 'Or Will.'

Nia guided her into the great room where they settled on the soft couch, their hands intertwined.

'You can fall apart with me,' Nia said softly, pulling Morgan into another tight hug. Morgan tucked her head against her friend's shoulder and let her tears fall. Daphne whimpered gently at her feet, pawing at Morgan's legs. She leapt onto the couch, pushing her head under Morgan's arms. They stayed like that for a while until Morgan caught her breath.

'Thanks for showing up,' Morgan said eventually, pulling back with an embarrassed smile.

Nia nudged the coffee toward her and pretended not to notice that her hoodie was soaked with Morgan's tears.

'You'd do it for me,' she replied. 'And I feel like a shit friend for missing the dance last night. I was wiped out. Now eat up because I know Ms. Vanessa is going to put us to work.'

Morgan noted that she hadn't asked about Miss Eleanor, or what her family planned to do. She simply showed up and that meant more to her than Nia would ever know.

In the kitchen, the business phone rang.

'Vanessa, it's for you!' Lionel shouted upstairs.

'Transfer it to my office,' she hollered back as she walked down the stairs. Morgan noticed her bedsheets in the basket clutched at her mother's side. Vanessa stepped into the living room, her mouth primed to fuss, probably about the forgotten sheets, when she noticed Morgan's guest on the couch.

Her eyes lit up. 'Nia, baby, nice to see you again.' She reached over and took a swig of the coffee Morgan wasn't drinking. 'Is this for me?'

'All yours.' Morgan smiled through gritted teeth, hoping that her mother couldn't tell that she'd been sobbing just minutes before. Vanessa Taylor thought tears were impractical. Tears never *helped* anybody. The only thing that helped was execution. Accomplishing was what mattered. A finished to-do list brought her mother more happiness than diamonds ever would.

Vanessa turned on her heel and stalked into the kitchen, taking another large swig of the drink that once belonged to Morgan. Daphne followed dutifully behind her, probably hoping for another instance of fallen shrimp.

'Who is it?' Morgan heard her mother ask, an annoyed tone lacing her voice. 'If it's some kind of reporter they can kiss my—'

Lionel cut off her rant. 'He said his name was Max Greaves.'

Morgan had never heard her mother sound so cold when she demanded, 'Hang up. Now.'

Chapter 8

Will

Will opened his car's roof to feel the sun on his skin warm like honey. It was shaping up to be another beautiful day in Cinnamon Falls. Soft, golden rays filtered through the branches that arched over Main Street, dappling the pavement in shifting patches of light. Above, sparrows traded songs from their perches on telephone wires, their cheerful notes carrying over the gentle hum of tires on asphalt. Storefront windows gleamed in the morning glow, chalkboard displays were freshly lettered with the day's specials; signs that small-town life carried on undeterred.

He snuck a sip of Angel's drink. It was way too sweet for his liking, but the cool creaminess of the vanilla ice cream soothed him internally. Tanya always had a way of riling him up, but that was no excuse for how he had responded. As much as he wanted to throw the past in her face, he knew she was trying her hardest to get on the straight and narrow. And despite what happened between them, she was still the mother of his precious baby girl.

'I shouldn't have snapped,' he muttered aloud. Angel, who was busy sketching on her iPad in the backseat, hadn't looked up. Will watched in the rear-view mirror. She was deep in concentration, shading in what looked to be the awning outside of The Cinnamon Scoop. He could barely draw stick figures, let alone buildings. Angel had an incredible mind and every day he felt himself grow more and more impressed by her.

Moments like this made him wish that Tanya were here to see their daughter bloom alongside him. There was something magical about watching their creation as she made new discoveries, and learnt valuable life lessons. The tiny baby he could once cradle with just his forearm was growing into a young lady and Tanya was missing it all.

Will brought the car to a smooth stop in front of Bones' Barbershop. Angel looked up.

'Got a client?' she asked.

'Uncle Jesse,' Will replied. 'It'll be real quick.'

Angel rolled her eyes. 'That's what you always say. Can I go see if Braxton is next door?'

Mrs. Guy's grandson usually helped his grandma at the grocery store on Sundays. He'd become fast friends with Angel after he came to get his hair cut by Mr. Bones months ago.

'Sure, but if he's not there, come straight back.

Don't go bothering Mrs. Guy about color theory and making things "aesthetically pleasing".'

Recently Angel had become obsessed with interior design. He had to apologize ten times to Mrs. Taylor when Angel asked why she chose to decorate one of the rooms at the Inn entirely blue.

Angel sighed dramatically, throwing her head back against the headrest. 'Alright,' she huffed.

Will made sure to watch her while she skipped across the empty street toward the grocery store, her curls bouncing in the wind. Main Street was slow for now. Will took a look at his watch. It was just past noon, around the time everyone would be on the hunt for a post-church snack.

While Will waited for Jesse to arrive, he unlocked the shop. Bones didn't work on Sundays but Will didn't mind the quiet, he needed some time to think. He turned on all the lights, and began preparing his work station. He wiped down the seat with a disinfectant solution and did the same with his tools. He unraveled a few sets of clippers and sprayed the blades. He was just about to pull out his shampoo and conditioner in case Jesse needed a quick wash when his phone started to ring.

He scrambled to answer it, hoping it wasn't Mrs. Guy begging him to come apprehend his overzealous daughter. Looking at the screen he saw it was his brother, Elijah. Normally, he would have let it go to voicemail. It wasn't that he didn't like talking to his brother, it was just that every conversation always turned back to Elijah and his perfect life. It was like he wanted to rub Will's nose in the fact that his straight and narrow ways during childhood had actually paid off. His condescending tone and backhanded compliments, always disguised as concern, were subtle reminders that Will "could have done more with his life".

'Yo,' Will answered, hooking the phone between his ear and shoulder.

'What's up, bro?' Elijah asked. 'Got a second?'

Will pulled the phone away from his ear. Since when did his brother ask permission to talk? He usually started the conversation without Will getting a word in edgewise. Dr. Elijah Reed fit everyone in his life on his schedule. He'd made it clear that his time was the only time that mattered.

Looking at the clock, Will knew he had about ten minutes before Jesse showed up. Just enough time to rush Elijah off the phone.

'Got a client in a few,' Will replied. 'What's going on?'

'What's going on with you? That's the question.' Elijah sounded like he had a smile on his lips. 'You told me nothin' bad ever happens in Cinnamon Falls. You see the news this morning? Someone dropped dead at that flower festival.'

'It's the Daffodil Inn, babe,' Will heard Renee, Elijah's wife, correct him with a laugh in the background. Did he always have to be on the phone with the pair of them? He couldn't remember the last time it'd just been him and Elijah without Renee being around.

Renee had always been cordial to Will, and even more so to Angel. As the baby girl in the family, Renee loved showering Angel with designer shoes that she'd grow out of in two months or real gold jewelry that Angel would almost always lose at recess. As a certified public accountant with a doctor husband, Renee Reed lived the perfect life.

Renee was distinguished and efficient. She ran a house full of synced calendars, polished countertops, and creased pants. She was a world away from what Will would ever find attractive, or at the very least, interesting. She was too rigid, too cold, and was the perfect woman for his brother.

Will clenched his jaw. 'It's really not funny, Eli. A woman died. Me and Angel were right there.'

'I didn't . . .' Elijah started, his tone shifting from playful to serious. Will heard rustling on the other end and then descending footsteps. His brother spoke again, all business. 'I didn't mean it like that, man. Is Angel okay? Are you okay?'

Will let out the breath that had been building in his chest. 'I don't know. Miss Eleanor was her buddy. She drinks chamomile tea now because of her . . . She wasn't really talkin' much this morning, but you know Peach. She'll come around.'

'Give her some ice cream and she'll be your best

friend again,' Elijah joked. It made Will chuckle too, because that was exactly what he had done. Maybe Elijah did know him better than he thought.

A beat passed between them before Elijah released a weighty sigh. Will braced himself for the real reason for the call. 'Man, I gotta ask. You weren't . . . involved with this, right? I'm just sayin', Pops isn't going to have to worry about—'

Will clenched his jaw so hard he heard the bones grind inside his head. Even after all the years that had passed, Elijah still saw him as the family fuck-up.

'I gotta go,' Will managed through clenched teeth. He refused to justify his question with an answer. Internally, he wondered, just for a second, what he ever had to do to prove to his brother that those years were behind him.

'Bro, come on, I needed to double check—' Elijah pleaded.

A bell tinkled overhead. Jesse walked inside the shop, clutching Angel's hand. She was interrogating him about Miss Eleanor, firing questions off back to back.

'I said I gotta go.' Will had never been so eager to end a phone call in his life.

Ignoring the buzz of his phone as Elijah tried to call him back, Will wished his brother would have the manners to apologize, but he knew Elijah Reed better than he knew himself. The man didn't apologize to anyone because, according to him, he was never wrong.

Angel slowed down just long enough for Jesse to get a word in. 'We still got a long way to go, so I'm not sure yet,' Jesse said. He'd dropped to one knee, coming face to face with the insatiable seven-year-old. 'The police are working very hard to find out what happened to Miss Eleanor.'

'Are *you* working hard?' Angel specified, crossing her arms over her chest.

'Of course I am, I'm the best,' Jesse declared.

Angel pouted, poking her bottom lip out. 'I don't know why she would die all of a sudden. We were having so much fun. Do you think she was annoyed with me? My dad says I ask a lot of questions some-times—'

Will's heart squeezed in his chest. Jesse looked between him and his daughter with sad eyes.

'Never!' he replied, hoisting Angel off her feet and into the air. 'Me and your daddy are so proud of you.' She let out a high-pitched squeal in response, and her laugh shocked Will's heart back into its rhythm. The rainbow lights embedded in Angel's shoes flickered happily as she kicked her feet with delight.

A fatherhood lesson he had to remind himself of over and over again was that Angel listened to everything he said even when he thought she wasn't. How he handled her was a direct reflection on how she showed up in the world. Will wanted to kick himself for all the times he played the 'quiet game' on the way home.

'Thank you, Uncle Jesse.' Angel blushed, as he placed her back down. She gave them both a twirl in her outfit of the day; an orange tiered maxi dress. Angel said that the balloon sleeves made it look fancy, and well, that was enough for Will to add it to the cart.

Will beckoned for her and she shuffled over to her father. He scooped under her arms and balanced her on one hip. She was growing so quickly that eventually he wouldn't be able to hold her like this anymore. He didn't want to think about the future. Right now, she was still his little girl.

'You're the best kid in the world, you get me?' Angel nodded, her bottom lip revealing that she was holding back tears. Will was losing his resolve so he quickly changed the subject. 'Was Braxton over there?' Will pointed with his chin toward Guy's Grocery.

She squirmed to get out of his embrace at the mention of her friend's name. 'Yeah, and I left him with the good coloring pencils Auntie Renee got me. I gotta go!'

'You've got thirty minutes, young lady!' Will called after her as she rushed toward the door. 'Tell Mrs. Guy please and thank you! Don't forget to use your manners!'

Angel gave him a thumbs up and he watched her curls bounce across the street until she disappeared within the grocery store once again.

Jesse walked over, giving Will a dap and settling into the barber chair. Will wrapped him in a plastic cape with a flourish.

'She cornered me at the door,' Jesse joked, pointing over his shoulder. 'I almost showed her my license and registration.'

'She plays no games,' Will replied, grateful that Jesse was there to help his daughter navigate a tough moment.

Having a community of people who cared was the only buoy keeping him afloat in the ocean of single fatherhood. Most days he was hanging on by a rope so thin it could have doubled as dental floss. But other days, like today, it was just a little less terrifying having someone else step in as backup.

'She's getting big, man,' Jesse commented while Will combed out his overgrown taper. As he suspected, Jesse needed his hair washed.

Will scoffed. *Big* wasn't the word to describe who Angel was growing to be. The girl was a force of nature. 'Sometimes I forget she's a kid,' Will admitted. 'She's so advanced it's hard for me to not share everything with her. It feels like she's my peer.'

Jesse turned to Will, straight-faced. 'Bro, you need more adult conversations in your life. She's seven, not your therapist.'

'She's my best friend, literally. We share everything. That's why this whole Eleanor thing is eating me alive. She hasn't said much of anything to me today, and normally she talks my head off and burns a hole through my wallet at the same time.'

The smile faded from Jesse's lips at the mention of Eleanor. 'Thanks for taking me on a Sunday. Raines is making us work overtime. I had to squeeze a cut in before she doubled my hours this week.'

'I gotta know, man,' Will all but pleaded with him. 'What's the latest?' He knew that Jesse respected the unspoken code of the barbershop. With them alone in the building, they could speak freely knowing that it wouldn't reach beyond the four walls. He was leaning on the bond they'd built, now more than ever before. He couldn't take another day of watching Angel pepper herself, and the people around her, with questions they couldn't answer.

Jesse removed his arm from behind the cape to find his watch. 'Chambers and Wade should be at the Inn right now, actually.' Will guided his head toward the shampoo bowl. He squirted a fair amount of shampoo in his hands and began to work the product through. 'Raines is on me about notifying the next of kin and getting the investigation going. She needs it solved, fast.'

'Did you talk to anybody at the Inn about her?'

Will rinsed out the shampoo and repeated the same steps with the conditioner. He sat Jesse upright and began to dry his hair for the cut. 'It was the first thing Raines did last night. We talked to that Caleb Brewster kid, too. I didn't know you started a gardening club at Cinnamon Falls High.'

'Yeah, a while back. It was just Caleb at first and then he recruited a couple of his friends. They're good kids, they remind me of myself when I was their age.'

Jesse grunted. 'I'm surprised kids like Caleb agreed to join a *gardening* club.'

Will sighed. 'I was restless as a kid too, you know? The only thing that really calmed me down was being in the dirt. I learned a lot about controlling my emotions and having patience from working with my Pops. This is a small town, but I knew there would be plenty of boys who were just like me at that age, teetering. They just need a push in the right direction. It sounds crazy, but I wanted to give those boys something they could hold in their hands; something that they took time to nurture. Just because you don't get shown a lot of love, don't mean you can't give it.'

Jesse grunted in acknowledgement while Will continued, 'We planted those daffodils right after the Fall Fest when the soil was cool. It gave the bulbs some time to root before the ground froze in the winter. They bloomed just in time for the Jubilee. I've never seen a bunch of dudes so happy about flowers, so I had to do something nice for 'em. Told them to get dressed up and come to the party to see their hard work in real time. My dad even had certificates printed.'

'Wait a minute. You're telling me a bunch of troubled teenage boys knew their way around the Inn?'

Will stepped back, the pieces falling into place. 'Those kids wouldn't hurt anyone.'

Jesse opened his arms. 'Listen, bro, as a friend, you did an amazing thing. You probably saved them from going down a dangerous path. But, as a detective, I'm going to need the names of every participant, past and present. It's not personal. I gotta follow every lead.'

Will stared at Jesse, warring inside. On one hand, he wanted to protect his boys over anything. He wanted to believe that they were innocent, but what if . . . what if they weren't?

Then he thought about Angel, who was on the verge of never speaking again if Jesse didn't find out what happened to Miss Eleanor, and fast. If Jesse needed to rule out Will's crew, then he would co-operate. Will knew that it was a waste of time, but that was what the police did best, waste time. He shot another text to Caleb to call him as soon as he could. Will was going to find the answers his way.

Will passed Wesley Taylor's red pickup truck as he pulled up to the Reed & Roots greenhouse. They gave each other a friendly wave, but Will could tell from Wesley's strained expression that whatever had just transpired with his father wasn't good.

Will maneuvered his coupe in the makeshift circle driveway, the grass long since worn to dirt by years of tire tracks and heavy boots. Across the yard, he noticed his father, with headphones slapped over his ears, hauling bags of soil toward the greenhouse like it was any other day of the week. Calvin Reed never stopped working, even on a Sunday afternoon. He was the backbone of Reed & Roots Landscaping, the family business that he'd built from the ground up with little more than a rusted pickup, a push mower, a pair of shears and an iron will.

Will and Elijah had grown up in the thick of it, with Will learning the names of plants and the rhythm of the seasons before he could ride a bike, his Sundays spent hauling mulch and trimming hedges alongside their father. Years later, he expanded the business to Cinnamon Falls and even when Will strayed off the ideal son path, Calvin kept steady, protecting the business like sacred ground, working well past the age most men retired. Will knew his father would spend the rest of his days with one hand in the soil.

Will and Angel stepped out of the car and journeyed across the expansive yard to join him. The Reed & Roots greenhouse sat like a quiet giant at the back of the Reed family property; a long, vaulted structure of clouded glass and weather-worn steel ribs that creaked when the wind blew too hard.

Inside, the heat hit them instantly, the air thick with moisture, fragrant with tomato vines and the sharp tang of fresh herbs. The scent was dizzying in the best way, like standing in the middle of a spring memory. Rows of raised garden beds ran the length of the structure, each labeled with small wooden stakes, labeled in Will's father's meticulously neat handwriting.

A rack of seed trays sat beneath grow lights that buzzed faintly, casting a lavender hue over the tiny shoots beginning to break through the soil. That was where he found his father, monitoring his new plants with a watchful eye, humming what sounded like an oldies record.

Angel ran over and jumped next to him, curling her fingers with a roar. Her grandfather stepped back, ripping the headphones off his ears.

'Little Peach! What are you—'

He turned to find Will in the doorway, one hand stuffed in his front pocket.

'Somebody had to come see their granddad before we headed back home.' Will nodded to Angel who was busying herself with the sprouting plants, inspecting them closely.

'What a nice surprise!' Calvin exclaimed.

'I passed Mr. Taylor leaving just now.' Will pointed over his shoulder. 'What was that about?'

His father sighed, looking between him and Angel. He picked up one of the sprouting plants and handed it to his granddaughter. 'Can you take this out to the field for me? This one's ready to be planted.'

Without hesitation, Angel snatched it from his hands and exited out of the back door, elated to be doing something to help.

'Yep, right there!' he called from the door, navigating Angel across the field. 'Cover it with lots of dirt. I'll be out to water it with you.'

He turned to his son and shook his head. He lowered his voice for good measure. 'Wesley wants me to salvage that garden of theirs. I told him daffodils are perennials. I can't make them sprout back up, good as new like nothin' ever happened. We'll have to start over,' he fussed. 'Now, I'm sorry 'bout that woman and their business and all, but I'm not a magician.'

His father had a point. In a year, the daffodils would bloom again. But it was clear Wesley Taylor didn't have the time to wait another year. He wanted it fixed now. As much as he could understand where Mr. Taylor was coming from, his father was right. There was no rushing nature. Calvin shook his head again and muttered, more to himself than to Will, 'And would you believe something ate up that foxglove in the back row?'

'An animal?' Will questioned.

'Something pulled it up. It was growing fine last week. Whatever it was didn't make it far, I can tell you that. Stuff's as dangerous as it gets.'

Will offered a noncommittal grunt and rubbed the back of his neck, unsure what to make of it. The garden was a buzz of activity all the time, between the Grow Squad on the weekend, deliveries during the week, and curious nocturnal animals; it could have been anything. Will's father hoisted another bag of soil onto his shoulder before heading out of the door.

'Anyway, Wesley told me that they've got some offers fishin' around. Won't be long before he sells it for pennies on the dollar, especially after last night.'

Will scoffed. 'The Taylors would never sell The Daffodil Inn.'

Calvin adjusted the bag and pushed the door open with his foot. Will spotted Angel in the field waiting for her grandfather, her hands on her hips.

'Everybody's got a price, son.'

Chapter 9

Morgan

Detective Terrance Chambers had one job: clear Eleanor's belongings from her room upstairs and then return to the station. While Morgan was walking Nia to her car, she overheard the directive on Chambers' cruiser radio from Chief Raines herself.

Thirty minutes later, Morgan found the chatty officer standing in her kitchen chowing down on a steaming bowl of Lionel's shrimp linguine, Daphne perched expectantly at his feet, her tail brushing the ground in anticipation. From Morgan's position in the great room, neither Lionel nor Chambers could see that she was listening in, too enthralled in their own conversation.

The last time she had properly seen Terrance Chambers was at the reopening of The Cinnamon Scoop roughly six months ago, and the time before that, she'd been thrown in jail for tampering with an investigation, but that was a conversation for another time. Ever since, she'd made a point to stay out of his way.

'And that's what I've been telling Raines,' he said around a mouth full of noodles. 'According to the people we talked to last night, anyone in Cinnamon Falls woulda killed this woman for five dollars.'

Lionel kissed his teeth. 'Eleanor wasn't *that* bad,' he responded, keeping one eye on a pot of cream sauce that he stirred every few seconds. He ladled some into Chambers' waiting bowl and continued, 'Like I said, she was a sweetheart to me and all the staff. She loved Angel, too. She took that little girl everywhere.'

Chambers responded with a grunt. 'Makes sense. Angel probably reminded her of the daughter she lost. We heard that after Bella died, things changed.' He slurped his noodles so loud it made Morgan cringe.

'That would change anybody,' Lionel replied, turning the heat down on the sauce and letting it simmer. He placed a top on the saucepan and returned to the island where he checked on his dough, which was proofing in a bowl.

'You're right,' Chambers relented. 'We've been hoping to talk to someone who really knew her; someone who could shed some light on who she's been dealing with, but it doesn't look like she had many . . . friends here.'

'That's for sure. Eleanor wasn't really the friend type.'

'We heard Vanessa wasn't her biggest fan either.'

Lionel paused, unmoving. The silence magnified. Morgan held her breath.

Chambers continued eating, never taking his eyes off his bowl, his slurps crowding the kitchen. Morgan couldn't tell if this was some kind of special detective tactic or if he really was ballsy enough to question her mother's motives standing in her kitchen. 'But Raines talked to the mayor and he had the same story that they were talking near the stage before the scream, so we cleared the Taylors right away.'

Morgan breathed again. 'Well, all I know is Eleanor got her hair done every week at CinnaCutz,' Lionel advised. Morgan leaned closer. 'I bet Ethel Lawson will know what she'd been up to. Her and Harold Bones get more gossip than a tabloid.'

Chambers held the empty bowl out to the chef. 'I'll do that, thanks, man.'

Lionel took it and placed it in the sink next to the mountain of dishes to be washed. 'What'd you think? More salt?'

'No, it's perfect,' Chambers replied, wiping his mouth with a napkin. 'I might need to send Alexis over here to get some lessons.' The men continued their conversation about the lack of culinary skills Chambers' wife possessed, but Morgan wasn't interested in that. The lanky detective backed out of the room and into the hallway where he found Morgan pretending to dust.

'Should be out of your hair soon.' He tipped his imaginary hat to her. 'See you at pickleball this weekend!' Chambers called to Lionel before heading upstairs to join his partner, Bud Wade, who'd been working alone since they arrived thirty minutes prior.

'Pickleball?' Vanessa and Morgan said simultaneously. Her mother ascended from the basement stairs and joined her and Lionel in the kitchen.

'That was supposed to be a private police interview,' Lionel deadpanned.

'Oh, please. You're in *my* house!' Vanessa took a seat on the bench. Morgan slid in beside her. 'I couldn't sit on my hands any longer. Did that man have the nerve to bring me up, or was I hearing things?'

'He said he cleared you right away. I don't think you have anything to worry about,' Lionel said.

Vanessa rolled her eyes. 'Did he say how long this would take?'

Morgan shrugged. 'I didn't hear that part.'

'But you heard everything else,' Lionel jeered.

Vanessa nudged Morgan with her elbow. 'Go up there and see what they're doing. They know you're Jesse's friend. They'll talk to you.'

'That man arrested me two years ago. I'm not going up there for him to try it again!' Morgan shot back. 'You heard what he said about you! I don't want to give him any more ideas about the Taylors.'

'Oh, please.' Vanessa waved her away. 'If we wanted

Eleanor dead she would've been buried in that garden a long time ago.'

The front door creaked open and Morgan's father stepped inside, catching the tail end of her mother's sentence. He looked like he'd aged ten years since Morgan saw him last. His shoulders sagged beneath his green windbreaker, his eyes dull, like all the hope had been wrung out of him. He trudged inside the kitchen, his boots thudding against the tile. He crossed the room with a sigh, opened the fridge, grabbed a beer, and popped the cap off on the edge of the counter with practiced force. He took a long sip.

'I don't even want to know what y'all are talking about,' he muttered, his voice low and frayed.

Vanessa studied him from her seat, concern laced across her face. 'Rough talk?' Vanessa asked.

Wesley didn't answer right away, not with words anyway. He gave a half-hearted shrug and turned toward the back door. 'I'll be in the gazebo if you need me.'

That wasn't good. Daphne rose from her spot and loped behind him, tail low, as if she could sense that he needed her in that moment. Morgan watched until he stepped through the doorway and outside. There was something hollow in the way he moved, slow and stiff. Whatever conversation he'd had with Mr. Reed hadn't gone well. Vanessa didn't push, just stared at the door like he would change his mind and come back through it, her lips pressed together in a tight line.

Lionel folded the proofed dough into a bread mold and tossed it in the oven. He set a timer on his watch and headed outside behind his friend, leaving Morgan and her mother to their own conversation. Morgan didn't know what was worse, her parents' controlled silence or their suffering.

'Morgan,' Vanessa started with a heavy sigh. 'I need you to stay here a few more days, at least until the last guest checks out. Your father and I need to figure out what will happen to the Inn and I can't be everywhere at once. You're the only person I trust to keep things running smoothly around here.'

Morgan froze. 'You know I can't,' she replied. 'It'll take days for admin to find a sub. Tomorrow is the first day back after break, I've got to reinforce everything we've learned. I've got lesson plans stacked and behavioral goals I'm tracking—'

Vanessa exhaled, turning slightly, not enough to meet Morgan's eyes.

'How hard could it be to replace you for a few days? I mean, it's not like you're teaching advanced chemistry. It's all primary colors and animal sounds. Anybody can do that.'

Morgan had never been physically slapped before, but her mother's words felt like five fingers to the face. Her face flushed, burning with humiliation, and then anger.

'Is that what you think I do?' Morgan rested fists on her thighs, her acrylic nails digging into her palms.

'The Inn needs all the help it can get right now . . .'

The Inn. Everything was always about the damn Inn. No, *anybody* could not do what she did. It took time, real skill, and lots of patience that Morgan was expeditiously running out of.

'I have a degree, Mom. From a real university. I spent four very long years learning how to teach children to read, how to identify learning delays, and how to manage classrooms with kids on every end of the emotional and behavioral spectrum. I have certifications. I write lesson plans. But sure, go ahead and reduce all my hard work to fucking animal sounds,' Morgan spat with more venom than she realized.

Her mother finally turned. 'You know that's not what I meant.'

'But that's what you said,' she snapped. 'You always do this. You think just because I didn't stay here and devote my life to folding sheets that my job doesn't matter. But I matter, Mom. What I do *matters* to those kids.'

'The Inn is—'

Morgan held her hand up. 'Don't say it,' she cut her off, her voice rising. She felt herself spiraling, but she couldn't stop herself. 'Let me guess, "the Inn is our legacy", "the Inn comes first",' Morgan mimicked. 'The Inn, the Inn, the Inn! You know what? Maybe if you spent half as much time investing in *me* as you do those damn daffodils, we wouldn't be having this conversation!'

Vanessa's lips parted in surprise, her fingers tightening around the edge of the table. 'Your father and I—'

'I've worked since I was sixteen to carve out a life outside of these reservation books. I love my students. I love my job. For once, I would like to come first.' To her disappointment, Morgan's voice cracked on the last word. 'Just once.'

Silence fell, thick and suffocating. The only sound was the ticking of the old wall clock and Morgan's uneven breath, her chest rising and falling.

Her mother threw her hands up, surrendering. 'I can't do this right now. Let's table this for another day.' She unfolded herself from the bench, leaving Morgan reeling with her own spiraling thoughts. Why did she have to fight tooth and nail for an ounce of respect from her mother? At the same time, her family was going through enough, so why couldn't she put her feelings to the side and be the dutiful daughter and stay without an argument?

And why did it feel like she was drowning?

After a steaming bowl of too-salty linguine and a slice of Lionel's freshly baked garlic bread, Morgan had quelled the hangry monster in her belly, feeling like a person again, but the sting of her mother's words still rang in her head.

Sitting cross-legged in the double rocking chair on the front porch of the Inn, Morgan swayed in the evening's cool breeze. The sun had retired behind a curtain of dusky clouds, leaving an amber glow that stretched across the horizon. The quiet hush of twilight embraced her, broken only by the rustle of tree branches overhead, and the distant chirp of crickets warming up for their nocturnal symphony.

She'd forgotten how quiet it was at the Inn, much different from her Juniper Heights apartment where there was a constant hum of other people's conversation floating through her vents, or the incessant slamming of doors.

Here, it was only the wind and Daphne's snores keeping her company.

Morgan had never been a smoker, all the throat cancer commercials from her childhood had scared her well enough. But if she wanted to pick up the habit, she'd choose right now to start. She mimicked holding a cigarette to her lips and inhaled, then expelled the air in a deep push, emptying her lungs. She felt better already.

A black truck rolled up the driveway, its windows darkened. Gravel crunched under its big wheels and Daphne's ears perked as she watched the truck get closer. She sprang to her haunches, crouching low, her eyes darting side to side. Morgan hooked two fingers under Daphne's collar, a fail-safe in case she let loose on whoever was about to step out.

A man with shoulders the size of a bear's got out and opened the rear door. Daphne growled, low and deep. Zara Wells emerged from the backseat, glowing like she'd just stepped off a magazine cover. A car door slammed, followed by the rhythmic click-clack of heels approaching.

The petite, brown-skinned beauty sported a skin-tight minidress that shimmered like oil underneath the porch light. Her makeup was flawless, her hair tamed into a glossy bun revealing the graceful slope in her neck and made her almond-shaped eyes pop. She was gorgeous, Morgan had to admit. But it wasn't just looks; Zara was an influencer, her curated life was shared with thousands online. She'd only been at the Inn for two days, arriving Friday just before the Jubilee, yet her presence felt larger than life.

Behind the beauty was a mystery. Morgan didn't know much about being highly desirable, but she knew women who looked like that didn't come to sleepy towns like Cinnamon Falls for the scenery.

'Hey, Morg,' Zara said softly, climbing the porch steps. Morgan released Daphne who began her sniffing exploration of the newcomer. Zara held her arms out and let Daphne do her canine investigation.

'Hey, you just getting back?'

Zara nodded, taking the open seat next to Morgan. She smelled citrusy like the Caribbean: sea salt, an ocean breeze, and ripe mangoes. 'Prime Society had a rooftop gathering; open bar, influencer only type of crowd. Asheville is doing this whole luxury rebrand thing and they pay girls like me to show up, drink champagne, and make it look irresistible.' She slid off her heels and stretched her legs. 'All I had to do was post three stories and tag the place. Easy five grand, enough for a new bag.'

Morgan blinked. 'Someone paid you five thousand dollars to . . . party?'

Morgan was in the wrong profession.

Zara shrugged. 'It's not my usual rate, but it's business. My face sells a lifestyle. You think I post that many outfits for fun?' She unclipped her hair, letting it fall around her shoulders in soft waves. 'But of course, the moment I posted from here, people lost their damn minds yesterday.'

Morgan stiffened. 'What do you mean?'

Zara pulled her phone out of her bag and scrolled. 'People are commenting like crazy about the Inn. "Isn't that where someone died?", "Are you safe?", "Cancel your trip, girl! You might be next". I got like, six DMs asking me to go live and spill the tea about what happened here.'

Morgan's stomach turned to stone. She braced herself for the worst.

'But I didn't do it.' Zara locked her phone and tucked it back into her purse. 'I'm not going to trash your family like that.'

'Really?' Morgan scoffed in disbelief.

Zara gave her a sidelong glance. 'You and your

parents have treated me better than half the sponsors I work with and you're not even paying me to stay here. To be honest, this has nothing to do with you guys. Someone died, yeah, but it could have happened anywhere. People just like a scandal.' She paused then added with a laugh, 'Give it three days and they'll be screaming about something else. Trust me, social media's attention span is basically at goldfish level.'

Morgan released the breath she'd been holding. 'I thought for sure you'd jump on the drama. I wouldn't have blamed you.'

Zara fanned her fingers over her heart. 'I may be materialistic and vain, but I'm not heartless. Just wait out the storm. By next weekend, nobody's going to remember a thing. You'll be back to normal in no time.'

The coils in Morgan's chest loosened. 'Thanks, Zara.'

'Don't mention it.' Zara yawned and stood, picking up her heels. 'I'm about to crash. That open bar wasn't playing and I need to record this "get un-ready with me".'

Morgan watched her go, the glint of her dress disappearing inside. For all her glitter and gloss, Zara had just given her more comfort than she realized.

Chapter 10

Monday

Morgan

As a naturally early riser, Morgan could have spent the whole morning in bed. The pillowtop mattress at the Inn cocooned around her body, supporting every achy nook and cranny, lulling her into a deep sleep. She'd been dreaming that she and Will were dangerously close to doing the horizontal dance, and if she had half the brains the good Lord gave her, she would have used one of her many sick days, called out of work, and continued her dream. But because she was her mother's daughter, she got dressed for work in the cool haze of dawn's first light. Work and responsibilities always came first, her pleasure, subconsciously or in real life, came last.

It'd been a painful three years since she'd been intimate with someone, and it wasn't because she wasn't trying, thank you very much. She'd been distracted.

With the influx of residents pouring into Cinnamon

Falls in just the last few years, her classrooms were getting more and more crowded. Last year, she had a mild-mannered sixteen kindergartners. This year, she had a rowdy and rambunctious twenty-four. It was a madhouse everyday, but Morgan always had a battle plan.

After much convincing from her father, Morgan compromised to stay one more night at the Inn. Thankfully, she'd packed an outfit that would double as business casual if you squinted one eye. Morgan dutifully ironed the creases out of her collared lavender blouse, and shook the wrinkles out of her purple polyester skirt. She wouldn't dare put any heat to it at this hour of the morning. She didn't trust that she wouldn't collapse into the ironing board and fall asleep.

Morgan rushed to the bathroom to do something with her hair. She studied herself in the mirror as she pulled all of her braids into a holder. Her eyes were still red-rimmed and tired. She tried on a smile and her teacher's voice.

'Good morning!' she said to herself, funneling all the enthusiasm she could muster into a plastered smile that felt dull and hardly believable. The minute she walked through the doors of Morningstar Elementary everyone would know that something was wrong.

She prided herself on being 'naturally high'; a person whose happiness radiated through their pores, no matter the circumstances. That was why she loved teaching kindergarten, children had no worries. Every day they brought her a new reason to be grateful, to realize life really *wasn't* that serious. But today, Morgan would have to fake it. She wondered for how long.

Morgan tied a deep purple ribbon around her high ponytail, knotting it into a bow atop her head. She slipped on a pair of flat sandals that were the same color and was satisfied with what reflected back to her. It was the best she could do today.

She took one last look at her room and rolled her luggage down the hall. Morgan tried not to look at the closed door to the Garden View room as she passed by. She dragged her luggage down the stairs, the bag thumping on each step as she descended.

Daphne met her at the bottom of the steps, her tail wagging so quickly Morgan thought it would jump off her behind. She reached down to pet her behind her ears.

'Good morning, Daffy,' she said while Daphne stretched out her back legs. She let out a big yawn and smacked her lips together, a sign she was hungry.

'Oh, no, you don't,' her mother called from the kitchen. 'I just fed you. Don't start pretending like you're hungry because your sister is here.'

Daphne whimpered, turning away from Morgan and padding into the kitchen. Morgan followed behind her.

The doorbell rang and Daphne unleashed a threatening bark. Morgan took a peek at her watch. It was just after six in the morning. Who would be coming to the Inn at this hour? Stepping into the hallway, Morgan made out a figure through the tempered glass that ran alongside the front door.

'The police, I bet,' her mother grumbled. 'What, they forgot something? They turned my house upside-down yesterday! It better be a hand-delivered apology for ruining my garden,' she fussed. 'A fruit basket at the very least—'

Morgan swung the door open expecting to see Jesse, or maybe even Chief Raines. Instead, she found an unfamiliar, and fantastically good-looking man with a leather duffel bag slung across his body.

He was the kind of man who looked like he belonged on the cover of a travel magazine, not the porch of a country inn tossed into the middle of a police investigation. His brown hair was tousled like he'd just finger-combed it on the way up the stairs, and his sharp blue eyes locked onto hers with a startling focus. His jawline could have cut glass, and his crisp white buttoned shirt, sleeves rolled to the elbows to reveal veined forearms, gave him a polished and casually confident look. He was tall and, Morgan presumed, athletically lean from lacrosse, or maybe even soccer. A warm tan graced his skin like he'd just gotten back from a tropical island vacation. She looked beyond him at the tan Oldsmobile tinkering in the driveway. He was driving that old thing?

Morgan blinked, momentarily thrown. The man's

smile was easy and polite, revealing two rows of straight, blinding white teeth. Daphne fought to get around Morgan, nosing her way between Morgan's legs.

The stranger looked between Morgan and Daphne, his smile deepening. 'A border collie!' he exclaimed, dropping to one knee. Daphne threw all her weight against Morgan, trying to get to the handsome stranger, nearly buckling her at the knees.

'Daphne!' Morgan yelled, but her dog was already on the porch, happily licking the stranger's face.

'That's a good girl,' he praised the unruly dog in a nasally voice that men usually reserved for cute babies.

Morgan grabbed Daphne by the collar, wrestling her off the man. 'I'm sorry, she's just a little excited.'

He righted himself, standing tall once again, well over six feet, Morgan noticed. He possessed the kind of height men on dating apps lied about. Morgan's breath hitched in her throat. A stranger, especially a handsome one, in Cinnamon Falls was like a UFO sighting.

'Apologies for the early visit,' he started, his baritone low and smooth. He cupped one hand over his heart. 'I'm Cameron Shore, Eleanor Langford's nephew. Is she here by any chance?'

Morgan's heart stumbled around in her chest. Her mouth ran dry.

He didn't know.

'I'm sorry to show up here unannounced like this so early in the morning.' Cameron pressed. 'I've been calling but no answer. She usually checks in on Sundays but I haven't heard from her since last week. I went past her house but then I remembered to check her favorite place.' Cameron coughed through his fist and shook his head like he was trying to stop himself from thinking the worst. 'I'm just worried about her, is all. She's getting up there in age and I just . . .' Morgan noted a bit of twang to his speech, an accent of sorts that she couldn't place. He closed his eyes for a beat, his unfairly long brown lashes grazing his rosy cheeks. 'I just need to lay some eyes on her, you know?'

Morgan stepped back instinctively, her heart skipping for reasons that had nothing to do with the investigation. How could she tell him that the very woman he was looking for had died just days before?

'Well, don't just stand there, let the man in!' Vanessa called from over her shoulder.

Morgan flinched, snatched out of the trance she found herself in.

'Sorry,' she said, pushing her luggage and Daphne out of the way to make room for Cameron in the tight foyer. She pushed too far and the front door slammed against the wall, knocking a picture from its resting place. Cameron rushed to grab it before it hit the floor and caught it with the smooth grace of a trained athlete. Maybe it was baseball, she considered.

'Sorry,' Morgan managed to say again, clutching the fallen frame to her chest.

'All good,' Cameron replied, a smile tugging at his lips; their eyes locked on each other. Morgan tried not to blush.

He followed behind Daphne as she led him to the kitchen. Morgan closed the front door and hung the picture back on its hook.

Her mother was busying herself making a fresh cup of coffee for their new visitor. Cameron sat at the kitchen island while Daphne sniffed all around him, curious.

'I'm Vanessa, and this is my daughter, Morgan. The Daffodil Inn is our family business.'

'It's beautiful,' Cameron replied as his eyes swept across the kitchen. 'My uncle Thomas loved it.'

The coffee pot percolated out a fresh batch. Usually, at this hour Morgan would have needed a cup or two just to get her going, but she was wide awake now. Vanessa slid the coffee over to Cameron.

Her mother's gaze latched on to hers and they silently argued who would be the one to break the news to him. Morgan was not the owner of the Daffodil Inn. She crossed her arms defiantly.

Vanessa rolled her eyes and took a deep breath. 'Cameron, I'm so sorry to tell you this, but Eleanor isn't here.'

Cameron's smile dropped. 'Oh, has she checked out already?'

You really do have no idea, Morgan thought.

Her mother fiddled with her fingers. 'She . . . passed away, Cameron, on Saturday night. We found her in our hedge maze during our annual jubilee. The police have been here and everything. I am so, so sorry for your loss,' she offered.

Cameron stilled, searching the ground for a long uncomfortable minute. He looked up at her with pleading eyes. 'H-How? Have they said anything about what happened to her?'

Vanessa shook her head. 'Nothing. They came yesterday to collect her belongings. Said they were having trouble notifying a next of kin, so it's a good thing you came down when you did—'

'They took her things?'

'Cleaned the whole place out.' Her mother pointed her chin upward. 'I'm sure they'd release her items to you since you're here now.'

'You think so?'

'Of course, Morgan can drop you by the station on her way to *work*.' Vanessa spat out the word with more venom than was necessary, considering she'd just shattered Cameron's heart to pieces.

Cameron's pleading gaze swung over to Morgan.

'Well, I have school—' she started.

'Nonsense,' her mother cut her off. 'She's friends with the detective on the case, Johnson. He can tell you more about it than we can.'

'Jesse,' Morgan corrected, rolling her eyes.

'Same thing,' Vanessa quipped, waving her daughter away. 'Put your things upstairs in the Garden Suite and I'll get Lionel to get you some breakfast started.' Her mother walked out of the kitchen and shouted for the cook.

'Lionel!'

'Garden Suite?' Cameron asked, dazed.

'Upstairs, on the right,' Morgan said.

'Lionel!' her mother shouted again into the depths of the house.

'I couldn't possibly,' Cameron replied. 'I can just grab a hotel. I—'

Morgan cut him off. 'This is Cinnamon Falls. We *are* the hotel.'

The last time Morgan was in a police station, she'd been handcuffed and tossed in a holding cell overnight with Nia at her side. The place was sterile, hauntingly so. Morgan could still feel the concrete slab that she'd slept on that night.

Angie, the receptionist, was just returning to her desk, blowing on a steaming paper cup as Morgan and Cameron walked in. Morgan watched her scald her tongue with a fiery gulp as she spotted Cameron swagger over to her desk.

'Cameron Shore.' He extended his hand. Dumbstruck, Angie fluffed her limp curls and shook his hand.

'Angela Robinson,' she responded, a flirtatious flash in her eyes.

In all the years Morgan knew Angie, she'd never seen the laid-back woman look so perky. Morgan couldn't blame her, Cameron was hot in a Ken doll kind of way; nice to look at, with a bit of mystery simmering under the surface. As much as she wanted to sink her teeth in him, she had to remember the man had just lost his aunt. It'd be wholly inappropriate, especially considering that she'd died at Morgan's family's place of business.

'This is Eleanor Langford's nephew,' Morgan supplied. Angie's eyes slid over to Morgan, startled that anyone else was in the room. 'Is Jesse in?'

'Um.' She began clicking around on her computer.

Just then, Jesse strolled in the door. The Cinnamon Falls detective was filling out his uniform more than ever before, Morgan noticed. Relationship weight, she figured.

Morgan couldn't have been happier for Jesse and Nia. They had been each other's first love, and despite Nia spending six years away from Cinnamon Falls, and getting a new man, she found her way home to Jesse. He'd been too happy to have her back. He'd been insufferable without her, moping around with a constant pout that had been starting to wear Morgan's patience thinner than it already had been.

Now that he'd made detective, he walked differently, carrying a weighed down plastic bag that

Morgan was sure was full of last night's leftovers and a few snacks to tide him over throughout the day.

He skidded to a stop when he passed her in the lobby, eyes bouncing between her and the new addition to the tiny town.

'Detective Shaw!' Angie clapped her hands in delight. 'Just the man we needed to see!'

Jesse cocked his head like Daphne did when she was confused.

'What's going on?' he asked.

Cameron stepped forward, all business, and extended his hand. 'I'm Cameron Shore, Eleanor Langford is . . . was my aunt.'

Jesse eyed the man in front of him, giving him a slow once-over from his feet to his head. 'Nice to meet you, I'm Detective Shaw. Why don't we have a sit-down in my office? My partner should be here shortly.'

Jesse beckoned the man ahead and Cameron reluctantly followed behind him. Cameron stopped short when he realized Morgan wasn't coming along.

'Thank you,' he called over his shoulder and Morgan replied with a wave of her hand. She wished that she could be a fly on the wall in that conversation. What had Jesse found out about Eleanor? Had there been any updates? More importantly, when could her life go back to normal?

When the two disappeared behind the partition

that led to the rest of the station, Angie finally broke character.

'You got to warn me before you bring a supermodel around here!' Angie cackled, settling into her office chair. 'I almost burned my esophagus!'

'How do you think I feel? I could barely keep my eyes on the road!'

'At least someone finally came around,' Angie said. 'Jesse's been trying to find anyone related to Mrs. Langford since Saturday night. I didn't think she had any family, let alone a hot nephew.'

'Well, he's here now,' Morgan replied. She took a look at her watch. It was closing in on 8 a.m. and she was about to be late.

'Yeah, he suuuuure is,' Angie responded, craning her neck past the partition to get another long look at the Cinnamon Falls newcomer.

Chapter 11

Will

Will cradled a warm mug of tea in his hands while standing cross-legged in the kitchen, keeping a watchful eye on the mounted TV in the living room and occasionally glancing at the pot of boiling eggs on the stove.

On the TV, flashbulbs popped as Chief Noelle Raines stepped up to the podium in Town Hall; her navy-blue uniform ironed crisp, her hardware gleaming under the fluorescent lights. To her left stood Jesse, arms crossed, his eyes scanning the crowd, sweeping from left to right. Jesse's haircut looked impeccable on screen, aligned perfectly on his head. Will mentally pat himself on the back for his handiwork. To Raines' right stood Mayor Sterling Tate, arms tucked behind his back with a firm look on his face. Detective Terrance Chambers stood next to Jesse, his posture open but his gaze serious.

Raines adjusted the microphone to her height and

a hush fell over the bubbling crowd. Next to Will, the toaster produced two pieces of white bread, drawing his attention back to the eggs on the stove. Will spun the knob, cutting off the gas, and removed the eggs from the heat. In the distance, the sound of the bathroom faucet shut off. Angel was still getting ready; probably trying to decide which headband matched her dress the best. That meant he had a few more minutes to himself.

Will tapped the remote to decrease the volume on the TV to a low hum, and turned on the closed caption. He didn't need Angel hearing this.

'Thank you all for being here on such short notice,' Chief Raines said. Her voice sounded steady, rehearsed. 'On the evening of Saturday, April 11th, at approximately 11.30 p.m., a woman was found unresponsive in the hedge maze at the Daffodil Inn. The victim has been identified as Eleanor Langford, longtime resident, and previous owner of the Daffodil Inn.'

Will's jaw clenched. He'd lived it, seen Eleanor's body with his own two eyes. But something about it being repeated, spoken aloud by officials, made it feel more real. More dangerous. He took another sip of his tepid water as his stomach churned. Will had experienced his fair share of dangerous situations in his lifetime, but nothing like stone cold murder. That was something different entirely; a new level of evil he couldn't wrap his mind around.

'Mrs. Langford was a guest attending the annual

145

spring festival, the Daffodil Jubilee. Emergency services were dispatched immediately, but despite best efforts, Mrs. Langford was pronounced deceased at the scene. We initially suspected natural causes given Mrs. Langford's advanced age and lack of immediate signs of struggle,' Raines continued. 'However, following an autopsy performed by the Whitfield Family Mortuary and toxicology results received from the Asheville crime lab late Sunday night, we can confirm that Mrs. Langford sustained a fatal stab wound. In addition, tests revealed the presence of digitalis, more commonly known as foxglove, in her system at the time of death. Based on these findings, investigators believe the poisoning may have contributed to or preceded the stabbing. At this time, we are treating the matter as a homicide, pending completion of the coroner's full report and the results of the ongoing investigation.'

Gasps rippled through the audience. In the crowd, someone shouted, 'Lord, have mercy!'

Reporters began scribbling, their murmuring getting louder.

A million thoughts collided at once: his daughter, Morgan, Mr. and Mrs. Taylor, Eleanor, the idea that someone slipped poison into a cup of tea, tea that his daughter drank on a nightly basis. His father, Calvin, mentioning that *something* ate his foxglove plant. He shuddered to think, had some*one* stolen it instead? But who? And why Ms. Eleanor?

Will reached to place his mug on the counter and missed the ledge. It hit the ground, sending splintered ceramic shards scattering on impact. Cursing under his breath, Will picked up the larger shards with his hands and then retrieved the mop from the nearby closet to remove the liquid. He kept one ear to the television, listening intently while he worked.

'We are opening the public tip line,' Jesse said, stepping into the frame beside Raines. 'And we encourage anyone with information, especially those who were at the Daffodil Jubilee Saturday night, to come forward.'

That reminded Will about Caleb. He opened their text thread and Caleb hadn't messaged back. He shot off another: **Call me**.

The camera cut to Elaine Matthias, already rising from her seat in the press pool. The gray-haired, sharp-witted, editor-in-chief of the *Cinnamon Chronicle* held nothing back when it came to policing in Cinnamon Falls, especially after Lyons' corruption scandal.

'Chief Raines,' she started, pushing her circle-framed glasses up on her nose. 'What *exactly* are you doing to ensure the safety of the Cinnamon Falls residents? This is the second homicide within two years. Should we be worried?' She pointed her ancient recorder toward the microphone, waiting.

Tension crept up Will's neck and he wasn't even the one being questioned. Elaine wasn't wrong, but he had no idea how the police would explain their way out of that question. He held his breath, waiting for Raines' answer.

Chambers leaned in, crossing over Raines to reach the microphone. Feedback screeched, making the audience wince and cover their ears. 'We have no evidence of an ongoing threat to the community.'

Raines could have sliced him in half with her glare. She elbowed him out of the way. 'This appears to be an isolated incident. Still, we are increasing patrols around major gathering areas and—'

Elaine didn't let up. 'With respect, Chief, a woman was murdered during one of our town's biggest festivals. Children were playing in that maze just feet away. Can you really expect us to sleep peacefully tonight believing that Cinnamon Falls is safe right now?'

Will could see the unease in Raines' posture through the screen but the Chief's voice didn't waver under the pressure. She leaned in, her eyes almost narrowed to slits, her finger punctuating each word.

'You can sleep soundly, Ms. Matthias, knowing we are doubling our efforts at every turn. My officers will investigate. We will follow leads. We will track them down. That's how we get justice for Eleanor. That's how we keep this town safe.'

'You didn't say "*our* town",' Elaine mumbled before collapsing into her seat.

Raines bristled, her fingers whitening on the podium. 'Excuse me?'

'You live here too, Chief Raines,' she spat. 'Act like it.'

Will heard the hardwood floor creak, announcing Angel's arrival. He snapped off the TV and the screen went black just as she walked into the kitchen. Angel's dress of the day was a grey short-sleeved number, with pleated ruffles. Her curls were away from her face with a black headband decorated with colorful gems. She slung her unicorn backpack on the counter, suspicious of the sudden silence.

'What were you watching?' she asked, eyeing the TV. 'Andrew Guy?'

'Weather,' Will fibbed quickly. He unpeeled Angel's eggs and slathered a dollop of butter on her toast. He grabbed a napkin out of the holder and started packing her eggs and toast into a reusable container. He took her lunchbox out of the fridge and handed both items to her.

'You'll have to eat breakfast in the car, Peach.' He rounded the kitchen island and bent to kiss the top of her forehead, pushing a stray curl back into place. 'If we leave now, we might be fifth in the drop-off line instead of fiftieth.'

Angel raced him to the front door.

Will waited impatiently behind Amanda Jenkins' vibrating Pinto in the drop-off lane at Morningstar

Elementary, drumming his fingers along the base of his steering wheel. The tiny semi-circle parking lot was crammed with minivans, SUVs, hurried parents, and finally, Amanda's rattling Pinto. He hadn't even known that they still made those cars, let alone would sell one shaking like the last leaf on a tree before winter.

Amanda's four children folded themselves out of the backseat, one behind the other, gripping a frosted pastry in one hand, their backpacks in the other.

Amanda stepped out too, all legs and attitude, and Will hoped Angel didn't notice the breath that hitched in his throat. He fisted a cough and promptly diverted his attention away from the woman in front of him wearing two tiny pieces of denim stitched together by what looked like only a hope and a prayer. Amanda turned, wiggling her fingers at Will, showing all thirty-two teeth, and more skin than a newborn. Will glanced at his digital dashboard. It was seven-thirty in the morning.

'Good morning, Will!' she called in a singsong voice, poking a hip out to flaunt her curves that didn't need a show. At that moment, Will knew exactly what it felt like to be a goldfish.

The worst thing about Cinnamon Falls was its size. Single women could sniff out a newcomer like bloodhounds. He'd always considered himself handsome, sure, but in a town this small, it didn't matter if he had a face for radio and three good teeth in his head, someone was going to hit on him.

They'd accidentally-on-purpose bump into him in the grocery store, or their son would mysteriously need a new barber. Once they found out he wasn't interested, they'd usually back off. His moral code wasn't the best for business, but he'd never been the player type. It involved too much lying, plus he had a shoddy memory.

Even so, before he could ever think about being physical with a woman, he craved a connection; something deeper than a date with dark liquor and tangled sheets. At thirty, he wanted something tangible; something he could hold on to, something stable. Besides, it was more than just his heart at stake.

Will cursed under his breath and lifted his hand in response, giving Amanda a curt nod. Angel, too busy in her sketchbook, hadn't observed the interaction, thank goodness. He didn't feel like explaining why she, too, couldn't have a pair of red platform pumps like Ms. Jenkins.

He wanted to melt into his seat when he noticed Morgan standing ahead of Amanda's Pinto, fiddling with something on her skirt. Today she sported a lavender collared shirt tucked into a loose-fitting skirt that featured a purple hibiscus flower stretched across the front. She looked up just in time to see Will and Amanda's exchange, and if she cared, she didn't show it on her face.

She seemed distracted, like she'd been chasing a thought that had disappeared when their eyes met.

Amanda glanced backward between Morgan and Will, a knowing smirk settling on her lips. A young girl in the front seat leaned over, her blond braids curtaining her face, and shouted, 'Let's go, Ma! We're going to be late!'

Amanda slid inside the Pinto and pulled away.

Will eased his car forward and stopped next to Morgan. She crouched down next to the door and hooked an arm through Angel's open window.

'Miss Morgan!' Angel exclaimed, scrambling to unlock her seatbelt. 'I haven't seen you in forever!'

'Twenty-four forevers to be exact,' Morgan replied jokingly with an easy smile that always made Will's heart stumble around in his chest.

Morgan looked amazing. Lavender was truly her color. It made her ebony skin sparkle with a radiance he could only liken to a spring morning's dawn. He didn't know if she had someone special. She never alluded to anyone in all the conversations they'd had, or in the flirty moments they shared. But he had to be sure for the sake of his own feelings. He didn't want to admit how devastated he'd be if it turned out she had a man somewhere, or that she wasn't interested in getting to know him on a deeper level.

Angel loosened the belt and gave her father a hasty kiss on the cheek before climbing out of the car.

'Have a good day, Peach!' Will called after her as she jogged up the sidewalk toward the building.

Angel whipped around. 'Not in public, Dad!' She stomped her foot, looking around sheepishly.

He knew she hated when he called her Peach, but he only had a few more years to embarrass her at school. He was going to get his time's worth.

'Love you, Peachy-Pooh!' Will puckered his lips, smacking them together for good measure. Angel covered her ears and sprinted inside the building.

'That girl is going to put you in a home,' Morgan laughed, shaking her head.

'And when I kick the bucket, I'll make sure to come back and haunt her,' Will replied. 'Sorry I didn't get to say goodbye yesterday morning. Things got a little . . . hectic.'

'It's fine, I know you have Angel to take care of. How is she doing?'

Will sighed, his fingers tightening around the steering wheel. How was Angel doing? That was the question that had been eating away at him since they'd left the Inn.

'She's quiet,' he said plainly, knowing it didn't even scratch the surface.

The truth was, Angel's silence scared him. Nothing, not even late-night TV, piled high pancakes, or those expensive gel pens could shake her out of it. It gutted him. The light in her had dimmed, and Will didn't know how to reignite it. He desperately wanted to fix it; to make the world safe for her again. It wasn't just fear, it was guilt, too. And exhaustion . . . that bone-deep loneliness that crept in late at night when he was folding her tiny socks and wondering if he was doing enough. If he would ever *be* enough.

He wanted to scream until his lungs gave out. He wanted someone who would listen, and not just to judge. He wanted someone to hear the words he was too proud to say: *I'm struggling*. What he really wanted – needed – was someone to lean on. Someone who understood what it felt like to carry the weight of everyone else's needs while burying your own.

But Morgan didn't need to hear all of that. Not with everything she had going on. He couldn't throw his pain at her feet and expect her to pick it up. She was going through enough. Still, just being near her made him feel like he wasn't completely alone.

'Will?' Morgan asked, snapping her fingers between his eyes. 'You okay?'

Her voice cut through his brain fog like a lighthouse in a storm. He blinked, refocusing on her face. She looked worried and beautiful, and real. In that moment he realized how badly he wanted more time with her. He wanted to know what made her laugh; what her deepest desires were.

The two of them were alone again, finally. This was his chance. He either said it now or walked away from Morgan with more regret.

He took a deep breath and cleared his throat. 'You got any plans Wednesday night?'

Will watched with sudden thirst as Morgan pulled her bottom lip into her teeth, thinking, his chest tightening with every passing agonizing second. She answered, 'I don't think so, I'd have to check my calendar.'

Will gripped the wheel until his knuckles went white. 'Pencil me in for eight-thirty?'

Morgan leaned in, her almond eyes narrowing, a playful lilt to her voice. 'Are you asking me on a date, Mr. Reed?'

A smile broke over his face. He couldn't remember the last time he'd smiled since Saturday night. 'That depends. Are you saying yes, Ms. Taylor?'

When Morgan agreed, Will programmed her number into his phone.

'Got a full day of cutting hair?' Morgan asked, strolling alongside his car as he kept up with the moving pace of the drop-off line.

'A few clients later on,' Will responded. 'I can't stop thinking about what Clarissa Hargrove said about Eleanor. Me and the little one stopped by the Toasted Pecan after we checked out of the Inn yesterday.' Morgan leaned in closer. 'She said that nobody in town cared for Eleanor except the people at the library, so I'm going to swing by and see if I can drum up some info about who could have done this.'

Morgan chewed her bottom lip, thinking. 'Good idea.' The school bell rattled and Morgan glanced over her shoulder as students filed inside the building. 'Let me know what you find out?'

Will nodded. 'Of course.'

'See ya!' She wiggled her fingers at him and ushered the lingering students inside.

He waited until he was well out of the parking lot of Morningstar Elementary and halfway down Main Street before he pumped a fist in the air.

The Cinnamon Falls Library smelled like old paper and lemon polish, both comforting and nostalgic in equal measure. The square brick building sat quietly at the end of Main Street, just a few blocks down from the police station and Town Hall.

Will couldn't get Clarissa's words out of his mind. No one in town would miss Eleanor Langford except a couple of librarians? Who was Eleanor Langford, really? He didn't know much about solving murders, that was Jesse's department, but Will did know that the woman he encountered was lightyears away from who Clarissa described.

If he could find out more about Eleanor Langford, maybe he could find out how she died, and if he could find out how she died, then maybe Angel could find some peace. He could get his daughter back and the Taylors could get their business, their reputation, back. The small, charming town he fell in love with would go back to what it used to be; a magical place that was safe for him and his daughter to exist. He'd found a community and he was going to do everything he could to protect it.

Will stepped through the double doors just as an older woman was leaving, not without her pausing to give him an unashamed once-over with her eyes. He tipped his chin in greeting, earning a flirty wink before the heavy oak doors closed behind him. He glanced around; there was a proclamation from Cinnamon Falls officials, even a plaque dedicated to an Edwina Rutherford who had been the head librarian for forty years before she passed. But there was no mention of Eleanor Langford.

Inside, the library was dimly lit by tall windows with diamond-pane glass, casting fractured light onto the scuffed tile. The air was still, like the whole building was holding its breath. High, wood-beamed ceilings gave the space a cathedral-like hush.

Will stepped further inside, his boots echoing slightly. The children's section was tucked off to the left, marked by a carved wooden arch that read 'Adventure Starts Here'. A dragon puppet was poorly taped to the arch, hanging on for dear life, his tongue spewing a burst of red flame. He caught a glimpse of finger paintings drying on a line that stretched across the room.

To his right, down a narrow hallway lined with faded posters featuring yesteryear's celebrities imploring children to read, was the archive room. That's where he was headed. But first, he paused, taking note of the bulletin board on the far wall.

Colorful flyers fanned out like patchwork: tax prep help, senior yoga, and after-school tutoring.

One, in particular, caught his eye.

Spring Drawing Club for Budding Artists
Bi-Weekly Saturdays at 10am. All Materials
Provided.
See Librarian for more information

Will's lips tugged into a smile. Angel would love that. Her sketchbook was already bursting with drawings of fairies, animals in tutus, sketches of daffodils, and even buildings. There was one of the Daffodil Inn's backyard she'd been working on tirelessly. She even drew her Aunt Nia's cat, Midnight, with a threatening glare.

He plucked the flyer from its home and brought it over to the front desk. A girl with electric blue braids and a 'Cinnamon Falls Reads' pin clipped to her lanyard looked up and grinned.

He found her nametag, Quinn. 'Need help with something?' she asked, closing the large paperback she was reading with a thump.

Will nodded and held up the flyer. 'Is this still open? My daughter is in second grade and loves to draw.'

Quinn's round eyes lit up. 'Absolutely! We have a few spots left. What's her name? I'll add her to the registration.'

'Angel Reed,' he responded.

Quinn grabbed a clipboard from under the desk and flipped a few pages before scribbling Angel's name on a list of what looked like six other children. Will rattled off his contact information.

'She'll get a sketchbook, colored pencils, and one-on-one instruction if she wants it. We do a spring showcase in May, this one is with the new mayor. The best drawing will hang in his office for the rest of his term.'

Will could already see Angel hoisting her creation in the air, her smile as big as the sun. 'She's going to be so excited.'

Quinn handed him a slip with the time and location. 'We'll see you next Saturday!'

With a nod of thanks, Will replaced the flyer.

'One last thing,' he added. 'Can you point me to where Eleanor Langford's plaque is? I heard she was fond of this place.'

Quinn's smile fell instantly. 'Eleanor meant a lot to us here. We were devastated to hear the news this morning. Her plaque is in the Archive room, above the door. She used to stay for hours in that place. It still feels unreal that she's gone.'

'I'm sorry for your loss,' Will supplied, hating that he only had placating statements and sorrowful looks to exchange.

Heading toward the Archive Room, Will hoped the quiet place would give him a moment to gather his thoughts.

The Archive Room was tucked in a far corner past the non-fiction section. Will passed by a locked glass case of rare books and sepia-toned photographs of the early days of Cinnamon Falls, next to a faded town charter, curled inward on itself with frayed, yellowed edges.

A brass placard over a frosted glass door read:

Cinnamon Falls Archival Collection

Under it was another:

Sponsored by Friends of the Library, Eleanor Langford and Ronald Hartley

Through the door Will noticed a woman wearing a cream-colored cardigan buttoned to her chin, perched behind a tall oak desk. Her hair was swept into a tight bun with square-framed glasses perched on the edge of her nose. He rapped lightly on the glass and she looked up without smiling. She adjusted her glasses with a practiced flick before allowing him to enter.

'Please sign in if you'd like to use the archive room,' she instructed, her voice polite but clipped. She gestured to a three-ring binder laid open. The top sheet showed today's date. Will had been the only visitor so far.

The golden nameplate on her desk gleamed,

Elizabeth. Will started to make conversation, hoping to lead to a talk about Eleanor, but she stopped him before he could get it out.

'There are a few rules for the archives,' Elizabeth began robotically. 'No pens, no food, no pictures, and under no circumstances are you allowed to handle any materials without wearing the provided gloves.'

A box of fresh white cotton gloves sat on the edge of the desk. Will slipped a pair over his hands. Elizabeth watched his moves, not with suspicion, but with the eyes of a trained master at the craft.

'If you need help finding anything, there's an index on the wall.'

He guessed he was fending for himself. He turned and took a deep breath. Beyond the desk, the archive room stretched ahead, dimly lit by brass lamps that cast a muted glow. The walls were lined as far as he could see with wooden filing cabinets and metal shelving filled with document boxes and large leather-bound books. A rolling ladder was affixed to one wall, a sign reading, 'Do Not Use Without Staff Assistance' above it.

The only sound was the soft tick-tick of the wall clock and the sharp page flick of Elizabeth's current read. It was colder here than the rest of the library, Will noticed. The air felt heavier too. Stepping cautiously into the stillness, quiet tension pressed into Will's shoulders as he made his way deeper into the room.

He gravitated toward the metal shelving that housed thick volumes of leather-bound books. The spines were gold-embossed and worn, each labeled by year. A laminated sign was affixed to the wall:

Cinnamon Chronicle Archives

He stood for a minute, considering. Where would he start? What was he even looking for?

Will recalled a picture above the fireplace in the Great Room of the Daffodil Inn. Morgan's mother, Vanessa, was cradling baby Morgan in her arms, smiling widely for the camera. In the bottom left corner was the year 2000.

But what was the Daffodil Inn before the Taylors arrived and before Eleanor and her husband, Thomas, had owned it? There had to have been a record of the land changing owners. Will steepled his fingers, thinking. *How long had the place been around? Twenty years? Thirty? More?* he wondered.

He trailed his gloved finger across the two thousands, the nineties, the eighties, and the seventies and stopped. His precious baby girl was seven, so he chose the 1977 edition of the *Cinnamon Chronicle*. With a grunt, he eased the weighty book from the shelf, the leather creaking like a saddle. He waved away the dust that puffed into the air as he opened it on the reading table.

The yellowed pages crackled under his touch as he

studied grainy photos of town parades, mayoral debates, and ribbon cuttings. The past sprang to life in flashes of names he'd heard Harold Bones mention in passing conversation, and places that didn't exist anymore. He wasn't sure what he was looking for; just something, anything, that could shed light on the woman who was at the center of the Daffodil Inn's chaos.

He paused on a small article. The headline near the bottom of the page caught his eye: Riverfront Property Purchased by Local Investor. The article was short, no more than a couple paragraphs wedged between an ad for garden fertilizer and a five-dollar pancake breakfast.

'The open tract of land along the Cinnamon River, long admired for its views and spring wildflowers, has been officially purchased by Thomas Langford from northern Georgia. Langford announced plans to build a private home on the property. The land was sold at county auction earlier this spring.'

There was a black and white photo beneath it, grainy and faded, but Will could just make out a man standing in front of a tree line, holding a rolled set of blueprints under one arm. He was smiling, proud. Will leaned in. The background of the photo showed the land as it once was, no daffodils, just a gentle slope of the riverbank and a thicket of trees behind.

Will took a second glance around the room and

noticed a drawer had been pulled out on the filing cabinet next to him. Its mouth, slightly ajar like someone had just finished researching and had been called away for another task. He stepped over, reading the sign above the cabinet:

Property of Cinnamon Falls Historical Society

He pulled the drawer open to reveal dozens of files of wire-bound documents separated and tabbed by year. The only file open was one from 2020. Will carefully pulled the book free from its file and brought it to one of the wooden study tables in the center of the room. It was heavier than he expected. Will winced as it landed on the table with a thud. He didn't have the heart to look over at Elizabeth, but he was sure she was watching him closely.

2020 Mayoral Election Financial Disclosures

As he flipped the first laminated page, he quickly realized that the figures he was reading were from Asad Lyons' most recent mayoral campaign. The entries were exhaustive, each donor listed alongside their address, company name, and contribution amount.

Why would someone be looking into Mayor Lyons now? Will wondered. The last time Will checked, ex-Mayor Lyons was rotting away in a jail cell awaiting his sentencing trial. This information was useless and still told him nothing about Eleanor.

Frustrated, he was ready to shelve the book back in its place when he noticed faint marks in the margins. He stood, holding the book closer to the light overhead. Two names had been circled in pencil, barely visible unless the light hit just right: Northbridge Management Group and Cedar Creek Solutions, LLC.

Both had donated sizable amounts to Lyons' campaign: $7,500 and $10,000 respectively. The names meant nothing to Will, but they meant something to someone, enough for them to make a note for the next person to find.

He turned toward Elizabeth. 'Is it possible to check this book out for a couple of days?'

She pointed to yet another sign next to her. 'All archive materials must remain in-house.' Will nodded, expecting as much. She rose from her seat, snapped on a pair of gloves and approached him with a slip of paper and a stamp. 'We keep circulation records for internal tracking, so I'll need to stamp it.' She gently turned the book over, noted the title and stamped today's date next to it. Will glanced over her shoulder at the list of previous patrons who'd also taken a look at the book as she wrote his name next to the date in neat letters.

The name above his, dated two weeks before the Daffodil Jubilee, was Eleanor Langford's.

Just then, his phone rang, making his heart stumble

around in his chest. Will clambered for his phone hurriedly, pinching the side through his jeans to prevent it from ringing out loud. The librarian looked at him with disgust.

Will put the phone to his ear. 'Yo, I'm at the library. What's up?'

Jesse responded, 'The library? I didn't know you could read.'

Will glanced over his shoulder. The librarian was staring at him with the heat from a thousand suns. 'No phones,' she mouthed.

'Man, what do you want? You're about to get me killed in here,' Will grumbled, scooting lower in his seat.

'Can you meet me at the Red Fern at eight? I got some news.'

'I can't, I've got Angel,' Will reminded him. He was jealous that his single, childless friends could go anywhere they pleased without a second thought. He missed that carefree life, but he wouldn't trade his daughter for anything in the world, including the cheap drinks at the Red Fern Tavern.

'Drop her off at the house. I'm sure Nia will love to babysit,' Jesse offered.

Will kissed his teeth. 'Does Nia know you're pawning off her evening?'

'I'm getting kicked out the house tonight,' Jesse responded. 'Apparently it's top secret wedding stuff. She'll be with Morg, so they can make it a girl's night.'

Will stood, carefully stripping the gloves from his hands and checked his watch. It was nearing mid-afternoon, and he needed to get ready for his first client.

'If she says yes, then cool. Otherwise, we might have to take a rain check.'

There was a brief pause and then Will heard a buzz through the phone.

Jesse said, 'She texted back in all caps. I think she's more excited about it than Angel is going to be.'

'My last client will be done right before Angel gets out of school. I'll meet you at your house around five?'

'Sir!' Elizabeth's eyebrows pinched together in frustration, fed up with Will.

He sprinted out of the Archives room before he was the next person to die in Cinnamon Falls.

Chapter 12

Morgan

Morgan could barely keep her focus. Between the argument with her mother, Cameron showing up, and Will asking her on a date, her mind was buzzing. She hadn't even had her second cup of coffee yet, and it was nearly noon. She should be grading her students' assignments while she had some quiet during their recess. The stack of papers was sitting in front of her, ready to receive marks from her trusty red pen or a sparkly golden star.

Occasionally, her students' screams filtered in through the open window beside her, jolting Morgan out of her thoughts that seemed to circle back to Will every few minutes, their morning conversation on a replay in her brain.

A date? With Will? Like, alone? Just the two of them? Morgan couldn't imagine it. She needed someone sane to give her advice so she pulled out her cell phone to text Nia: **Red Fern tn?**

Nia messaged back almost immediately: **We're picking my second dress tonight, remember?** Another text buzzed in: **Plus I've promised Will that we would watch Angel.**

Morgan nearly catapulted out of her seat when she heard a knock at her classroom door. Her cell phone jumped out of her hand, clattering across her desk. She looked up to find Ms. Shanice, the other kindergarten teacher, with a concerned smile on her face.

Shanice Brooks was a young teacher, fresh out of her collegiate courses, with big dreams and even bigger hair. Morgan had been dodging her since the beginning of the school year when Shanice suggested that Morgan could facilitate a school-wide training session on classroom management.

It was no secret that Morgan had the most behaved class in Morningstar. Even though it was 'just kindergarten' to everyone else, Morgan knew the difference. She had the track record to prove that the students who left her class went on to excel afterward.

Morgan had a long while to go in the education system, but she knew, deep down, that teaching children was her calling. She'd never been more sure about anything, and she wasn't going to let her mother's comments affect that.

'Knock, knock,' Shanice mouthed through the rectangular window above the doorknob. Morgan glanced at the clock against the far wall. She was

169

late. She rushed over to find a hallway full of kinder-gartners staring back at her.

'Forgetting something?' Shanice motioned to the gaggling line of children fresh from recess, a sheen of sweat over their faces, dirt caked on their clothes and in their hair.

'Shit,' Morgan murmured under her breath. In all her years of teaching she'd never forgotten to pick her class up. Plastering a smile on her face, her mind whirred for an excuse, but she knew her kids were smarter than whatever she was about to come up with. Perfect Miss Morgan steeled herself to get ripped a new one.

'Miss Morgan, you forgot about us!' a little voice accused from the back of the line. The chatter continued, nonstop. The best place to start with a mob of unruly tiny humans was to apologize.

'I'm sorry, guys, I—' Morgan started.

They did not accept her offering. Questions and accusations flew at her faster than she could respond.

'We was burnin' up out there!'

Then came the requests, which quickly turned into demands. 'I need some water!'

'I'm so thirsty, I could die!'

'How can you talk if you're dead?'

'Don't say dead!'

'My mom said that's a bad word!'

It felt like tennis balls were being volleyed around in Morgan's head. The children's voices were transforming into the argument with her mother. The scream from Saturday night flashed through her brain, all of it melding together into one voice that echoed: *It's all your fault!*

Her heartbeat pulsed out of her ears, pressure rising in her chest, until she married her hands together in a deafening slap that silenced the chaos immediately, inside and out.

'If you can hear me, clap once,' she instructed, pushing a breath through her teeth.

One singular clap resounded.

'If you can hear me, clap twice,' she requested again.

There were two claps this time.

Morgan said in a calm voice. 'Lips zipped, hands on hips.'

Silently, the children placed one finger over their mouths, the other hand on their hip and fussed over one another until they were in a straight line.

Ms. Shanice's class stared, blinking in awe.

Morgan pointed over her shoulder inside her classroom.

'In,' she instructed.

They followed each other inside the class in a single-file line. Chairs scraped across the tile floors as the children found their normal seats, and waited for further instruction.

'Thank you, Shanice,' Morgan said, turning to the open-mouthed teacher. 'I apologize for being late. I wasn't watching the time. It won't happen again.'

She smiled back, all toothy and apologetic. 'It's really no problem, we love hangin' out with Class A.' She opened her classroom door and her students fell inside, a barrage of happy screams echoing into the hall.

She closed it behind them and stepped closer to Morgan. Morgan did the same, not before giving her students a sharp look.

Shanice ran her manicured hands together, her eyes searching the floor for the words, and Morgan already knew what was coming.

'I, um, heard what happened at the Inn. I'm surprised you're back at work. We all thought you would have taken some time off and I'd have to run both classes for a while. But Ms. Alston said you hadn't requested a sub?'

We all? Morgan questioned. Had the entire faculty gathered together in the break room and gossiped about her behind her back?

'I'm okay, Shanice, really.' Morgan wasn't sure who she was trying to convince more, Shanice or herself. 'It's no big deal.'

Shanice placed a gentle hand on Morgan's shoulder. Morgan glanced down at her perfectly almond-shaped French-tipped nails. 'I bet it's a big deal for your mom and dad.'

Morgan reeled backward, shoving Shanice's hand away.

'Don't bring up my parents,' Morgan warned with a heat inside she didn't know she possessed. Her parents were too sensitive of a subject right now; a bruise too tender.

'I don't mean to be insensitive, I just want to help. I know this must be difficult to deal with. Go be with your family. Work can wait.'

Morgan glanced back at her children through the window. She thought about her mother's comments: *primary colors and animal sounds*. Then, she thought about her readiness goals that she was on track to smashing. There was no way she could stop now. If one thing had to give in her life, it wasn't going to be those children. Besides, she needed the distraction, something to hold on to, because the rest of her world was in the wind.

'No, it can't,' Morgan replied, and stepped back into her classroom.

At dismissal, Morgan hadn't made it past the front office when her path was blocked by a rhinestone-wrapped speed bump in the figure of Ms. Alston, the school's administrative assistant.

'Principal Allen wants to see you, hon,' she said, hands out, offering to hold Morgan's belongings with a warm, but pitiful smile.

Morgan hesitated. 'Right now?' She glanced at

her sports watch. 'I've got ten minutes before the pick-up line wraps around the corner. If it can wait—'

Over her glasses Ms. Alston gave her a firm look that let Morgan know it couldn't, and wouldn't, wait.

'Come on.' Ms. Alston beckoned her ahead into the front office.

Morgan sighed, surrendering her belongings.

Ms. Alston had to have been a drill sergeant in a former life. She took slack from no one, students, teachers, and parents alike. She wore lavender perfume so strong it could have its own zip code. Today, her fingernails were painted a stunning lime green that made Morgan question Ms. Alston's after-work life. She'd heard she spent her nights and weekends at the casino over in Asheville, but Morgan wouldn't dare repeat it.

The front office was a haven of chaos. Phones trilled at a deafening volume that no one reached to answer. The air hummed with the grind of the ancient copier machine in the corner. Bright construction paper signs about flu season, PTA meetings, and the lunch schedule covered the walls. A tempting glass jar of lollipops sat on the edge of the desk, a bribe for well-behaved visitors. Judging from the sheen of dust growing on top, there hadn't been many given out in quite some time.

Mr. Wallace, the fourth-grade math teacher, stood near the copier, waiting for his print job to finish.

He gave her a curt nod then a shrug. If he knew about her unexpected meeting, he wasn't sharing.

She followed Ms. Alston as she parted the sea of clutter like a practiced general. They passed the dual secretary cubicles, and she knocked gently on the closed door in front of them. She didn't wait for permission to walk inside.

Principal Allen was finishing up a phone call when Morgan stepped in. He gestured to the tufted leather armchair across from his desk. Ms. Alston backed out of the room and Morgan sat down, her knees stiff, her heartbeat quickening with every passing second.

While she waited, Morgan filtered through all the potentially fireable offenses she'd committed in the last several years. Had one of her students snitched on her after her sarcastic rendition of *The Hungry Caterpillar*? Honestly, how could that little guy eat so much? Or was it the time she warmed up her leftover salmon in the teacher's lounge? Fishgate lasted for three weeks without anyone confessing to the crime, remaining unsolved to this day. Morgan would take it to the grave.

She glanced down at the manila file on his desk. Her name stuck out in typed letters on the tab. It was thick, about half the size of her pointer finger. Six years of teaching and a file that big couldn't be good.

Principal Allen ended his call and placed the receiver

down with a soft click. Even sitting in his winged-back chair, his shoulders boasted his broad stature. He scrubbed his hands against his close-cut beard that had more salt than pepper these days. His usually kind eyes were shadowed by something deeper. Morgan braced herself for the bad news as he removed his glasses and took a long look at her.

'Thanks for stopping in.' He folded his hands on top of the file. His smile didn't reach his eyes as he continued, 'I know dismissal is hectic, so I'll make this brief.'

Morgan's stomach doubled over. She regretted gobbling down the shrimp salad she had for lunch.

'I watched the press conference this morning with Chief Raines. I had no idea your family was so close to what happened.'

Everyone knew, even her boss. Morgan's internal temperature rose rapidly and she gripped the armrests.

'It's been tough,' she mumbled, unlatching her tongue from the roof of her mouth.

'I truly can't imagine,' he said gently. 'And I won't pretend I can. But I want you to know that this school, your colleagues, we all care about you. Which is why I'm requesting that you take the rest of the week off—'

'Is this about recess? Because I explained to Shanice—'

He held a hand up. 'This isn't about Shanice, although she's been on at me about making you take some time off. You've been a rock here, Morgan, but you don't need to be a hero right now.'

'I haven't written any plans for a sub,' Morgan said weakly, listing all her thoughts on her fingers. 'It's the first day after break. We've got to do a review before we move on—'

'We'll take care of everything,' he assured her with a soft smile. 'Go be with your family.'

Morgan shook her head. 'The kids need structure. If I'm not there . . .' Tears sprang into her eyes before she knew it. 'I just ca–can't leave,' she stuttered, caught off guard by the emotion building in her chest.

The last place she wanted to be was at the Daffodil Inn.

Principal Allen pressed his lips together and handed her a tissue. 'You're one of the best teachers I have at Morningstar. You show up every day, fully present, and fully prepared. That's what makes you great at your job. But, the truth is, you can't pour from an empty cup. You've got a lot going on and we want to support you in showing up as your best self.' He plucked the folder in front of him. 'This is six years' worth of commendations. Letters from parents and students.'

He opened the file. On top was a construction paper drawing of planet Earth. Morgan immediately recognized Angel's depiction of her standing on top of the world. Over her head were the words: Best Teacher In The Universe.

The pressure in Morgan's chest released and the

dam of emotions she'd been holding in finally broke. The folder wasn't full of written reprimands or warnings, it was all praise. Still, something about being told to step back felt like a punch in the gut.

Principal Allen's voice remained steady and warm while she snotted all over his desk. He handed her the box of tissues.

'Take your time. We'll handle things here.'

Morgan swallowed the lump in her throat and nodded. 'Thank you for not firing me.'

'I wouldn't dream of it. See you next week, bright and early, Miss Morgan.'

Morgan shook his outstretched hand, gave him a tight-lipped smile, and stepped out.

Back in the front office, Mr. Wallace was clearing a jam from the copier, frantically checking the clock on the wall. He stood upright when she passed by, giving her the same pitiful smile Ms. Alston had.

Morgan's belongings were waiting on Ms. Alston's desk. 'I added a bottle of water,' she said, patting Morgan's lunch bag. 'You looked like you were going to faint.'

Morgan laughed softly. 'Thank you.'

Ms. Alston shooed her away. 'Go on now before the kids see you.'

As she walked through the parking lot she realized how strangely illegal it felt to leave school before all the buses had gone. Like she was skipping, even though she'd been given permission. It would only be a short drive back to the Daffodil Inn, but Morgan had never felt further from home.

Later that evening, Morgan arrived at Jesse and Nia's house with her bridesmaid binder and two bottles of wine. Before she could make it up the staggered concrete steps, Nia wrenched open the door.

'Please tell me there's alcohol.'

Morgan held up a plastic bag that contained two brand new bottles of Pinot Noir. Nia stepped back, relieved, and let Morgan pass her to enter.

Morgan immediately recognized that Jesse had redecorated since they'd all been together last, celebrating the happy couple's engagement. The tan leather couches Jesse's mother called 'frat house furniture' had been swapped with a tufted soft grey sectional sofa that made the place more elegant.

The previous pictures of Jesse that lined the mantel were gone too, replaced by photos of him and Nia in various vacation spots, smiling widely at the camera, love dancing in their eyes. His parents were pictured too, with their hands clasped together in places all over the world. There was one of Niles at his high school graduation. Morgan recognized herself, linking arms with Nia at the grand opening of The Cinnamon Scoop. Their love oozed from every corner of this house. She tried not to gag.

'Both bottles are for me,' Morgan announced. 'I'll let you take a sip if you ask nicely.'

On the couch, Jesse chuckled. Morgan greeted him by swatting him on the back of the head. He held the spot in mock offense while they shared a laugh.

'That kind of day, huh?' Nia inquired, joining Morgan in the kitchen while she unpacked her bags.

'You have no idea,' she mumbled, shaking her head.

Before Morgan could unload her woes on her best friend, Jesse interrupted and said, 'You ladies enjoy yourself, I am retreating to the man cave.'

'You got that one trained up real good,' Morgan commented, one hand on her hip. 'I like a man that knows how to leave when the grown-ups are talking.'

Jesse rolled his eyes and Morgan held a finger up. 'Not so fast, Mr. Officer.'

Jesse grumbled, 'I thought I was getting away.'

'What's the latest on the investigation? It's been radio silence since Chambers came to pick up Eleanor's things. And what happened with Cameron this morning?'

'Wait, who's Cameron?' Nia questioned, on her tiptoes while she rooted around in a cabinet for wine glasses.

'Look, Morg. It's complicated. I can't really speak about—'

Morgan waved him away. 'Everybody's seen the news by now. What should I tell my family? What do we need to prepare for? You gotta tell me something, Jay.'

Jesse looked at Nia before responding, their un-spoken language bantering back and forth.

Morgan fisted her hips. 'So now he's doing the cop thing with me?' She looked between the two of them. Morgan considered both Jesse and Nia her best friends. Was he icing her out of this? She deserved to know, too.

'As soon as I hear something, I promise you'll be the first to know. For now, just take it easy, okay? Stay offline, it's nothing but bullshit anyway. We'll get through this, alright?'

Morgan narrowed her eyes, her finger gliding between the two of them. 'Y'all practiced this, huh?'

'Of course not,' Jesse scoffed. As soon as she turned to Nia, Jesse slipped through the side door and out of sight. The garage was where he kept his frat boy recliner, a TV as long as the wall, and his most prized possession other than his fiancée: his '87 Caprice.

Harvey Briggs gifted it to him after Jesse proved that he was innocent of Rosie's murder. Its only twin in all of Cinnamon Falls belonged to Grace Whitfield. That reminded Morgan, she was not going to forget to tell her best friend that Grace was getting a little *too* friendly with Jesse on Saturday night.

Nia wrestled the wine open and poured them both a generous amount.

Morgan commented, 'Don't think I don't know when I'm being bribed into silence with red wine.' She flipped out her binder and settled into the seat at the kitchen table. She spread out some color palettes, centerpiece options, and finally dress options.

She turned to her friend and they kissed glasses. The cheerful *ping* lifted Morgan's mood immediately. 'Let's get down to the real business!'

Nia pushed away the samples. 'Not until you tell me what happened today. Who is this Cameron guy?'

'Eleanor's nephew. He came early this morning to the Inn around, like, six. And he is so hot! Gorgeous hair, big broad shoulders, perfect teeth, bright blue eyes to die for. Me and Angie almost had it out over who would get him first!'

'So, wait. He just showed up unannounced at six in the morning?' Nia inquired, one eyebrow raised in skepticism.

'His freakin' aunt just died two days ago!' Morgan responded. 'If it were Marjorie or Walter, you'd be on the first thing smoking for your parents.'

Nia nodded. 'You're right about that. Where did he come from?'

Morgan shrugged. 'I dunno. I didn't ask. I just drove him right to the station.'

Nia's eyebrow hiked impossibly higher. 'You? The most suspicious person I know didn't ask where the gorgeous stranger with perfect teeth came from?'

'He seemed like he was in shock. I was just trying to be helpful. I wasn't trying to get in his boxers.'

'Why not?' Nia screeched. 'When's the last time you even got some?'

'Keep your voice down!' Morgan shushed her. 'I need Jesse's parents to keep thinking I'm the wholesome one between you and me.'

'They are on a cruise to Bermuda.' Nia waved her hand dismissively. 'Those two won't be back for two weeks.'

'Y'all got engaged and they never came home again.' Morgan slapped the table with laughter.

'They couldn't wait to pawn him off,' Nia replied with a cackle. 'What does Will think of this Cameron guy?'

Just the mention of his name made Morgan's skin flame, or it was the wine catching up to her, Morgan couldn't be sure. She braced her hands on the side of the table.

'Will asked me out, like on a real date,' Morgan admitted, keeping her eyes downcast so she couldn't see Nia's goofy expression.

Nia squealed dramatically, nearly toppling off the chair. The wine sloshed around in the glass while she righted herself.

'Finally, girl! It's about damn time! Wait till I tell Jesse. He owes me fifty dollars and I want that cold cash in my hand tonight!'

'You two took *bets* on us?' Morgan asked, incredulous.

'A friendly wager,' Nia clarified. 'I bet that Will would ask you out before the Fall Fest, and I won by a mile!'

'You two are pathetic,' Morgan scoffed.

'Don't be like that.' Nia poked Morgan in her side. 'I knew he wouldn't be able to resist you once he saw you in that dress at Petals N' Promises.'

Morgan did a terrible job at hiding her blush. 'Don't start wedding planning yet, he's probably just being nice.'

'Tell me you don't believe that.' Nia sobered, her expression serious. Morgan didn't have the heart to say the thing she'd been dreading out loud. Nia grasped her friend's hand in hers.

'You're beautiful, Morg! You're hella smart, seriously the funniest person I know. Your heart is genuine . . . you're a real-life gem! He can see what we all see, which is why he asked you on a date! I can promise you, it isn't just because he's a nice guy.'

Morgan couldn't stop the tears from prickling her eyes. She wished that were true. 'Sometimes it just feels like I'm always the second choice. The side character, the funny friend, the helper—'

'Not anymore,' Nia cut her off. She scooted her chair closer to her friend and knocked away the tear rolling down Morgan's cheek. 'This is your story now.'

The doorbell echoed through the house, pulling Morgan and Nia from their debate about sweetheart necklines. Nia claimed to have broad shoulders and wanted something that covered her arms. Morgan couldn't understand why she wanted to wear a long-sleeve T-shirt as a reception dress on supposedly the best day of your life. Thankfully, Nia chose a few better options, much to Morgan's approval, and had made an appointment to try on more suitable dresses at The Velvet Fox the next day.

'I'll get it,' Morgan said, crossing through the living room to open the door.

She opened it to reveal Will standing with Angel, a sketchpad in one hand and a vanilla Shirley Temple in the other.

'Miss Nia!' Angel bolted past Morgan toward the kitchen. 'Your brother never makes my drink like you do. It's not enough cherry.' She pouted, holding up her plastic cup for Nia to inspect. Angel was right. The normally deep cherry red drink was a paltry pink.

Nia tsked. 'He's not as smart as us. I'll see what Uncle Jesse has around here.'

'Just dropping her off,' Will said, presenting two greasy paper bags. 'I didn't know if you ladies had eaten. I got some burgers from The Golden Grille on the way over.' He handed the bags over to Morgan. 'Jesse's dragging me to the Red Fern tonight so pray for me.'

'I nearly got a staph infection last time we were there,' Nia said, walking over to give Will a hug. 'Thanks for dinner. Your friend is in the cave.' She pointed to the side door.

'Thanks,' Morgan finally managed to say. Her palms were perspiring so much she was grateful she didn't drop the bag of food.

Jesse emerged from the garage. 'I thought I heard some testosterone in here,' he joked, giving Will a friendly dap. 'You ready?'

Will nodded and turned to leave. 'Bye, Peach!' he called over his shoulder.

In the kitchen, Angel rolled her eyes. Morgan pretended not to watch as Jesse pulled cash out of his wallet and slapped it in Nia's hand before leaving. He planted a kiss on her lips and walked out behind Will.

Morgan removed the food containers from the bag, dividing them up among the girls.

Angel flipped open her sketchbook, turning it around for Morgan to see.

'I drew this at school today.'

'In class or during your free period?' Morgan asked in her teacher's voice.

Angel raised her pointer finger in the air. 'I plead the fifth,' she responded.

Morgan turned to get a better view and she recognized the place immediately. It was a bird's eye view of the Daffodil Inn's backyard; the garden maze, the daffodils, and even the river. In the maze were two figures, a woman and a child, one unmistakably Angel and the other . . .

'Is that you and Miss Eleanor?'

Angel nodded solemnly. 'She said that I could always find her where things are hidden.'

The room felt like all the air had been sucked out of it. Nia and Morgan exchanged an uneasy look, something unspoken hanging in the air.

'Is this like one of those hidden object games?' Nia asked, holding the sketchbook up to the light and turning her head this way and that, attempting to lighten the mood. Angel did not find it amusing.

'Never mind,' she said, glumly. Hopping off the chair, Angel walked into the living room and turned on the TV. 'Miss Nia, can you find the detective show my grandpa watches?' she asked. 'Andrew Guy, P.I.'

'Sure, honey,' Nia responded.

Morgan snapped a picture of Angel's drawing and closed her sketchbook. She sent the picture to Will in a text: **Angel's latest masterpiece. She mentioned finding Eleanor where things are hidden. You know what to make of it?**

No idea, Will responded. *I'll see if I can get it out of her.*

Let me know what you find out? It sounded kinda cryptic.

Should we come back? Is she okay?

Morgan glanced over at Angel who was demanding that Nia turn up the volume on the TV. On the screen, an older man in a trench coat peeked around a street corner and held a magnifying glass to his eye, then the screen faded to black.

Morgan responded: **She seems okay, Andrew Guy is on now.**

Good. She won't move for the rest of the night. Thanks for watching Peach tonight. We should be back soon.

See you then.

Chapter 13

Will

Will had been to the Red Fern Tavern with Jesse only once before. It wasn't his preferred establishment for eating or drinking because the place was filthy. He could appreciate a cheap happy hour as much as the next man, but drew the line at fruit flies and sticky countertops.

He walked in, preparing to hold his breath for as long as he could stand, but the Red Fern didn't smell like the Red Fern. Will stopped short just inside the doorway, nose wrinkling at the scent of lemon cleaner and something vaguely floral wafting toward him. The old pub usually smelled like cigarette smoke, old grease and watered-down beer. But tonight, it was almost — Will sniffed — fresh.

It didn't even look like the same place. Gone were the sticky floors and dust-cloaked shelves. The battered beer top had been polished within an inch of its life and the booths along the far wall had tea lights flickering in the center of the table. Even the old jukebox in the corner glowed like someone had finally wiped the grimy fingerprints off the glass for the first time in over a decade.

A hand clapped him on the back. Jesse grinned beside him, guiding him to two open seats at the bar.

Will narrowed his eyes. 'It's too clean in here.'

'Seriously,' Jesse agreed, as they swung their legs over the bar stools to sit. The usual cracked leather on the stools had been patched. They even felt sturdier, as though the wobbly wood had been replaced.

'Under new ownership, or something?' Will inquired, taking another long look around.

On the wall, a chalkboard had been erected displaying the weekly specials. Draft beers were half off today, along with a few specialty cocktails. They even had a premium menu featuring top shelf liquor and select appetizers: various flavors of bone-in chicken wings ranging from mild to inferno, pretzel bites, hand-cut parmesan fries, fried pickles, and nachos.

'They sell food in here?' Jesse asked aloud.

'We do now.' Behind the bar, the slim bartender finished fiddling with her phone and brought two menus over to the men. Will tried hard to concentrate on the diamond dimples in her face and not her hot pink push-up bra that sported her name tag, Amber.

'The big boss wants to test out a new menu,' she explained. 'Bring in a different crowd. Interested in anything?' she asked, keeping her eyes on Will a little too long for his liking.

Jesse jumped in, oblivious. 'I am, actually. I don't want you to take this the wrong way but why is it so clean in here?'

'It's cool. You're not the first person who's asked.' She shrugged. 'Like I said, the big boss is in town, a guy named Max Greaves. Apparently, he owns this whole strip mall, and he's cracking down on all the businesses to clean up. My manager, Rick, called and said he'd pay us time and a half to get this place spotless before Max arrived. He's never offered overtime before so there was no way I was passing up that kind of money. We scrubbed that kitchen, he fired Microwave Benny who'd been back there forever and hired a real cook.'

'A real cook, huh? What do you recommend, then?' Jesse asked.

'Nachos are good. Wings are better,' she commented, leaning over the counter, her bra on full display. Will found himself suddenly interested in the color of the walls.

He decided on the fries with a light draft beer and Jesse ordered buffalo wings and a cocktail. He hoped the food was as good as Amber said it was because he was starving and fries were hard to mess up.

Once Amber walked away to get started on their drinks, Will turned to Jesse. 'So, what's up? You said you had news?'

'First, let's talk about your news. I heard you asked Morgan out.' Jesse gave Will a sly smile. 'Only took you two years.'

'How did you . . . ?' Morgan must have told Nia. Did that mean she was excited for the date? Nervous? If he were being honest with himself, he was nervous too. He knew they'd have good conversation and plenty of laughs, that was a given. He reminisced on their slow dance under the stars Saturday night and how soft Morgan's body felt against his. In the moment, he wanted to comfort her, but looking back at it now, could it have been more? Did she really see him as more than just a friend?

'You know Nia told me, man,' Jesse admitted. 'Cost me fifty bucks, too,' he grumbled.

'Serves you right,' Will laughed, shaking his head. 'Back to you, tell me the latest on Eleanor.'

Jesse glanced around surreptitiously, scanning the bar. For the most part, they were alone. A couple sat cozily together in a corner booth in the back of the pub, lost in their own world. Three women sat at the far end of the bar, indulging in their own conversation, laughing over wine. Lastly, a lone man sat at the table near the window, staring blankly at the sidewalk. No one was giving them a second glance.

'I'm assuming that's why you dragged me all the way out to Red Fern?'

Jesse nodded as Amber slid their drinks across the counter and gave them a quick smile before disappearing down the bar. He took a long sip, then leaned in. 'Too many eyes and ears in town. I needed somewhere neutral.'

'So?' Will pressed.

'I had a visitor this morning. Eleanor's nephew, Cameron Shore.'

Will frowned, thinking back to the brief conversations he'd had with her while they stayed at the Inn together. 'Eleanor never mentioned family.' He shrugged. 'She told me she was a widow and Angel kept asking why she wasn't see-through. Matter of fact, Clarissa Hargrove was the one who told me she'd lost a daughter, figured that's why she took to Angel so well.'

Jesse nodded, listening.

'So, what about this nephew?' Will asked.

'Morgan brought him down to the station this morning—'

Will's brain slammed to a halt. 'Wait, Morgan brought who . . . where?'

Jesse smirked mischievously. 'All I have to do is mention her name and you're like a bloodhound.'

Will punched his arm playfully. 'Be serious, man.'

'I am serious!' Jesse chuckled, rubbing his arm. He laughed around a swig of his drink. 'I shouldn't be telling you this anyway, but apparently he dropped by the Daffodil Inn early this morning looking for his aunt. He didn't know she'd been . . .' Jesse trailed off.

Will's jaw clenched as he remembered the look on Morgan's face that morning, like she was chasing ghosts.

'Said he was from Maryland, claimed to be related by marriage, and when he hadn't heard from her, he came down to check on her. But aside from that, nothing useful. No insight into her life other than what we already knew about her from gossip around town and the staff at the Inn.'

'That's it?' Will asked, his voice flat with disbelief.

Jesse nodded. 'We've searched her house. We're digging through her financials, combing through her phone records, but nothing shady has turned up. We've got nothing to go on besides petty neighbor disputes. Nash reported that there were fifteen calls from her just last year about the kids hanging out after hours at Barkwood Bridge, using the guys on patrol duty like her personal police force.'

'Fifteen?' Will repeated, his eyebrows hiking upward.

Jesse nodded. 'Mostly the Brewster kid and his crew in those souped-up low riders. You know how it is around here. All the seniors get their first old school and parade them around all hours of the night. Even I've hit the drag down Main Street once or twice.' Jesse coughed. 'Before the badge, of course.'

Will couldn't imagine straight-laced Jesse Shaw breaking the law in any capacity, but everyone had a past. If racing down Main Street was the height of his criminal activity, he knew Jesse would be horrified at Will's juvenile rap sheet.

Jesse let out a breath, then scrubbed a hand down his face. 'I can't wrap my mind around the fact that someone *stabbed* Eleanor, bro. To get up close to someone like that—' He pushed his fist into his palm. '. . . that's personal. Who could have done that? I'm just . . . starting to feel like the Cinnamon Falls I grew up in, that safe haven, is disappearing.'

Will leaned back, dragging his fingers across the condensation on his glass. 'There's still good people here.'

'Hard to tell who's who anymore,' Jesse said quietly. 'Feels like everyone is a suspect.'

Will sat forward and met his friend's eyes. 'Then we find the truth. We owe her that.'

Jesse nodded, but the crease in his brow didn't fade. Speaking of the truth, Will couldn't hold it in any longer. He had to tell Jesse what he found at the library even if it was just a coincidence, even if it had no connection to Eleanor's death.

'Listen, I went to the library today and—'

Just then, Jesse's phone clattered on the bar top, vibrating with insistence.

Grace Whitfield was calling. Jesse held one finger up, bringing the phone to his ear and answering with a clipped, 'Detective Shaw.'

Will watched his friend closely, noting every shift in his posture. He waited a beat while Jesse talked with Grace, every few seconds grunting with either approval or dissatisfaction, he couldn't tell. His brow creased. He pressed the phone tighter to his ear, closed his eyes briefly and exhaled. That wasn't good.

Will's gut twisted.

Jesse pinched the bridge of his nose and let out a breath heavy with frustration.

'So, what are we looking at?' Jesse asked.

There was a pause when his gaze met Will's and that's when he knew something was deeply wrong.

'Alright,' he replied, his voice lower now. 'I'll call Chambers and have him meet me at the mortuary. I'm about twenty-five minutes out.'

Jesse hung up the phone and stuffed his cell phone back in his jeans. He flagged Amber over and asked for their food to be boxed up.

'What happened?'

Jesse took a moment too long to gather himself, almost like he was bracing himself for something awful. 'That was Grace. She found something.' Will waited, not wanting to push. When Jesse finally spoke, his voice was low.

'She just finished processing the clothing Eleanor was wearing the night she died. There was a cufflink tucked into her undergarments, like it'd fallen off.'

Will's pulse quickened. 'What do you mean, a cufflink? Eleanor was wearing a dress.'

'Exactly,' Jesse replied, not looking over.

'What kind?'

'Gold, heavy, expensive.'

Will exhaled slowly. 'So, whoever did this . . . they were dressed for the festival.'

A cold chill crawled up Will's spine, his brain finally registering as goose pimples rose on his arms, making the hair stand straight up.

'Blended right in,' Jesse grunted through gritted teeth. 'Right under our *fucking* noses. I'm going to head over with Chambers to see what we can make of it.'

Will nodded, his pulse rising with every passing second. Jesse didn't have to say anything, he could read it in his friend's face. He was pissed. The killer wasn't some stranger. They'd already been inside.

Chapter 14

Tuesday

Morgan

The rain had stopped sometime before dawn, but the sky still looked bruised; lavender and gray smudged together like forgotten watercolors. Morgan cracked the window in the Wildflower room, just enough to let some air in, hoping the breeze might sweep away the ache that had settled in her chest.

She hadn't slept well; tossed and turned all night, drifting in and out of a shallow, anxious haze, Angel's voice chasing her with every turn of her pillow: 'I can always find her where things are hidden' echoed like a nursery rhyme.

Was it a warning? A clue? A child's imagination running wild? Or had Eleanor trusted Angel with something more? And what in the world did it mean? Morgan didn't know, and that was the worst part – the not knowing.

She could still see the confusion in Angel's eyes

when she and Nia hadn't understood. The way her small shoulders curled inward like she was embarrassed; like she said too much and immediately regretted it. After that, she'd withdrawn completely; quiet, distant and unreachable; not even an offer of a triple-scoop sundae or a cherry soda could coax a smile from her. She stirred the cream until it became soup, never digging in for a bite.

Will hadn't been exaggerating yesterday when he said that Angel had been quiet since Saturday. Quiet didn't feel like the right word at all. It was like a light had dimmed behind her eyes.

Swinging her legs over the edge of the bed, Morgan braced her hands on her knees. She swallowed the lump rising in her throat.

She couldn't help but feel partially responsible for Angel's suffering. *What if I made it worse? What if she was trying to tell me something important and I brushed it off?*

The thought carved a hollow space in her chest, deeper than she expected. Children carried things in strange, tangled ways. Morgan should have known better, should've done better.

Morgan pressed the heel of her hand against her eyes. Today was not about her feelings. She had to push them aside, at least for now. Nia needed her; their dress appointment started in just a few hours. It'd be a brief escape into something joyful. Morgan owed her that. She had a full day ahead and no time for foggy thinking. Still, the unease lingered like the morning's mist.

By the time she reached her apartment in Juniper Heights, a small community stuck between Cinnamon Falls and Asheville, the sky had brightened just enough to cast soft gold along the rooftops. Juniper Heights wasn't much, a sliver of a neighborhood carved into a wooded ridge with winding streets; the kind of place where the houses leaned close together by necessity.

Morgan's building sat at the end of a cul-de-sac lined with overgrown juniper hedges. It was a quiet place, not like Cinnamon Falls, but still hadn't quite found an identity. Young professionals passed through on their way to Asheville, and students sublet rooms until they figured themselves out. It was where Morgan went once she graduated college, and she'd stayed ever since.

Her sandals slapped against the pavement as she unlocked the door and stepped inside. The air was stale, still clinging to the time of yesteryear before the Daffodil Jubilee.

Her apartment was small but charming, every detail curated in her image, or who she was before Saturday night. Lavender throw pillows were stacked neatly on top of an indigo velvet couch. A gallery wall of framed quotes about wine, books, and one-liners from her favorite TV shows. A desk by the window with a rainbow of pens lined up like soldiers sat beside her laptop and planner. Everything was for her, or at least, the version of herself she believed in before Saturday.

Now, it all looked foreign, like she stepped into a showroom made to mimic Morgan Taylor. She paused in the bedroom doorway. Her bed was still unmade from Friday. Her work blazer hung on the back of her vanity chair, a pair of heels were slung aside where she'd kicked them off without a second thought.

She moved through the room quickly, heading straight for the closet. She tucked a dress into her overnight bag along with a pair of strappy heels, a few more sets of clothes, and some extra toiletries.

She glanced at her reflection in the mirror, and for a moment, she didn't quite recognize the woman staring back; tired eyes and a mouth set tight with worry. The smile she tried on didn't hold.

Zipping her duffel bag shut, she slung it over her shoulder and turned off the light. She left her apartment and didn't look back.

The Velvet Fox sat on the corner of Rosewood and Maple, nestled next to Inkwell & Ivory, Delilah Marks' stationery shop that specialized in handmade journals and pressed flower notecards. On the other side sat an herbal apothecary, Moonlight's Howl, run by Rowan Bell.

The outside of the Velvet Fox was deceptive; charming, whitewashed brick and stained-glass lettering, the logo of a mischievous fox winking at the passing crowd.

The real magic was inside. A silver bell above the door chimed softly, announcing the arrival of Morgan, Nia, and Nia's mother, Marjorie.

The scent of rosewater slapped Morgan first. Velvet armchairs dotted the open floor, flanked by vintage gold mirrors that reflected soft light. Gowns of all kinds floated on racks like clouds, some sleek and modern, others with miles of tulle and sparkle.

In the back corner, a circular dais stood surrounded by three full-length mirrors. Crystal chandeliers hung from exposed beams, and at the center of it all stood Frankie 'Fox' Templeton, a sharp-suited man adjusting a dress on a mannequin with the reverence of a sculptor. He was tall and elegant, with salt-and-pepper hair slicked back and a measuring tape coiled around his wrist like a bracelet. He'd only gotten more handsome as he aged, the silver fox moniker ringing true.

'Well, well,' Frankie purred around a mouth of stick pins, not looking up. 'If it isn't Cinnamon Falls' notorious crime fighting bride.'

Marjorie stepped around Nia proudly, planting her hands on her slim hips. 'And if it hadn't been for my girl, Rosie's murder would still be unsolved.'

Frankie finally turned to face them, smirking. 'Ah, Marjorie Bennett, always a pleasure. Tell me, are you here for opinions, or to remind me how you broke my heart in the nineties?'

Marjorie laughed, unbothered. 'Frankie, I told you then, and I'm telling you now: I am in love with Walter Bennett.'

'The ice cream guy,' Frankie deadpanned.

'I'm sure you've had your fair share of women you've fallen for over the years.'

Frankie reached for Mrs. Bennett's hand and pressed his lips to the back of it. 'None as gorgeous as you.'

Nia cleared her throat with a sarcastic grin. 'I didn't take a day off work for this. We've got an appointment to try on reception dresses, Frankie. Morgan said you'd pull a few for me.'

Frankie looked over, assessing Nia. 'Gorgeous like her mother,' he mumbled, giving her a once-over. 'Feisty, too.'

'The Bennett way.' Nia smirked.

Morgan followed the trio deeper into the boutique and took a seat as Frankie sorted dresses for Nia.

'At Morgan's request, I've selected some options for you.' He pulled out a rack of dresses from behind a curtain. 'A few vintage pieces and more modern hemlines. I know how the Bennett women love tradition.'

Marjorie found a rack of mother-of-the-bride gowns. 'And what about me, Frankie?'

'Only the best for the best,' he answered, his voice a low purr.

As Mrs. Bennett hid her blush behind her hands, Nia gagged. 'This is disgusting.'

'Oh, please. How do you think you got here?' Morgan chuckled. She flipped the tag over on a white pantsuit with mesh cut-outs. Her eyes bulged out of her head. 'Let her keep talking, maybe she can flirt her way into a discount.'

Seven dresses and three pantsuits later, Nia finally agreed on a possible option, and even though it had a sweetheart neckline, it was nothing short of breathtaking. It featured a structured, corset-style bodice with delicate vertical seam work that sculpted her petite frame. The neckline dipped into a subtle plunge, framing her collarbones. The ruched satin drape swept across one hip and gently cascaded to the floor; elegant with an understated drama.

Morgan stared, momentarily speechless, as Frankie spun her around in the mirror. Tears sprang to Marjorie's eyes.

'You look . . . gorgeous,' she eked out.

Frankie placed a veil atop Nia's head that cascaded around her bare shoulders, completing the look.

'You gotta choose this one,' Morgan said breathlessly. 'It was made for you.'

'A few alterations here.' Frankie pinched the fabric and slipped a pin in where the ruching gathered. 'And it'll be perfect. I can start the alterations as early as next week.'

Nia said, 'Thank you so much, Frankie.' She spun around on the platform, the train sweeping the floor. 'It's going to be perfect at the wedding.'

'Anything for Marjorie's girl,' Frankie added, walking over to the checkout counter.

Nia stepped off the platform and disappeared behind the curtain. 'I'll help you take it off,' Marjorie volunteered.

Morgan caught Frankie's eye and headed over. 'Can I ask you something?' She leaned on the glass counter.

'Of course, love. If it's about the alterations, I'm afraid I can't push it up any earlier.' He trailed his finger down his appointment log. 'I've got a few customers ahead of Nia that I still have outstanding—'

Morgan dropped her voice low. 'It's about Eleanor Langford. I know she was a regular customer of yours. She was staying at the Inn when . . .'

Frankie's posture stiffened just slightly, but enough for Morgan to notice. 'Mmm,' he responded with a deep sigh. 'Eleanor bought my very first custom piece. She was one of my best customers; I'll miss her and those gaudy ruffles dearly.' He placed one hand on top of hers. 'I saw all the backlash your family's getting online. People really ought to be ashamed of themselves.'

Morgan silently thanked him for his sympathy. She

couldn't bring herself to log into social media since Saturday night in fear of what she'd find in her direct messages. Her phone was in constant Do Not Disturb mode. Radio silence was a better option than fighting in the comments with people who didn't have all the facts. And the facts were what mattered.

'The last time you saw her, did she seem okay to you? Did she say anything strange?'

Frankie hesitated, pressing his hands to the glass. 'She came in twice last week,' he admitted. 'Once with that darling, Angel.' He clutched his hands to his chest. 'An icon in the making. But the first fitting for her Jubilee dress . . . she seemed rattled, nervous, always checking over her shoulder. I asked if everything was alright.'

'And what'd she say?'

He looked up at her with an uneasy expression.

'You won't get in any trouble,' Morgan assured him. 'I'm just trying to piece together what really happened to her.'

Frankie glanced over her shoulder as Marjorie and Nia's laughter floated from behind the counter. His eyes softened. 'She said she thought she was being followed.'

A chill crept its way up Morgan's spine. 'Did she say by who?'

Frankie shook his head. 'Nope,' he sighed. 'I implored her to go to the police, but she didn't think anyone would believe her, or care.'

Morgan stepped back. 'What would make her think that?'

Frankie pursed his lips. 'You know Eleanor's reputation. They would probably think she deserved it; karma for all her run-ins with people over the years,' Frankie continued, 'but the way she said it . . . she was genuinely scared. Eleanor's a tough bird, but this had her rattled.'

'Thanks, Frankie,' Morgan responded, sadder than she had been before.

Regardless of what people thought about her, Eleanor didn't deserve to be stabbed and left for dead. And from the looks of it, if Morgan wanted to save her parents' business, she had to find out who killed her. And fast.

Morgan pulled into the gravel driveway of the Daffodil Inn, tension riding shotgun. She parked and shut off the engine, resting her head against the steering wheel. She didn't know how many more days she could spend at the Inn, walking on eggshells around her family with guests in earshot.

The press conference yesterday morning hadn't helped their strained dynamic. The Cinnamon Falls Police Department officially ruled Eleanor's death a homicide. Another murder in Cinnamon Falls, and this time it was at their doorstep. Would they survive this? Morgan wasn't sure and it was the uncertainty that fueled the anxious thoughts running laps in her mind.

Her eyes roamed the exterior of the Daffodil Inn – the weathered shingles, wrap-around porch, and the daffodil garden peeking out from the backyard. It looked the same as it always had, a photo locked in time. Her chest tightened when she noticed the sleek luxury car parked next to her father's truck.

Inside, she'd barely made it through the front door before cologne greeted her. It was a unique scent with a burst of persistent citrus and heady, warm spices. It smelled expensive like one of those clothing stores in Asheville mall that had only three racks of jeans and constant *oontz-oontz* music pumping into the hallway.

An unfamiliar man was standing at the kitchen island, his arms stretched across the length of it like he owned the place. His back was turned so she couldn't see his face. Her father's expression read that he was concerned. And her mother looked like she could shoot lasers out of her eyes.

He wore a crisp white dress shirt. A gold Rolex peeked out beneath one cuff. The jacket to his charcoal gray suit was folded neatly over the island bench. His tailored pants stopped just short of his designer loafers. He wore luxury casually.

Wesley looked up at Morgan, his face folding into an uneasy smile. Daphne, stationed between his legs, scurried over to her, vacillating between her curious sniffing and playful licking. Absentmindedly, Morgan petted her as she moved further into the kitchen, her eyes darting between her parents and the stranger.

Morgan stood next to her mother at the sink, who was strangling a dishrag behind her back. All three of the Taylors faced the man now, Morgan finally getting a good look at him head on.

His jet-black hair was combed back with precision, every strand locked into place with just enough sheen to signal wealth, not vanity. His features were angular: razor-sharp cheekbones, a square jawline and eyes the color of wet slate. He was handsome in a way that babies were cute, on principle, like there was never a time in his life where he'd been considered unattractive.

His eyes latched onto hers and he smiled, calm and courteous. 'You must be Morgan,' he said, his voice smooth and mellow, like slipping into a silk robe.

He extended his hand across the island. Morgan took it out of reflex. His grip was firm, but not aggressive. There were no calluses or hangnails in sight. He had the hands of a man who called the shots. He didn't do the shooting.

'Maximillian Greaves,' he introduced himself. Morgan frowned, her memories racing backward. Where had she heard that name before?

'I was just telling your parents how impressed I am with the Daffodil Inn,' he went on. 'The history, this location, is such a rare find. And this view.' He gestured over their shoulders and out of the window where the backyard opened up to a magazine cover-worthy shot of the lazy river and golden garden. 'Incredible.'

Beside her, her mother sighed loudly.

'Your parents and I were just talking about a potential opportunity. Something mutually beneficial.'

Judging from her mother's disposition, it wasn't mutual, and he'd been doing all the talking. The thought dropped into her mind like the season's first rain.

'You're here to buy the Inn?' Morgan asked, tightening her grip on Daphne.

Max smiled again and Morgan had to stop herself from smiling back at him. His good looks were disarming in the worst way.

'I'm here to offer a solution to your . . . situation. With the right investment, the Daffodil Inn could be turned into a tourist paradise.' He patted the seat beside him on the bench and Morgan joined him without resistance.

He raised his arms in the air, forming a box with his thumbs and pointer fingers touching. He brought them to his nose and peered through. 'Picture it: a riverside spa, modern retreat, and curated guest experiences. A rejuvenation of the entire lot of land. I'm thinking of calling it Cinnamon Waters Resort and Spa.'

'The Inn is not for sale,' her mother stated, her voice firm.

'Of course not. Not officially, anyway. But anything can be bought for the right price.'

Wesley piped up, 'My wife is right. Besides, this is historical land, declared so by Mayor Lyons—'

Max chuckled, unaffected. 'You mean the mayor who's fighting a prison sentence for corruption right now? I'd love to see the decree if you have it.'

Her father stumbled over his rebuttal. 'Well, I would assume that the new mayor would uphold Lyons' recommendations—'

Max pulled his lips inward, giving my father a skeptical look. Morgan had never seen her mother madder than this moment, except for when Morgan spilled a can of yellow paint down the freshly polished stairs when she was eleven.

Vanessa's lips were pinched so tightly they nearly vanished. Her father shifted in place, not saying a word. He kept one arm laced around his wife's waist, holding her close. Morgan knew it was so she didn't slap Mr. Greaves in the mouth with the dishrag she'd been twisting.

'I don't mean to overstep,' Max added smoothly. 'But I know an undervalued property when I see one. Whether you agree or not, Cinnamon Waters will happen, Mrs. Taylor. The wheels are already in motion. I'd rather do this the easy way, with the family's blessing, of course. I'd cut a check, save your family the headache of bouncing back after a nightmare of a PR situation, and leave everyone happy.'

He leaned over to scratch behind Daphne's ears. She growled, showing him her sharp teeth.

Max pulled his fingers back just in time.

'Good girl,' Morgan whispered.

Max said, 'I'll need an answer by Friday.'

Morgan swallowed hard. Max glanced at her once more, his gaze lingering a bit too long. He cleared his throat and Morgan realized she'd been sitting on his jacket. She lifted up, handing him the finely tailored specimen like a bomb.

'I'll leave you to discuss,' he said, making a show of swinging it over his shoulder. 'You know where to find me.'

He snapped a crisp white business card out of his pocket. His name was embossed on the front: Maximillian Greaves, in bold black letters. He left it on the table, tapping it twice with his fingers. Without fuss he slipped out of the kitchen, and then finally, out of the front door.

The door clicked shut softly behind Max and a heavily quilted silence settled over the kitchen. The only sound was Daphne's claws across the tile as she paced nervously between them. Morgan folded her arms, still watching the front door long after Max had left.

She spoke first. 'He makes a good point.'

Vanessa's head snapped toward her, eyes wide with disbelief. 'Excuse me?'

'The Daffodil Inn just became the scene of a homicide. Or did you miss the news? This place isn't going to bounce back overnight. All of the guests have cancelled. There's no new bookings—'

On the wall the phone rang. Vanessa lifted the receiver and screamed, 'No comment!' before placing it back on its hook.

Morgan gestured to the phone. 'Reporters won't stop calling.'

Wesley hovered in the corner, his gaze flicking back and forth between his wife and his daughter like a referee waiting for an opportunity to blow his whistle if things got out of hand.

'How much is he offering? At least we can walk away with something rather than struggle through a "PR nightmare",' Morgan offered, using finger quotes to mimic Max's statement.

'I can't believe this,' Vanessa snapped, slamming the dishrag into the sink with the finality of a gavel. 'You want to sell our legacy? Just like that?'

'Our legacy?' Morgan echoed, crossing her arms tighter. 'You mean yours and Dad's legacy. This place has never been mine.'

'You just said "we",' Wesley pointed out.

'Suddenly everyone speaks French,' Morgan mumbled.

'Never been yours?' Vanessa scoffed. 'Why do you think that is?'

Morgan tilted her head, confused. 'What's that supposed to mean?'

'It means we were waiting for the right time,' Wesley

finally cut in, his voice gentle, soft and pleading. 'We wanted to tell you after the Jubilee, but . . . we're planning on retiring, sweetheart. We were going to hand the Inn over to you.'

Time slowed to a grinding halt. Reality collided into her; a runaway train meeting a brick wall.

'You . . . what?' Morgan could barely breathe.

Vanessa stepped forward, bracing herself on the opposite end of the island. 'We thought it was time. We've put in almost thirty years here. We want to enjoy the rest of our lives . . . live off the fruits of our labor, maybe live closer to your Aunt Joyce in Charlotte—'

'And what? You thought I'd just give up my life and run the Inn?' Morgan looked between her parents, incensed.

Wesley tried his hand. 'We thought—'

'You didn't think!' Morgan jumped in, her voice cracking with brimming emotion. 'You assumed! You didn't even talk to *me* about it! I can't just quit! I have a career; students who depend on me.'

'So we've heard,' her mother grumbled.

Morgan growled, 'I didn't get my education degree to become a bed and breakfast host!'

'You teach the alphabet and make paper turkeys on Thanksgiving, it's not exactly—'

'Don't you dare belittle what I do!' Morgan warned, her voice shaking now. White hot rage pulsed out of her ears. She shivered as anger radiated through her body.

'Like you do to us? As if we didn't work day and night to keep these lights on, to keep these people paid, to keep these rooms booked! If it weren't for us, you wouldn't have that fancy degree that you throw in our faces every chance you get! You should be thankful your father had the foresight to build a legacy that could sustain us for all these years!'

Morgan pushed away from the table, the wooden bench striking the wall behind her. She stepped back from them both, her chest rising and falling, while Daphne whimpered at her feet.

'Save the lecture for someone who wants to hear it.'

Without waiting for a response, she crossed the kitchen and stormed out of the back door that led to the gazebo. The door slammed behind her like a punctuation mark on the conversation they wouldn't get to finish.

Chapter 15

Morgan

In a blind rage, Morgan stormed across the inn's backyard toward the rickety gazebo. Daphne loped beside her, tail low and ears alert, sensing the storm brewing inside her. The river's spring breeze did nothing to cool the fire smoldering underneath her skin. She flopped onto the splintered bench, not caring about the rough wood scraping at her thighs beneath her jeans.

Her breath came out in shallow bursts. She gripped the edge of the seat, trying to ground herself, but her thoughts were spinning.

We're planning on retiring, the words echoed on a loop in her head like a cruel joke. They want *me* to take over the Inn? Morgan barked out a sarcastic laugh. What did they think? She'd hug her students goodbye and tuck her dreams into her pockets?

'Is it early onset dementia?' she muttered aloud. 'What would make them think that I'd say yes?'

Her father looked genuinely shocked that she wasn't jumping for joy at their announcement, like it was the opportunity of a lifetime. Her mother had already been planning the handoff, like Morgan had been groomed for this since birth. And maybe she had, right under her own nose.

Unwelcome hot tears pricked the back of her eyes when the realization twisted into her gut. Had it all been leading to this? Every chore, every family holiday skipped because the Inn was 'too busy', every birthday party cut short due to some random emergency . . . was it all training for a life she never wanted?

Could they not see how the Inn they *loved* so much ruined her life?

'They love this place more than they'll ever love me,' Morgan whispered, her voice shredding to slivers. Daphne whimpered, nudging her wet nose on Morgan's leg before resting her head on her knee.

Her throat thickened as she bit down on her lip, hard, willing herself not to cry. The memories came anyway: sitting backstage during her fifth-grade play, scanning the audience for her parents' faces until she finally realized they weren't coming. Every time she convinced herself that *this time* would be different, and it never was. They were always too busy, too tired, too *anything* to show up for her. She hated that still, after all those years of cold hard evidence, she continued to look for them in the crowd, knowing they wouldn't be there.

And now they wanted her to take the Inn on with pride as if it was her dream, and not theirs.

The sound of raised voices snapped her out of her mental spiral. Across the yard, Morgan spotted Max Greaves spin on his heel and fold himself into the driver's seat of his luxury car. The engine purred to life and the tires screeched as he sped out of the driveway, showering Cameron with a spray of gravel dust as he sped off.

Cameron covered his face, brushing the dust off his clothing. He looked up and caught sight of her, watching.

Morgan stiffened and turned her head away, suddenly interested in the wood grain of the bench, but it was too late. Seconds later, she heard Daphne's wagging tail *thumpthumpthump* against the wood as Cameron approached.

'Didn't mean to intrude,' Cameron said as he stepped into the gazebo. He was wearing a navy henley that clung to his body just enough to suggest that he worked out, paired with medium wash denim, worn at the knees like he'd had them forever. His hair was a mess of dark waves, still damp from a recent shower. A hint of aftershave floated on the breeze toward her, clean and woodsy. He leaned casually against one pillar, crossing one foot over the other. His ocean eyes watched her with a careful curiosity. 'I wasn't trying to eavesdrop, but it was kinda hard not to hear.'

Morgan wiped at her eyes quickly. 'Thin walls,' she muttered, fidgeting with her fingers. 'Didn't mean to make a scene. Just stupid family drama, sorry you had to hear that.'

'You don't have to apologize.' He slid onto the bench opposite her. 'It sounded like a lot happened. Are you okay?'

Morgan scoffed softly. 'Define "okay". My parents just dropped a bomb on me and told me they're retiring. They assumed I'd take on the Inn, like that was always the plan. Apparently, a plan I didn't know about.'

Cameron nodded, folding his arms and leaning backward. 'That's a huge ask.'

'And then this guy shows up offering to buy the place like it's a pair of shoes. I don't know, everything just happened so fast.' Morgan shook her head, feeling more embarrassed than before. She'd known Cameron for one day and here she was telling him all about her family's personal problems.

'I, uh, went to talk to that guy, Max.' He scrubbed the back of his neck with one hand. 'Figured I might be able to get more details on this offer.'

Morgan sat up straight. 'You *what*?'

He held his hands out in surrender. 'I work in real estate,' he explained. 'Nothing like that guy obviously but I've had enough run-ins with big developers like him to know a thing or two.'

'What did he tell you?'

He hesitated for a bit before saying, 'Let's just say he wasn't too thrilled about me asking questions. But his offer is pretty generous, considering.'

Morgan frowned. 'You're *siding* with him?'

'Never,' Cameron said, his voice gentle but steady. 'I'm saying if your parents are seriously thinking about selling and need help navigating the deal, I could look it over for you. I've seen these kinds of offers go sideways and I know what this place means to them . . . what it meant to my aunt. I'd hate for it to fall into the wrong hands.'

'You'd really help us out?'

'It's the least I could do. You guys took care of my Aunt Eleanor in her last days.' He placed one hand over his heart, his eyes downcast. 'And I can't thank you all enough for your hospitality. Plus, you've got enough on your plate. If your parents sell or not, it should be on their terms. And yours too.'

She held his gaze longer than necessary. Cameron never broke eye contact. 'Thank you . . . that actually means a lot.'

He smiled, the edges of his lips curling just enough to make her heart flutter. 'Anytime,' he responded.

A breeze kicked up, washing over both of them, warming Morgan all over.

'I'm exhausted. Today has been all over the place,' she said with a sigh. 'Sorry, I'm being a disaster of a host.'

'You don't have to be anything right now,' Cameron

replied, lacing his hands behind his head. A far-off expression settled over his face. His voice softened. 'You get to just be.'

The simplicity of the words wrapped around her. No one had said that to her in years, maybe ever. Not to be strong, or responsible, but just to be.

Surprised by his kindness, Morgan relaxed into their comfortable silence. The tightness in her chest and the spiraling thoughts slowly unraveled. And for the first time that day, she felt like she could breathe. Cameron's face was unreadable, his face angled toward the sky. He didn't look like he was reeling from a loss. She couldn't believe how composed he was. If her aunt had just been declared the victim of a homicide Morgan would be an emotional landmine. How was he so calm, so grounded?

'They told me she'd been stabbed,' Cameron murmured, his voice so low she almost missed it. He studied his palms like they held answers he hadn't discovered yet. 'Bled out on the ground like cattle after someone tried to kill her with . . . poison. Who would do that to m-my aunt?'

'I am so sorry, Cameron.' It was all Morgan could think to say.

He nodded in acceptance, but didn't meet her eyes. 'I'm so angry.' His fists clenched at his sides. 'It feels like I'm separated from myself, floating above it all.' His gaze flicked toward her, searching. 'Does that make sense?'

'It does,' Morgan replied. 'Shock can give you an outer body experience, like it's happening to someone else.'

It was how she'd been feeling for days. But this moment, right now, she'd never felt so clear-minded.

She wasn't going to let the life she'd worked so hard for slip away from her that easily. She was going to fight, just like Nia had. Nothing, not even a man in a slick suit with deep pockets was going to stop her, especially with Cameron by her side. If Max Greaves thought the Taylors were going to roll over and go quietly, he had another thing coming.

Morgan hesitated for a brief moment and then turned to face him. 'Listen, I'm going to fix this.'

His brow creased. 'How?'

'My family isn't going anywhere. I've been asking around and I'm going to find out what happened to your aunt.'

Cameron raised one eyebrow, skeptical. 'You're serious?'

'Almost two years ago, my best friend Nia and I figured out what happened to our best friend, Sienna, and her mom, Rosie. She owned the diner in town and was like our second mom growing up. Everyone thought Sienna's death was an accident, it wasn't. We proved it. I know we can do it again.'

Cameron's expression was unreadable. 'I . . . don't know what to say.'

Morgan continued, 'I don't know who would have

wanted to hurt your aunt, but I promise you, I'm going to find out and when I do, I'm going to save my parents' business.'

For an unbearable moment in time, Cameron said nothing. Then a smile tugged at his lips, nothing flirtatious, but something gentler laced with understanding and a soft acceptance.

'You're kind of amazing,' he said matter-of-factly.

Their eyes connected in a way that made her stomach flutter. Heat flushed her cheeks.

'You've got murder board energy.'

Morgan guffawed despite herself. 'Murder board energy?'

'You mean to tell me you don't have colored string and a corkboard around here, detective?' Cameron teased.

'I prefer the term amateur sleuth,' Morgan replied, a smile lingering on her lips.

The sun was higher in the sky now, breaking through the trees. At her feet, Daphne panted.

Morgan inhaled deeply and broke their silence. 'Thank you,' she said.

'For what?'

'For just letting me be,' she responded.

Cameron's smooth hand landed on top of hers, sending a jolt of electricity through her body. 'You don't have to pretend with me, Morgan.'

Chapter 16

Will

The Pit pulsed with strobe lights and the heavy bass beat of a rap song that sounded like a foreign language to Will. The arcade in the basement buzzed with noise: Skee-Ball machines clattering, bowling pins falling and being cleared, kids chasing each other, their voices competing with the music that vibrated in his chest. Sweat, fryer grease and teenage bravado clung to the walls like wallpaper. Will swaggered through the teen hangout, which was next to the Red Fern Tavern, on the hunt for one person.

He thundered down the steps and passed under a glowing red EXIT sign that cast neon shadows over kids crowding around a series of old-school pinball machines, claw games, and low-lit booths. He pushed through a crowd of boys doused in too much body spray and defiant attitude. They sported designer sneakers, jeans two sizes too small, and fake chains as thick as dog collars.

He spotted Caleb almost immediately, slouched in the back corner, half-hidden, with a girl Will didn't recognize perched on his lap in a shirt that exposed too much of her midsection for his liking.

Will had texted Caleb twice since the Petals N' Promises Dance. No response. Now here Caleb was, in the middle of a school day, hunched in a cracked leather booth eating flimsy fries like he didn't have a care in the world.

'You ignoring me on purpose, or are you too preoccupied to text me back?' Will asked.

Caleb glanced up, the faintest flicker of guilt flashing in his eyes before it morphed into defiance.

'Didn't know I was on a leash.'

Teenagers were exhausting; on one hand they didn't want to be treated as children, but were literally cosplaying as adults. Caleb had no idea how real life could get and Will was more than ready to deliver a reality check.

The girl on Caleb's lap looked up at Will, attitude in full force. She pushed long blond braids out of her face. He'd seen her before, he was sure of it. 'You his parole officer or something?'

Will's gaze turned to steel when he recognized Amanda Jenkins' daughter. Caleb leaned up and whispered in the girl's ear. He patted her on the thigh and she took that as her cue to leave. Will stepped back as she passed, her eyes relaying the message that she was not happy he'd interrupted their alone time.

Exhaling through his nose, Will tried to keep his voice even. 'I need to talk to you.'

Caleb leaned back in the booth and crossed his arms over his chest. 'I didn't see anything.'

'I haven't even asked you a question yet.' Will took the seat across from him. 'Besides, that's not what I heard.'

In truth, Will hadn't heard anything. All he knew was that Morgan had told the police that Caleb was the person who pointed her to the maze before she discovered Eleanor. Caleb had to have seen something, and judging from his response, he had something to hide.

The teen's jaw flexed.

'You're lucky I found you before Jesse did,' Will started, 'because if you're mixed up in this somehow—'

'The cops already talked to me that night. I'm telling you like I told them, I didn't see anything. Why are you popping up here acting like my dad?'

'I'm not trying to be your dad.' Will made a point to soften his tone, but he didn't back down. 'Listen, I promised your mom that I'd look out for you. If you saw something that night, I need to know.'

Caleb scrubbed his hands over his face, looking over at the girl who'd been sitting in his lap. She was engaged in a conversation with one of the guys Will pushed through earlier. She was being handsy, with a toothy grin. Caleb had fire in his eyes. He shifted in his seat, turning his shoulder toward Will.

'I didn't ask you to do that,' he grumbled, 'she did.' He took a long sip of the cola in front of him, before sitting it back down so hard that the dark soda spilled over the side.

'I didn't have to be asked. I'm genuinely concerned about you. Look, you're not the only one who lost something when your uncle went down. But you don't have to throw away the rest of your life.'

Caleb rolled his eyes. 'You sound like my mom, always on this sentimental bullshit! This isn't about my uncle. I wish everyone would stop saying that.'

Will snapped his mouth shut. The tension between them settled for a moment, stretched thin and taut. Will had to see the situation from Caleb's point of view. He was once this kid, too; angry and misunderstood. A tough persona on the outside, but crying himself to sleep when he was alone, night after night, wishing he had someone he could talk to; someone who would actually listen and not judge.

'Listen, Caleb. My child won't say more than three words to me because of that night. The grief she is carrying around is eating me from the inside out. I'm here to get answers for her, not to coddle you, or whatever you've got going on. You want to run around with them? Cool. I won't stop you.' Will gestured toward Caleb's friends. 'But a woman was killed Saturday night, you get me? And you might have been the last person to see her alive. Tell me what you saw and you can get back to . . .'

'Her name's Kelsey,' he supplied.

'Kelsey,' Will repeated, fighting for eye contact with the teenager who had begun to study the table in front of him.

Caleb sighed, pulling his hood tight around his head. 'I saw that lady, okay? In the maze.'

Will's heartbeat quickened. 'What time?'

Caleb shrugged. 'I wasn't looking at my phone, man. I was . . . busy.'

'Busy?' Will repeated, raising one curious eyebrow.

'Preoccupied,' Caleb corrected, leveling him with a knowing look.

'With Kelsey?' Will asked.

'I didn't want to get caught making out with my girl, okay? She was on the clock. My folks were there and my mom doesn't like her coming around like that so it was our only time to, y'know . . . That's why I didn't say anything to the cops. I didn't think it was a big deal.'

'You didn't think a dead woman was a big deal?' Will asked, incredulous.

'She wasn't dead when I saw her! She just looked lost, like dazed, you know? She was stumbling around like she was confused. I mean, it *is* a maze so I didn't think anything of it. We just waited for her to pass like everyone else.'

'Was anyone with her? Did you hear anything?'

'Just some shadows, people trying to find the center

and then giving up halfway through. It wasn't like y'all made it easy. Me and Kels got lost plenty of times before we found it and when we did she was just . . . laying there. Kelsey screamed and that's when Miss Morgan showed up.'

Will exhaled slowly, pushing his breath through his teeth.

'Look,' Caleb said, panic in his eyes. 'I didn't kill her, I swear.'

Will responded, palms out. 'I believe you, Caleb. But you can't hide when things get hard. That's how you end up down the same road as—'

As me, Will thought.

A cloud thundered over Caleb's face. His lips pulled into a tight knot. 'As my uncle. You can go ahead and say it.'

'That wasn't what I was going to say, and you are not your uncle.' Caleb's eyes flicked up to Will, then over at his friends. 'You get to choose what kind of man you want to be. Make the right choice for you, for your future,' Will advised. 'Last thing, foxglove is missing from my father's garden. You know anything about that?'

'Nah,' Caleb answered quickly, shaking his head.

'Aight,' Will responded, deciding not to push him any further. He paused for a moment, looking around the busy room. He'd taken up enough of Caleb's time now. He reached over for a dap, a sign of solidarity, of peace, and slid out of the booth. Before he got too far away from Caleb he said, 'And next time I text you, answer.'

Kelsey eyed him as he passed through the group of guys.

Caleb called, 'Are we still on for next Saturday at the greenhouse?'

Will nodded, his heart lighter. 'Same time, same place.'

As he stepped out of the cool arcade and into the sticky spring heat, a sick feeling twisted in his gut. It was getting clearer by the minute that someone had it out for Eleanor Langford, and that someone was still out there.

That evening, Will found himself so distracted replaying his interaction with Caleb that he burned the garlic bread. When he pulled the scorched hockey pucks out of the oven, a plume of black smoke rolled out after them. The smoke detector hanging on the opposite wall roared with a deafening alarm while Angel, waiting patiently at the wooden kitchen table, clapped her hands over her ears.

The sound echoed in all corners of Will's cozy, two-bedroom bungalow. The kitchen was the heart of the place, with walnut-stained cabinets and brass accents. The marble patterned countertops made the icy blue backsplash pop, giving the kitchen a larger feel than its specs allowed.

The living room was decorated with a well-worn couch that had caught all of Angel's messes since birth. It was the only thing he'd brought with him from Macon. A couple of framed photos graced the walls: Angel's artwork and pictures of her at all stages of her life. Their rooms were small, but warm, just the way Will liked it.

He rushed to grab a dish towel to fan the smoke out of the kitchen, coughing out the acrid taste of burned bread.

'Dinner's ready,' he announced to Angel with a wide smile.

She rolled her eyes and helped herself to a plate of spaghetti and meatballs while Will stood under the smoke detector, fanning the stubborn smoke.

He watched as she carefully positioned the step stool next to the stove, climbed up, and doled out a spoonful of noodles and sauce on her waiting plate. Without words, she returned to the table and propped her tablet up on its kickstand. Will immediately recognized the theme music of *Andrew Guy, P.I.*

'No tablet at the table,' Will reminded her, still fanning.

Angel sighed so deep that Will almost let her keep it. She paused the show and tossed it on top of her sketchbook in the seat next to her.

Will shook his head, warring with himself inside. It was another day of silent treatment from Angel, and he was starting to lose his resolve. As much as he wanted to keep her on schedule, he also needed to make space for her feelings.

Maybe I should back off a bit, he wondered. Her friend just died, and she is still a little girl. Angel has big emotions and nowhere to put them.

He wanted to kick himself. He should have listened to his father and enrolled her in camp during spring break, some place where she could run wild and be around her peers. But Will had needed the money from the job at the Daffodil Inn. Cutting hair was getting him by – he'd built up a solid clientele of men, and a few women – but Angel was getting older and more expensive. He had to make smart money decisions, especially since he was practically doing it all on his own.

The detector finally shut off and Will started a fresh batch of bread, setting a timer this time. He scooped out some spaghetti into a bowl and joined his daughter at the dinner table. She was picking at her spaghetti, twirling the noodles around her fork, but never bringing it to her mouth.

'Eat a little, Peach,' Will implored. 'You barely touched your breakfast,' he recalled, remembering how she nibbled on the corner of a piece of toast. Had she gone on a food strike too? 'You've got to be hungry.'

'I'm not,' Angel lied. Will could've heard her growling stomach from outside.

'I stopped past the library yesterday.' He decided to lighten the mood. He flipped out his phone and showed Angel the picture he took of the Drawing Club flyer. 'Signed you up for this art club that meets on Saturdays. The librarian said the winner's portrait gets hung up in the new mayor's office.'

Angel's eyes brightened just a little. She pulled the phone closer to her, reading it slowly, one finger trailing the words as she sounded them out.

'Will they have markers, too?' she whispered after a minute.

Will grinned harder than he ever had in the last few days. 'Every color under the sun.'

Angel brought her fork to her mouth, and took a bite out of the sauce-covered meatball. It smeared on her nose and she wiped the marinara sauce with the back of her hand. Will stopped himself from fussing about using a napkin. Eating was the victory, he wasn't about to lose it over the little battles in between.

They ate in silence and that was enough for Will. Once she was satisfied, he cleared their plates, and Angel disappeared into the living room with her sketchbook. She curled up into the arm of the couch, her favorite spot.

Will put away the leftovers and rinsed the dishes and pots enough to stick them in the dishwasher. He cleaned the stove and swept the kitchen, returning it to its default state. He joined his daughter on the couch, a cherry popsicle in hand.

She ripped into the wrapper hungrily and Will leaned over to look at her latest creation. Will froze when he realized it was a bird's eye view of the Daffodil Inn, the same image Morgan had sent him yesterday. The hedge maze, the river, even the gazebo, which still made him shudder with embarrassment, was there. He squinted, honing in on a small detail in the maze.

Gently, he asked, 'Is that you and Miss Eleanor?'

Angel nodded, her mouth turning redder by the second as she enjoyed her ice cream.

'Did you draw this from memory?'

She nodded again. 'Miss Eleanor liked the maze a lot. She said I could always find her where things are hidden.' She paused, thinking. 'Can we go back to the Inn, Dad?'

The words hit Will like a punch to the gut.

That must have been what Morgan was talking about. 'Where things are hidden?' Will shook his head, confused.

'Mmhmm,' Angel said, finishing her popsicle in record time. She picked up a coloring pencil and began shading in the sky. 'That's what she told me.'

An icy chill crept down Will's spine. 'Why do you want to go back to the Inn?'

'To see if I can find her,' Angel answered without looking up. 'She said she'd always be there. She's got to be there.'

And there it was, the thing that broke the dam inside of him again. Angel still couldn't wrap her mind around the fact that Eleanor had passed away. Will steeled himself and pulled his daughter and her sketchbook in his lap, enveloping her in his embrace.

Will coughed out the emotion in his voice and said, 'Peach, Miss Eleanor is gone, okay? But I promise, Daddy will find out what happened to her. You've got my word.'

Angel looked up at him, her eyes shining with tears.

'Okay,' was all she could muster. Will fought with all his might not to crumble in front of her. He had to figure out who did this to Eleanor, for both their sakes.

Hours later, after Tanya called to say goodnight, Will was lying down in bed, listening to Angel's faint, rhythmic snores coming through their shared bedroom wall. The house had settled into silence for the night, but his mind was still spinning in circles, refusing to succumb to his body's tired demands. The low hum of the humidifier did little to quiet the questions looping through his brain.

She said I could always find her where things are hidden, he remembered Angel saying, her voice quiet but certain. What did she mean by that? Where were things hidden? And what *things* was Eleanor referencing? And why was she looking into Mayor Lyons?

Will shifted against the cool cotton sheets, staring at the ceiling. His bedroom was the most modern room in the house, his only indulgence besides Angel's pink princess room, in an otherwise simple home.

The king-sized bed was pressed neatly against the back wall, sheets tucked with military precision, but getting tangled from his tossing and turning.

Tall bookshelves flanked the walls filled with a thoughtful mix of worn paperbacks, miniature model cars, and potted plants that gave the room a little more life. A framed photo of he and Angel at last year's Fall Festival sat on his dresser, the both of them smiling through the blur of powdered sugar across their mouths.

Will reached for his phone on the nightstand and checked the time. It was just past 11 p.m. and he wondered if Morgan would be asleep at this time of the night. It was only a few hours until tomorrow, his date with Morgan.

The thought sent a wave of nerves through his belly. He opened a new message and stared at the blinking cursor until he finally built up enough courage to type: **Hey, just checking in. You still up?**

The reply from Morgan came almost instantly: *Doom scrolling before bed as usual. Wyd still awake?*

Will smiled and typed what he'd been really thinking: **Thinking about you.**

He'd grown used to seeing her every day during spring break, sitting cross-legged on the porch steps with Daphne at her feet, chatting with guests about Jubilee plans while he trimmed the hedges within earshot. Those small, ordinary moments had stitched themselves into his days so quietly he hadn't noticed the comfort they brought him, until now. He was painfully aware that they hadn't crossed paths today. She'd been drifting in and out of his mind all day. Not just because of Angel or the Inn, but her. Her laugh, the way her eyes crinkled when she was trying to hide a smile, or the way she said his name, with such finality like she savored it. His finger hovered over the arrow to send the message.

'Too much?' he asked aloud. He hit backspace until the message cleared.

Same, lol, he sent instead. It was safer. **We still on for tomorrow?**

8:30, right? she responded. *You mind picking me up from the Inn? I'm staying here for the rest of the week until we get everything sorted out.*

Not a problem, I'll be there.

There was a pause before her next text.

I can't wait :)

Will's heart skipped at the smiley face. He stared at the message for a beat too long, then typed: **Me too. Goodnight, Miss Morgan.**

Sweet dreams, Mr. Reed.

Will placed the phone face down on the nightstand but his smile remained. Sleep came slowly, but sealed with a guarantee that Morgan would be first on his mind in the morning.

Chapter 17

Wednesday

Morgan

Wednesday morning arrived with a sweet song from a morning dove that floated through the cracked bay window of the Wildflower Room. In bed, Morgan stirred, but just barely, not ready to face the day yet. She couldn't remember the last time she'd had a chance to sleep in during the week, and now her body craved the extra precious minutes of rest.

She wanted to bask in that subconscious dream land where all was right in her world. Where the Daffodil Jubilee went off without a hitch and Eleanor was still alive. Where her parents hadn't lied to her and there was no threat to their livelihood. All she wanted, more than anything, was a few stolen moments of peace.

On the bedside table, her phone vibrated, her weekly alarm shattering the glittery realm between possibilities and choke slamming her back into reality.

Morgan flung one arm out from under the sheets and blindly fumbled for her phone. It clattered to the hardwood. It sounded like a gunshot in the quiet morning hours.

She prayed she didn't wake Zara one floor below, or Cameron at the other end of the hall. Morgan steeled herself listening for any indication that she'd disturbed their sleep. The only sound she could make out was Daphne's faint snores at the foot of her bed, after returning to her own canine dreamland.

It was a little after six, and even though she didn't have school today, Morgan was too awake to go back to sleep now. Throwing off her covers, her feet met the cool hardwood. Her neck and shoulders felt like they were being held together by a rubber band pulled taut. No matter which way she stretched, the tension stayed.

She slipped her feet into a pair of mauve slippers that matched her bonnet and satin night dress and crossed the room to the ensuite bathroom. Daphne watched her move through cracked, sleepy eyes.

'I know,' Morgan mumbled. 'Mornin' to you too.'

Daphne sighed in response, her tongue lolling out of her mouth as she released a belly-deep yawn. She stretched backward and shook her coat out from her ears to her tail; the daffodil charms on her collar jingled together. Daphne paced in a circle once then twice, her expectant eyes landing on Morgan with a quiet insistence.

'We might as well,' Morgan sighed, grabbing her robe on the way out of the bedroom.

Downstairs at the door she pushed her feet into a pair of sneakers and grabbed Daphne's leash off the waiting hook. The collie sat dutifully, her bushy tail swaying, while Morgan clipped it to her collar.

They stepped out onto the porch, greeted by the morning sun peeking over the tops of the trees. Even Daphne stopped to admire the sunrise before she began her daily sniffing tour of the yard. The sky was awash with a breathtaking kaleidoscope of colors; a rainbow with an orange center, its promising pinks giving chase to the indigo remnants of the leftover night.

Morgan stood, taking it all in. She wished every moment felt like a sunrise over Cinnamon Falls. Just then, Daphne lowered herself to the porch, her ears flattening to her head. A growl, low and threatening, rumbled in her throat as she geared up for a series of barks that could wake Old Man Milton miles away. Morgan squinted and focused her attention on the figure running up the driveway. With the sun at their back, their face was covered in shadows.

Morgan stilled, her heart in her throat, Daphne rising to her haunches as they got closer, baring her teeth. If Morgan knew nothing else, whoever it was wouldn't make it past her dog.

'Daffy girl, don't act all brand new with me,' Zara Wells warned as she jogged up the driveway, dressed in an olive-green two-piece jogging set. Double white trim ran around her unfairly tiny waist, accentuating her hourglass frame. Morgan felt increasingly aware of her own slobber-stained robe as Zara got closer.

Daphne transformed back into her normal attention hog self and wiggled her way over to Zara, turning over on her belly for scratches. Her legs kicked in satisfaction as Zara's coffin-shaped nails hit the spot.

'You run every morning?' Morgan's question was more out of judgment than curiosity.

'Run?' Zara scoffed. 'As much as my hair costs? I wish I would work up that kind of sweat. Ten thousand steps, that's all it takes.' Her smart watch made an appearance, the pedometer glowing, when she raised her wrist in the air.

'Oh,' was all Morgan could manage to say. She couldn't tell if Zara was sharing her routine or giving out unsolicited advice. Either way, she took it as disrespect. Next time, Morgan would let Daphne bite her.

'Besides, I'll be traveling all day so I need as much outside time as possible,' Zara continued, propping one leg on the steps. Morgan tried her hardest not to ogle her muscular calf and thigh as she lunged backward, stretching.

'You're checking out?'

'Headed out west,' she replied after a nod. She pulled one arm over her head, then the other. 'Got a friend out in LA with an insane view of downtown. Look at this.'

Zara slid her phone from her pocket and held it out to Morgan, swiping quickly past a few recent selfies she'd taken on the property in full glam with different angles, the sun hitting just right.

'Wait, go back,' Morgan said, pointing at the screen. 'That one.'

Zara paused on the photo. 'Oh, that's from Saturday night. I had to catch golden hour. There was some good lighting in there—'

Morgan leaned in, her eyes widening; not from Zara's stunning face but from who was in the background of the photo. 'That's the hedge maze.'

Zara blinked, looking between Morgan and the phone. 'Is it bad? I already posted it, but it's not too late to delete—'

'No,' Morgan said slowly, her mind zooming in different directions. 'It's just that the photographer is scheduled to drop off the pictures today, so I haven't seen any clear photos of that night yet. This would look amazing on the website. Do you mind sending me this?'

Zara shrugged and hit the share button. Morgan typed in her phone number.

'Done.' Zara smiled, tucking her phone back in her pocket. She tilted her head and asked, 'So what's the deal with the tall drink of water that checked in a couple days ago?'

Morgan knew immediately who she was referencing, but tried to play it cool. 'Oh, Cameron?'

'That's his name?' Zara fanned herself dramatically. 'Girl, if I had one more night here I'd be doing anything to get his attention. But he's definitely into you. I saw you guys out here in the gazebo yesterday. Looked pretty co-zy,' Zara singsonged, playfully eyeing Morgan.

Morgan flushed. 'You think so?'

Zara stepped closer. 'I know so. I'm around men for a living, and men like that? They don't linger around unless they're hoping you do too.'

Morgan's stomach flipped at the idea of a man as handsome as Cameron finding her attractive, but then she remembered Cameron's reason for his visit. He wasn't sticking around because he was into Morgan. He was sticking around because his aunt died at her Inn.

Morgan decided to change the subject. 'I couldn't. Cameron's a guest here. Besides, I have a date tonight.'

'Oooh.' Zara grinned like a proud older sister. 'With who?'

'Will,' Morgan admitted bashfully.

Zara snapped her fingers. 'The landscaping guy? I knew it! The way he looked when he saw you in that dress at Petals N' Promises. I thought his eyes were going to pop out of his head!'

'Not you keeping tabs on my love life.' Morgan couldn't help but laugh as Zara shrugged innocently. 'I don't know if it's *that* serious—'

'Oh please!' Zara threw her hand up, stopping

Morgan mid-sentence. She spun her fanny pack around to the front and unzipped the top compartment, pulling out a small rollerball perfume.

'This is my signature scent; it drives 'em wild!' She pushed the perfume into Morgan's hand. 'Consider it a thank you for not letting your dog maul me for the millionth time.'

Morgan accepted the bottle and gave it a cautious sniff; sweet jasmine with a vanilla base. At the end, a floral note lingered. It was unexpected yet captivating.

'Thanks,' Morgan replied genuinely, clutching the perfume to her chest.

Zara nodded then looked down at Daphne, holding out her hand for a shake. 'No hard feelings?'

Daphne huffed reluctantly, giving Zara her paw.

'You might've won her over,' Morgan laughed.

Zara looked up at her and grinned. 'All in a day's work.'

When Zara passed Morgan on the way into the house, she gave her shoulder a squeeze. Morgan waited until she was out of sight before she checked her phone.

She opened the new text message containing Zara's picture. Morgan gasped, clutching her phone tighter, zooming in on the background.

The gorgeous almond-eyed influencer had her arm outstretched, blowing the camera a kiss, the sun highlighting her unblemished skin.

Just behind her head, partially secluded by fingers of tangled branches and leaves, was Caleb Brewster with a sinister look in his eyes.

Chapter 18

Will

Angel was not being very angelic Wednesday morning. She sat slumped in the backseat, facing the window, doing everything she could to avoid making eye contact with her father.

It had started with her hair. Will had failed miserably in replicating the braided zigzag pattern she saw on the front of one of her kiddie magazines. In his defense, he was under way too much pressure for 7 a.m. and neither his brain nor his fingers had fully warmed up yet. He also couldn't understand why pigtails, which she wore every other day to school, weren't good enough for this random Wednesday. But Will digressed.

After the hair debacle had reached a low simmer, the shoes had been next. Will had refused to let her wear snow boots from two winters ago on a mild day in April just because Angel said they went better with her dress. After she got home from running around in school, the smell of the shoes would probably knock the both of them unconscious.

Will glanced at his daughter in the rear-view mirror. Angel averted her eyes quickly, crossing her arms over herself even tighter. Thank goodness her school was only a short distance away. By the time he picked her up that afternoon she would have forgotten all about their fight from this morning.

He hoped that today was the day she'd go back to being his normal talkative child. The way she was before Eleanor was killed and their world was flipped upside down. As much as it nagged him before, he would give anything to hear about the random world facts she'd learned that day, or her roundabout stories detailing the drama of a second-grade classroom.

Things hadn't been normal in quite some time. Hell, he had Tanya to thank for that. He shook the memory out of his head and found her name in the recent callers displayed on his digital dashboard.

It only rang once before she answered, 'Peachy-Pooh!', Tanya's familiar velvet voice booming through the speakers in Will's car. The sound of her mother's voice made Angel perk up in the seat.

'Mommy!' she exclaimed, a mega-watt smile taking over her face.

'How's my sweet peach?'

'Not good,' Angel reported, listing on her fingers. 'Daddy messed up my hair this morning—'

'Excuse me!' Will cut in.

Angel barreled over him. 'And then he wouldn't let me wear those boots Auntie Renee got me—'

'They've got to be way too small by now, Peach,' Tanya responded. 'It's been almost two years since we went to Stone Mountain.'

Will threw his hands up. 'That's what I said!'

'Although I'm not sure why you would even still have those boots. Your father should have donated them a while ago. I bet there's a penguin somewhere right now who's dying for some pink fur-lined boots just like those.'

Angel giggled. It'd been days since Will had heard that sound. His heart felt like it was melting.

'Penguins don't wear boots, Mommy,' Angel responded between laughs.

'Well, why?' Tanya feigned ignorance. 'Isn't it cold in the North Pole? They must wear something on their little toes.'

Will laughed to himself while he maneuvered his car through the drop-off line at school. Thankfully, Amanda Jenkins' Pinto was nowhere in sight.

Angel replied matter-of-factly, 'All penguins don't live in the North Pole.'

Dramatically, Tanya questioned, 'Ohhhhhhhh, they don't?'

Angel smacked her palm to her forehead. 'Shouldn't grown-ups, like, know this stuff by now?'

'You're just so smart, Peach! What would I do without you?'

'I dunno, Mom. This is pretty basic stuff. I mean, even kindergartners know that.'

'Well, when you get out of school today, make sure you tell me about what you learned so I can be smart like you.'

Will brought his car to a stop in front of Ms. Shanice. He searched the crowd of teachers for Morgan, but didn't spot her. He settled back in his seat, deflated. Angel's voice brought him to the present moment.

'I gotta go now. We're first in line. Bye, Mom!'

Angel leaned forward and pecked her father on the cheek absentmindedly before pushing out of the door.

'Have a good day, Peach,' Will called behind her. He watched her bookbag until it disappeared within the building.

'You still there?' Will asked.

'I'm here,' Tanya replied. 'What was up with the hair thing?' A patronizing laugh held itself together between her words. 'She sounded pissed.'

'Man, she wanted these criss-cross braids and I didn't have the mental bandwidth for all that this morning.'

'Last time she tried that you called me in tears almost,' she joked.

'That girl has me stressing first thing in the

morning!' Will pulled away from the curb of Morningstar Elementary, making his way toward Main Street to open the barbershop.

'You gotta learn how to do her hair, it's only going to get harder the longer you take. If I were there everyday, you wouldn't have to worry about it but, well . . .' Tanya's voice frayed at the edges. He didn't need her to finish her sentence. He'd already thought about it a million times over.

If Tanya hadn't this, if Tanya hadn't that. Those were just excuses. But she had a point. He did need to make more of an effort to do her hair in different styles. She was blossoming into a young lady and pigtails, let Angel tell it, were for babies. If it were up to Will, she'd stay a baby forever.

'How's everything going otherwise?' Tanya asked, her voice laced with concern. 'I haven't seen an update since Monday. How's Angel taking it?'

Will ran his hands over his face. 'She's not speaking, T. Won't hardly eat. She's obsessed with this detective show she watches with her grandpa. I think she thinks she can solve this quicker than the actual police.'

'She probably can,' Tanya replied jokingly. 'That girl can do anything she puts her mind to.'

'You're tellin' me,' Will mumbled. He pushed the gear into park and idled next to Bones' Barbershop on Main Street.

Inside, the shop was dark. His boss, Harold Bones, normally didn't come in until closer to midday unless it was Monday, when Mrs. Guy, the widowed grocery store owner across the street, changed her display signage. Then and only then was he ever a morning person.

'It's gotta be you then.'

'Excuse me?' Will choked out, hoping he'd misheard her.

'You need to do something about this. You're telling me our daughter is on the brink of depression and you're sitting on your ass about it?'

'I'm doing everything I can, T, alright? I'm not Sherlock Holmes.'

'You *are* the man I share a child with; a child who's suffering, by the way. You need to do something about this, Will!'

Will opened his mouth to argue, but a succession of beeps told him that his discussion with Tanya was over.

'So much for a reassuring conversation,' Will said aloud. He shut off his engine and got out.

Chapter 19

Morgan

Jabari Rhodes of Chosen Moments Photos arrived right after lunch. Morgan had polished off the last of her potato soup, the bowl still warm on its platter. She pulled off her headphones just in time to hear Lionel announce, 'Photographer's here,' in a punctuated tone, nodding his head toward the front door, his lips twisted in irritation. He stacked her dishes with a theatrical sigh. He hated being interrupted from prepping dinner.

Today's dinner menu would feature tender short ribs, a cloud of creamy garlic mashed potatoes, and a mix of seasonal vegetables, filling the Inn with a tantalizing scent. If Morgan hadn't been going on a dinner date that night, she'd have Lionel save a plate for her.

'Where's my mom?' Morgan asked, filtering the annoyed inflection from her voice.

Lionel shrugged, wiping his hands on a dish towel.

'I haven't seen Wesley or Vanessa since I got here this morning. Duty falls to you.'

Morgan glanced at the time on her laptop screen. It was nearing 2 p.m. When she had returned to the house after Daphne's morning walk, she thought her parents had gone out to run errands. But now, as the afternoon stretched on with no word, she felt uneasy.

'Want me to tell him to come back?' Lionel asked.

'I'll talk to him,' Morgan replied. She stood and pushed her feet into a pair of slippers.

Jabari Rhodes was standing just outside of the frosted glass. He was carrying two thick white envelopes, his expression sunny as always. He wore his usual red and black baseball cap, and wire circle-shaped glasses; his camera slung across his chest like a trusted companion he never let out of his sight.

'I come bearing memories,' he greeted with a wink. Morgan stepped aside to let him in. He pressed one envelope in her hand and dug around in his pants pocket until he found a small black flash drive.

'Every shot from the Jubilee. Figured I'd drop them off here before turning them over to the police. Thought you and your folks should get the first look.'

Morgan accepted the envelope and the flash drive with a grateful smile. 'Thanks, Jabari, you always come through. Any updates from the station?'

Jabari's shoulders hiked up to his ears. 'No idea. Detective Chambers called me early this morning, didn't say much, just asked for copies of everything

I had. But something tells me they're working over-time on this. He sounded desperate.'

Morgan gestured to the second envelope. 'Those the copies?'

He nodded, a sly smile tugging at his lips. 'Even got a snap of you stuffing one of those corn dogs into your mouth behind the balloon arch.'

Her eyes widened in horror. 'Delete it!'

'No promises!' He dodged the swat of Morgan's hand and stepped backward off the front porch, heading out. She watched until his tail lights disap-peared onto the road and stepped back into the house.

Morgan walked back into the kitchen. On the island, Lionel julienned onions, peppers, and carrots with careful concentration. Daphne waited impa-tiently at his feet, her eyes trained on his hands, probably wishing for a morsel of anything to drop over the side.

Lionel pointed his knife at the envelope. 'Those from the Jubilee?'

'Yep, let's see how bad he got me.' Morgan cracked open the envelope and pulled out a stack of glossy photos. The images were crisp, vibrant and alive with joy.

The Daffodil Jubilee came rushing back to her in images frozen in time: children jumping in the bounce house, their mouths agape, mid-laughter, their shoes kicked off in a rainbow pile nearby.

Seniors hand danced to the oldies, their smiles

beaming. Two teenagers Morgan didn't recognize blew kisses to the camera, sun shades in the shapes of daffodils covering their eyes. Morgan herself, caught in motion, laughing beside Nia as they both stuffed a corn dog into their waiting mouths. She smiled and put that one to the side for her own safekeeping.

'You look happy there,' Lionel said as he pounded potatoes with a wire masher.

She wished she could go back to that Saturday afternoon, knowing what she knew now. She'd relive every moment of chaos. More importantly, she'd stop Eleanor from going into that maze.

Morgan flipped through the next set of prints: photos of vendor booths, food trucks, the pie-eating contest, and the face painters. There were candid shots of townspeople she knew well and even some strangers from out of town.

As the stack thinned, a frown took over Lionel's face. His hand stilled on the masher. 'I haven't seen Eleanor yet.'

Morgan froze. She flipped back through the photos, quicker now, her eyes scanning every frame, studying every background. There were plenty of faces she didn't recognize, but Eleanor Langford, with her burgundy hair and ruffle kimono, would have stood out.

'I remember seeing her,' Morgan mumbled. She plugged the flash drive into the waiting laptop. 'I'll check the rest, maybe she's in the digital files.'

She didn't want to say what she was thinking out loud. But the pit in her stomach was making it hard to breathe. Lionel joined her on the other side of the island, looking over her shoulder as she flipped through the files.

Lionel found it first, his finger tapping on the thumbnail. 'There.'

Morgan enlarged the photo. Angel Reed made an appearance; victorious, clutching a giant unicorn, while Will and Eleanor looked on with prideful grins.

Goosebumps rose on her skin when Lionel said, 'You know what this means, right? That was the last time anyone had seen Eleanor alive.'

Chapter 20

Will

Will cut three heads back to back, barely pausing for a bite to eat and a sip of water. Surprisingly, his Wednesdays were always busy; a constant rotation of familiar faces, small talk, and careful precision. He usually found the rhythm calming; finding peace in the weight of the clippers in his hands. But today his mind vacillated between his conversation with Tanya and counting down the seconds until 8:30 tonight, his date with Morgan.

His first client was Alvin Grady, the retired postmaster who'd lived in Cinnamon Falls for over fifty years. Mr. Al came in every other Wednesday like clockwork, offering Will one of the butterscotch candies from his truck's console and asking for the same cut every time: 'Line me up but keep it square in the back. None of that fancy city stuff.'

Today, Alvin wore his trusty khaki pants, hiked

over his belly button and strapped in place by a sturdy brown leather belt.

'You seen that press conference?' he asked Will, as Will draped the cape over Alvin's front.

Will nodded. 'Caught a bit of it Monday morning.'

Alvin shook his head slowly. 'That poor woman, can't imagine ending up dead in a maze. I been goin' to that Jubilee since Wesley opened the Inn.' He grunted and continued, 'Truth is, things been crazy 'round here ever since Rosie passed.'

Will didn't respond. He'd heard countless stories about Rosslyn 'Rosie' Rose in the months that followed her murder. He wished he could have known the golden age of Cinnamon Falls like Mr. Alvin, Jesse and Nia did. They talked about their hometown like it had a heartbeat of its own.

'You still takin' those boys out to the garden?' Alvin asked after a few moments of silence.

'Every other Saturday,' Will answered.

'Good.' Alvin nodded his approval. 'Keep 'em busy. Idle hands and all that. I know you know.'

'Yeah,' Will commented. He knew all too well.

He finished the cut quickly, spraying down Mr. Grady with a sheen and removing the cape with a flourish.

His second scheduled client was rookie Officer Reggie Nash, who had recently joined the Cinnamon Falls Police Department as a patrolman. He was green and eager; too eager, and Will planned to use that to his advantage.

Reggie's request for a low fade was always met with finesse, and he spent the rest of the appointment talking about his ambitions for a detective position. Will didn't know if Reggie knew about his friendship with Jesse, but he preferred keeping that bit of information to himself. It wasn't often that he had an unsuspicious officer in his chair. Maybe he could talk him into telling him something about the investigation.

'How you likin' it so far?' Will started, adjusting the height on his chair.

In the mirror, Will noticed Reggie's grin. 'Man, it's good. Chief Raines is a little intense. But it beats writing parking tickets up and down Main Street, that's for sure.'

Will buzzed a clean line around Reggie's temples, brushing away the cut hair that had fallen into his face. Will nudged a bit more. 'Heard y'all been working around the clock since Saturday.'

Reggie exhaled. 'That's for sure. We've been pulling double shifts, chasing down every lead, tip, and rumor in this town. Folks won't stop calling about ghosts or some secret passageway under the maze.' He chuckled. 'Cinnamon Falls has gone full *Dateline*.'

'What's the word?' Will asked flat-out. 'You guys getting close to wrapping it up?'

Reggie glanced at Will in the mirror and pulled the cape off his neck. 'We think so. We're making an arrest tonight.'

Will paused. His hand stilled mid-fade. 'That right?'

'Yeah,' he responded. 'Chief says I should be back to regular patrol by the weekend.'

Will resumed the cut, carefully and slowly, taking in the words. 'Who's the arrest?'

Reggie stiffened. 'Can't say, you know, protocol.'

Will gave him a nod in the mirror, trying to play it cool. If they were ready to arrest someone, that meant they'd solved it. The investigation was moving faster than he thought. Maybe Jesse, Chambers, and Raines were really *that* good and he was one step closer to getting his daughter back. Arresting someone meant closure for the town; for Morgan and her parents, too. Will finished the cut and shook off his cape with a snap.

'Guess I'll keep an eye out for Charlie Kent in the morning when he delivers the paper.'

Reggie smiled. 'You and everyone else.'

When eight-thirty rolled around, Will found himself climbing the front steps of the Daffodil Inn. He couldn't tell if it was his nerves or the sticky spring night that had him sweating. A bouquet of daffodils rotated from one hand to the other as he wiped his moist palms on his pants.

He'd opted for a simple outfit, one he couldn't mess up: a pair of slim-fit black chino pants, paired with a black buttoned shirt and blazer. The gold buttons matched the gold watch that peeked out from under his tailored shirt. His beard was freshly lined; his normal loose locs were twisted away, positioned in a holder at the back of his head. Still, he felt wildly unprepared the moment the front door swung open.

An unfamiliar man stood in the doorway of the Daffodil Inn; tall, tense, and very much in Will's way. His blue eyes narrowed, trailing Will from his feet upward. The men were eye to eye, Will taller only by a hair.

The stranger's eyes dropped to the flowers. In a perturbed tone he asked, 'You lost?'

'Nah,' Will replied calmly, squaring his shoulders to the man. 'Here for Morgan.'

His face didn't register any emotion, but Will noticed his jaw tick. 'You two have plans tonight?'

Will's brow furrowed slightly, keeping his cool. Since when did the Inn hire security? 'We do.'

'Right,' he responded, glancing over his shoulder toward the ascending staircase. 'She'll be down in a minute.'

As if summoned by fate, Morgan's voice floated down the hall. 'Is that Will?'

Security stepped back just as she appeared at the top of the steps, looking like the kind of woman that drunk men spend their nights reminiscing about in dive bars. Will felt his breath catch in his throat, and he knew then that this view would be imprinted in his memory for the rest of his days.

Morgan's indigo dress clung to her curves in all the right places, hugging her waist and falling just above her ankles with a tasteful slit that gave Will a peek of her thigh. Her braids were pulled into a bun at the top of her head, a few purple strands artfully left out to frame her heart-shaped face. Simple gold teardrop earrings caught the light as she swayed down the steps. Her merlot lipstick made his mouth run dry.

Morgan's cheeks reddened at his stunned expression. She grinned as she reached the bottom step.

'Rescue those from the river?' she asked, eyeing the daffodils, a laugh playing at her lips.

Dazed, Will nodded, finally finding his voice. 'Cut fresh from Pops' garden. You, uh, look amazing.'

Amazing would never live up to what Will was feeling inside. Pressure mounted in his chest by the second, he could barely breathe.

'Thanks,' she said, her voice syrupy sweet. She reached for the flowers, their fingers brushing in the exchange, causing Will to feel like he'd internally combust. 'You clean yourself up nice too, Mr. Reed.'

'Y'all have fun.' Security's voice cut in, sounding like nails on a chalkboard. Will had forgotten he was even standing there. His tone was pleasant, but tight, and Will knew exactly what that meant.

There was a code between men, one that let each other know when a woman was spoken for. It was a good thing he'd gotten to Morgan first. He gave the guy a knowing smile and reached for her waiting hand.

'We will,' he said, leading Morgan out toward the driveway. As he did, he caught her magnetic scent; something warm, vanilla, spice, and a deep floral. Irresistible.

Will clicked the fob on his '59 Eldorado and the headlights cut across the yard, bathing them in a soft spotlight. The car's sleek black chrome paint almost glittered in the night.

Morgan paused. 'This is yours?'

'First classic car I ever bought with my own money,' Will said, holding the passenger door open for her. 'Thought I'd dust it off tonight for something special.'

Morgan slid inside, laughing softly. 'So, this is something special?'

'Absolutely,' he replied. *More than you know*, he said to himself.

Closing Morgan's door gently, he walked around to the driver's side. Morgan reached over and pushed his door open, and he slid in beside her.

As the engine rumbled, she looked over at him, smiling. 'Ready?'

He shifted the car into gear, his gaze lingering on her, memorizing every inch of her. 'I've been ready.'

Peeling out of the driveway, Will left the stranger in the doorway, seething.

Prime Society had a sizable crowd for a Wednesday night. The newest upscale steakhouse restaurant in Asheville had a waiting list as long as his arm for reservations, but after Will and his father completed the landscaping job out front, he'd asked for one small favor from the owner: to be pushed to the top of the waiting list if he ever needed it. Tonight, his favor pulled through.

The teenage valet balked as they pulled up to the restaurant-slash-lounge. Will smirked, watching the kid's eyes widen at the sight of his car. The Eldorado was sleek, waxed to perfection, with swooping tailfins and polished chrome accents that gleamed under the streetlights like midnight on wheels.

Tripping over himself, the valet reached for the door handle. He let out a low, impressed whistle. 'Sir, this car is . . . wow. Is this a restoration?'

Will stepped out slowly, adjusting the sleeve of his blazer. 'Original parts. Custom paint. A few upgrades.'

He nodded, awestruck. 'It's the nicest car I've ever parked.'

'If you scuff it even a little bit, I'll know,' Will warned, tossing him the keys.

Will ventured around to Morgan's door, opening it for the main attraction. When she stepped out, the valet's jaw nearly hit the pavement. Her dress shimmered under the entry lights, hugging every curve with a sophisticated elegance. The valet looked from

Will to Morgan and back again like he was witnessing a movie.

Will offered his date his arm and winked. 'Let's give them something to talk about.'

He heard the Eldorado's engine purr its way into the underground garage.

'Reservation for Reed,' he informed the waiting hostess at the door. She nodded without words, as if she'd been waiting for them to arrive.

Morgan's heels click-clacked along the tiled floor as the hostess led the couple past velvet ropes and a curated cluster of low-lit tables until they were seated in a private booth.

The modern interior glimmered with polished concrete and black walnut accents; flickering candlelight, gold-trimmed menus, and live jazz humming softly in the background. A wall of windows offered a panoramic view of Juniper Heights in the distance, glittering beneath the stars. It wasn't Atlanta or some big city, just a few buildings clustered together, but he figured Morgan would appreciate the view, nonetheless.

Will pulled out Morgan's chair and waited until she sat before sliding in across from her. She looked absolutely stunning; the candlelight danced across her skin, catching the subtle shimmer on her high cheekbones and defined collarbones. He noticed a beauty mark just below the bone. He decided he would kiss her there first, if he ever got the chance to get that close.

Suddenly, he was thirsty.

'You're staring,' Morgan said behind the rim of her glass of water.

Will broke his concentration by straightening the napkin over his lap. 'I'm just trying to figure out how the hell I got so lucky to be here with you right now.'

Morgan rolled her eyes, her fingers fiddling with the stem of her water glass. 'That smooth talk work on all your clients?'

'Only the ones in purple dresses who make the whole restaurant stop and stare.'

'You're trouble.' Morgan smirked, shying away from his gaze.

'Only the good kind.'

'Speaking of trouble, have you found anything new on Eleanor?' Morgan asked, sitting up straighter in her seat. The playfulness drained from her voice, replaced by an edge of curiosity. 'I spoke to Frankie Templeton the other day and he told me that Eleanor thought she was being followed.'

Will balked. 'Followed? By who?'

Morgan shrugged, swirling the condensation around her glass before taking a sip. 'Frankie didn't say, just that she was spooked by it.' A shiver crept up her arms, and she rubbed them briskly. 'Eleanor didn't have lots of friends, but I can't imagine anyone here actually killing her.'

Will frowned, his mind already racing ahead. 'Ms. Hargrove over at the Toasted Pecan told me that she was friendly with the librarians, told me she even had a plaque with her name on the door.'

Morgan nodded with a dry laugh. 'Over the Archive room, right? She bragged about it constantly like she owned the building or something. You said you were dropping by there on Monday. What did you find out?'

Will leaned in closer. 'Eleanor had been digging through Mayor Lyons' old campaign donations from the last election cycle.'

Morgan's brow furrowed. 'How do you know that?'

'Her name was listed as the last person who handled the book I was reading, dated just two weeks before the Daffodil Jubilee.'

Morgan's gaze drifted to the tabletop as though the wood might hold the missing pieces. 'Frankie said that she noticed somebody following her. It must have been right after she saw those records.' Her voice dropped to a whisper. 'But why would Eleanor care about Asad Lyons anymore? They've got him dead to rights, I heard.'

'It must've meant something to her,' Will replied.

'Enough to get her killed?' Morgan asked, the words falling off her trembling lips.

Will's hand tightened on the edge of the table. 'I keep thinking about how someone was out there, watching her while she was out with my daughter. They could've hurt Angel. If they had—' He cut himself off, unwilling to give shape to the thought. Rage flickered in his chest, dark and consuming.

Morgan reached across the table and pressed her palms flat to the surface, her fingers grazing his hand, calming him. 'Some ground rules for the night?' Morgan stated firmly. 'No more talk about Eleanor, or the Inn. Let's forget everything for just one night.'

Will exhaled slowly, then pulled an invisible zipper over his lips. 'Your wish is my command.'

Their waiter, Brianna, returned to take their orders. Will went for the signature ribeye filet, medium rare, topped with chimichurri butter and a side of potato gratin featuring a garlic asiago cream sauce. Morgan settled on the miso-glazed Chilean sea bass paired with sauteed bok choy. They shared a side of crispy Brussels sprouts and lobster mac and cheese. Will ordered a cherry wood smoked old-fashioned while Morgan requested a blackberry thyme margarita. It matched her dress. By the time their meals arrived, their nerves and flirty banter had melted into something softer.

'So, tell me about you,' Morgan inquired, twirling her fork on the edge of her plate. 'I know Angel is your world but . . . what about her mom? What's the story there?'

Will's jaw flexed around a delectable chunk of steak. He swallowed it down with the help of the aged whiskey that gave his chest a warm burn on the way down.

'We were high school sweethearts. Inseparable . . . until we weren't.'

Will didn't want to elaborate. He wanted to get back to talking about her, and why she thought the Teenage Mutant Ninja Turtles could take the Power Rangers. She had a fair and very valid argument: *Four talking turtles who just happen to be badass ninjas, raised by their elderly single father rat, versus a couple of teenagers who take fifteen minutes to morph, isn't even a fair fight. The turtles are taking them down, and devouring a pepperoni pie right after.*

She reached over and took a forkful of lobster mac in her mouth. Will forced himself to keep talking and got back to the subject. When Will talked, Morgan didn't press, just nodded, listening. She was *so* easy to talk to. She could probably get him to confess his heart's most cherished desires. All she had to do was level him with those toffee brown eyes and he was like putty in her hands. Cupid's arrow shot straight through his heart.

'Tanya was a force in my life.' Will smiled, the memory of his and Tanya's love rushing back in Technicolor; their life unfurling in memories he'd shelved years ago. 'In high school, she was smarter than I could have ever hoped to be, and was quicker than me, too, in academics and wit. I hated school and didn't care to go, or finish. Tanya saw something in me that I just couldn't see for myself at the time.

It wasn't until she was going away to college that I decided I'd get my life together. I couldn't lose the best thing that had happened to me.'

Morgan took a sip of her cocktail, and Will had never wished he was a margarita glass more than that moment. He shook the thought out of his head and continued.

'We spent our summers together, inseparable, and when Angel came along, it was the happiest we'd ever been. I had someone to live for.'

He paused. He hated this part; reliving it was the worst. 'She was involved in a hit-and-run. Some asshole slammed into the back of her at a stoplight one night, caused one of her spinal discs to bulge . . . most nights she could barely move.' Will stilled. 'Then came the painkillers. At first, they were her saving grace. She could tolerate the injury. We danced in those days, something we hadn't done in a long while; but it didn't take long for her to become—' Will swallowed, trying his best to get through it. 'Addicted. It was a Tuesday morning when the sheriff came to my house and told me that if it hadn't been for a good Samaritan, Tanya would have rolled into a busy intersection with Angel in the backseat.'

Morgan gasped as she brought her trembling fingers to her mouth.

'We separated. I got primary custody of Angel and moved to Cinnamon Falls shortly after.' He took a breath. 'Tanya's better now, ten months clean. I know she's trying to do right by Angel, and back when I was going through a rough patch, it was Tanya who extended her hand. I feel a duty to do the same for her, even if we aren't together anymore.'

Morgan exhaled. 'That couldn't have been easy,' she said gently.

'It wasn't. Still isn't,' Will sighed. He took another sip of his drink. The familiar burn welcomed him once again. How many nights back then had he spent drowning his sorrows in brown liquor? Too many to count. He put the glass down. He was *not* going there again.

'Tanya knows Angel is our priority. I make it a point to make the drive to Macon on the weekends when I don't have the gardening club. I would never let anything come between that.'

Morgan tapped her fingernails against her glass. 'I respect that. It's admirable after everything you've been through. It sounds like you've had your share of let-downs.'

Will finally looked up. That was an understatement. 'Yeah. What about you?'

Morgan surrendered a dry laugh. 'I've had the same; liars, ghosters. Men who say one thing but mean another. They only want one thing from me but pretend to be romantic and understanding for, like, two weeks.' Her eyes flicked in his direction and Will straightened in his seat. He wasn't pretending.

He had much more romance to give . . . for the right woman, and he hoped that that woman was seated across from him now.

'The last one almost got me to believe in forever.' Morgan pulled her fingers and thumb apart just barely. 'But then I got a butt-dial in the middle of the night. My phone is normally on 'Do Not Disturb' during the week so it went to voicemail.' Her eyes trended down, meeting the tablecloth. Will braced himself for the rest of her story. 'Let's just say I heard everything he *really* thought about me. Everything he'd made me believe was a lie. He was just baiting me; stringing me along until he could hit.'

Morgan gave a hollow shrug, like the memory was just another box she'd shoved into the back of her closet. 'That was the last time I let myself fall for words without action. Now I watch what a man does, not what he says.'

Heat rose in Will's body, roiling around in his veins. He couldn't imagine someone hurting Morgan, especially on purpose.

Will tapped the paper napkin in front of her. 'Write his name down for me.'

Morgan's eyes bulged. 'What for?'

'I know some people who can pay him a visit, maybe a few bites of the curb will set him straight, or maybe some concrete shoes . . .' Will joked.

Morgan snorted, trying to hold back her laughter. Just then, Will's phone vibrated, clattering on the table, capturing both their attention. Will didn't recognize the number. He pressed 'Ignore'.

'I don't want to be too forward, Morgan, but I want to be clear with you. I know I come with a lot—'

'I love Angel,' Morgan inserted quickly, shaking her head as if having a daughter wasn't a big deal. There were women who would scream bloody murder if Will dared bring up the fact that he had a child. But Morgan didn't flinch. Will felt his smile building from the inside. The butterflies fluttered around his stomach double time. He had to spell it out now or he'd lose his nerve.

'I want to get to know you, and not just as a friend. I can't say I'll be the perfect man, but you deserve happiness, someone who makes you feel safe, someone you can trust.'

Their eyes met across the table, and for a moment, the noise around them faded. Something passed between them; recognition, maybe, or pain survived; of walls cautiously lowered. She nodded slowly, as if she'd been digesting his words; silently acknowledging that she'd seen him, really seen him, for the first time.

She said the words he'd been waiting to hear since he met her. 'I'm open to that.'

Just then, a figure rounded the corner, pulling Will and Morgan out of the moment. He glanced up to find a man he'd never seen before.

'Evening,' he said smoothly, his voice slick with charm.

A tall, broad-shouldered man in an expensive navy suit was standing beside the table, a curvy woman clinging to his arm in a tight red dress. Will kissed his teeth when he recognized her smirking face: Amanda Jenkins. She smiled low and smug and Will rolled his eyes.

'I don't believe we've met,' the man said, extending a hand. 'Max Greaves.' Will couldn't help but notice his Audemars Piguet watch. He was casually walking around with a watch the cost of a home on his wrist.

Will stood and took his hand, firm grip to firm grip. 'William Reed.'

'Ah, the infamous Will Reed, one third of Reed & Roots.' Max's grin was all teeth, bright and gleaming. 'I've heard good things. How's business?'

'Excellent,' Will replied, not elaborating. 'And you?' He gestured to his watch.

'Excellent,' he responded, still smiling. Will couldn't tell if Max was mocking him.

'Max *owns* this place,' Amanda butted in, her hands trailing the lapel of his suit jacket.

Max stammered, 'Well, I own the casino on the other side of the building.'

Will frowned. 'I thought Greg Jenkins owned Prime Society?'

'Greg manages the property. I'm the owner.' Max winked. 'You know how that goes. Can't be in so many places at once.'

Before Will could reply, Max flagged down a waitress.

'Be a dear and bring a bottle of the best champagne to this table. Clearly, they're celebrating new love.'

Not-Brianna nodded and scurried away. Will glanced over and Morgan was bristling while she kept her eyes on Max.

Max leaned in, just slightly. 'Remind your parents that Friday is the deadline. I'd hate to push the paperwork through without their blessing.' He straightened with a satisfied smile and turned to leave.

Amanda Jenkins gave Will a long once-over, her smile curling like smoke. Will didn't move. He watched as she snuggled closer to Max and the two of them sauntered away without another glance.

Will eased back into his seat and Morgan let out a slow breath.

Not-Brianna returned in a flash; a frosted bottle of champagne with a gold label rested in a bucket. She had two upturned glasses between her fingers. Carefully, she removed the cork and poured them both a glass.

'On the house,' she said. 'Enjoy.'

At first, Will and Morgan stared at each other in disbelief. But he was not one to let a free drink go to waste. He raised his glass, getting back to the moment they'd lost. They clinked glasses, never breaking eye contact, and took a sip.

'I know we said the Inn talk is off-limits, but who was that guy? And why did that reminder feel like a threat?'

Morgan sighed. 'Maximillian Greaves, some real estate developer dead set on my parents' place.'

'Wait, so they *are* selling the Inn? I didn't want to pry, but was that what he meant by a deadline?'

She nodded. 'They're considering it,' Morgan said, her eyes meeting the table. 'He made an offer to buy the Inn outright for something called Cinnamon Waters, a luxury retreat that's apparently already in the works. My mom is furious with me because I want her to consider it.'

'You're asking her to sell her life's work.'

Morgan scoffed. 'Have you been online? There's a petition boycotting the Daffodil Jubilee *next* year! It's our biggest event of the season. Without it, they're dead in the water, Will. Isn't it better if they just cut their losses?'

Will sat back in his seat. 'And give up?'

Morgan shook her head. 'Cameron offered to help them navigate the process. He works in real estate. He can at least make sure they're not getting a raw deal.'

Cameron. Will had heard that name before from Jesse.

Morgan continued, 'Sorry, that's the guy who answered the door. He's Eleanor's nephew, sticking around until the investigation gets sorted.'

'Got it,' Will responded, holding his breath for the next statement.

'Charming guy,' Morgan added.

Charming, huh? Will thought. He wondered what words she used to describe him when he wasn't around. With everything that had transpired, Will had forgotten all about Mr. Unfriendly. It was good to put a name to a face.

'Okay, serious talk over. Let's change gears.'

Will liked that suggestion. 'Alright, what's something I don't know about you?'

Almost immediately, Morgan supplied, 'I got suspended for fighting in middle school.'

He nearly choked on his drink. Morgan? A fighter? 'No.'

'Yep, this girl Ruth Evers told the whole class I was dressed like a very popular purple dinosaur one day. I said she smelled like wet dog food. Things escalated quickly.'

'What if she was just jealous of your coordination?' Will asked between laughs.

'She had every right to be, I looked damn good.' Will was still laughing when she added, 'Your turn.'

Will decided to go a different route.

'I write poetry,' he blurted out. In truth, he hadn't written anything down on paper since high school, but it was the last thing he remembered loving more than cutting hair, or digging his fingers in the dirt.

Morgan leaned her elbows on the table. 'You? Mr. Tough Guy?' She reached over and squeezed his biceps through his shirt.

'Shakespeare would've wept,' Will teased, wishing

to feel the warmth of her fingers on his body again. 'My middle name is Romeo.'

Morgan sat back, lacing one arm behind her chair. Her seductive brown eyes roamed him hungrily. 'Lay one on me, Romeo.'

Will grinned. 'You'll have to stick around long enough to see if I've still got it.'

Will's phone buzzed on the table. Another unknown number. He'd dropped Angel off with Elijah and Renee earlier that evening at their house. If something was wrong, she wouldn't call private. Will's mind raced with possibilities, but he pressed 'Ignore' again.

Brianna walked over, offering the dessert menu.

'Anything pique your interest?' she asked Morgan, her handheld tablet at the ready to take their order.

'The cheesecake, extra strawberries.'

She looked at Will but his phone was vibrating a third time, pulling him out of the conversation.

What was going on?

'Sorry,' he murmured, and picked up his phone. 'Hello?'

There was a pause, then a shaky voice came through.

'Mr. Reed? It's Caleb. I–I'm at the station and they ar-arrested me and I d-don't know what to do.' Caleb sounded panicked on the other end.

Will's heart dropped to his feet. He stood abruptly, his chair scraping the floor. A rage he hadn't known since grade school sprouted in his belly.

'What happened?' Will roared.

'They're saying I killed her but I swear I didn't! Please can you come get me, Mr. Reed? I can't stay here all night!'

Will's heart pounded; his brain filled with static. His fingers tingled with electricity. Through gritted teeth he said, 'I'm on my way.'

Morgan stood too, concern laced in her eyes.

'I'm sorry, I have to go. One of my students is in trouble.'

'Of course. Go.'

Will dug around for his wallet, slapping his card on the table. 'Get whatever you want, okay? Call a car to take you home. I'll make this up to you, I promise.'

Morgan smiled, too soft and too understanding. Will wanted to punch himself as he skidded out of Prime Society into the spring night.

The next person he was going to punch would be Jesse Shaw for ruining the night of his dreams.

Chapter 21

Morgan

Morgan didn't cry when Brianna took Will's card with an apologetic look that said everything she already feared: *Poor girl, he must not have been into her.*

She didn't cry when Brianna returned with the steak dinner she'd ordered to-go for her pain and suffering, boxed up neatly, pity disguised in the folded corners of the bag.

She didn't cry when Nia came to pick her up from Prime Society, the fanciest restaurant she'd ever been to, with thick white tablecloths, gleaming marble floors, and a wine list with its own leather-bound menu.

She didn't cry when she realized she'd wasted her time, again. She'd worn her best dress; the dress she'd been saving for a very, very special occasion: Nia's wedding. She even soaked her braids in hot rollers to have bouncy, voluminous curls. She shaved her armpits *and* her legs for Chrissakes.

She didn't cry while she waited outside the restaurant under the neon sign, the valet's stare burning a hole in her side. Her heels stung the pads of her feet, each second spent standing being admonished with a pinprick of shame.

She didn't even cry when she noticed Nia's sedan cut through the parking lot, almost clipping the curb as Nia jerked to a stop alongside Morgan.

But the minute Morgan folded into the passenger seat, and the soft interior lights dimmed above her, something inside of her collapsed. Her fingers trembled as they reached for the seatbelt but couldn't find the latch. Her chin quivered, threatening. Her breath hitched. Then the first sob escaped, tearing through her chest, raw and violent, like she'd been sucker-punched in the gut.

Nia said nothing. She reached across the console and gently took the belt from her best friend's shaking hands, clicking it into place. Then she pulled off without a word while Morgan kicked off her heels, pulled her knees to her chest and sobbed.

Morgan didn't dare look back at the restaurant, she couldn't. She watched its sleek facade shrink in the side mirror and then disappear totally out of view like a cruel joke.

The night had started with butterflies and banter and ended in gut-wrenching silence, tears, and the smell of her pain-and-suffering steak dinner wafting up from the passenger seat floor.

Her best friend reached across the console, linking her fingers in Morgan's.

'I really . . . liked him,' Morgan whispered between uneven breaths. 'I thought w-we were having a good time,' she hiccupped.

Maybe she was wrong.

Maybe she misread it.

Maybe he didn't like her like he'd said he did.

Maybe she was memorable enough, funny enough, sexy enough, but not worthy enough to finish a date. The thought sent her spiraling. It burned behind her eyes, down her throat. Her shoulders hunched, her entire body folding into itself as more tears slid free.

'I hate crying,' she mumbled, feeling more foolish by the second; ashamed that she cared this much already. Ashamed that one date – half of a date – was enough to send her heart into freefall with a man she barely even knew.

But it wasn't just one date. It was all of them. All the times she dared to believe that someone might stay; that someone might choose her first this time. She cracked the door to her heart open, just a little, and this was the outcome.

Again, her brain screamed at her. When would she ever learn?

'Do you want to talk about it?' Nia asked gently, her thumb massaging slow circles into Morgan's hand, anchoring her.

Morgan shook her head, shame settling into her

bones, too mortified to want to relive the last thirty minutes of her life. All she wanted to do was curl up in bed with her cheesecake and watch re-runs of her favorite sitcom with the laugh track that didn't require her to participate.

Morgan's silence wasn't just about Will and every other guy who'd come before him, too.

The last few years she'd convinced herself she wasn't looking for anything serious. She was too busy with lesson plans and SMART goals, and that her heart was doing just fine. But deep down she knew. She wanted to believe in something real again. And now she felt stupid for trying, for believing that anything as life-changing as love could happen to someone like her.

'Do you want me to punch him? Because I can. Jesse's been letting me join his 6 a.m. workouts, and let me tell you, I'm as strong as an ox right now.' Nia removed her hand from Morgan's and flexed her arm. 'One punch to the nose and he's out, I promise.'

Morgan smiled ruefully. The thought of sweetheart Nia punching anyone was hysterical, but it was a nice gesture. It should have made her laugh, but she didn't have the strength to muster one. Absolutely nothing was funny, not anymore.

When Nia suggested a whiskey sour at the Red Fern to drown Morgan's sorrows before heading home, Morgan had agreed. One reluctant drink had turned into three, and now she was hammered and felt much better. She couldn't speak for how she would feel in the morning, but right now, the only thing on her mind was making it up thirteen stairs and falling face first into bed.

Morgan had expected to find the Daffodil Inn shut down for the night. She thought she'd be greeted with complete silence; at the most hearing the soft hum of the refrigerator or Daphne's nails tipping against the hardwood to meet her at the door.

But it was just after midnight and the sight of the unexpected glow spilling from the kitchen stopped her in her tracks. She rounded the corner and found her parents seated at the farmhouse kitchen island, sending a finger of anxiety crawling up her spine.

Shit.

The rich aroma of freshly made coffee told her that her parents had been up for quite some time. Her mother had both hands wrapped around a cracked mug that Morgan had decorated in grade school, a lifetime ago.

The purple paint had long since faded, the ceramic chipped over the years. The once vibrant red heart with the words '#1 MOM' painted through it was a sad shade of pink, the words barely visible after years of wash cycles. Her father looked weary, his glasses perched low on his nose as if he'd just been reading something, though there were no papers in sight. They both looked up when she entered, eyes tired. Morgan was certain she looked like death warmed over, but she did the best she could to play sober.

Her mother frowned, glancing over her shoulder at the time on the clock shaped like a rooster.

'You're home late,' Vanessa said softly, sitting the mug down.

Morgan let out a long breath. It was the first time she'd seen both her parents since their fight yesterday. She was hoping to artfully avoid the pair of them until the investigation concluded or until Max Greaves came knocking, whichever came first. She owed them an apology, a sober one, which meant she'd have to take a rain check on serious conversations tonight.

From the living room, Daphne padded over, sniffing Morgan's feet and legs as if she could retrieve the exact coordinates for where she'd been all night.

'I didn't expect anyone to be up.'

'Couldn't sleep,' Wesley offered, patting the bench for her to sit. 'How'd it go?'

Morgan ignored the request and crossed the room to stash her food in the fridge. She'd come back for it in a few hours once she felt like herself again. Her mind filtered through excuses to tell her parents, but she couldn't bear to talk about Will anymore. In fact, she wanted to forget he even existed.

'It was fine,' she answered, pushing her bag to the

back of the fridge. She was hot from the inside out. The cool blast of air on her face felt like a heavenly reprieve from the liquor working its way through her system. She turned to find her parents with skeptical expressions.

Her mother had one eyebrow raised. 'That's it?'

Morgan crossed her arms, indignant, doing her best to keep herself upright. 'I really don't want to talk about it.'

Her mother squinted at her. 'Are you . . . drunk?'

'God forbid a girl has a few cocktails after a shit date,' Morgan mumbled. Now that the cat was out of the bag she didn't have to keep up the sober act. She was failing miserably anyway. She hunted for a glass of water, opening and slamming nearby cabinets until she found a clean glass.

Vanessa pursed her lips in disapproval. 'What'd you say to him? Not everything is a joke, Morgan. I've been telling you that since you were little.'

Morgan paused, an empty glass in her hand. *She* was responsible for a man leaving her stranded? Was it her fault that Will decided that a phone call was more important than finishing their date? Was it her fault that someone killed Eleanor Langford? Were they blaming her for Max Greaves' arrival, too? As usual, every failure of the Daffodil Inn rested squarely on Morgan's shoulders.

Her mother's comment had pushed Morgan over the edge of the cliff, sending her free-falling in the crevice between anger and irrationality. Thunderclouds rose in her chest, bolts of anger felt like electricity shot through her veins. Her heart splintered open, the last pieces of her life she'd been holding together by loose stitches frayed at the edges. Her vision blurred, tears crowding her eyes. She was undone.

'Morgan . . .' Her father's voice was soft, but laced with warning.

'You know, I hope Max Greaves does buy this place. Maybe then you'll know what it feels like to want something so desperately and have it dangled just out of reach. Maybe then you'll know what it feels like to have the thing that means the most to you, snatched away right in front of your eyes.'

Vanessa looked stunned, but Morgan couldn't stop now. Her hands trembled as she continued, 'I've been wearing purple since the first grade, did you know that? Every day! Because I thought maybe if I stood out enough, you'd actually see me. Not as the Inn's next owner, not as your helper, but as your daughter, your own flesh and blood.' Morgan sniffed, wiping her nose with the back of her hand. Her makeup was ruined, just like everything else in her life. 'So, no, I don't want to tell you how my date went. It's not like you even care. And if you absolutely must know, it was terrible, okay? It was pathetic, actually. It reminded me why I stopped letting anyone in a long fucking time ago.'

Vanessa stood, her shaky hands reaching for her

daughter, tears shining in her eyes. 'Oh, Morg, I didn't know—'

Morgan backed away. 'I don't need your pity,' she snapped.

Wesley stood, as his voice cut through the tension. 'Sit down,' he boomed.

Something about the weight of his tone disarmed Morgan and her mother. Slowly, they moved to the island, and Morgan sank onto the bench. The room spun and she braced herself with both hands on the table in front of her.

'I'm sorry,' her father said, his voice softer now. 'We're sorry. We thought that giving you the Inn, keeping it alive . . . we thought we were doing the right thing. We thought that was enough. But I realize now how much you needed *us*, not the business.'

Vanessa's eyes glistened. Morgan blinked, slapping away the tears out of her own eyes. It was the first time she'd seen her mother cry. She said, 'I just wanted you to be strong, to be successful. I never wanted you to struggle like we did. Baby, your father and I didn't have a dime to our names for years. We told ourselves, not *our* child. Our child would have a legacy, something to pass down to her children, and their children.'

Wesley said, 'We tried our best to do both, but the business demanded more from us than we ever imagined.'

'Don't think for a second we didn't want to be

there. Every performance or game we missed, hit me like a blow to the chest. You were just so . . .' Vanessa grasped at the air.

'Independent,' Wesley supplied.

'Independent,' Vanessa echoed. 'By the time we had more time to spare, you were grown. You had your own personality, your own thoughts, hell, even your own style.'

'Your own job,' her father added.

'I didn't know how to reach you. We're sorry for not being the parents you needed.'

Was her mother, who was allergic to admitting her wrongs, actually apologizing? Morgan felt like she was in a fever dream. The very thing she'd wanted from her parents for years, she'd received in an instant. The hole she'd carried in her heart since adolescence felt a tiny bit smaller. She shook her head, stunned, and hoped that she'd remember this moment in the morning.

Swallowing the lump in her throat, Morgan extended both her hands to her parents. Wesley grabbed one hand, his callused grip strong and enduring. Vanessa took the other hand. Her embrace was softer, warming Morgan from the inside out.

'That's all I ever wanted,' Morgan said, the emotions overtaking her. She was so tired of crying, but this time, it was from relief. Vanessa scurried around the table and took the seat next to Morgan on the bench. The anger, the disappointment, the burden of neglect, she could put it all down. She didn't have to carry it with her anymore.

As the emotions passed, Morgan asked, 'Why were you both still up, anyway?'

At that, her father stripped his glasses off and sighed. 'All of Mayor Lyons' files have been seized, tied up in the corruption case. There's no record of the Daffodil Inn on the historical registry.'

Morgan blinked, unsure if she'd heard correctly. 'What do you mean there's no record? There's got to be something *somewhere*. What does that mean for us?'

'We're unprotected,' Vanessa admitted. 'Without that decree, we're up shit's creek.'

Wesley added, 'Greaves gave us until Friday and it's already Wednesday night.'

'Thursday morning,' her mother corrected. Her father nodded gravely.

Morgan's hands curled into fists. 'I'll go to Town Hall first thing tomorrow morning. I'll talk to Mayor Tate myself! There's a record somewhere.'

Wesley shook his head. 'We tried that. I sat in that building all day. There's nothing,' he insisted.

Morgan refused to hear that. 'I've got this,' she responded. 'No one is going to take the Inn from us.'

As much as she hated the Inn for monopolizing her parents' time, it was the only home she'd ever known. She had every creaky floorboard memorized. She'd watched her father hand-paint each bird fluttering around the doorknobs. She'd spilled the yellow paint that adorned the walls of her old room. She had bounced from store to store right beside her mother, one summer after the other, to weigh in on every piece of furniture: from tiles to lamps to carpets.

What would happen to Lionel and Tiana? Where would they go? What would they do without the Inn? And what about Daphne? Could she even survive without a big backyard to chase squirrels and wild rabbits in, to roll around in grass, to be free?

Her mother was right; they weren't just selling a business. They were giving up their home, their safe place. In that moment, Morgan understood her parents more than ever. She'd been wrong about everything.

She was going to save her parents' business and that started with solving Eleanor's murder. She hadn't forgotten Caleb Brewster in the background of Zara's picture. In the morning, she'd turn it over to the police.

Her mother nodded slowly. 'Thank you,' she responded. Her eyes met Wesley's, hopeful.

For now though, she needed to sleep; to curl into the safety of her childhood bed and pretend the evening's events hadn't happened.

The floorboards groaned beneath her feet as she made her way to the Wildflower Room. Her heels and purse felt like cinderblocks slung over her shoulder, her thoughts foggy from the whiskey sours, or maybe just the disappointment of it all.

'Morgan,' a low voice called from the landing.

She squinted into the hallway light and there he was, Cameron.

Shirt unbuttoned, pajama pants slung low on his hips, chest defined and arms casually crossed like he belonged in the pages of a fitness magazine. His hair was slicked down, wet around the edges.

'What are you doing awake?' Morgan muttered, straining to keep her eyes on his and not the bulge screaming for her in his thin pajama pants.

'I heard the door,' he said. 'And the argument after.' He gave her a once-over, his voice dipped in easy concern. 'You okay?'

Morgan gave him a weak nod and turned to the door. Her bed was just a few feet away. 'I'm fine, just tired.'

'You don't look fine.' He crossed his arms and leaned against the door jamb. 'Was the date that bad?'

'I've had a long night—'

Cameron stepped back and held his door open. 'Come sit, you don't have to say anything if you don't want.'

Morgan hesitated, but the thought of not being alone, even for a moment, was enough to make her feet drift forward. She entered quietly, sitting on the edge of the bed while he shut the door behind them. His room smelled like his cologne; cedarwood and something warm like honey or musk. It didn't help that the soft lamplight highlighted every toned line of his damp chest. Morgan squeezed her legs together.

He sat beside her, close, but not too close. 'You don't deserve that, you know, whatever happened tonight . . . however he made you feel.' Cameron glanced over at her, eyes soft and voice low. 'You're smart and thoughtful, selfless. Any guy would be lucky to have your attention. I don't know what that guy's deal is, but if he can't see what's in front of him, that's on him, not you.'

Nia had all but told her the same thing, but why didn't she believe any of it? If she was so special, why did Will leave? Morgan let her head fall forward, fingers pressed to her temples. 'I don't think it's that simple.'

'It should be,' he said gently.

She exhaled, letting herself lean back slightly, resting her weight on her palms. Cameron shifted to mirror her posture, their arms brushing.

'I'm trying not to overstep,' he said, his voice barely above a whisper. 'But I see the way you hold everything in, trying to be strong for everyone else. You don't have to be that way with me.'

The weight of her emotions, the cocktails, the argument with her parents, the sting of the evening – it all caught up to her in that quiet moment. Cameron reached out, tucking a braid behind her ear with almost a reverent touch. Morgan didn't stop him.

'You're worth more than second thoughts,' he murmured. 'Or half-effort apologies.'

Her throat tightened. Tears burned behind her eyes, but she blinked them back.

'It's been a long night. Just rest.'

She was too tired to argue. Too raw to move. Morgan curled onto the edge of his bed, facing the window. Cameron adjusted the chunky knit blanket over her. She felt his warmth climb in bed behind her, not touching, just . . . near. He reached over and turned off the light.

The last thing she remembered was his whisper in the dark. 'I wouldn't have walked away from you.'

Morgan closed her eyes. Soon after, she was asleep, and the nightmare she'd endured in reality, didn't exist in her dreams.

Chapter 22

Will

The all-black Eldorado screeched to a halt outside the Cinnamon Falls Police Department. Will jumped out, his chest tight, heart thrumming with adrenaline.

His mind was spinning so quickly in different directions, steam should have been billowing out of his ears. On one hand, Morgan would probably never speak to him again. Every time the two of them were alone together it seemed like things never went the way he'd intended them to. There was always something standing in the way. Was it fate or the universe stopping them from developing a deeper connection? Were they simply not meant to be?

Will was helplessly attracted to the woman, drowning in his own desires. Her laugh, her smile, those eyes, especially when they were on him, made him feel like he was the only man on the planet; like she was meticulously crafted in her mother's womb special for him.

Why could they never get it right? She'd opened up to him tonight, showed him another side of her, and he blew it. She would never get close to him again, but he needed to apologize, at the very least. He would have time to plan his apology tour right after he dealt with Jesse.

A black rage roiled angrily in his veins as he stomped into the police station. At this time of the night it was deserted. A lone woman sat at the front desk, a romance paperback trapped between her fingers. On the cover, a shirtless man and a scantily clad damsel embraced. The golden name plate facing out read Angela Schmidt.

Angela looked up, startled, just as Will thundered up to the desk. He looked past her, into the depths of the station, but the hallway behind her was dark and unoccupied.

'I need to see Caleb Brewster. Now,' Will demanded. He gripped the edge of the counter to keep himself steady. He wanted to rip the desk from the floor and drag Caleb out of his cell by the back of his shirt. How in the hell had he gotten mixed up in this?

'It's midnight. I'm sorry, sir, but you'll need to come back during—'

'I don't need to do anything but see that boy! He's just a kid!'

Will heard the thunder of boots on tile get closer. As Jesse rounded the corner, Will used every muscle in his body to restrain himself from lunging towards him.

Jesse's eyes were narrowed and serious, his shoulders and chest pronounced. Will knew what that meant.

Don't push me, Jesse warned.

Don't make me have to, Will answered back, gripping the desk impossibly harder.

'Will.' Jesse took measured steps toward him. 'Let's talk.'

Will reminded himself that he was in a police station. The second he put one finger on Jesse he'd be in the cell next to Caleb.

'You arrested him,' Will growled. 'Without even giving me a heads-up? What the hell is wrong with you?'

Jesse exhaled loudly through his nose. He glanced over his shoulder at Angela who was pretending she wasn't listening.

'Ang, you mind getting Mr. Reed here a cup of coffee?'

'The coffee here sucks. Trust me, he doesn't want that. He's already mad enough.' She flipped a page in her book.

Jesse spun on his heel toward her. 'Coffee. Now, please.'

Her eyes brightened when it dawned on her that Jesse was requesting privacy.

'Coffee, riiight. Comin' right up, Detective Shaw.' She took her romance novel with her as she left the two of them to rip each other's heads off in peace.

Jesse watched her go, making sure they were alone.

Will didn't waste any more time laying into him. 'He's just a kid, Jesse! You know what he's been through; what this town has done to him.'

Jesse sighed like it hurt. 'I'm just doing my job.'

'Your job?' Will took a step forward, almost nose to nose with him. He stuck one finger in Jesse's chest, meeting the hardened vest beneath his uniform shirt. 'Your job is to protect people. You know Caleb is not a killer.'

Jesse took one step backward, keeping a safe distance between them. He glanced down the hallway again, before he spoke.

'We've got evidence that he was in the maze at the time of the murder, we found foxglove on his clothing, and his prints are on the knife, man.'

Will felt the air leave his lungs. 'This is bullshit! Come on, you know that!'

'You know I don't want this to be true either,' Jesse snapped. 'But this is my job. Look at the facts, Will.'

Will shook his head in disbelief. 'You're a better cop than this. You ever think that maybe someone wants you to think that?'

Jesse folded his arms. 'The Brewster kid's been hauled in a dozen times. I saw the fingerprint match with my own two eyes.' He threw his hands up, frustrated. 'You're wasting your time with conspiracy theories. I cut corruption out at the root two years ago. We're running an honest ship here and you need to face the truth about the kid you're protecting.'

Will rolled his eyes. All of a sudden Jesse was a supercop that could do no wrong, that missed nothing. Now that he was lead detective, he could protect little old Cinnamon Falls with just a puff of his chest. As always, he wasn't seeing the forest for the trees.

'What about this Max Greaves guy? Morgan told me he turned up just a couple days after Eleanor was murdered, pushing to buy the place.'

Jesse shook his head. 'You must think we're sitting on our asses in here, huh? We've already checked him out. He was at Cinnamon Crest Country Club in Asheville, in the Ember Room in a private poker game Saturday night. It started around 8 p.m. and ended after midnight. There's multiple witnesses *and* surveillance footage. I even had Chambers cross-check the timestamps with the security team there. There's no way it could have been him.'

'Convenient,' Will muttered bitterly. 'You throw a kid in jail because some rich man, who owns half of Asheville, by the way, smiled and said he didn't do it?'

Jesse squared his shoulders to Will, the air of camaraderie between them thin.

'What about the guys Caleb rolls with? They're bad news, bro. He could have been framed! Just let me talk to him.' Will craned his neck over Jesse's shoulder, but couldn't see much of anything down the darkened hall.

Jesse's eyes hardened. 'My hands are tied in this,

man. I told Nia this two years ago, and I'm telling you now. Let the police do our jobs.'

Will stared at him, the betrayal settling in his bones. 'I'm not your nosy-ass girlfriend, alright? I'm asking you to reconsider.'

Jesse looked stricken, his jaw tight with tension. Will had gone a step too far, but he couldn't take it back. 'I'm going to let that slide because you're on one right now.'

Silence crackled between them, tiny fissures in a fragile friendship.

Jesse cleared his throat. 'If you want to help him so badly, get him a lawyer. He's going to need it.' Then, he turned to walk away.

Will's voice rang out before he got too far, 'You better be right about Caleb. Because if you're wrong, you'll lose more than your goddamn badge!'

The dark hallway swallowed Jesse whole.

Chapter 23

Thursday

Will

Will made the drive to Elijah and Renee's house with both hands on the wheel, enraged, until he reached Astoria Glen, a polished and prestigious tree-lined town tucked into the rolling hills on the outskirts of Asheville.

Even at three in the morning, Will could make out the ivy-covered estates as he cruised through the neighborhood at a moderate pace. The streets were clear, all cars sequestered behind tall, ornate gates that stretched toward the sky. The residents fast asleep in their four-poster beds, didn't have a care in the world.

He couldn't lie and say that he hadn't wished for a life like this at one point with Tanya. But those dreams died the minute she decided that her comfort was worth more than her daughter's life.

Will scanned his visitor's badge at Elijah's gate. The scan pad turned green and the gates swooped open, welcoming him in. The plan had been to pick Angel up early in the morning, but with the night he'd had, he needed to crash someplace outside of Cinnamon Falls. When he'd arrived back home from the police station, his bungalow felt too empty, too quiet without his daughter. Only his racing thoughts had filled the silence.

Elijah's house was the opposite; a flurry of timed activity. Outside, the built-in sprinklers showered the vibrant green grass with filtered water. Frogs croaked, belting out their nightly song.

When Will hopped out of his coupe he heard the faint tinkle of cascading water. Peeking over the fence around the side of the house he saw the family's pool glow, washing the three-level home in a neon glow. A vacuum scooted its way around the sparkling turquoise beauty.

Across from the pool sat a one-level house: Will's domain for the rest of the evening. He reached one hand over and unlatched the gate, ready to feel the pillow-top mattress against his tired body. Closing the gate behind him, Will crossed the yard toward the pool house. Motion sensor lights illuminated his path.

Once he turned the doorknob, he knew sleep would come much later. His brother was seated on the expansive tan couch, one hand on the remote, the other clutching a cigar burned down to the size of a thumb. His red eyes swung over to Will in a sleepy haze.

'S'late,' Elijah muttered, stubbing the cigar out in

a waiting ashtray, his words slurred. 'Wasn't expecting you until tomorrow.' He waved the smoke around.

Will kicked off his shoes at the door and stripped off his jacket, necessary for the cool spring night.

'Shitty night,' Will replied sleepily, folding himself into the recliner nearest the door. On the screen, Elijah was watching sports highlights that featured reruns of the week's biggest plays. He turned the volume down.

'That bad? We heard all about *Miss Morgan* at dinner.' Elijah chuckled, mimicking Angel's voice. 'Tell me about it.'

Will scrubbed his hands over his face, more tired now than he had been before. The last thing he wanted to do was talk about Morgan Taylor, especially to Mr. Perfect Wife himself.

'Nothin' to tell,' he replied, tight-lipped.

Elijah rolled his eyes and sat forward on the couch, his elbows resting on his knees. 'I'm your brother, man. Talk to me. For real, how'd it go?'

'Eli, it's almost three in the morning. I just want to go to bed.'

He pressed anyway. 'What, she rejected you?' He released a patronizing laugh that made Will's blood pressure rise. 'It's not 'cause you're ugly.' Elijah pretended he had a mirror in front of him and stroked his perfectly lined shape-up and goatee. 'You get your good looks from me.' His brother looked over when Will didn't join him in laughter.

'What's up? It can't just be the date that's bothering you. Be real with me, for once.'

'For once,' Will repeated, shaking his head. The man with the manufactured life was asking him to be *real*, how ironic.

'Yeah, for once,' Elijah shot back. 'You didn't drive all the way out here to pick up Angel. You couldn't have expected us to wake her up at this time of the night. So, you planned on sleeping here, right? What, you'd sneak into my pool house and sleep it off till morning? Keep it real with me, you been drinking again?'

'Fuck you, Eli.' Will surprised himself with how effortless the insult had leapt out of his mouth. Judging by the look on his brother's face, he was shocked, too.

'Fuck me?' he scoffed. 'Who was there for you, huh? When you fell off the wagon after Tanya. She was the easy scapegoat, the one the whole family pointed our finger at. But who took in Angel? Cleaned you up, called in favors and put you through that apprenticeship so you could cut hair. So you could—'

'Thank you, almighty one. You'll never let me live it down,' Will sighed, giving a mock bow.

'I'm not trying to throw it in your face. I'm trying to show you I'm on your side but you're too damn stubborn to let anyone in.'

'So you can talk shit about me to your doctor buddies? Your perfect wife?' Will asked, heat creeping over him in a slow roll. Will spread his arms wide. 'Introducing my brother, the family fuck-up.'

Elijah frowned, confused. 'You think I talk about you behind your back? If anything, I catch so much heat from Renee about *defending* you. I don't let anyone, not even my "perfect wife" talk about my family. Not one person in that house would dare to bring you up in a negative light around me. You know how much you and Pop mean to me. I don't play that, Will.' He paused, mulling over his next sentence. 'The only person who could ever disrespect me without getting seriously hurt, is you.'

Will felt like he was an eight-year-old again, ashamed that he had to call his big brother out to defend him against a group of older boys. Elijah was primed to play football and his stature alone – broad chest and strong shoulders – was intimidating enough that he didn't have to fight. Will, on the other hand, had always been the slimmer of the two, and was used to solving his problems with his fists. His anger had gotten him in trouble more times than he could count. It was doing the same thing now, pushing people away that meant the most to him.

'I'm sorry,' Will murmured.

Silence stretched between them. Elijah flicked his lighter, the flame brightened the room, then plunged the brothers into darkness once it extinguished. The end of his cigar glowed while he took another long drag.

'I'm sorry, too,' he stated around a plume of smoke. 'I got about two hours before Renee gets up and it turns into the same ol' rinse and repeat. This right here is my only reprieve.'

'I thought you quit smoking?' Will asked.

'I did,' he responded, taking another long inhale. That was Will's cue to leave it alone.

'I had to leave in the middle of the date,' Will started. 'Got a phone call from the jail. One of my gardening kids, Caleb, was arrested.'

'You left her at the restaurant?'

'I wasn't thinking,' Will said, wishing he could redo the moment. It was true what people said about hindsight. He should have taken Morgan with him, or at the very least, ignored the phone call. There was nothing Will could have done for Caleb until the morning. 'I was pissed that Jesse would arrest him without giving me a heads-up. I didn't want Morgan to see me angry like that.'

'So you thought you'd walk out on her instead?'

Will laced his hands behind his head. 'It's . . . more complicated than that.'

'I hope you know that your chances with Miss Morgan are blown. If I were her, I'd never speak to you again. In fact, the moment I saw your back leaving the restaurant, I would have blocked your number.'

'Thanks for the vote of confidence,' Will grumbled.

'What'd your cop friend say about Caleb? Is he guilty?' Elijah asked.

'Said they found traces of foxglove at his home and evidence that put him in the maze at the time of Eleanor's murder.'

Elijah chuckled, slow and easy. 'Please. Get him a good lawyer and those charges are out the window. He's in your gardening club, of course there'll be traces of foxglove. Pop grows it as a pollinator if I remember correctly. You invited the guys to the Jubilee, right? You're tellin' me a bunch of kids weren't running in and out of that maze all day? They've got nothin',' Elijah assured him.

Will waited for the gut punch. 'His prints are on the knife.'

Elijah let out a low whistle. He paused, considering. 'I know a good attorney who does some pro-bono work here and there. I'll send him your contact information. No promises, but he's gotten real criminals outta some tight jams. A little small-town murder should be a walk in the park for him.'

It was a longshot but Will would take all the help he could get right now. For the first time in hours, Will smiled. 'Thanks, Eli. He's a good kid. I just know he couldn't have done it.'

'Shoulda called me first before walkin' out on that woman. Renee looked up her Instagram. I had to act like I wasn't looking! You sure she's into *you*?'

Will wished. 'Not anymore.'

'Get some sleep, little brother. Call your girl in the morning, see what you can work out.' Elijah crossed the room and brought his hand down on Will's shoulder. He stopped short at the door. 'If I were you, I'd beg. I'm talkin' 90s R&B style. You got a leather outfit?'

At 7 a.m. Will was back on the road with Angel fast asleep in the backseat. He was dead last in the drop-off line, but Ms. Shanice made sure Angel got inside before the first bell at eight.

Will wanted to make a pitstop to The Daffodil Inn before heading to work, but his Thursday client, Miss Martin, was not one to tolerate tardiness. Besides, Morgan hadn't answered any of his phone calls on the drive back into town. Her phone was going straight to its voicemail. As much as he needed to make things right, the money came first.

Ms. Lorraine Martin, an eighty-one-year-old fire-cracker, lived two streets over from the Daffodil Inn. She insisted on coming in every week to taper down the sides of her gray mohawk after she got a wash and style from Ethel Lawson over at CinnaCutz. Will arrived at Bones' Barbershop just as Lorraine pulled up in her midnight blue '65 Cadillac Calais.

'Mornin', sugar,' Lorraine called out, swinging her door open with a dramatic flair. Today, she sported a multi-colored kaftan that cinched at the waist.

'Morning, Ms. Lorraine,' Will answered, unlocking the shop's door. 'Got your favorite seat ready.'

Lorraine was already perched in the chair by the time he flipped on the lights, sipping a frosted can of ginger ale like she owned the place.

'You're late,' she accused, pointing at him with a manicured finger.

Will grinned. 'A whole two minutes. Don't make me tell Bones you've been sneaking his sodas out the fridge.'

Lorraine clutched her imaginary pearls. 'Lies and slander!'

They bantered as Will worked, lining up the edges, careful not to disturb the curls of her mohawk with practiced ease. Harold Bones shuffled inside with his usual copy of The Cinnamon Chronicle and a half-eaten cinnamon roll.

'What's the word?' he announced, plopping onto the couch near the door.

Will tipped Lorraine's head so he could hit an angle just right.

Lorraine yapped, 'I was talkin' about how they picked up that Caleb Brewster boy last night.'

Will pretended he didn't know. Bones was the neighborhood gossip. Will wanted to hear what he knew first before he offered his two cents.

'Caleb was arrested?' Will faked concern.

'Mhmm,' Bones confirmed, rubbing one knee in a slow circle. 'Late last night, I heard. Dragged him out of his house right in front of his momma. Surprised Jesse didn't call you and let you know they were holding him.'

Will bit his tongue so hard he tasted blood in his mouth. Bones wasn't the only one who was surprised by his so-called friend.

'Nah. This is my first time hearing it,' he lied.

Bones leveled him with a look but didn't mention any further.

'Something ain't right,' Lorraine piped up. 'That night after the Jubilee, I saw somebody sneakin' around behind my house, walkin' fast like they didn't want to be seen. When I yelled, they booked it down the street. It wasn't Caleb, 'cause he knows better than to play around like that.'

Will raised a brow. 'You tell Jesse?'

She snorted. 'I told the other one, the stick figure lookin' one. That boy don't listen, thinks I'm just some nosy old lady.'

'You *are* a nosy old lady,' Bones said without looking up from his paper.

'And proud of it!' Lorraine shot back. 'Nosy people keep towns like this from fallin' apart.'

Will added in, 'I don't like the way things are movin' around here. Wesley told my dad he's thinkin' of selling the Daffodil Inn to Max Greaves.'

Bones looked up now, his attention fully snagged. 'Greaves tried buying half of this town after Lyons got caught up. I heard he practically owns all of

Asheville now; spends all of his time down at that casino.'

'Wants to make it some kind of luxury wellness retreat,' Will confirmed.

Lorraine shook her head in disgust. 'He called me last year offering me pennies for my house, too. I told him to kiss my entire—'

'Lorraine,' Bones warned. 'I thought your New Year's resolution was to stop cursing so much? You stood up in front of the whole congregation and said so.'

'I did stop, in January! I'm just saying, Bones, nobody is runnin' me off my land for some rich people spa. When I didn't hear from him again I thought it was a done deal.'

Bones shook his head. 'Goes to show you how much he thinks about us. The Inn can't be touched anyway, it's historical land just like Barkwood Bridge and Old Man Milton's farm. Lyons issued a decree years ago during the centennial Fall Festival. I remember it like it was yesterday. It was to keep our place protected; to stop greedy companies like Northbridge from putting a casino on Main Street like over in Asheville.'

'Say what you want about Lyons, but he cherished Cinnamon Falls. Can't say the same for that new guy, Tate. I haven't seen him since he started,' Lorraine chimed in with a disapproving grunt.

'If that's true then maybe the paperwork conveniently

got lost in all the mess with the mayor last year because Greaves wants it, bad,' Will stated.

'No, sir,' Bones replied. 'Ronald Hartley and Eleanor Langford made sure the historical society archived everything in the library; paid for it out of their own pockets. Hard copies with detailed logs. You can't change history.'

Will rubbed the back of his neck, his mind spinning. That name; he'd seen it over the door at the library, and Angel had mentioned him at the Toasted Pecan. She and Eleanor went to the big white building. There was only one big white building in all of Cinnamon Falls: Town Hall.

'That'd be enough to stop Max then, right? If it's protected—' Will asked. *'She said I could always find her where things are hidden'* – Angel's cryptic phrase had taken on a new meaning. What better place to hide – or preserve – something, than in a library? Maybe Mr. Hartley knew exactly where the historical decree was.

Hartley had been one of the few people to see Eleanor alive last. If she told him something, anything that could help Will figure out what happened to her, he could be one step closer to getting his life back on track.

'It will stop anybody,' Bones guaranteed. 'Can't nobody take that land from the Taylors unless *they* sell it, or Sterling Tate amends that decree.'

Will was in a trance, lost in his own thoughts, so

deep he'd forgotten he was supposed to be cutting hair. He flipped his clippers back on. Lorraine turned around, giving Will a sharp look. 'Before you run off and save the day make sure you finish my hair first.'

Will did as he was told, watching the clock and his clippers at the same time.

Once Lorraine was satisfied with her neck taper, she slapped a wad of bills in Will's hand and moseyed out the door, not before cracking a few more jokes with Bones.

Will wiped down his station hurriedly, checking his phone once more.

'You expect me to believe you didn't know about Caleb?' Bones asked, grabbing a cold soda out of his fridge.

Will hung his head. He couldn't get anything past ol' Bones. 'I knew last night, okay? Caleb called me and I dropped everything to get to the station.'

'What did Jesse say? Why didn't he call you first?'

Will shrugged. 'Beats me. I'm still trying to figure that out myself.'

Bones cracked open the soda, the hiss of the carbonation slicing through the quiet hum of the shop. He took a slow sip, watching Will like he was trying to read every muscle twitch in his face.

'Let me guess,' Bones said, settling deeper into the couch. 'Y'all had words.'

Will huffed a bitter laugh. 'That's one way to put it. He told me to let the police do their job. He's forgetting who stood by him when he was getting that detective spot. We built everything on trust, and now he can't even give me the courtesy of a heads-up? He knows how much I've invested in Caleb.'

'You're hurt,' Bones clarified as if it were that simple. Will was more than hurt, he was disappointed. 'But you and Jesse are like brothers. You fight, you argue, but you show up for each other.'

'Tell that to him,' Will said, tossing the towel in the soiled bin beside him. 'I can't imagine forgiving him right now.'

'Who said anything about forgiveness? You need to make amends though. Y'all both care about the same thing, keeping this town safe. Caleb is going to need all the help he can get from the both of you. Don't let pride cost you a friendship, son.'

Will grabbed his keys and his phone and headed toward the door. 'I'll think about it, Bones.'

'That's all I ask.'

Will stepped out into the soft embrace of a spring morning. Main Street buzzed with the illusion of normal, with fresh paint on shop fronts – soft pastels to reflect the season – and flower baskets of petunias swaying gently from lampposts. Overhead, birds hopped from one structure to the next, chirping all the way. But the weight pressing against Will's chest didn't budge.

Chapter 24

Morgan

Morgan had a headache that spanned the length of her body. Every bone thrummed in a rhythm all its own. But she had more pressing matters to tend to than her own comfort.

Last night was a blur. When she woke up just after 5 a.m. in Cameron's bed, she had to pinch herself just to make sure she wasn't still dreaming.

Cameron had been fast asleep beside her, one hand behind his head, the other draped across his chiseled chest. They hadn't moved all night. He'd been the perfect gentleman, just what she needed after being left at Prime Society. When she'd plugged her phone in to charge, she'd found no apology texts and no missed calls from Will.

It was like nothing had ever gone wrong between them. Cameron had shown up when Will walked away, and for that, she was thankful. Especially for those abs. Will's loss was just that – his. She was worth more than he could ever afford and she wasn't wasting another tear on him.

Morgan gathered her things and crept out of Cameron's bedroom and down the hall to her own. She had an early start to her day and didn't have any time to waste on second guessing.

The Cinnamon Falls Police Station was too quiet on Thursday morning. The usual movement: chatter of radios and banter between officers was noticeably absent. Had Raines given them the day off? What happened to 'doubling the effort'?

She approached the front desk, her bag tucked under one arm and the phone clutched in her hand. The photo had to mean something. She just needed Jesse to see it. She hated that it was Caleb, but Eleanor deserved justice.

Angie looked up from her desk, her eyebrows lifting in surprise. 'Morgan, what are you doing here?'

'I need to speak with Jesse, it's important. I have something he needs to see.'

Angie hesitated, her fingers pausing over the keyboard. She referenced the computer screen in front of her. 'He's not available. Actually, no one is really available right now.'

Morgan frowned. 'It's seven-thirty in the morning, what if I had a real emergency?'

Before Angie could answer, Chambers stepped out of the hallway. He spotted Morgan and let out a sigh, as if her mere presence was an inconvenience.

'What does this one want?' Chambers asked Angie, plopping a stack of files down on the desk.

Angie parroted, 'Says she's gotta talk to Jesse. She has something he needs to see.'

Chambers turned to her full on, doubt oozing out of his pores. He folded his arms. 'Jesse's with me, so anything you need to tell him, you can tell me.'

Morgan shook her head. 'No way.' She turned to Angie. 'Could you tell him to call me when he gets in? It's important.'

'Don't be like that,' Chambers called before Morgan walked away. 'Seriously, what's going on? Something happening at the Inn? We've been monitoring the discourse online. If something has materialized into a real threat, you need to let us know.'

Morgan flipped her phone around, showing him the picture. His eyes scanned the screen but made no recognition. Morgan was hand delivering him the smoking gun and this was how he reacted?

'She's gorgeous, but I'm a happily married man,' Chambers said, looping his thumbs through his belt.

'Look again, doofus,' Morgan spat. She zoomed in on the picture. 'There. That's Caleb Brewster in the maze right before Eleanor was killed.'

'Is this a joke?' Chambers deadpanned, sticking a thumb in Morgan's direction.

Angie's face turned beet red. Morgan's stomach sank. Why did she get the feeling that everyone knew something she didn't?

'You're too late,' Chambers said. 'Caleb Brewster is in holding right now.'

Morgan blinked. 'What?'

'His prints were found on the knife,' he said with a clipped tone. 'The case is solved. We have everything we need.'

Angie butted in. 'Jesse's meeting with the Chief right now, preparing for another press conference. It's over, Morg. Everything should go back to normal for you and your family real soon.'

Morgan's pulse thudded in her ears. Her throat tightened, working to tamp down the jumble of sudden emotion. Did Will know? It wasn't her job to tell him if he didn't. She shoved her phone back in her bag.

'Right,' she murmured. 'Normal.'

She turned on her heel and walked out of the station. Outside, the air felt sharper. In her mind, when this day came, she would rejoice. Her world hadn't gone back to normal, only shifted. Solving Eleanor's murder was no longer priority number one, now it was finding the historical decree.

Morgan dry-swallowed an ibuprofen as she ascended the steps to Town Hall. She hadn't been since her kindergarten class took a trip to meet Cinnamon Falls' newest mayor, Asad Lyons, all those years ago.

Town Hall was postcard worthy. The white colonial building rose three stories high, crowned by a golden domed clock tower. The manicured lawn had just been mowed, filling the air with the sharp, earthy scent of fresh cut grass.

The stately white columns along the front entrance gleamed in the morning sun, casting long shadows across the brick steps where city employees and locals alike, lounged with brown paper bags and flasks of coffee, their voices light with gossip and laughter. Someone had propped open the heavy oak doors, letting a playful breeze drift into the marble-floored lobby. Echoes of conversation bounced off the high ceilings and enormous windows flooded the county building with light.

Inside, the spring cheer faded into the stiff hush of government formality. Morgan ignored the buzzing in her purse. Deep down she hoped it was an apology text from Will, but she didn't have the heart to look, just in case it wasn't. Last night was for mourning, today was for justice.

She adjusted the strap of her purse on her shoulder and marched through the lobby, the hem of her violet skirt fluttering in the breeze from the open door. Taking the elevator to the mayor's office, Morgan reached a set of chrome double doors that gave way to a modern office layout: beige cubicles with rows of dark wooden doors lined the hallway like a maze of secrets. She'd skipped her morning coffee, thinking it would be a quick stop; a simple misunderstanding that could be solved by a brief, but serious, conversation.

As soon as Morgan approached the front desk, where a receptionist sat behind a thick pane of glass, she realized her grave error. She could recognize that permanent scowl anywhere: Ruth Evers.

Ruth's perfectly lacquered nails clacked across her keyboard as she pretended not to notice Morgan standing there. She wore a crisp white blouse with an enormous bow knotted at her neck, and ironically, a lavender pencil skirt. Morgan's eye twitched as she placed her purse down on the ledge next to a lime green lanyard curled around what looked like a key card.

Ruth didn't look up as Morgan said, 'Good morning, I'm here to see Mayor Tate.' Morgan made sure to use her best professional voice just in case Ruth didn't recognize her. But if Morgan were Ruth, she would definitely remember the can of whoop-ass Morgan unleashed on her all those years ago.

'Do you have an appointment?' Ruth switched to thumbing through a container of breath mints with the urgency of a snail on vacation.

'I didn't think I needed one. He's a man of the people and all,' she joked, but quickly sobered after Ruth didn't laugh. 'It's urgent.'

'Well,' Ruth said, finally lifting her gaze, 'unless you're dying or on fire, I'd say it can wait.'

'Seriously? You're not even going to check?'

Ruth tapped one nail on the keyboard. 'Oh, looks like Mayor Tate is in another appointment right now. His next available appointment is November tenth at ten forty-five.'

'Seven *months* from now?' Morgan looked around, making sure she wasn't being watched and lowered her voice. 'You're still mad about middle school?'

'You started that fight, not me!' Ruth shot back, fire in her eyes.

'You were making fun of me, what did you expect—' Morgan pressed her hands to the counter, realizing that rehashing conflicts from yesteryear would not help her right now. She needed Ruth's help. 'Can you please tell him that someone is waiting to speak with him?'

Ruth tilted her head. 'Not without an appointment. His calendar is booked all morning.'

'Fine then.' Morgan crossed her arms. 'I'll wait.'

Ruth's desk phone rang. She shrugged at Morgan before she reached to answer it, hooking it between her neck and shoulder. 'Suit yourself.'

Morgan positioned the lanyard under her purse as she dragged it off the ledge. She turned and found a seat. 'Should be mad at your mother for giving you that New Testament ass name,' she mumbled.

Two hours passed.

Morgan paced.

She'd memorized every flyer on the community bulletin board, one advertising a STEM summer camp for boys with limited spots; another about an art club on Saturdays at the local library. She snapped a picture for Angel then remembered with a pang that her evening with Will had turned half past tragic. She drank two cups of lukewarm coffee from the open coffee bar, and played six games of solitaire on her phone.

Ruth didn't look up once, until the phone rang.

'Mayor Tate's office,' Ruth said in a forced bright voice. 'Oh, hey, Frank.' She deflated. 'Mhm, this is his third time calling this week,' she scoffed. She listened for a beat and then decided. 'Fine, transfer him.'

She pushed her shoulders back as she prepared for the call. 'Mayor Tate's office.' The counterfeit voice returned. 'Yes, Mr. Greaves, this is Ruth, we spoke last week.'

Morgan froze. Her ears perked up faster than Daphne's.

'I've passed your message along to him, sir . . . I understand it's urgent, but the mayor hasn't signed off on the appeal yet . . . No, I can't rush him. It's on his to-do list as I stated the last time you called.' She waited, rolling her eyes. 'As soon as he signs off, you'll be the first to know. Yes, you too, sir.'

Ruth slammed the phone down. She shot out of her chair and leaned over the cubicle wall, talking to someone out of sight.

'You won't believe who just called again!'

'That Greaves guy?' the headless voice replied.

Ruth pinched her nose, jutting her chin in the air, and clamped one hand on her hip. 'He needs the rezoning appeal signed immediately.' Her impression was spot-on, but Morgan wouldn't give Ruth the satisfaction of laughing at one of her jokes.

The two laughed together until Ruth remembered she wasn't alone. Her eyes slid over to Morgan, then back to her coworker.

'Rosie's for lunch?' she asked.

'I thought you'd never ask,' her coworker responded. Ruth spun around and retrieved her purse (also purple) out of her cabinet. 'Wait, I can't find my badge,' they said.

Morgan stiffened, stopping herself from looking at the badge and lanyard lying in her bag. The headless voice rounded the corner and Morgan was surprised to see that it belonged to Sasha Daniels, one of Ms. Pearline's great nieces, and Shawna's sister. She looked past Morgan like she was part of the furniture, which was exactly how Morgan preferred it. Ruth, however, cast Morgan a smug look on the way out.

'The mayor won't be back until after three,' she quipped.

'I'll keep waiting,' Morgan chirped happily like her ass wasn't starting to go numb from sitting in the chair for so long.

'Building closes at five,' Ruth called over her shoulder as she stepped into the waiting elevator.

Morgan waited until the ticker on top of the elevator showed that it was idling on the first floor. She shot out of her seat and crept down the carpeted hall. She passed empty offices stealthily and undeterred. Morgan knew the mayor sat behind the locked double doors at the end of the hall.

One swipe of the badge and the pad glowed green, allowing her to enter into another tiny reception area preceding a set of double doors. A golden nameplate was screwed into the wall: Mayor Sterling Tate.

A set of matching sage green chairs and a small coffee table sat to her left, and another receptionist with an attitude sat to her right. A bespectacled young man with a nondescript haircut looked her up and down with contempt.

'You the new mail girl?' he asked, his lips pursed with disapproval. 'You're late. Mail gets collected at ten on the dot.' He tapped the face of his watch. It was just after ten fifteen.

Morgan nodded quickly, reading his name plate: Benjamin Crowder.

Benjamin rolled his eyes. 'Ruth is always letting y'all back here without an escort,' he huffed. 'I'm taking it all the way to Hartley this time.' He held his hand out, gesturing for the badge. Morgan handed him the lanyard dangling from her fingers. 'Can't wait to see her weasel her way out of this,' he said. Morgan was pleased to know that Ruth still had her fair share of enemies.

'Outbox is in the blue bin.' He pointed over his shoulder toward the double doors. 'The top folder goes to Records, make sure Deb gets that pushed through *before* her lunch. The rest can get sorted as normal.'

'Got it,' Morgan replied like he wasn't speaking a foreign language.

'Well, what are you waiting for? Go in.' Benjamin shooed her away in the direction of Mayor Tate's office. Morgan plastered on a smile and pushed through the double doors.

Mayor Tate's office stretched wider than any office had the right to; mahogany furniture basked in morning sunlight that spilled in through a row of arched windows lining the far walls. The ceilings soared, crisscrossed with dark wood beams that gave the space an old Southern charm. The walls were painted a soft ivory, the kind of neutral that looked expensive and calming. Crown molding adorned every edge, framing the room, and an antique bronze chandelier hung overhead.

The mayor's desk sat like a throne at the end of a wide, woven rug. The massive, dark desk had papers stacked neatly in labeled trays. Morgan identified the blue outbox just where Benjamin said it would be, a manila folder inside, waiting. A ceramic coffee mug emblazoned with the town's crest sat beside a crystal pen holder in the shape of a leaf. Behind the desk stood a high-backed leather chair, turned slightly as if the mayor had just stepped away.

Morgan scanned the room quickly, knowing that Ben probably had her on a timer on the other side of the door. A large display case on the right held plaques, proclamations, and framed black-and-white photos of every mayor since 1919. A tall filing cabinet stood flush against the wall beside it, its top drawer slightly ajar. Her heart pounded.

Morgan stepped closer, eyes scanning the neatly labeled folders inside. There was only one folder left open: ZONING – ACTIVE REQUESTS. She pitched forward slightly to see inside. It was empty.

She spun around to the desk and picked up the folder in the blue bin, scanning the top sheet.

Rezoning Request: Maximillian Greaves
Date Submitted: January 1, 2024
Location: The Daffodil Inn, Parcel 4089
Request: Rezone flower fields as preserved land; All remaining structures rezoned for luxury commercial development (Cinnamon Waters Wellness Spa & Retreat)
Previous Action: Denied by Ronald Hartley, Planning Commissioner; citing historical decree

#218; February 28, 2024

Override: Approved via Rezoning Amendment #63-4A, Mayor Asad Lyons, presiding; August 9, 2024

Override: Denied; See community testimony, Appendix B, Mayor Sterling Tate, presiding, April 3, 2025

Appeal: Request submitted; Maximillian Greaves April 6, 2025

Status: Pending; see attachments

Morgan's mouth went dry. Max had been trying to get a hold of the Daffodil Inn for two years! The latest, just two days before the Daffodil Jubilee . . . just before Eleanor had died.

Had her parents known about it all that time? She flipped through the papers, forward and backward, snapping photos of all the documents; her eyes scanned a bunch of construction mumbo-jumbo that she couldn't make sense of, but there was no historical decree.

She stared at the mayor's signature line on the first page, still unsigned. He hadn't made it official yet, which meant Morgan still had some time. She gathered all of the files in the blue bin just as she heard Ben's footfalls approaching.

'Found them!' Morgan reported brightly, just as he swung the door open, eyes blazing. She sped past Benjamin and back out into the vestibule.

'What'd you say your name was again?' he asked, his eyes narrowed suspiciously. He held a phone to his ear.

'Thanks again, Ben!' Morgan called as she booked it down the hallway and past Ruth's desk.

'Hey, wait!' She heard Ben's voice behind her, closing in, but Morgan didn't stop, not even when the elevator opened invitingly, giving her a clean getaway. She opted for the stairs instead.

Barreling down the steps, her heels echoing against the concrete until she reached the ground floor. She slipped out of the side door opening to the expansive grass field. She didn't stop running until she was a good way down Main Street, then she chucked Max Greaves' rezoning request in the trash.

Chapter 25

Will

Will parked his coupe beneath a row of oak trees outside Town Hall and shrugged off his jacket. The dewy morning chill had since burned off, the sun climbing into the sky with slow reverence. The air was soft and sweet, carrying the fragrance of freshly mown grass. A gentle breeze stirred the budding branches overhead, scattering shadows across the walk. Another gorgeous day in Cinnamon Falls, the kind that made the whole town feel alive.

He paused for a moment, leaning against the car door, scanning the quiet street. He finally understood why people stayed here; why they built simple lives that didn't need skyscrapers, digitization or endless hustle. Once, he thought Cinnamon Falls was just a postcard town. The kind of place people passed through on the way to somewhere better.

It was a place people visited like a museum that housed a preserved relic. He'd driven through a dozen times as a kid, seen Barkwood Bridge from the car window, admired the river bend, and then forgotten about it by the time he hit the next gas station. He never gave it a second thought that someone could *live* here.

But then Tanya's accident happened. And Macon felt like a slow collapse. His father was stretching to keep Reed & Roots afloat and proposed the idea of opening a new location near the river. Will volunteered to help out. He'd needed a fresh start.

Three years later, Cinnamon Falls had quietly become something more than a pit stop. It'd given him a second chance. A steady job. It nurtured a daughter who made his life matter. Friends. Even a spark of something new with Morgan.

This town, with its nosy neighbors and slow mornings and annoying festivals; it was his now. It'd crept in while he wasn't looking and made itself a home in his bones.

And he couldn't let anyone, especially not Max Greaves, threaten that.

He climbed the stone steps slowly and pulled open the heavy wooden doors. He made his way to the directory just before the front desk, scanning the names listed until he found it: **Ronald Hartley: Planning Commissioner, 203**

Second floor.

A bang sliced through the quiet lobby. Gasps rippled as workers turned just in time to hear the side door slam shut. Hurried footsteps approached and Will leapt out of the way just as the stairwell door banged open. A red-faced young man in a sweater vest doubled over, bracing his hands on his knees, taking deep breaths. He pointed a shaky finger toward the door.

'Did anyone . . . see . . . a woman come this way?'

'Ben, what's going on? Sit down.' The receptionist guided the panting man to an open seat. She fed him slow sips of water.

'The mail girl,' Ben croaked out. 'She—' His chest heaved. 'Where's the mail girl?' he demanded.

'What mail girl?' the receptionist implored.

'She had on all purple!' Ben shouted.

Will's skin flamed.

The receptionist looked confused. 'Her name is Ruth Evers, Ben. How many times has Hartley told you, you need to learn their names. She's your admin, not your mail girl. You really need to get that together—'

Frustrated, Ben groaned and shot to his feet. He punched the button for the elevator and it opened to let him inside. 'If you see her again, call security,' he spat just before the steel doors shut.

Relieved, Will opted for the stairs. If he ever got the chance to talk to Morgan again, he couldn't wait to tell her that her middle school enemy was now sporting her favorite color, too. Will had been right. She was jealous.

He jogged the flight with ease and found the second floor even quieter than the lobby. He stepped out to the carpeted office suite; hallways of closed doors stared ahead. Will followed the signs until he found the 200 suite. He knocked on the glass-paneled office door, his jaw tight. He didn't know what he was chasing exactly, just that it had Eleanor's reputation at the end of it.

'Come in,' came a voice.

The man behind the desk was wiry and silver-haired, glasses perched low on his nose. His gray suit hung off his shoulders in a tired fashion. He looked up from a stack of paperwork and blinked, startled but not unkind. He pulled the glasses from his nose, resting them on the stack of papers in front of him.

'Can I help you?'

'I'm William Reed. My father is the owner of Reed & Roots and—'

'Business permitting is on the other side of the hallway. Make a left when you leave my office. Charles' office is the last door on the right.'

Will explained, 'Sir, I—'

'Listen, son. Can't you see I've got a shit ton of work to do? Waste someone else's time, will ya?'

'I'm here about Eleanor Langford.' Will straightened, his heart knocking against his ribs.

Hartley's jaw tensed, the crease between his pinched brows softening. He motioned for Will to shut his door, and Will took the seat across from him. Will leveled eyes with the photograph of a younger Ronald, holding his daughter's tiny hand at an amusement park. A six-foot rat in a costume held up a thumb with an animated smile.

Hartley extended his hand. 'Ronald Hartley, everybody calls me Ron. Sorry for the misunderstanding, I've been swamped here lately. As you can tell.' He sputtered out an awkward chuckle. 'What about Eleanor? I was so sorry to hear that she'd passed.'

Will decided that he was going to cut to the chase. He had a whole speech planned for Mr. Hartley about his relationship to Eleanor, in the hopes that he'd share what he knew with a practical stranger. But judging from his inbox, he didn't look like a man who had a lot of time to be bothered.

'Eleanor was a very special person to my daughter. She's heartbroken over the loss. Father to father, I'm here to find out what happened to her.'

Hartley leaned forward, blowing air through his teeth. 'I wish I knew.' He threw his hands up.

'You met my daughter, Angel.' Will flipped out his phone and showed Hartley his lock screen, Angel in her Halloween costume last year dressed as an angel, clip-on wings sprouting out of her dress and a halo headband.

Recognition glowed in Hartley's eyes. 'Yes, and what a delight she was! You have a very clever young woman there, Mr. Reed.'

That wasn't the first time he'd heard that about

his daughter. Angel made friends everywhere she went. She got her extrovert personality from her mother.

'Thank you, sir. She's the light of my life, and right now, she's not doing well. I believe you were one of the last people to see Eleanor alive. I need to know what she was up to.'

Hartley nodded, considering. 'She came by to tell me that Vanessa Taylor was on the brink of losing the Daffodil Inn to Max Greaves. He'd been calling, harassing, for upward of two years.' Hartley pulled open a drawer next to him and revealed a thin manilla folder. 'Two weeks ago, Eleanor had spoken to the mayor, on record. Right after that, Tate denied Greaves' request for rezoning and he put in another appeal immediately after. He's like a dog with a bone.'

Will stared at the file, unmoving. 'She gave me the transcript,' Hartley said, handing it over to Will. 'We were hoping it was enough to stop Greaves from taking the Inn.'

Will read:

[TATE]: Speak your name and today's date for the record, please.

[LANGFORD]: Eleanor Caroline Langford. Today is Friday, April 4, 2025.

[TATE]: What is it that you would like to tell me, Mrs. Langford?

[LANGFORD]: First of all, I don't know what you heard about me, but . . . well, I know I'm not

the most beloved person in Cinnamon Falls. I'm
nothing like Rosslyn Rose, I don't make no
qualms about that. I don't bake pies for fundraisers, and I don't wave at people in the
grocery store. I've never pretended to be something I'm not. But I love this town just as much
as the next person. My husband, Thomas, and I
moved here after he retired from the Navy. He
kept his promise to me. That we'd move someplace safe together and raise a family. We
bought that little house by the river with the wild
garden . . . that garden kept him alive longer
than the doctors said he had. We'd already lost
baby Bella decades before, barely survived that.
When I lost him, I lost the house . . . the only
thing that made me stay here was the Daffodil
Inn. The land, that place . . . it's more than a
property, sir. It's part of the fabric of this town.
Vanessa told me that Greaves is hounding her
for it. Probably offerin' a real pretty penny, too.
Now, I know he made promises to Mayor
Lyons, probably the same ones he made to
you. But he was crooked, that Lyons. He could
be bought; took campaign donations through
Greaves' companies; shell corporations is what
they call them, learned that down at the library.
Got my name on the door and everything —
You ever been to the Archives? You're lookin' at
me like I'm crazy but I can prove it—

[TATE]: I'm not saying anything, just listening.

[LANGFORD]: Well, listen good. I don't want
nothin' special from you, Mr. Tate. Not even
recognition or to shake my hand. I just want
the place that my husband loved to stay whole.
I'm asking you, as a concerned citizen and all,
please don't sell it to a man who'll gut it for
profit.

[TATE]: I certainly will take everything you said
into consideration, Mrs. Langford. Thank you
for stopping by.

[END OF TRANSCRIPT]

Will looked up at Hartley and swallowed the lump in his throat.

'She brought me two names of shell companies that supposedly donated to Mayor Lyons; ones she suspected were tied to Max Greaves. We did some digging, but couldn't find anything. She said she had more, but . . . she never got the chance to bring it in.'

'Because she was killed,' Will murmured, his voice low.

'Tate is stalling Greaves' amendment request. Said he wanted to do things by the book going forward. But I don't think that sat well with Max.'

Will sat back in the seat. The room felt smaller somehow. Heavier.

Eleanor Langford had been painted as a bitter old

woman by nearly everyone in town. But here she was, trying to save the very people who shunned her.

Hartley leaned back, rubbing his temples. 'I should've gone to the police—'

Will shrugged, remembering. 'It wouldn't have done any good. Max's got an airtight alibi the night Eleanor was murdered. It couldn't have been him. We need all the facts if we're going to nail him.'

'It should have never gotten this far. I denied Max's request years ago. The Inn sits on historical land. The decree expressly forbids it. We made sure to archive all of that information in case something like this ever happened.'

That reminded him, Will had one last stop to make. If he could get his hands on the decree, he could stop Max Greaves once and for all. Eleanor's death wouldn't be in vain.

'Thank you for your time, Mr. Hartley.'

He stepped into the hallway, softly closing Hartley's door behind him. He exited Town Hall the same way he came and walked the short distance to the library, his chest full of sharp things: anger, guilt, and most of all, hope.

Chapter 26

Morgan

Morgan threw open the door to The Cinnamon Scoop, the little brass bell overhead ringing with such force that both Nia and Niles jumped behind the counter. Midnight, who'd been fast asleep in the window, hissed at the sudden commotion. She paced in a slow circle and curled into a cozy ball, her yellow eyes flashing annoyance in Morgan's direction.

'Someone's had a day,' Niles commented, pausing mid-scoop of mint chocolate chip. 'You good, Morg?'

'I just committed a minor crime,' Morgan blurted, breathlessly. She rushed to the counter, planting her hands down, thankful that the ground underneath her was no longer moving.

'Without me?' Nia cried.

At the same time Niles said, 'Define "minor".'

'I broke into Mayor Tate's office,' Morgan admitted. 'I need a double scoop of cinnamon swirl, stat.'

'Morgan!' Nia dropped the scoop she'd been

holding. It clattered into the empty metal tin with a hollow clang. Niles scrambled behind the counter and started Morgan's order, enthralled by the gossip.

'How'd you get past Ben?' he asked.

'I had a badge.' She shrugged, brushing past the minor felonious detail like she hadn't stolen it first. She pulled out her phone and showed Nia the pictures. 'The point is, I found Max's rezoning request. He's been trying to get the Inn for a while.'

Nia crossed her arms over her chest, disapprovingly, her eyes scanning the pages, Niles perched over her shoulder.

'There's no signature,' she pointed out. She shrugged her brother off her back, taking the phone in her hands. 'You think Mayor Tate plans to honor Lyons' override and push the thing through?'

'Well, he won't have the chance to,' Morgan mumbled, heat pulsing in her face. Niles slid a double scoop of cinnamon swirl toward her and handed her a spoon. Morgan pushed the ice cream into her mouth hungrily. 'I got rid of it.'

'Did you two *like* jail?' Niles asked earnestly. 'I've never seen two people more hellbent on spending the rest of their days behind bars. It's mind-blowing.'

They ignored him. 'Where's this historical decree?' Nia handed Morgan her phone back.

'That's the problem.' Morgan's heart sank. 'There was no decree in the file, nothing that said the Inn or the land is protected, which makes no sense.'

'Hold on,' Niles said. He grabbed his bag from behind the counter and pulled out his laptop. He powered it up, pulling one lip into his mouth, concentrating. 'Let me check the internal database. If there's anything active on the property, it should've been digitized by now.' He typed furiously, his fingers flying across the keypad.

'How would you know?' Morgan asked.

'I'm the digitizer at the County Clerk's office, remember?' Niles flashed Morgan his badge. 'My office is in Town Hall. Next time you need to break in, just let me know. No stealth needed.' Morgan filed away that tidbit of information – too little, too late.

Niles' expression darkened. 'It's restricted. Everything tied to Mayor Lyons' office is sealed, probably for his upcoming trial. Even my login doesn't have clearance anymore.'

Morgan groaned, leaning against the counter. 'So, there's nothing? No backup files, no proof?'

'There is one place you can try,' Niles said slowly. 'The library's archives room. Every document gets a physical duplicate; zoning records, proclamations, everything. They've got files dating back to the fifties.'

'Worth a shot.' Morgan shrugged, already moving toward the door.

Nia threw off her apron. 'Hold on, I'm coming too. There's no way you're breaking into another place without me.'

Morgan rifled through her wallet and found what

she was looking for. 'No need for a break in.' She flashed her library card.

'You delinquents better not leave there in handcuffs!' Niles called after them.

'Shut up!' they yelled back in perfect unison.

The Cinnamon Falls library hadn't been open long by the time Morgan and Nia hurried up the stone steps. They passed by baskets of pastel-colored tulips and butter yellow pansies that lined the walkway and pushed through the wide doors.

'Archives are in the back.' Morgan pointed, leading the way. She spent at least one day a week here, exchanging books and finding new ones to read during storytime with her kids. All the librarians knew her by name.

She and Nia passed the children's section, where a group of toddlers giggled through a puppet show; Aisha, the head librarian, gave them a quick wave as she straightened shelves.

Morgan slowed as they approached the Archives room. Her steps completely halted when her eyes locked onto the familiar silhouette bent over the desk, signing in.

Will.

Morgan's breath hitched in her throat. There he was in a soft gray shirt, sleeves pushed to his elbows.

She froze; her stomach twisted, not out of anger, but out of that awful, aching place in her chest that she hadn't been able to name since their date was interrupted.

Nia stepped up beside her, one hand bracing her side. 'You okay?'

'Yeah,' Morgan lied. She wasn't okay, not at all.

Will looked up. Their eyes met and for a long while, neither of them moved.

Chapter 27

Will

Will froze.

Morgan stood in the doorway of the Archives room. Sunlight streaming in from the tiny clouded window above the librarian's desk caught the highlight in her braids, throwing a soft glow across her face.

For a suspended moment, the hum of the lights above dropped away; so did the crick in his neck from sleeping on a hardened couch for three hours, so did the constant ache in his chest that had been there since last night. The pen he'd been holding felt like cement in his hand. His throat worked, but nothing came out of his mouth.

There she was, standing in front of him. But she wasn't alone. Nia stood tall at Morgan's side, one hand shielding her best friend, with a scowl so mean it cut deeper than a blade. It was Morgan's expression that did him in, stoic but vulnerable around the edges, like she was trying not to feel anything but was failing miserably.

Will's feelings were too intense, too scattered for him to express them right now. He straightened, unsure of what to say. 'Sorry' felt too trivial, bland. Apologizing wasn't enough.

'Hey,' he said quietly.

Morgan stepped inside without a reply, her heels planting soft thuds as she closed the gap between them. His heart hammered in his chest. She reached inside her purse for something and pulled out a small rectangle.

His bank card.

She held it out between them like it stunk. He took it and was all too aware that their fingers didn't touch.

'Thanks,' he said, but it felt hollow as it came out his mouth. He didn't care about the card. He cared that she wasn't looking at him like she used to, like he mattered, like she still felt something for him.

Will swallowed hard and finished signing his name, but the air in the room shifted. It was thick now, heavy with unsaid confessions. He couldn't stop himself from stealing glances at her; her face, her hands, the tension in her shoulders.

He wanted to say so many things: *I wasn't thinking. I was stupid.*

I didn't mean to hurt you.

Even Eli's suggestion was an option: *Baby, I'm begging.*

Morgan stepped around him and took an extra pen from the cup on the librarian's desk and signed in. Nia moved beside her, jotting down her name in the three-ring binder, walking around him in a wide circle like he was patient zero.

'Hey, Liz,' Morgan whispered to the librarian who'd given Will the death stare a few days ago. 'We're looking for the original copy of the historical decree for my parents' place.'

Liz looked up from the paperback she was in the middle of, her brow knitted together behind her thick, oval-shaped glasses. She stuck a receipt in the place she'd been reading, and stood, pulling her cardigan around her. 'I have to say, I haven't seen the Archives get this much action in years. A guy was here last week looking for the same thing.'

'What guy?' Morgan and Nia said at the same time.

Liz picked up the binder and flipped a few pages. She ran her finger down the length of the printed page until she found the entry she'd been looking for.

'It was the Friday before the Jubilee. He was pissed I made him sign in. I told him he could sign in or he could leave.' She placed the binder down on the desk and pointed to the name signed in an obnoxious flair, taking up half the page. 'Maximillian Greaves.'

The three visitors gasped at the same time.

She walked from behind the desk and pulled on a pair of white gloves. 'The historical decrees are just that, historical. These pages are decades old. They are not to be tampered with or handled without a trained professional.'

Morgan, Nia and Will followed Librarian Liz into the depths of the room.

'Of course,' Morgan responded. 'But is there a way we could make a copy?'

'A copy?' Liz stopped in her tracks and spun around to the group, bewildered.

'Before you have a conniption,' Morgan started. 'I need proof that the Daffodil Inn sits on protected land.' Morgan gave Liz a weak smile. Will noticed that it didn't reach her eyes.

His fingers itched to touch her, to tuck a runaway braid behind her ear, to hear her tell a joke that would have him doubled over in laughter. But he stayed rooted to the floor.

'Morgan, you know I adore you, but Aisha would have a fit if she found out—'

'She won't!' Morgan showed Liz her palms. 'One quick photo. We won't even take it out of the plastic thingy or whatever.'

Liz pulled a step stool from behind a shelf and climbed up. She leaned on her tiptoes and dragged a thick book off the top shelf, its leather spine worn with age.

'This is the decree index.' She trailed a gloved finger

346

down the tabs until she found the section labeled 'D'. She flipped and flipped with careful hands until she reached the next section, 'E'.

'That's not right,' she mumbled, turning the pages even slower this time.

'What is it?' Will asked. He couldn't take the suspense.

'The page for The Daffodil Inn is missing,' Liz admitted, fear written all over her face.

Not torn. Not dog-eared. Gone. Removed like it hadn't existed at all.

Morgan stared at the empty space, tears welling in her eyes. 'You've got to be kidding me,' she said under her breath.

Nia jumped in. 'Wait, you said these pages couldn't be handled without a trained professional. So, that's not normal, right?'

Will shook his head. 'Unless someone had a reason to make it disappear.'

'Did Max ask about this page in particular?' Nia inquired.

Liz, frozen in fear, looked like her mind was in a different place. 'Not in particular, he asked to see the index. He said he was mostly looking for old zoning maps. We chatted about the Red Fern and he told me he owned the whole strip mall. He was sweet and charming. He . . . you think he *stole* it?'

'It had to be him!' Morgan said, frustration radiating off her in waves.

'I would have seen him,' Liz muttered, her eyes searching the ground. 'There's no way. We were standing right next to each other.'

Nia offered, 'What if he didn't steal it? What if he hid it?'

The thought hit Will like a bolt of lightning. 'Eleanor!' he blurted out.

'What?' Morgan looked at him like he'd sprouted another limb.

Will shook his head, his brain moving faster than the words could form. 'What if Eleanor hid it? Angel told us that Eleanor said she could always find her where things are hidden. At the time, I thought she was just being dramatic but—'

The color returned to Morgan's face. Her eyes lit up like a firework.

'I know where it is.' She stepped back so quickly she bumped into the tall shelves. They swayed upon impact, threatening. Liz rushed to the racks, cradling the shelves in place like her children.

'What are you saying, Morg?' Nia asked, one hand on her friend's shoulder.

She wrestled out of Nia's hold. 'No time. I'll explain later!' Morgan took off, skirting through the tables and chairs until she reached the door, her skirt fluttering in the wind.

Will and Nia barreled after her, but she was gone. Only the echo of her heels and the soft thump of the Archives door closing behind her remained.

Will stared at the empty doorway, his chest swelling, his heart in his hands.

Nia stepped forward, blocking his view. 'We need to talk. Now.'

Rosie's Diner still looked the same. A long counter ran the length of the front, lined with stools. It'd been two years since he'd actually been inside. Most of the time, he used the to-go window Eddie installed for quick orders around the side of the building. Stepping inside again felt like a homecoming.

Will had only met Rosie a few times, but the way Morgan, Nia and Jesse revered her – part matriarch, part myth – he felt like he was part of her family too. Besides, he still hadn't found a cinnamon bun in all of the Falls that was better than Rosie's: soft as a cloud in the middle, caramelized at the edges and slathered with a rich glaze so delicious that it should have been a felony.

The place was half-full, thick with the lunch crowd's conversation crowding the rest of the unoccupied place. Will spotted a back booth tucked beneath the window and slid onto the leather bench. Nia didn't sit right away.

'This was the exact spot I sat in the last time I saw Rosie alive.' Nia turned, staring at the workers behind the counter, unseeing.

'I'm sorry, Nia. We can choose someplace else,' Will replied.

Will expected there to be tears, but Nia spun around with fire in her eyes. 'And this is the perfect place for you to get what's coming to you. Rosie was a big fan of retribution.' She sat across from him like a Mafia boss, arms crossed, all business.

Will groaned, letting his head rest against the back of the booth.

'Go ahead,' Will relented. 'Let me have it.'

She leaned in. 'You've managed to piss off two people I care about most in the world,' she said flatly, resting her elbows on the table. 'My man and my best friend. With both of whom, I don't play about.'

Will winced, taking it all in. He deserved it. 'Comin' in hot, okay.'

She raised one eyebrow. 'I haven't even gotten started.'

A server came by and Nia ordered a medium rare burger with fries with a sweet tea to go. She didn't even look at the menu. Will didn't order anything, suddenly not hungry.

'You stormed into that police station like you were in an action movie. And for what? To embarrass him? You think you know more than an actual trained detective?'

'Nia, that's not—'

'Jesse is just doing his job, Will. You think he wanted to arrest Caleb in the middle of the goddamn night? He was following orders. Then, he has to deal with you going off on him at work when he already feels like shit about it? That was low. And reckless. And stupid. And—'

'Alright! I got it!' Will cut her off. He looked away, jaw tight. 'I know, okay? I just . . . lost it. Caleb called me in tears and I saw red.'

'That doesn't make it right.' Her tone softened. 'And then there's an even bigger issue: Morgan.' Hearing Morgan's name hit him harder than expected. Another wave of shame washed over him. Nia cracked her knuckles and Will braced himself.

'You left her at that dinner table,' Nia said, voice steely and low. 'Do you know how humiliating that is? She liked you, Will. And I mean *really* liked you. I don't think I've seen Morgan that excited about anyone in . . .' She paused, looking up to the ceiling. 'I don't know how long!'

Will wanted to scream but he knew nothing would come out. He let his head drop into his hands. 'I screwed up, Nia,' he admitted.

'Yeah, you did,' Nia replied, giving him a sarcastic look.

'I want to fix it,' he said, quickly looking up. 'I'll make it right with Jesse. But, Morgan . . . I'll do whatever it takes, and I mean that.'

Will had never been one to back down from anything: win, lose or draw. Calvin Reed had taught him that. He was willing to own up to his mistakes;

to look shame in the face and accept his fate, but he couldn't let Morgan go, not like that. He owed her an explanation if she would let him get close to her again.

Nia raised a skeptical brow. 'Morgan is many things, Will. Funny, loyal, brilliant, drop-dead gorgeous.' She listed on her fingers. 'But forgiving? Not in her top five qualities.'

Will pushed his shoulders back. 'I can handle hard things.'

Hell, he'd been knocked out by life, cold, flat on his back and he still got up swinging. This time would be no different.

Nia snorted. 'She still has beef with a girl from the sixth grade who called her . . .' She lowered her voice and glanced around like Morgan would leap out of a corner and suffocate her. ' . . . a certain infamous purple dinosaur. I can't even say his name out loud or—'

'You mean—'

'Don't!' Nia hissed. 'The point is, she doesn't forget, and she damn sure doesn't forgive easily.'

Will leaned forward, resting his arms on the table. 'Then I'll work harder. I'll show up. I'll prove that she means everything to me, because she does. It's not an excuse but I was upset, Nia. I couldn't let her see me that angry. I was . . .'

'Scared she'd see the *real* you?'

Will couldn't deny it. He was scared; scared that

the version of himself that flared up in moments like that – blinded by loyalty, quick to defend, slow to think – would be the version she remembered. She'd mistake his anger for recklessness, for violence, for the same things that made his family treat him like a ticking bomb. He didn't want Morgan to think he was like every other man who chose rage over reason.

'Yeah,' he said finally. 'Scared she'd see a version of me I've worked too damn hard to bury.'

'Then show her the man you are now.'

Will nodded slowly, letting the words sink into him. He wished he could have talked to Nia before he ruined things with Morgan.

'You can't brute force your way out of everything. Love takes time, patience, and compromise. It's a lot like gardening.' Nia studied him for a moment, her eyes roaming, narrowing with the kind of scrutiny only a best friend could wield.

She stuck a pinky out. 'Promise me you won't mess this up again. No running. No losing your temper. No treating her like a backup plan when your world falls apart. She's not a princess, Will. She can handle hard things, too.'

He hooked his pinky in hers and sealed the deal. 'You got my word.'

The server arrived with Nia's food boxed up neatly.

She nodded, satisfied, and patted the plastic bag. 'Thanks for buying my man lunch. You're already starting off on a good foot.' She slid out of the booth and sauntered away.

Will chuckled and couldn't believe how easily he'd gotten played. He flipped out his wallet and in all the chaos he realized he'd left his bank card at the library. He paid for Nia's lunch with the cash from Ms. Lorraine and checked his phone. He still had some time before Angel got out of school. He thanked the server and headed back toward the library.

Elizabeth was still hunched over the wide oak table, her nose buried in a precarious tower of old books. The historical decrees were splayed out before her like puzzle pieces waiting to be reassembled with the visitor's log beside it.

Will spotted his bank card at the reference desk stationed in the front of the room. He slipped it back in his wallet and journeyed deeper into the room next to Elizabeth.

'You're still here,' he said, unsurprised she hadn't moved from that spot.

Elizabeth didn't look up. 'Figured you'd be back for your card. I've been trying to make sense of this mess. Someone knew exactly what to look for.' She tapped the logbook absently. 'No one ever comes to the Archives. I get the occasional visitor during library tours or a tourist wanting to learn about the history of Cinnamon Falls. But I checked the sign-in sheet. Over the last two weeks, only two people have come down here besides you, Nia, and Morgan.'

Will moved closer, curiosity sharpening. 'Who?'

She tapped the page. 'Eleanor Langford and Maximillian Greaves.'

Will turned, bringing his fingers to his mouth, thinking. 'Why would Greaves come to the Archives? He already knew about the decree and his request had gotten approved without it. He couldn't have been concerned about a piece of paper, his campaign donations had it handled.' Will gulped, his brain churning into overdrive. 'Plus, he was seen at the country club the night Eleanor was murdered.'

'I'm telling you, the Greaves guy was here.' Elizabeth's pointer finger stabbed the sign-in log.

There's no way Greaves could have been in two places at once. Will didn't know why he hadn't seen it before. Greaves had to have known that Eleanor was the one who had stopped his approval. If he had killed her himself, the trail would lead straight to him. And if he couldn't get the Daffodil Inn through bribery, he only had one other option, murder. He had to send someone in his place, someone *charming* enough to find more information and backdoor their way into the deal; someone who could get close to Eleanor without being recognized, close enough to kill.

Will growled, curling his hands into fists. 'Cameron.'

Liz looked alarmed, removing her glasses from her face. 'Cameron?' she asked, invested.

Will's jaw clenched, remembering every detail about the man who tried to block him in at the Inn yesterday. 'Tall guy, new in town—'

'Messy brown hair, eyes blue as the ocean.' Liz paled, her voice airy. 'Th-that's Maximillian Greaves.'

Will cursed under his breath, already fumbling for his phone. He jammed his thumb into the screen when it landed on Morgan's number.

'Pick up,' he pleaded.

The phone rang once.

Twice.

Voicemail.

He hung up and tried again, pacing now. Still no answer.

'She's not picking up,' he muttered. Fear snaked around his heart, squeezing.

'You think she's in trouble? He seemed like he wouldn't hurt a fly. He was so—'

'Charming? Yeah, so I've heard.'

Liz started, 'But—'

Will didn't need to hear the rest because he was already out of the door.

Chapter 28

Morgan

Morgan's tires skid over the gravel as she threw her truck in park in front of The Daffodil Inn. She ignored her vibrating cell phone, too focused on the task in front of her. She was almost there. Her heart thundered with every step toward the front entrance. She'd been on pins and needles the whole ride over. She couldn't believe she hadn't thought of it earlier.

She kicked off her heels and bolted up the stairs, not bothering to stop and check if anyone was home. When she reached the top of the steps she turned right and shoved Cameron's door open without knocking.

He was on the phone, lounging at the edge of the bed, his shirt half-unbuttoned exposing his washboard abs. His voice caught in his throat when he saw her, jumping up, covering the mouthpiece with his hand.

'Morgan! What's going on?'

'I know where it is!' she said breathlessly, unknowing

if her lack of oxygen was due to all the running she'd done today, or the sight of Cameron's V-cut abs.

'Where what is?' he asked, catching her staring. Morgan ripped her eyes away from his perfect body and remembered why she'd burst into his room in the first place.

'The decree!' She crossed the room in quick strides toward the old cedar chest. It had always been there, holding Eleanor's secrets, but today it felt like a door waiting to be opened; her parents' ticket to freedom. Morgan's fingers tingled with anticipation.

She pushed Cameron's clothes to one side, revealing the vanity bench. She pulled it down, and in the gap she felt around until her fingers found the latch that housed the cubby hole. She pushed her hand in deeper, bracing her shoulder against the door. She felt around blindly, Cameron hovering over her shoulder, until her fingers brushed what felt like a roll of papers. Morgan strained, her fingers catching hold, and pulled gently. A paper from the stack unfurled and it was the most important one.

There it was. The original decree from the Cinnamon Falls Historical Society. Signed, dated, stamped, and official.

'I knew it,' she breathed, lifting it carefully to the light overhead.

She did it.

She turned to Cameron, happy tears pricking her eyes, gripping her family's saving grace.

'It's real,' she sobbed, clutching the paper to her chest.

It was over, finally.

She heard the silence first.

'Morg, I'm so sorry.' Cameron didn't sound like himself. She turned toward him, confused. It wasn't the tone of his voice that made her stomach drop. It was the look in his eyes.

The mourning nephew was gone. In his place was someone Morgan had never seen before. Cameron's ocean blue eyes were steely and cold, and he was inching closer. Morgan backed up instinctively, collapsing into the vanity, but he was already on top of her, she was trapped.

'Cam—'

A shadow swept over her vision. Morgan opened her mouth to scream but the darkness came first.

Chapter 29

Will

Voicemail.

Will cursed under his breath and lowered the phone back into the cupholder. He tried Morgan's number again, his thumb hovering over it like she might change her mind and answer.

'She doesn't want to talk to you, Mr. Reed. Just accept that,' Caleb mumbled through a mouthful of cheeseburger. 'You're probably blocked.'

Will shot him a glare across the console. 'Man, shut up,' It came out sharper than he intended. What did a jailbird know anyway?

Outside the windows, Cinnamon Falls shimmered under a fading spring sun. Pink dogwood blossoms scattered across sidewalks like nature's confetti. People strolled along Main Street with iced coffees in hand, pausing to wave at shopkeepers. It looked like joy out there; like fresh air and new beginnings.

But inside Will's car was the stale scent of fries, frustration, and silence.

'You better be thankful I have a brother with connections.' Will gripped the wheel tighter. 'Or you'd still be in that holding cell crying to your momma.'

'Too soon, man.' Caleb shook his head solemnly before funneling a handful of fries into his mouth. Grease smeared across the side of his cheek.

In the cramped backseat, Angel looked on, disturbed. 'You're going to choke,' she warned, tsk-ing her tongue at him. 'Slow down.'

'Can't help it,' Caleb said between bites. 'This is the first real food I've had in a day and a half.'

'Looks like years,' Angel commented, crossing her arms over her chest, disgusted.

Will maneuvered his coupe out of the Golden Grille's parking lot and headed toward Caleb's house. After the release, Caleb hadn't asked to see his mother. He didn't even mention his so-called girlfriend, Kelsey. His only request was beef and Will had obliged. The kid had spent the night in a cold cell. He'd earned a burger.

Will's phone vibrated in the cup holder. He clambered to answer, a flash of hope in his heart, but it disappeared just as fast when he saw the caller ID.

Elijah. Will connected the call to his car's Bluetooth.

'I take it everything is all good. I've got Jacob and Rhonda on the other line. You still with Caleb?' Elijah asked, his voice like espresso; smooth, strong and annoyingly confident.

Will didn't answer right away. He slowed at a stop sign, watching a couple jog by with matching water bottles, a golden retriever keeping in time with their steps running between them. Austin Jacobs, Cinnamon Falls' go-to guy for general contracting, lifted his hand in a friendly wave, and jogged on. A woman stepped out of a boutique with a shopping bag tucked under her arm, retail satisfaction lacing her grin. Everything looked picturesque like Will's whole world hadn't spun off its axis.

'Yeah,' Will lied. Everything wasn't all good, not even in the slightest, he wanted to say but he had too many ears around.

Morgan was icing him out. Caleb could be looking at charges he didn't deserve, and Eleanor's killer was still out there. But the silence from Morgan cut the deepest. She could hate him, that was fine, but she needed to know that that Cameron dude was manipulative and potentially dangerous. And where was the decree?

'We're here,' Will said.

'Great,' Jacob said. Jacob Lawson, one half of Lawson & Lawson Law, made a fool of the Cinnamon Falls police department when he showed up, expensive suit and briefcase in tow. He had Caleb out within the hour. Will was sure it cost his brother a pretty penny no matter what pro-bono stories Elijah had told him. An attorney doesn't get a Maserati by doing work for free. He was born at night, but it wasn't last night.

'My apologies I couldn't stick around, but I've got a business dinner to jet to. Miss Rhonda, we didn't get to connect tonight but I'll cut right to the chase, Caleb is on his way to you safe and sound for now, and that's what matters the most.'

Rhonda's voice filtered in, tight with nerves. 'Mr. Lawson, thank you so much for helping us out. My bitch of a boss wouldn't let me off until just now. I was on my way to the station but I guess I'll head home.'

Will pulled onto the highway in the direction of Caleb's house. Caleb sank lower in the passenger seat like his mother was standing next to the window with a disapproving glare.

'I'm okay, Mom,' he managed with a mouth full of fries.

'Mhmm, I'll deal with you when you get home,' Rhonda snapped.

Caleb threw his head back against the headrest. Behind him, Angel snickered in the backseat. Will shot her a warning look in the rear-view mirror. She positioned her headphones back over her ears and returned to her tablet.

'The police told me they found something called foxglove and that his fingerprints were on the knife. I was so worried I wouldn't get to see him again.'

She hiccupped. 'What happened? How does he get to walk out just like that?'

'Rhonda, take a breath, okay?' Jacob's tone softened. A professional blend of practiced calm. 'Your son was in a gardening club, it's very possible that he could have brought traces of foxglove home on his boots from that morning. As far as the knife, fingerprints prove that your son touched the knife at some point that night. They don't prove he killed anyone, and that's the big difference. The police know that, too. Without more concrete evidence, they didn't have a strong enough case to hold him.'

'W-what if they do find something? My family isn't very popular in Cinnamon Falls anymore, I can thank my damn brother for that. What if they drag him back in?'

'They might ask more questions. That's their job. At some point, Caleb may have to testify about what he saw Saturday night. But he's not a flight risk. He's got no violent arrest record. If they want to push this, I'll be with you every step of the way.'

Rhonda exhaled sharply. Will imagined her shoulders dropping from around her ears, finally able to breathe. 'I still don't know how you did it, Mr. Lawson—'

'Call me Jacob, please,' he insisted. 'You've got a good kid who was in the wrong place at the wrong time. The detectives saw that and if we have to, we'll convince a judge and jury of that, too.'

Rhonda let out a laugh that was half relief, half

disbelief. 'He's going to wish he was in the right place once he gets home.'

'We're fifteen minutes out,' Will announced.

With pleading eyes, Caleb groaned and mouthed, 'Drive slower.'

'I can't thank you enough, Jacob, for helping us out,' Rhonda added in. 'I owe so much to you, Will and Elijah.'

'We're all in this together,' Jacob replied warmly. 'You'll be hearing from me soon. For now, take care of yourselves, alright?'

'Thank you, Mr. Lawson and the other Mr. Reed.' Caleb looked up sheepishly and swallowed the last bit of burger.

'No problem, son,' Eli responded, before hanging up.

Will looked across at Caleb who, behind all his humor, looked exhausted. 'Let's get you home.'

Will pulled the coupe up to the curb and killed the engine. Caleb's house sat at the edge of a quiet street. The porchlight flickered, casting long shadows across the generous lawn where a worn basketball sat abandoned in the grass. The front door swung open in anticipation and Rhonda's silhouette made an appearance. Caleb sighed and Will didn't miss the way he hesitated before reaching for the door handle.

Will looked over his shoulder at the backseat. Angel was fast asleep, her unicorn headphones tight around her ears, her tablet on her lap, an episode of *Andrew Guy, P.I.* rolled on without her.

'I know what you're thinkin', Mr. Reed. I don't need some big speech about responsibility and choosing the right friends.' Caleb looked down at his lap and back toward his house. His mother, waiting in the doorway.

He sighed, his shoulders rolling forward. 'Everybody's going to think I killed her.'

'If they thought that, trust me, the police wouldn't have let you walk out of that station. Jacob is going to take care of everything. You just keep your head down and your nose clean until then.'

Will clapped his hand against the back of Caleb's neck like his father used to do to him when he really needed Will to listen and understand him. Will tried not to feel geriatric when he said, 'You got a second chance tonight, make it count.'

Caleb nodded. 'Yeah, I hear you.' He threw his weight against the passenger door and hopped out. Before he got too far, he leaned in and said, 'Thanks again, Mr. Reed. I owe you one.'

'Go be somebody and all your debts have been paid.'

The teenager nodded again, the words seeming to soak into his brain. Will watched him trek across the yard, walk up the steps and go inside. Rhonda threw her arms around her son's neck and Will could only imagine the relief she felt knowing that her son was finally home. She waved at Will before shutting the door with a finality that Will hoped meant change.

Chapter 30

Morgan

The last place Morgan thought she'd ever be was face down on her own hardwood floor, teetering on the brink of unconsciousness.

Who had she wronged to receive such karmic retribution? If she ever got out of this, she was going to go on one of those spiritual journeys to figure out who she was in a past life, because whoever she used to be, was getting her ass handed to her in this lifetime. And this version of Morgan was dancing with death because of her shenanigans.

Morgan's head throbbed like a bass drum against her skull. The taste of copper rested on her tongue. She stirred and her world tilted sideways as a crescendo of pain crashed over her body. Stars popped behind her eyes.

For a moment, she didn't move, keeping as still as possible while her other senses sharpened. Morgan blinked, fighting against the haze of her mind. She forced one eye open at a time, wide enough to see Cameron swim into view. He paced the floor, a phone pressed to his ear.

'Yeah, I got it. She ran straight to it just like you said. Eleanor hid it in an ugly chest in this room up here. It had some kind of hidden latch, but all our problems are solved now.' He chuckled menacingly, lowering his voice. 'That will be taken care of too, after we destroy the decree. I called earlier and Mayor Tate is going to approve the rezoning by tomorrow. It's done.'

Morgan's heart plummeted. Cameron had pretended to be on her side and Morgan had walked right to the very thing he needed to make sure the rezoning went through. She'd been played. Again.

Cameron continued, 'She's still out cold. What should I do with her?'

Morgan held her breath and squeezed her eyes shut. Her heart thrummed in surround sound while she waited to hear her fate.

'Nah, no one's seen me. I fed the pooch the rest of that foxglove you gave us for lunch. They're going to be tied up at the vet for the rest of the night. Yeah, I'll get changed and bring her now. What about the rest of the family?' Another pause, too sinister. 'Copy that.'

The cold barrel of a gun pressed into her back. She whimpered, quickly forgetting that she was supposed to be unconscious.

'I'd keep quiet if I were you,' Cameron whispered. 'Unless you want your daddy's heart to give out before sunrise when he finds out both his business and his baby girl are dead.'

Cameron slipped into a plain black suit. He meticulously folded his belongings into a bag, making sure every speck of his presence at the Inn was gone.

Then she was being yanked off her feet. Her head swam while she gained her balance. Her knees buckled. Unimaginable white-hot pain engulfed her body, black dots clouding her vision. She was losing it, reality folding on its creases.

'Move!' She stumbled out of the room and into the hallway. She clutched onto the railing, her saving grace, or else she would have gone over the side of the landing. She parted her lips to scream, but the cool metal against her spine made her reconsider.

Think, she told herself, but her brain felt like it was in quicksand.

Slowly, she descended the stairs, Cameron tight on her heels, one arm around her waist keeping her upright. When she reached the bottom, she noticed Daphne's leash was gone. There was no light spilling from the kitchen, no conversational laughter from Lionel. She was alone. No one could save her.

Cameron forced her outside, into the night. When she got home earlier, there was light outside. She must have been out a while, she thought, as he dragged her over to his car, and forced her into the back of his sedan. She squeezed her knees to her chest, too terrified to make a move. He climbed into the driver's seat.

'Don't try anything stupid,' he said over his shoulder. The gun rested on the console. 'I'd hate to get blood on the leather.'

The doors locked with a click of certitude and Morgan wondered if this was truly how it ended for her, in the backseat of a mom car. She hated that for herself.

Morgan used all of the strength she had left to push herself up. She watched the Daffodil Inn, her home, her world, shrink from view.

Chapter 31

Will

Somehow, Will managed to cook dinner without burning anything, which was no easy feat considering how distracted he was. He even let Angel watch her favorite show at the dinner table, only pausing to have a quick (heavy emphasis on quick) video call with Tanya. After the customary cherry popsicle and some sketchbook time, he put Angel to bed. Will spent his evening staring at his phone.

Was Morgan even seeing his calls anymore? Was Caleb right, had she blocked him? He couldn't be mad. It was deserved. All he needed was two minutes of her time to explain, and she could hate him for the rest of her life, if she wanted. She wouldn't be the first woman.

Will threw himself back on his couch and used his last resort. He called her mother.

The phone rang twice before Ms. Vanessa picked up. 'Daffodil Inn, Vanessa speaking.'

'Mrs. Taylor, it's Will. I was wondering if Morgan was around? I've been trying to reach her.'

A pause. Then a rustle and an even longer pause. Will pressed the phone to his ear but all he could hear were mumbles he couldn't make out. Was Morgan standing right there, giving her mother instructions to hang up? Was he doing all this worrying for nothing?

'We haven't heard from her. We've been at the vet all night, but I think she left with the young man staying here, Cameron.'

Will shot upright. 'You . . . think?'

'She's not here and his car is gone. They probably grabbed dinner or something, though it's not like her to leave and not text.'

Will glanced at his phone. It was close to 10 p.m.

'Have you tried calling her?'

More rustling. 'Try calling Morgy,' he heard her say.

'She didn't answer,' Wesley reported back. 'What's going on? Who is that?'

'It's Will!' Vanessa snapped. 'He's looking for Morgan.'

Will jumped when he heard Wesley shout through the other end of the phone, 'You tell that low-life sonofa—'

'Wesley!' Vanessa cut him off. Will was thankful for that.

Morgan must have told her parents about their date. He thought he only had Morgan to deal with.

Wesley Taylor, the man of few words, was another beast on his own.

'Listen, I'll find her. Is it okay if I drop Angel off with you?'

'Of course, bring her by.'

Angel slept from door to door until they arrived at the Daffodil Inn.

'If she wakes, she likes *Andrew Guy, P.I.* Right here. That should do the trick.' He tapped on the green streaming app to show Ms. Vanessa, who was too busy fussing over tucking his sleeping daughter in her bed, tablet be damned.

'I'll just be out in the hallway if you need me.' Ms. Vanessa left him with his daughter.

Will had never been in the basement of the Daffodil Inn. Morgan had told him her parents stayed downstairs with the rest of the crew that made the Inn run so smoothly. In his mind, the servant quarters would be twin bunk beds and minimal amenities. But Morgan's parents' domain could easily rival the rooms upstairs.

The bedroom was warm, richly decorated with thick burgundy drapes framing a pair of arched windows that looked out into the back garden. A carved cherrywood headboard anchored the king-sized bed where Angel was laid, curled up, her hair sprawled across the embroidered quilt. In all the fuss he'd forgotten her bonnet. She would not be happy about that in the morning.

A vintage armoire stood against one wall, its polished surface reflecting the glow of an old school glass lamp in the shape of a daffodil on the night-stand. The scent of lavender lingered in the air, calming and nostalgic. It reminded him of his grand-mother's bedroom.

Family photos lined the dresser; Morgan as a little girl in pigtails on the couch in the great room, a Teenage Mutant Ninja Turtles T-shirt hanging off her; Wesley and Vanessa posing on the front porch, smiling for the camera.

Will stood next to the bed a moment longer, watching Angel's chest rise and fall, then leaned down and put his lips to her forehead.

'Daddy loves you,' he whispered. 'More than anything.'

Angel stirred and attempted to roll over but she was tucked too tight. She gave up, returning back to a peaceful sleep. Will knew she was in good hands.

He stepped out into the hallway. He didn't know where Morgan was, but he had to put his pride in his back pocket. He needed Jesse's help.

The argument had been still heavy on his heart. Bones' advice played on a loop in his head. He swallowed hard, his thumb tapping the screen to call before he could talk himself out of it.

'Shaw,' Jesse answered, exasperation already baked

into his voice. It was late. The face of his phone told him it was nearing midnight. Morgan still hadn't shown up.

Will's fingers clenched around the phone. 'It's me,' he started. 'I need your help.'

Jesse sighed. 'What now?'

'It's Morgan. She hasn't come back after leaving the Inn with Cameron. Her parents haven't heard from her. Neither have I. I think something's wrong.'

Jesse went quiet. Will could picture him on the other end, rubbing his temples, his detective brain working overtime.

'When's the last time you talked to Morgan?' Will heard Jesse ask Nia, he assumed.

'Not since lunch time before me and Will went to Rosie's. She was going back to the Inn, I think.'

Jesse was back on the phone. 'You think this Cameron guy has something to do with it?'

'Yeah.' Will nodded. 'I think he's involved with Eleanor's death too, somehow. I don't have proof, just weird coincidences.'

Another pause. 'What's he driving?'

Will looked to Vanessa who was standing beside him, close enough to hear the conversation, worry lining her face.

'A tan Oldsmobile, if you can believe it. I haven't seen one of those since the nineties,' Vanessa commented. 'I have to go get Wesley.' She walked away and up the stairs. Will heard her soft footsteps overhead.

'I'm going to reach out to Raines to put out an alert. I'll have the patrols start to look for the vehicle.'

Will's head dropped forward, relief snaking through his limbs.

'Thanks, man, I—' His throat tightened. 'I didn't know if you'd pick up.'

Jesse was silent for a long beat then said, 'We've both been stubborn.'

'I didn't mean what I said,' Will admitted. 'You're a damn good cop and you've always had my back. I was scared for Caleb and I took it out on you. That's my bad.'

Jesse's voice was softer now. 'You're like a brother to me, Will. I know how much Caleb means to you. You have to know I'd never do anything to jeopardize our friendship or my badge.'

'It wasn't about Caleb, or Morgan. It was about me. I've been carrying so much, I just snapped.'

'Preaching to the choir,' Jesse responded. 'Thanks for lunch.'

Will gave a quiet laugh. 'No problem.'

'We'll find her,' Jesse added. 'You have my word. I'm about to hit the streets now. I'll check in once the patrols have an update.'

Will's eyes burned. He clenched his jaw and nodded again. 'What should I do?'

'Stay there in case she returns.'

Will bounced on his toes. He wanted to be out there with them, searching for her. He didn't feel right doing nothing, but if she returned, he wanted to be the first person she saw.

'You know I can't do that.'

Will stood in the hallway for a moment, staring at his reflection in the mirror on the other wall; his eyes tired, jaw tight, hope flickering behind the worry. Jesse had his back again, and now he didn't feel quite so alone. But there was no way he could stay put.

Jesse sighed. 'I'll be there in ten.'

Will hurried upstairs.

Chapter 32

Friday

Morgan

Morgan hadn't considered how she'd die. Old age, she was sure; maybe in one of those mechanical hospital beds surrounded by loved ones; children she hadn't had yet, and a loving, rheumy-eyed husband clutching her hand.

She damn sure didn't think it would be like this, in an itchy skirt, her least favorite work blouse, and a pair of purple thong kitten heels. If she ever got out of this, she vowed to buy more casual clothes; something that was easier to perish in.

Her head throbbed with a steady pulse that matched the echo of the music above her. The casino's basement was cold, damp, and smelled like mildew and sawdust. She could hear the rhythmic *ding-ding-ding* of winning slot machines from the casino floor, people cheering, coins cascading into metal trays; life going on, completely unaware that a woman was about to be unalived beneath them.

Her back was pressed to a support beam, zip-ties cutting into her wrists so tightly they'd gone numb. Duct tape was slapped over her mouth. She gagged on a rag that tasted like motor oil as she breathed through her nose. The concrete might as well have been steel under Morgan's body. She shivered uncontrollably.

Broken slot machines surrounded her like forgotten relics, their cracked screens flickering with phantom lights. Rolls of unused carpet and plastic wrapped signage cluttered the far wall. The whole place was a graveyard of half-built dreams, and Morgan was sure she was going to be buried inside of it.

She twisted her wrists, panic rising with every failed attempt to break free. Her heart thundered in her chest, her breaths coming faster as she strained to hear what was happening around her.

She couldn't die here. Not in this moldy basement. Not without seeing her parents again. Not without telling Will—

She jumped as a door slammed shut somewhere behind her. Footsteps approached. Voices followed. And then she saw them: Max Greaves and Cameron arguing, getting closer. They were a few feet away from her; their prisoner. From the floor, Morgan could only see Max's cold eyes over Cameron's shoulder.

'I'm not doing it,' Cameron protested, his voice lower, more serious than Morgan had ever heard it before. 'The deal was Eleanor. I did what you asked. Where's the rest of my money?'

She froze. Her heart pounded impossibly harder, hammering through every limb. She strained against the column again and it only dug into her wrists more, the sting forcing out a whimper.

Max's shoes clicked against the cement floor as he stepped closer. 'The deal was to make it look like she died of old age, in her bed! They would have never suspected that she'd been poisoned. It would have all worked out if you hadn't deviated from the plan,' he said icily.

'Yeah, well, your plan didn't work, alright? She didn't drop dead like you told me she would. Your little poison angle didn't work on her. I told you it would take more than one slip in her morning tea, asshole!'

'I paid you for a clean job, in and out, but you stuck around, followed her.'

'How many times do you think I could get close to her without her recognizing me in a town of, like, a hundred people? Plus, she had a kid with her. You know I don't do kids.'

'And I don't do sloppy,' Max snarled. You stabbed her on the biggest night of the year around dozens of witnesses.' He grabbed Cameron's sleeve, holding his arm in the air. 'Left behind evidence—'

Cameron protested. 'I didn't expect her to be so strong. She grabbed me . . .'

' . . . Even used my name at the damn library, looping me into this mess! That wasn't part of the deal.'

Cameron killed Eleanor . . . for Max? Morgan's thoughts spiraled into madness. Cameron must have looked surprised as Morgan heard Max laugh, bitter and low. 'Oh, didn't think I'd find out? I've got my eyes on every single person in Cinnamon Falls. I'm going to own this town, snatch it right from under their little country noses.'

Cameron snapped, 'Regardless of how I did it, she's dead. That's what you wanted, right? The stupid paperwork is getting pushed through.' Cameron fished the decree from his pocket and handed it over. Morgan strained to no avail. 'I'm done with this bullshit, Max. You want the Taylors dead, do it yourself.' Cameron unholstered a gun from his waist and slammed it on an abandoned billiards table like a challenge. He glanced backward at Morgan, a smug smile on his lips.

Morgan narrowed her eyes, thrashing toward him. The zip-ties bit through her skin and she clamped down on the grimy towel in her mouth, growling through the pain.

'Or triple my rate.'

Good to know her life was worth only thrice his normal rate, whatever that was. Morgan stared at Cameron's back, searching for any sliver of the man who once made her laugh in that gazebo, who'd slept next to her in bed, who reminded her how special she really was. That version of him was counterfeit. It was all a lie, a twisted fantasy he got her to believe in. If Morgan ever got out of this, she was going to hunt him down.

'Triple?' Max scoffed. '*You* messed up and now you want a bonus?'

Cameron held his ground. 'You want your name kept out of this? Then pay me my money. You can afford it. I've seen the—'

Max cut him off. 'I've got your bonus right here.'

The gunshot sounded like an explosion in the cramped basement. Morgan tried to scream but nothing came out. Cameron staggered backward, looking between Max and his outstretched arm in disbelief. Max gripped a smoking pistol.

Cameron collapsed in a heap next to her, his head banging against the concrete. He turned, his ocean blue eyes rolling toward Morgan slowly as a gigantic wound as black as night flooded the front of his shirt, spreading quickly. His body spasmed and a soft smile tugged at his lips once his eyes settled on her face. His final breath left his body in a wet gasp.

Morgan's heart seized in her chest. She screamed around the gag, her throat on fire, her body lurching with panic.

Max turned to her, his eyes as empty as the machines surrounding him.

'And now for you,' Max growled. He pumped another bullet into the chamber.

Morgan stared at the gun in Max's hands and shut her eyes.

Chapter 33

Will

It took seven agonizing minutes for concerned citizen, Ms. Lucretia Alston, to respond to the mass message and report that she'd seen a tan Oldsmobile pull into Diamond Jack's Casino after her Thursday evening poker game.

Jesse picked up Will on the way from the Daffodil Inn, his overheads flashing, clearing the traffic on the highway. Cars leapt out of their way, trees whizzed by in a blur as Jesse's truck accelerated on the slick asphalt.

'Listen, I know you want to find Morgan, but if she's in danger, you need to let me handle it,' Jesse advised, expertly switching lanes around a slow-moving vehicle.

Will shook his head, trying to keep his thoughts steady. He wanted to believe that she was sitting at a slot machine, nursing a drink, and drowning in Cameron's boring conversation. That would have been better than what he was thinking – she was somewhere hurt, with only minutes left in her life. If she was in danger, there was no telling what he would do.

'If she's got *one* mark on her . . .' Will worked hard to tamp down his anger. He pounded one hand in his palm, a temporary relief. 'Just let me get one crack at him before you arrest him.'

Jesse barked out a laugh. 'I'll think about it.'

By the time Jesse threw his cruiser into park at Diamond Jack's, Will was leaping out of the truck. He passed the same valet who parked his car days ago at Prime Society. The lanky, pimple-faced teen was scrolling aimlessly on his phone.

Will slowed, long enough to ask him a question. 'Did Max Greaves come this way?'

Jesse met Will at his side and unholstered his weapon, his eyes sweeping the facility.

'Who?' the valet asked, glancing between the two of them through a sheet of greasy black hair covering his eyes. He pushed his bang out of his face.

'Tall guy, too much cologne,' Jesse supplied.

'That's every guy who walks through these doors, man,' he deadpanned.

'Detective,' Jesse corrected.

'The owner, Max,' Will said.

The valet shrugged. 'I just park the cars. The owner wouldn't come this way anyway. There's a private entrance around back for, like, "VIP clientele".' He air-quoted. 'Big spenders and celebrities or whatever.'

Jesse slid his weapon back into the holster with a click, and the two men clambered back into the truck. The valet jogged over and approached Will's window before Jesse pulled away.

'Yo, I just gotta say, I hope you apologized to that young lady from the other night. She looked devastated when you sped outta here without her, bro. She held it together, I'm not gonna lie, but the look on her face was the saddest thing I've ever seen.'

'She's my first priority,' Will promised.

Jesse floored it, sending Will careening back into his seat. He managed to snap on his seat belt just in time for Jesse to make a sharp right around the back of the building. A floodlight from above blasted the fenced area. He slowed once he passed the loading dock, and sure enough, a tan Oldsmobile sat alongside several other luxury vehicles at the service entrance, shameless and undisguised among its counterparts.

They hopped out. Jesse crept toward the vehicle.

'Empty,' he reported. He ran his hand over the hood. 'Warm,' he told Will.

Ahead, the door was propped open by a man's foot. He sat slumped on an overturned milk crate in a chef's apron while he puffed on a limp cigarette. Will was not one to come between a man and his vices, but this was an emergency. He started to think of ways he could convince this man to let them inside, but as soon as the chef spotted the two men he pushed the door open with his foot.

He tipped his imaginary hat to Jesse. 'Detective.'

'Thank you, sir.' Jesse clapped him on his shoulder as he passed him.

Will guessed it paid to be a cop.

A short, round woman wrapped tightly in a black sequin jumpsuit paced in the white hallway, leading to an elevator. Will recognized Ms. Alston immediately. When he and Angel were late in the mornings, she always slid him a late pass with a flirty smile.

Ms. Alston explained, 'Officers, I'm the one who called. Ms. Angela told me to wait here for the detective—'

Her eyes narrowed in recognition. 'Mr. Reed? What are you doing here? You're a member of Diamond Jack's, too?'

'I'm here with Officer Shaw. We're looking for Morgan. Have you seen her?'

She took a step backward. 'Morgan? Is she in trouble? That poor girl can't catch a break—'

'What is this place?' Jesse asked, eyes darting side to side.

'The basement,' Ms. Alston said. 'The elevator at the end of the hall takes you upstairs to the main floor.'

The unmistakable blast of a gun sounded off nearby. Instinctively, Jesse leapt for Ms. Alston, pushing her head down. Will ducked, crouching low.

Jesse ordered, 'Get her outside! I'll find Morgan.'

'I'm coming with you!' Will protested.

'Not a chance.' Jesse spoke into the radio clipped

on his cargo pants, announcing that he'd heard gunshots and needed backup.

He crept down the hall slowly, his gun trained in front of him. He tried the knob of a closed door to his left. Jesse reared back and put his boot through the frame. It flew off its hinges after one swift kick.

Will turned to find Ms. Alston running as fast as she could toward the exit, casino chips spilling out of her pockets with each laborious step. Will sprinted in the door behind Jesse.

Sheets of plastic hung from exposed beams, blocking his view as light spilled in from far windows. He crept slowly, putting one boot carefully in front of the other.

'Drop your weapon!' Jesse ordered.

Will spun, Jesse's voice booming from the opposite direction in which he was heading. Will picked up the pace, swiping at the plastic holding him back until he found a clearing. He slowed behind Max Greaves who had Morgan by the neck, his pistol trained to her head, his finger balancing on the trigger, threatening.

'Can't do that, Shaw,' Max panted. 'I've got too much money invested in this. Lyons understood that, he was a businessman like me. But that bitch Eleanor and her bullshit decree was the only thing standing between me and that Inn.'

'So, what? You got your guy here to do your dirty work?' Jesse questioned, nudging Cameron with the toe of his boot. His body didn't move. 'Giving you the airtight alibi.'

Max kissed his teeth. 'It would've worked if it weren't for that damn kid.'

Jesse frowned. 'Caleb Brewster.'

'You'd be surprised what women will do for a little attention and some extra cash,' Max responded, a sinister lilt to his voice.

Kelsey, Will thought, shaking his head.

It'd been her that night at the Inn. The serving platter had covered her face, but he remembered passing a girl with long blonde braids in the hallway. She was the same girl that was screaming for her mother in the front seat of Amanda Jenkins' Pinto days ago. She'd also been at The Pit, the one sitting on Caleb's lap.

Will's heart squeezed as the scenario formed in his mind. Kelsey must have convinced Caleb to take the foxglove from Reed & Roots. Posing as event staff, she was the only person who could have gotten close enough to Eleanor's drink. Kelsey poisoned Eleanor's tea that night and caused her to stumble into the hedge maze, lost and confused. She slipped Cameron Caleb's knife, giving Cameron the perfect opportunity to grab Eleanor from behind and plunge it into her back. Caleb would take the fall, none the wiser.

'I couldn't trust that Cameron wasn't seen. Amanda would kill me if she knew about her daughter and someone had to go down for it. It wasn't going to be me.'

Jesse edged closer. 'You really think you're getting out of this, don't you?'

'Oh, I absolutely am. I'm going to start by shooting you,' Max replied confidently. 'After all, you're the one who shot Cameron. He lunged at you after you witnessed him shoot poor Morgan here. I heard all the gunshots and ran inside. You're out of uniform, officer, I thought you were an intruder.'

Will crept closer, holding his breath. A pile of unfinished wood beams were stacked together next to him. He slid one out of the pallet slowly, inch by inch until he got a good enough grip between his shaky palms.

'Shitty plan,' Morgan muttered around the gag. She wrestled to get out of his grip and he pulled her in tighter, making her whimper.

Will saw red. Jesse's eyes went wide as Will hoisted the beam over his head. Max spun around, loosening his grip on Morgan who shrieked, leaping out of the way just in time for Max's face to meet the board. A powerful vibration zigzagged up Will's arms as blood exploded out of Max's face. His body crumpled, falling to the floor with a satisfying wet smack.

Jesse looked up at him, his eyebrows flattened. 'I told you to let me handle it.'

'You were taking too long!' Will argued. He tossed the wood to the side and dropped to his knees. He crawled over to Morgan who was curled in the fetal position. Jesse snipped the zip-ties from behind her wrists with a pocket-knife while Will gingerly removed the tape from around her mouth. She spat the dirty rag out, gulping down air.

'Remind me to never trust the two of you with my life again,' she fussed. 'You let that man talk for twenty minutes!'

'I was waiting for a confession and then a clean shot. Excuse me for trying to save your life,' Jesse replied.

'The only person who saved my life here is . . . you.' Her venom died immediately as she turned to face Will.

Adrenaline pumped through his veins, electricity shooting to his fingertips. He felt like he could run through a wall right now, but once her eyes leveled him, nothing else mattered.

'Let's get out of here,' Jesse advised. He clipped the phone off his hip. 'Ang, I need emergency services here at Diamond Jack's . . .'

Will hung back as Jesse led Morgan out of the room. He crouched close to Cameron's body and just as he suspected, he was wearing a suit with a missing cufflink. He faced Max, who was still gurgling; half-conscious. He felt around in the man's pockets until he found the yellow, folded piece of paper. The historical decree. He knew more than one person who'd be elated to have it in the right hands.

391

The chaos waned. Max Greaves was already in the back of a squad car, slumped against the window. His split lip and eye looked four times its size from the wood Will cracked across his face. Will knew he should've felt some satisfaction, instead he was raw, rattled, and exhausted.

He stood outside the ambulance, arms crossed, watching as the paramedics finished checking Morgan over. Her skin was pale under the harsh lights, a nasty bruise on her temple where she'd been knocked out cold. But those fire and honey eyes of hers were still sharp, still alive. Morgan was safe, and that's all that mattered.

He didn't realize he'd been holding his breath until she turned toward him and nodded. Just a little tilt of her head, but it was permission to approach. He took a step forward, but paused, unsure if he deserved to.

Jesse swaggered over, notepad in hand, blocking him in. 'She gave a full statement. They're going to search the Garden Suite at the Inn. She said there's a chest in the bedroom with more files, maybe some material that will prove that Max has been planning this for a while. Tate is pissed. Apparently, he'd just met with Eleanor a few weeks before she was killed. He's bringing the big guns out, the state police, so it's out of our hands now. He's making sure that Greaves will be going away for a long time.'

Will nodded, jaw tight. 'Talk to Ronald Hartley,

the planning commissioner. He can piece everything together. In the meantime, she needs to rest, Jay.'

'She's clear to go. We'll get all of it buttoned up.'

The two shook hands, then pulled in for a back-slapping hug.

'Thanks, man,' Will said. 'For everything.'

'You're practically family now,' Jesse responded, releasing and pointing his chin toward Morgan.

Will didn't wait another second. Morgan was sitting on the bumper of the ambulance, the scratch on her cheek turning purple, zip-tie marks etched in red around her wrists. When he stopped in her line of sight, she looked up slowly, like seeing him settled something within her.

'I should have protected you,' Will apologized. His voice cracked in the middle, rough and uneven. 'I shouldn't have let anything come between us.'

'You didn't make this happen.' Morgan sounded tired, but steady. 'Cameron and Max made their choices.'

Will shook his head and ran a hand over his jaw. 'I left you. I never should've done that, Morgan. I was angry and ashamed, and I didn't want you to see that part of me. I thought if you saw it . . . you'd stop seeing the good; change your mind.'

She stood, slowly, pain flickering across her face, but she didn't flinch when she reached for him. 'I don't need you to be perfect, Will. I just need you to be real.'

That cracked something wide open inside of him. He pulled her into his arms, wrapping her tight, grounding them both in the moment. She buried her face in his chest, and the weight of everything they'd survived caught up to them all at once.

He hooked one finger under her chin, tilting her tear-soaked face up to his. 'You mean everything to me, Morgan Taylor.'

Tears were rimming her eyes, but she smiled, small and full of light. 'Then shut up and kiss me already.'

He did just that. He took apart the top button of her blouse, then the next until her collarbone was exposed, revealing the beauty mark he'd seen on their date. Morgan's breath tangled in her throat.

'Will . . .' she breathed.

He placed his lips so close to her skin he could feel her warmth radiating over his lips. 'I read in a book of poems once that moles were places lovers kissed in a past life.' He looked up at her. 'Tell me, Morgan, does this feel like déjà vu?'

He brought his lips to her skin and the sound Morgan made, he'd replay in his mind for years to come. Pressing one hand into her back, keeping her upright, he trailed kisses from her neck to her chin and finally they were face to face, their mouths a whisper apart.

He leaned in, hungry, until their lips met. He'd been waiting forever for this moment; to have her in his arms, a dream come true. Their kiss was slow at first, hesitant; gentle and reverent. Then deeper, aching, as if he could make up for every missed chance. Every unsaid word. Every moment they'd spent apart.

When he finally pulled back, breathless, Will released her braids from the bun on top of her head. The long strands cascaded around her shoulders like a waterfall. She'd never been more gorgeous.

'When you're ready,' he started, 'I want to take you to Macon. I want you to meet Tanya.'

Morgan stepped back, surprised. 'Your ex?'

Will pulled her back into him. 'Angel's mom. She's still part of my life. But I also want you to see where I'm from, what made me. I want you to know all of me, Morgan.'

She nodded, eyes glassy. 'Okay,' she relented. 'I'd like that.'

Will leaned in again, brushing a kiss against her temple.

The spring night was still cool, the flashing lights casting blue and red shadows across their skin, but for the first time in days, Will felt steady. As he held Morgan close, he knew: this was only the beginning.

Chapter 34

Saturday

Morgan

The golden sun broke over the wild cinnamon trees like a promise kept, steady and unrelenting. Morgan rested her head against the cool window of Will's Eldorado, her eyes tracing the golden streaks slicing through the trees. Morning haze clung to the edges of the highway, softening the world around them.

In the backseat, Angel was fast asleep, her head tipped back, mouth open, clutching her sketchbook. Daphne lay curled at her feet, snoring. Will's hand rested on her thigh and for the first time in what felt like a century, Morgan let herself breathe.

Everything was going to be okay.

She turned her head, watching the side of Will's face as he drove; shoulders forward, brows relaxed, jaw unclenched, the lines of tension around his mouth finally gone. He glanced over, caught her staring, and smiled. That crooked, slow-bloom smile that always made her chest tighten in the best way.

Seven days. One week. That's all it had taken for her world to tilt on its axis. A week ago, she was convinced her life was crumbling; unsure of her future, her place in the world, the Inn, or her own heart.

And now? She was on the way to Macon with a man she . . . loved? His daughter was in the backseat fast asleep. She was bruised, still piecing things together, but she felt whole.

She reached for Will's hand and laced their fingers together. He squeezed and focused on driving. Morgan let her head fall back against the seat as the memories rushed in, flashes of chaos and heartbreak and revelation.

Eleanor Langford had saved her life – her parents' lives – without ever knowing it. Every scrap of paperwork Eleanor collected, carefully tucked in the hidden compartment of the Garden Suite chest. Ultimately, it had been Angel, curious, and fearless Angel, who was tiny enough to slip inside the chest's hidden compartment and pull out the documents before the police resorted to breaking it apart.

The files were all there. Eleanor's meticulous research and handwritten notes. Diagrams, payment records, bank transfers. And the most damning of it all: the zoning map with falsified overlays.

Max Greaves had been laundering money through

shell companies that donated to Mayor Lyons' campaigns. A large sum was paid the same year the zoning decree was suspiciously amended. The other trail of payments? Wire transfers to Cameron Shore, all there in black and white.

The whole twisted web unraveled in front of the Cinnamon Falls police department, all because one woman refused to be erased. Mayor Tate wasn't taking the crime lying down, either. He personally escorted Greaves into the hands of the state police, to make an example out of him, and anyone else in the future who dared to cross the good people of Cinnamon Falls.

Morgan blinked against the sudden sting in her eyes. She still couldn't believe Eleanor, her mother's most annoying guest, had had their back all along. As for Cameron, she wasn't ready to untangle all her thoughts on him. Not yet, anyway. She'd need a couple whiskey sours, a brave therapist, and her best friend for that.

She glanced out the window again. The road to Macon stretched long and straight, flanked by wild-flowers and swaying grass.

Somewhere up ahead was Tanya, waiting to be reunited with her daughter, and oddly, Morgan wasn't nervous. Not because it wasn't complicated, because it was, but she didn't feel like she was about to fall apart. She felt grounded; dare she say it, she felt loved. She caught her reflection in the mirror; her lip was still healing, but her eyes were focused. She smiled at herself. How quickly life changed.

As they passed the welcome sign into Macon, she leaned into Will's shoulder and whispered, 'Let's see where this story goes next.'

Chapter 35

Six Months Later

Morgan

The mic was too close to her mouth. Morgan gently batted it away, only for the bespectacled sound tech, appearing behind her out of nowhere, to immediately reposition it under her nose again.

'Just pretend it's not there,' he advised.

Will scoffed from the seat beside her. 'Easy for him to say. He's not about to have his secrets broadcast to a million people.'

Angel, ever unbothered, swung her feet from the office chair and grinned like the whole setup was made for her.

A tiny microphone was secured neatly to her lemon-yellow cardigan. Her dress of the day was a white linen maxi dress. Clipped to the other side of her cardigan was the blue first place ribbon she'd won at the library months before.

Her art, a portrait of Eleanor Langford, was now

hanging in Mayor Sterling Tate's office, and would stay there until his term ended. She refused to take the ribbon off. Her *Andrew Guy, P.I.* action figure (not a doll) sat proudly in her lap, and her hair was done in the zigzag style she begged Morgan for at six-thirty that morning, and Morgan couldn't refuse a woman who knew what she wanted.

'Don't worry,' Angel whispered. 'I'll do all the talking.'

Will gave her a tight smile. 'Oh, I'm sure.'

Rosie's Diner buzzed with pre-show chatter. LED lights glowed softly from the recording rig overhead. Across from them, the hosts of the *Untold* podcast, Brooke Slade and her partner, Jake, were flipping through their notecards with the energy of two people who'd had one too many of Eddie Rutherford's espressos and not enough sleep.

'Okay.' The woman host looked up, eyes gleaming with excitement. 'Let's make some podcast magic.' Brooke had curly auburn hair, oversized glasses, and an insatiable curiosity for crime.

Her co-host and husband, a hefty, bearded guy in a flannel, offered them a friendly nod as Jake adjusted his headset.

Brooke leaned across the diner's table, while techs worked behind the scenes to ready the production. 'We are so honored to have you three here today. Angel, you are officially the youngest sleuth we've ever interviewed.'

Angel beamed and flourished her pointer finger. 'I prefer investigator extraordinaire.'

She sent the crowded room into a frenzy.

'Absolutely,' Jake responded. 'That's our bad. And your doll, Andrew Guy, played a key role in cracking the case?'

Will put his head in his hands. 'She's never going to let us live this down.'

Brooke held up the doll dramatically. 'You pull the string and it says—'

Angel pulled the string in Andrew Guy's back: 'You can always find me where things are hidden,' the two said in sync.

Morgan rolled her eyes affectionately. 'Which just so happened to be the exact thing Eleanor Langford told Angel right before she passed.'

Brooke gasped like it was the first time she'd heard it, even though she and Morgan had been emailing the details for weeks.

'Incredible,' Jake said, shaking his head. 'From a cryptic message, to a treasure trove of zoning fraud documents. I mean, this story has everything – murder, small-town corruption, a creepy maze, and a secret compartment! If you tried to pitch this to Hollywood, they'd say it was too much!'

'You forgot the romance,' Will said, grinning. 'That part is still unfolding.' Morgan flushed, hiding her face in her hands.

From the back of the restaurant, the crowd

whooped, Nia's voice leading the pack. Jesse sat with his arms crossed, next to Calvin and Tanya, with a satisfied smile on his face. Renee argued with Elijah through video call while she readjusted her tripod to get the best angle of the show. Marjorie and Vanessa were both almost in tears, though Morgan couldn't tell if it was from pride, or Angel's comedic timing. Walter and Niles fought for Midnight while Daphne was curled at Wesley's feet, wholly unamused by the lack of food.

Jake flipped a page on his notes. 'Now, according to your statement, Morgan, you were zip-tied in a basement beneath Diamond Jack's Casino. And Angel, you were asleep?'

'Out cold,' she deadpanned.

'Absolute legend,' Brooke whispered.

Just then, someone from the audience shouted, 'Ask about the kiss!'

Morgan's eyes went wide and Nia stood. 'Apparently it was very cinematic. It deserves to be included.'

'You weren't even there!' Jesse fussed.

'Shut up, you told me you almost cried.' She slapped his shoulder.

'Want me to recreate it?' Will offered, inching closer to Morgan's face.

'Please, we are here on business.' Angel faked a gag. 'Let's be professionals.'

Everyone burst into laughter, and the producers gave Brooke and Jake a thumbs up. From a speaker,

Morgan heard the familiar *Untold* intro music begin.

'Okay,' the producer called, clapping his hands and silencing the crowd. 'We start in three . . . two . . .'

Just before the red light came on, Morgan took a deep breath.

This was it, she thought. *Time for main character energy.*

Acknowledgements

Friday, November 7, 2025

Dear Reader,

For me, writing the acknowledgments is the hardest part of writing a novel. This book began, as most of my stories do, with family. Writing *Death at Daffodil Inn* reminded me how deeply our roots shape us. I think a lot about the paths we walk; the ones we're sure we're forging on our own, only to realize someone has already walked them for us, laying down pieces of themselves to make the way smoother for whomever comes behind.

I owe so much of who I am to the people who came before me; those who showed me what true strength looks like while still leaving room for laughter, for wonder and curiosity. The ones who've made faith my foundation, and the ones who keep me afloat when life feels too heavy.

At its core, writing is a solitary act, but the heart behind it never is. So much of this novel comes from the love, grief, humor and resilience from my real life.

Although fictional, when I write about Cinnamon Falls, I'm picturing my grandmother's home in small-town Virginia. It's where I learned that love is in the little details; a sprinkle of sugar over your Saturday morning cereal, the porch light left on for late-night arrivals, the lift of your hand when a neighbor drives past or a chilled glass of lemonade for an unexpected visit from a friend. Consideration, that is the heartbeat of Cinnamon Falls.

If you've found comfort within the pages, thank you for being part of this journey. You are the reason I keep writing, and the reason this little fictional town feels so real.

Until we meet again,

R.L. Killmore

R. Killmore

Welcome back to Cinnamon Falls...

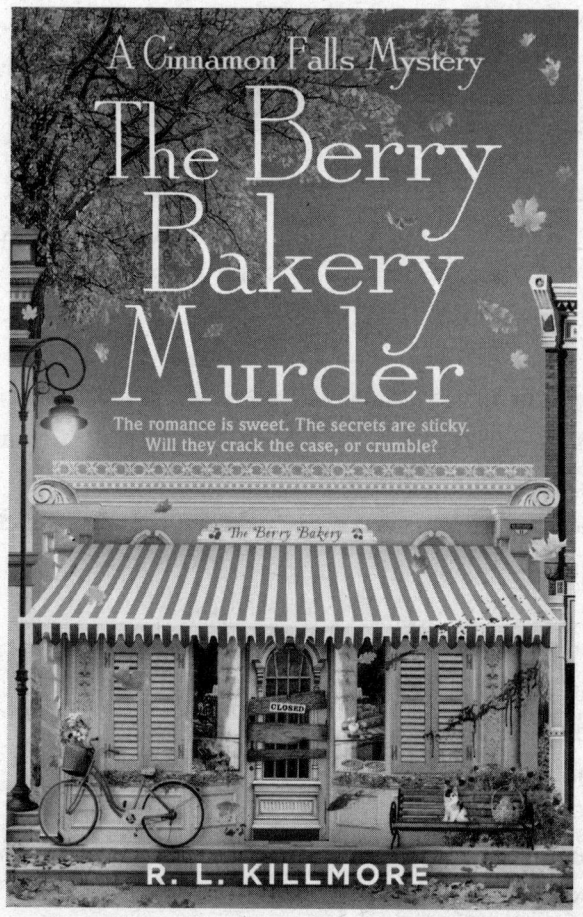

Join Ginger, Cinnamon Falls' new girl, and local heartthrob Austin, as they team up to solve the town's latest murder case.

AUGUST 2026

In Paperback, eBook and Audio

Bringing a book from manuscript to what you are reading is a team effort, and Simon & Schuster UK would like to thank everyone who helped to publish *Death at Daffodil Inn*.

Editorial
Charlotte Osment
Gail Hallett
Aneesha Angris

Copyeditor
Nia Bragg

Proofreader
Amanda Raybould

Marketing & Publicity
Kate Kaur
Polly Osborn
Sabah Khan

Sales
Olivia Allen
Madeline Allan
Jade Unwin
Alice Twomey

Jonny Kennedy
Richard Hawton & the rep team

Design
Pip Watkins
Jill Tytherleigh (map)

Production and Operations
Karin Seifried
Mike Messam

Rights
Amy Fletcher
Ben Phillips

Finance and Contracts
Luke Shaller
Maria Mamouna
Keely Day
Meshach Yeboah